D1521411

DR. WESTON

THE BILLIONAIRE BOYS CLUB

LM FOX

Copyright © 2023 by LM Fox

This book is a work of fiction. Any references to real events, real people, and real places are used fictitiously. Other names, characters, places, and incidents are products of the Author's imagination and any resemblance to persons, living or dead, actual events, organizations or places is entirely coincidental.

All rights are reserved. This book is intended for the purchaser of this book ONLY. No part of this book may be reproduced or transmitted in any form or by any means, graphic, electronic, or mechanical, including photocopying, recording, taping, or by any information storage retrieval system, without the express written permission of the Author. All songs, song titles, and lyrics contained in this book are the property of the respective songwriters and copyright holders.

Editor: Readers Together

Proofreader: Cheree Castellanos, For Love of Books4 Editing

Formatter: Bearded Goat Books/Kate Decided to Design

Cover/Graphic Artist: Hang Le (Discrete cover: Kate Decided to Design)

Cover Photographer: Wander Aguiar

Cover Model: Felipe M.

To believers in second chances...
May all of your dreams come true!

Ask, believe, receive, and be immensely thankful
for all is possible
when we live in gratitude and joy.

CHAPTER ONE
BROADIE

"Beatrice, I'm headed to the doctors' lounge a little early. The OR asked if I could move my next case up about an hour." I reread the text from the pre-op nurse, Patricia, stating they needed to adjust the schedule to make room for an unstable ER patient.

"Don't forget, Dr. Weston, they're…"

I make my way to the elevator, and quickly text back a reply letting Patricia know I'll be there as soon as I can. It's tempting to dive right in and get things moving when there's a crisis. Yet, in this hospital, there's *always* a crisis. It's best I grab something to eat before jumping headfirst into the next case. Otherwise, I'll likely go all day without more than a cup of coffee in my system.

I should know. I've worked as a general surgeon at St. Luke's Hospital in Hanover, Virginia, for over ten years now. After finishing residency, I was so eager to start my career that I hit the ground running and never looked back. However, I've learned the hard way about the toll this career can take on you. And not just physically.

As I approach the doctors' lounge, my eyes narrow at the large sign taped to the door. That's odd. Coming closer, I read the bright yellow paper.

CLOSED FOR RENOVATIONS

We apologize for the inconvenience.
Our physicians' dining and office areas are
overdue for a remodel.
We look forward to serving you in the main
dining room until the new space is complete.

This shouldn't come as a surprise. That doctors' lounge has definitely seen better days. Scratching the back of my head, I seem to recall Beatrice and Pearl, our office manager, chatting about this. Yet I thought they were merely bantering about what might be coming in the future. But then again, it could've been months ago they were having this conversation. I admit I get fixated on my patients and the never-ending meetings I'm required to attend. These details don't stay on my radar.

"Well well, if it isn't *the* Broadie Weston. Renowned general surgeon and frequent winner of Richmond Magazine's Annual Top Docs in Surgery award. I wouldn't have thought you'd know the way here. Did someone escort you?" Jarod snickers.

"Ha ha. I come to the cafeteria."

"Oh yeah? When's the last time?"

I actually have to stop and consider this. It's not because I think I'm above coming here. It's just more convenient to run in and grab a coffee or fix something off the buffet in the doctors' lounge before heading back to work. Not to mention, I skip many meals. It's the nature of the beast in this line of work. "About six months ago, I missed lunch because a case ran long."

"I'm just shitting with you, man. How've you been?"

"Good. Just busy." It's odd, really. My close friend, Jarod Snow, and I have worked together in our practice alongside five other surgeons for years. Yet we rarely see each other unless we're in a meeting due to our operating room schedules. "Finished a scheduled hernia repair before completing a lumpectomy on a twenty-six-year-old."

Jarod's frown mirrors my concern for that sweet young woman. We try to detach emotions to these cases as often as possible, but some tug at your heartstrings. All we can do is pray the biopsy shows no sign of cancer.

"I thought I had an hour before my next case, until the OR called. They have a patient in the emergency room they're trying to squeeze in. Thought I'd grab something before I head back."

"I don't know how you do it, Broadie." Jarod shakes his head.

"What? Your schedule is as insane as mine."

"No. It's not. I turn cases down when it gets too much. I've trained people not to come at me for more. But they know you'll do whatever it takes."

This statement makes me pause for a moment. He's probably right. But it's just the way I've always operated. I never want to keep anyone waiting, time can be crucial in this line of work.

"Hi, Dr. Weston," a young brunette in navy blue scrubs greets from across the salad bar. Her smile is served with a side of flirtation.

Jarod snickers, reaching for a packet of salad dressing.

"Good afternoon," I answer with a cordial grin as I grab what I think is a chicken salad sandwich wrapped in cellophane. Yet, prior visits to this cafeteria have proven I could be wrong. I have no earthly idea what this nurse's name is and don't want to encourage continued conversation by looking at her nametag. Lifting the sandwich to my nose, I take a deep inhale. It can't be tuna. Must be chicken. *What else could it be?*

"Hell. I just got back from vacation with the family. I haven't managed to get my mind in work mode. I definitely wouldn't be able to keep up with your pace."

Jarod and his wife, Mandy, have two young boys. I don't get to see as much of him as I did when we were both single. It goes without saying that we're always here for one another, but there simply aren't enough hours in the day for spending bro-time outside of work.

There are days I'm jealous of his life. Coming home to a wife and kids, attending little league games. But it's my own doing. If I want the life he has, I need to make it a priority. And I've already failed at it once. Not going to do that again until I'm all in.

"Oh, yeah? Where'd you go?" I ask as I examine a fruit cup and decide against it. Who am I kidding? I'll be lucky to choke down this sandwich if I don't' get moving.

"Jamaica. It was amazing. But any island is that way for me. Sun, surf, and all the fresh seafood you can eat. I haven't finished my first day back, and I'm already planning our next island getaway."

We head to the refrigerator to get water when something grabs my attention from the corner of my eye, and I do a double take.

Who is that?

A striking blonde in a long white lab coat stands in line for the cashier. She's holding a plastic container and what seems to be a bottle of lemonade, staring off into space as if deep in thought. I'm not one to be taken in easily by an attractive female, especially one who works at the same hospital. However, something about her makes it nearly impossible to turn away. Is she new to St. Luke's? I'd remember meeting a woman who looks like that.

She's probably about five foot eight. Her blonde hair is pulled back in a loose bun, allowing an unobstructed view of her slender neck. Her skin is fair, and besides those tantalizing red lips, she doesn't appear to be wearing much makeup. As I continue to observe her, her face remains expressionless. I wonder what's going through that pretty head.

"Who is that?"

"Who?" Jarod answers, startling me. I hadn't realized I'd asked it aloud. I watch as he follows the trajectory of my gaze. "Poppy?" His voice carries an odd tone of disbelief.

"Who?"

"Poppy. The pharmacist."

"When did she start working here?" I reach into the glass case for a bottle of water as a chuckle rumbles behind me.

"Are you for real? Probably not long after you did. She's worked here at least seven or eight years."

I stop dead in my tracks. "There's no way."

"Yes, way. Have you been working under a rock?" He shakes his head mockingly. "You're ridiculous. You're so fixated on the next case you've probably talked to her a dozen times and didn't know it. Add to it, you usually have your head buried in your phone… or you're talking shop to a colleague." He laughs. "You've probably sat next to her in a meeting and didn't pay any attention."

Hell, am I that bad?

There's no way I would've been in the same room with that gorgeous creature and not noticed her. "I usually get Frank or Marshall when I call the pharmacy. How could I have missed her all these years? Maybe she only works the evening shift."

"Yeah. Well, they consider you a pretty big deal around here. There's probably a sign on the wall over the phone that says to send all of your calls directly to the big dogs."

"Whatever. I'm not a bigger deal than anyone else."

Jarod nearly chokes on his sip of water. "Right. That's why the administration is constantly putting on the heat to get you to take the medical director position."

He's not wrong. However, I've worked hard to build a solid practice over the last ten years. I know the key to a successful career in medicine is compassion. Long hours and dedication to your craft are one thing, but patients going under the knife want to feel safe. Their concerns need to be validated. I honestly think some of my partners could stand to go back to residency. A lot more is required of a surgeon than an expensive education and a God complex.

"Hi, Dr. Weston," a giggly blonde dressed in white scrubs greets.

Unlike the previous nurse who said hello, this young woman's nametag happens to be front and center. "Hi, Brittany." Her giggles seem to intensify as I walk past her. Good grief. She's probably my daughter's age.

"If this is how it's going to be every time you come to the cafeteria, could you warn me before your next visit?"

"Shut up." I chuckle. Looking ahead as we make our way to the checkout line, I notice a radiant smile overtake Poppy's face in response to something the cashier has said. *Jesus. She's luminous.* Unless she's recently dyed her hair blonde, there's not a doubt in my mind I've never seen this dazzling woman before. She outshines everyone else in the room.

At this exact moment, the beauty in question turns, and our eyes connect. An electric current travels at the speed of light from her gaze to mine, my breath catches in my throat as her deep blue irises seem to penetrate right through to my soul.

What the fuck is happening to me?

"Don't even let your mind go there, man," Jarod's voice breaks through the silence, causing my stare to snap to his. "She won't give you the time of day. Not about anything beyond work anyway. Don't think several of us haven't tried."

My brows jump to my hairline at his admission.

"Chill. It was long before I got married. I got shut down faster than a nurse with juicy gossip." He laughs. "But from what I hear, I'm in good company. So it didn't hurt my ego as much as it might have otherwise."

How has grabbing a quick bite to eat before diving into my next case turned into this?

I need to get laid. I'm sure that's all this is. I'm simply desperate for some female companionship. And Poppy is undeniably beautiful. There's no question why I or anyone else wouldn't find her attractive. But I know better than to consider anything with someone I work with. I've never slept with a colleague or a patient. Hell, I barely slept with my wife.

My first love has always been my career. Maybe if I'd figured out early on to keep my priorities straight, I'd be vacationing in Jamaica with Camile and my daughters instead of working myself into an early grave.

"Well, hello, Dr. Weston," a pretty surgical tech I recognize says from the line next to us.

"Good afternoon, Samantha." I grin. Moving ahead, I scan my items as the cashier smiles, waving me through given there's no charge for my meal. "I'll catch you later, Jarod. I'm going to the OR to scrub in after I finish this sandwich." I inspect it again questioningly, wondering if this is really a good idea.

"See ya, Broadie."

Walking toward the surgical center, I find Poppy sitting on the other side of the glass at a bistro table in the shade, solely focused on the book before her as she lifts her bottle of lemonade to her pretty red lips. What is she reading? A mystery? A Jane Austen classic perhaps?

How is it possible that in seven or eight years I've never noticed her? Am I really so focused on my work that I could've missed this enchanting creature? Is she married or living with someone? Is that why she turns men away, or is she merely as committed to keeping her work and dating life separate like I am?

And the biggest question... what is it about this mysterious woman that has me so entranced?

CHAPTER TWO
POPPY

TAP. TAP. TAP.

Knee deep into this angsty romance that I've put off way too long, I nearly jump from my chair at the sound. I glance up to see my sweet friend, Katarina, beaming at me and pointing in my direction. As if she'd ever need permission to join me. I nod repetitively with an ear-to-ear grin.

"Hey, stranger. It feels like forever since I've seen you," Kat greets, engulfing me in her warm embrace.

"It has been. It's funny how we can work under the same roof, yet between our different schedules and the chaotic pace of this place, I go forever without connecting with anyone."

"You're right. I seem to only see the people from my department." Kat reaches over, steals a cherry tomato from the top of my salad, and grins.

"I didn't think the ER ever let you leave long enough to eat."

"It's rare. But there was a brief lull where I could make a break for it. Now, whether I actually get to eat my food once I return is a whole different story." Kat may be complaining, but I know her well. She loves working in the emergency room.

I've known Katarina since she was a teenager. We met when she worked her way through her undergraduate degree as a pharmacy tech at the drug store I managed. At that time, Kat had briefly entertained applying to pharmacy school. I'd coached her on what was required and even donated some of my old flashcards so she could learn the names of the more common drugs. However, having volunteered as a paramedic for several years, Kat ultimately decided to pursue a career as a physician assistant. Her job is a lot more hands-on and appears to be a perfect fit. She seems to thrive on the adrenaline rush of her work as a PA.

"You ever miss the days of working in the drug store?"

"God, Kat. That seems like ages ago." Taking a sip of my lemonade, I ponder her question. "The hours were better. This twenty-four-hour gig can be draining. Luckily, I don't have to work as many overnight shifts now that I've been here a while. But even working until eleven o'clock can be hard." I laugh. "I'm not getting any younger."

Kat pops up from where she'd been sitting on the wrought iron chair beside me. "You're only thirty-six, Poppy. You make it sound like you're approaching retirement."

"I'm thirty-eight, missy. And feeling it." If I'm this tired all of the time at thirty-eight, I can't imagine what life in my forties will be like. Then again, it could be that I spend most of my free time with my mother at the nursing home. They're probably rubbing off on me. I wince. *It's like I'm turning into one of* The Golden Girls. Maybe I should volunteer with a youth group. Or try a different multivitamin—.

"Hi, Kat." A delicious, gravelly sound from my periphery interrupts my thoughts, and causes a surprising quiver in my limbs. It's been decades since a man's voice has affected me. Pushing a wayward lock of hair behind my ear, I look up to see the attractive surgeon from the cafeteria. Shocking, given I thought this man was too important to inhabit the more common areas of this hospital.

"Oh, hi, Dr. Weston."

"Sorry to interrupt. I hadn't seen you or Nick in ages and thought I'd say hello before my next case."

Kat has such a radiant personality. It doesn't surprise me that she'd be so familiar with the likes of Dr. Broadie Weston. She probably interacts with him regularly, having to consult him on patients in the ER. Plus, her husband, Nick, is an orthopedic surgeon. I'm sure they run in much different circles than I do. Heck, they probably 'do lunch' and whatnot. Lately, I don't have many friends outside of the fictional ones in my books. I'm lucky to 'do lunch' with my mother and her roommate, Agnes, once a week.

"Hi."

I realize a hush has fallen onto the three of us, and I look up to see the handsome doctor is speaking to me. "Oh. Hi." My cheeks flush in embarrassment. Had I missed what he'd been saying before that?

"It's Poppy, right?"

Broadie Weston knows my name? Feeling timid, I lower my gaze only to land on the nametag pinned to my lab coat, and inwardly roll my eyes. *Get over yourself, Poppy. You've only worked here eight years. I'm sure he knows who you are.* I can feel my ears turn red under his stare. *Ugh.* Why must my fair skin always give me away when I'm feeling self-conscious? "Yes. It's nice to see you, Dr. Weston."

He appears to stand a little taller, a sexy smile crossing his dreamy face. There's a flutter in my lower belly as the deep dimple in his right cheek sends morse code that goes right to my lady bits. *Jeez.* Is this how he is with everyone? His mere presence is charming and charismatic.

I'm sure this is all a front. Every surgeon I've had to deal with here is a pompous asshole. They want everything yesterday as if we should all be mind readers and know exactly what they need before they order—

"Poppy?"

"Oh, I'm sorry." I clear my throat, mortified my inner ramblings have caused me to be so distracted. "I don't know where my mind keeps going." *Get it together, Poppy.*

"I was just saying I have to run." Kat leans in for a hug. "The cafeteria seems busier than normal, so I better grab my lunch and get back. Please say we can catch up sometime. Or better yet, come out to the lake one day and hang out. Text me your schedule. We can go to The Belleview Cafe for brunch."

I really need to make more of an effort to reach out to her, both here and outside of work. She's one of the few people outside my family I've kept in touch with over the years. "Oh, Kat, I'd love that. I will. Goodbye." I wait for Dr. Weston to walk away with Katarina, but I'm stunned to find him still standing silently before me. He's holding a sandwich that looks like it's seen better days. Do I ask him if he wants to sit down? I see how everyone flocks to him like he's some celebrity, yet I wouldn't know what to say if he took me up on the offer.

Bzzz. Bzzz.

Saved by the phone, I reach into my pocket and pull out my hospital zone phone in case someone from the pharmacy is trying to contact me. Not that, in all the years I've worked here, I've ever had a pharmacy emergency that required me to cut my lunch short. Okay, maybe that one time the ER needed antivenom for a patient who'd been bitten by a snake.

When the zone phone shows no calls, I retrieve my cell phone as that rich baritone voice floats down to my ears, reminding me I'm not alone.

"I apologize. I have to get to the OR. I—"

Looking up, I feel confused. Had I missed something? Peering from side to side, I wonder if anyone else sees what's happening. What was he going to say? And why is he still standing here wordlessly? *Is he having a stroke?* Maybe he's having some sort of breakdown. It's no mystery that Dr. Weston works all the time. He's practically considered a caped crusader around here.

Without another word, he shakes his head, seeming to gather himself, turns, and walks briskly down the hall.

What the heck just happened?

~

"Hey, Poppy. Can you run this to the ER? The charge nurse called and said there's a plastic surgeon there who needs this stat."

"Sure." I walk over to where Marshall is standing and retrieve the lidocaine from him. "They don't have any of this in the ER?" Seems strange given how often it's used down there.

Marshall shrugs. "I think they have it with epinephrine. He wanted plain, and they're out."

I gather the patient sticker and apply it to a clear plastic bag before dropping the medication inside and heading toward the emergency room. As I walk briskly down the hall, I say a silent prayer this plastic surgeon will either be too preoccupied to notice me or will take his ire out on someone else. I've had one too many confrontations with surgeons who feel the world revolves around them. I'm really not interested in dealing with that today. Okay, let's be real. I'm never interested in that.

But who is?

Why do these people think they're better than anyone else who works here? I get their job is stressful, but there's no need to take it out on your peers.

I make it to the ER in record time and swipe my badge to allow entrance. I barely make it through the doors before spotting Katarina. *Thank god!* Waving to get her attention, I call, "Hey, Kat."

"Hey. Long time no see." She laughs.

"Any idea where this patient might be? I suspect the surgeon's probably waiting on this."

Kat looks down at the medication bag before a knowing look crosses her face. "Oh." She grimaces. "Yeah. This is probably for that sweet ten-year-old bitten by her family's new Great Dane."

My hand flies to my heart. "Oh, god. Is she going to be okay?"

"I think she's more traumatized than anything else. But it got her in the chest wall, and Dr. Peck wants to make sure there's as little scarring as possible. The wound's not bad enough to require going to the OR. We've given her something to relax her." Kat's expression is heartbreaking. "She's being so brave."

Now, I feel guilty complaining about surgeons taking their stress out on their peers. Their outbursts still suck, but I can't imagine having to deal with this type of pressure on a regular basis.

"It's not my patient, but I'll run it down to him." She hesitates momentarily. "Hang tight. Don't run off, okay."

"Okay."

As I stand out of the way, taking in the commotion, a mix of emotions surrounds me. I'm proud of Kat. The determined, hard-working girl I watched grow into a woman has made such an incredible life for herself.

My thoughts are cut short as an almost gray-appearing man sitting on a gurney rapidly flies around the corner, surrounded by nurses and patient care techs. Dr. Hart, one of our cardiologists, brings up the rear. The patient's skin tone appears to make more sense now. I suspect he's having a heart attack, and they're headed to the cath lab. I'm grateful that I chose a less stressful career path. I couldn't do this day in and day out.

As I await Kat's return, my mind travels to a time I've tried hard to forget. My more personal memories of this emergency room. It's as if I've been teleported eight years in the past. The sounds of beeping monitors and phones ringing, combined with the sight of nearly lifeless bodies lying on stretchers, bring it back as if it were yesterday. It all feels so familiar.

And painful.

"Sorry about that. I think I got stopped about ten times trying to get back here." Kat's laughter startles me for a moment, bringing me back to the present.

"Did Dr. Peck get after you? About having to wait?"

"Nah. I think he knows me well enough that it wouldn't get a response. So why bother if it doesn't garner the attention he's looking for." She shrugs.

"I'm so proud of you, Kat. I don't say it enough. You're so capable and confident."

She immediately pulls me in for a hug. "Thank you. I'm not as put together as it appears. Ask Nick." She giggles. "And I owe a lot of it to you. You were such a huge role model for me."

"Me?"

"Yes, you. Oh, Olivia and I used to dream of having a life like yours back in the day." She practically swoons. "You seemed to have it all together." I recall the two of them, so young and determined. Kat wanted a career in medicine, while her friend, Olivia, worked at the drug store to afford head shots for a chance at Broadway.

My face falls, thinking of how different my life has become. I really did have it all. At least, it felt that way until it was gone.

Instantly, Kat grabs my arms, rubbing her hands up and down to comfort me.

"Oh, Poppy. I shouldn't have—"

"Don't. Please." I hate that I can't control my emotions better after all these years. "I'm getting there. But I'm still a work in progress, I'm afraid." And here I thought I'd come so far.

"Maybe Dr. Weston could help hasten your progress." Kat waggles her brows at me teasingly, and my jaw drops. The thought of that sexy surgeon helping me with *anything* has my interest. But he's way out of my league.

"What on earth are you talking about?"

"Oh my gosh, Poppy. You couldn't see the way he was looking at you?" Her face is almost animated with the gleeful expressions she's wearing.

"Did you ever eat, Kat? I think your sugar might be low."

She giggles, dancing from foot to foot. "Oh, come on. He's got his eyes on you. I know it." She claps as if unable to contain her excitement.

Has she completely lost it?

"What gave you that impression? Hi. Poppy, right?" I mimic his words from earlier. "Yes, I'm expecting a ring any day now." I shake my head, realizing I need to get back to the pharmacy where I can focus on something productive. Not this silly matchmaker's imagination.

"You could do far worse."

"Than an arrogant surgeon?"

"But he's not like that, Poppy. I swear. He's so nice. I've known him since before I started working here. He took care of my granny before she died. He's not your typical surgeon. He was so compassionate, and I genuinely felt he cared about all of us. Not just her surgical outcome but how our family was dealing with her situation. Plus, he's so handsome," she adds, steepling her hands in front of her with a dreamy expression on her face.

"Well, I'm glad to know such a surgeon exists. It's a shame I only tend to deal with the self-righteous ones." Looking down at my watch, I realize

I've taken Kat away from her patients for far too long. "None of this matters. I'd never date anyone who worked here. The only thing I have going for me right now is my job. I'm not about to do anything that'll rock that boat."

Kat comes closer, lowering her volume, "Word on the street is he's loaded. And not like, surgeon money, but millions. Maybe billions." Her eyes are as big as saucers. "So you might not have to work." Kat is beaming at me like she's trying to sell me a lottery ticket she secretly knows is the big winner.

I lean in toward her and whisper, "You're ridiculous."

"You still owe me brunch." Kat brings her hand to her ear as if she's answering a phone, giving the universal sign for 'call me.'

I shake my head at her antics, turning abruptly for the exit doors and running right into a wall of muscle. A familiar frisson travels from my head to my toes, and I immediately know it's him.

Wow. Who knew this was hidden under his tailored suits and lab coats? I fight the urge to trail my hands up and down his chest, yet can't resist leaning in. God, he smells good.

"Well, hello."

Peering up, I find Dr. Weston's whiskey-colored eyes smiling down at me and that deep dimple joining our impromptu get-together. How long has he been standing there? Could he have heard any of that preposterous conversation?

Placing my hands on his chest, I slowly push back to regain my footing. It's honestly of no consequence to me if he heard anything. I never gave any indication I'd be interested in what he had to offer.

Not that he's offering.

"I'm sorry. I really need to pay more attention to where I'm going."

"Don't apologize. I didn't mind at all," he adds with a wink.

Um, what?

CHAPTER THREE
BROADIE

"Dr. Weston, I'm sorry to bother you. But the surgical floor is on the phone. They've been trying to get in touch with you. Apparently, a patient you operated on recently seems to have developed an infection."

"Who, Mr. Utterly?" I had a sneaking suspicion his wound wouldn't heal well. This gentleman has been a heavy smoker for years, and uncontrolled diabetes has caused additional circulatory problems. It's always painful to explain to a patient they'll need an amputation. As life-altering as it may be, there's usually no other choice. Yet, the same risk factors that led to the loss of the limb also create a poor environment for wound healing. Add to that his multiple medication allergies, and it's been a complicated course for this patient.

Checking my phone, I discover I haven't received any calls. "Can you double-check with the hospital operator as to why I didn't receive any of the floor's pages, Beatrice? Please let them know I'm on the way."

"Yes, sir."

I make my way to the inpatient surgical wing and hope the nurses are being proactive about the appearance of the wound, given his risk factors.

As I approach the nurses' station, I hear cackling and find they're all crowded around Ashton's phone. With long dark hair and a voluptuous figure, she's a beautiful girl but comes across as overly flirtatious and doesn't have the same work ethic I observe with the nurses who've been here for some time.

Clearing my throat, I watch as they quickly retreat from the area, returning to their computer stations like children caught with their hands in the cookie jar. I don't fault them for having some downtime once in a while. Their jobs aren't easy.

"Hi, Dr. Weston," Jenny says, appearing embarrassed.

"Hi, Jenny. I heard you guys were trying to get in touch with me. I'm glad you contacted the office. I'm not sure why the calls weren't going through to my phone. Is it Mr. Utterly?"

"Yes. I'm worried the antibiotic isn't working. There's some mild discoloration along the surgical site and some slight drainage from the area."

"No fever?"

"No. I just didn't want to wait too long to bring it to your attention."

"Thank you. I can always count on you. I guess I'll need to add a second antibiotic. It's tricky given his medication allergies." I grab a seat next to her and sign on to the computer to review his chart. I click on multiple prior admissions attempting to locate an antibiotic he's tolerated in the past. He's had numerous skin infections leading up to his amputation. But with his extensive allergy list, I'm unsure if the medications he's received were given before or after his allergy was identified.

Reaching for the phone, I dial the inpatient pharmacy number and can't contain my smile when I hear the unexpected greeting. *I admit this woman has unknowingly joined me in the shower several mornings this week.*

"Pharmacy, this is Poppy."

"Poppy, hi. This is Broadie Weston. I'm taking care of Robert Utterly in room 3214. He's had a below-the-knee amputation and appears to be developing an infection at the surgical site despite the use of antibiotics. He's likely going to need another. I'm hoping you can help me determine the best one, given his extensive allergy list. This man already has an uphill battle ahead of him. So I'm leaning on your expertise."

There's a slight pause before she answers me, causing me to think I've lost the connection. "You're right." Her voice sounds a bit shaky. I pull the receiver back and verify the cord is fully connected before returning it to my ear. "This is a pretty long list. Plus, his kidney function isn't great either. So we'll need to be careful there also."

The line grows quiet once more, and although I'm confident she's doing her job, I feel the odd impulse to make small talk with her. Ask her how her day is going. *Or if she'd consider having a drink with me.*

"Dr. Weston, would you mind if I take a closer look at this and call you back?"

"Of course. I still need to examine him. But I'm fairly certain that's the direction we're headed. I'll be at this extension when you come up with something."

"Okay. Shouldn't take me too long." As she disconnects the call, I realize I have a dumbass smile on my face. My eyes quickly dart about the room. I must look like a goof. How would I explain grinning like this over a pharmacist calling me back?

What the hell is it with this woman?

I may avoid relationships like the plague, but I don't suffer from a lack of opportunity. Sure, Poppy is alluring, but so are the women at the private club I frequent. And they don't expect a call the next day. Not to mention, dalliances with the women there won't affect my job.

While finding a willing partner through the club is an option, I haven't needed to in a very long time. I have one steady girl I've spent time with over the years. There's no love connection. It's merely two adults enjoying in the other's physical company. We initially met at the club. However, Brandee now works as a paid escort. She's no more interested in a relationship than I am. Our association is purely carnal. I'm not capable of more. Just ask my ex-wife.

Returning from Mr. Utterly's room, I sit back down to document my physical exam in his medical chart when I'm interrupted by a pleasant surprise.

"I think this is what you are looking for."

My head snaps up from my computer screen, and that fucking grin takes over my face again before I can stop it. "Wow. Now that's service for you," I tease. I immediately grimace as I replay the statement in my mind. *Shit. That sounded condescending.*

I swear this woman has turned me into an overeager, hormonal teenager. I manage to articulate complex lectures on state-of-the-art new surgical procedures, yet struggle to say the right thing around her.

"Happy to be of help," Poppy says reassuringly. *God, this woman is beautiful.* She's wearing her hair down today. It falls just below her collarbone, styled in loose waves. Her lips are stained cherry red, and her skin has a soft glow about it. Yet, it's likely her aura. Her radiance seems more than physical.

The royal blue top under her lab coat brings out the vibrant indigo shade of her eyes. But there's a different sparkle present today I hadn't noticed before.

A gold one that's wrapped around her left ring finger.

She's married? Why didn't Jarod tell me that? No wonder she turns everyone down who expresses any interest.

"Thank you. I appreciate your taking the time to deliver this so quickly."

She must have noticed my undeniable change in mood. Why do I feel so defeated? It's not like I was going to make my move. I don't date people who work in this hospital. Fuck, I don't date, period. Why would I set up another woman to get hurt as I did with Camile? I'm a selfish asshole who's incapable of giving a partner what she deserves. Let's call it what it is.

Before I can come up with a polite way to excuse myself, Poppy hands off the IV antibiotic to the nurse in charge of Mr. Utterly's care and walks away. I'm not sure why I'm getting caught up in disappointment over spotting a ring. It's obvious I have no impact on her anyway.

"I'd be happy to call you if anything changes, Dr. Weston," Ashton advises as she runs her well-manicured hand dramatically down her dark tresses. "Maybe you should leave us your number so we can call you directly versus utilizing the operator since you're having trouble receiving pages." She stares at me expectantly, a hush falling about her peers.

It hits me that had Poppy offered this, I would've jumped all over it.

However, something tells me giving my cell number to Ashton is dangerous.

"Thanks. I've got my office looking into the problem with the service." I turn my focus to Jenny. "I'll check on Mr. Utterly again before I leave for the day."

"Yes, sir."

"Bye, Dr. Weston," another nurse calls from behind me. Lifting my hand, I give a curt wave as I head back to my office.

"Broadie, everything okay?" Jarod asks as I walk by his office door.

"Yeah, why?"

"Beatrice said there was a problem with the BKA you did the other day."

My jaw flexes at his statement. I hate it when people refer to my patients as anything but their names. They aren't their surgery any more than they are their room number. "Yes. Mr. Utterly looks like he's developing a wound infection." My response has more of a bite to it than it should. I know Jarod doesn't mean anything by it. I have to admit I'm feeling a bit surly after seeing that ring on Poppy's finger. Why, I have no idea. "But I think Jenny caught it early."

I start to head to my office, then stop myself. "Hey, why didn't you mention the other day that Poppy was married?"

"What?"

"The other day, when we were in the cafeteria, you joked that she wouldn't give anyone the time of day. You even laughed that it was before you were married. But she's wearing a wedding ring. It would've been a much shorter conversation to say she's off the market."

Jarod rubs his hand knowingly over his stubbled jaw. One corner of his mouth lifting in a shit-eating grin. "Somebody's been doing his homework. What's up, Broadie? Thought any woman employed at St. Luke's was strictly off limits."

"It's not like that," I reply dismissively. "She brought some IV antibiotics to the floor, and I noticed she was wearing the ring. Thought it was odd you didn't mention it. Was curious, that's all."

He looks at me skeptically. "If you say so." Jarod turns as if returning to sit at his desk, giving me the signal this conversation is over.

I start to make my way to my office when I hear him.

"I think he's dead."

CHAPTER FOUR
POPPY

"Good morning. How many?"

"Oh, I think my friend is already here," I tell the hostess. "She's a tall, beautiful brunette."

"Oh, yes. Right this way."

Following along behind this pretty young hostess until I reach Kat's table, I look about the place. The Belleview Café has been a popular spot in Hanover for what feels like forever. It's a small, family-owned place. If I'd looked past the hostess stand, I'd likely have seen Kat. The café has been our go-to spot for breakfast or lunch for years. I admit, I haven't been here in a very long time. But then again, I haven't been much of anywhere in a long time.

"Oh, it's so good to see you outside of the hospital, Poppy," Katarina greets. She's wearing a pretty white sundress covered in lemons. Her hair is down but pulled back on the sides to reveal matching yellow teardrop earrings.

"You look so cute, Kat."

"Thank you. So do you." On impulse, I look down at my outfit. I'm wearing white linen capri pants and a sleeveless sweater. And now that I think about it, I'm not one hundred percent sure my shoes match. I really need to take a little more time to get ready before I leave the house. Heck, I've only returned to using makeup about a year ago and thought that was a big step.

Grief is a funny thing. You finally get one foot in front of the other after losing your spouse, only to feel guilty about everything you do. If I try to look nice or spend the evening doing something that brings me joy, it causes such heartache because he isn't able to do the same. Even laughing feels disrespectful. I know Dan wouldn't want me to feel this way, but I've needed to handle my sadness in my own way. It's much better than it was in the years immediately following his death. But I realize I have a long way to go.

"Can I get you ladies something to drink?" the handsome young server asks, pen in hand.

"Oh, just coffee and water for me, please," Kat answers.

"I'll take the same. But could I have a slice of lemon in my water? Her outfit's causing lemony cravings." I giggle. My hand flies to my mouth, surprised at my own comment. It's been years, and I still find lighthearted banter a bit jarring. *God, what is wrong with me?*

As if Kat can sense what I'm feeling, she reaches across the table to take my hand. "How are you, Poppy? I feel terrible I haven't made more effort to connect with you over the last few years. But I admit, I was struggling with my own demons. But now that things are brighter, I should've reached out."

"Don't be silly, Katarina. You've reached out more than most. And early on, I couldn't handle spending time with anyone." I haven't really left the door open for someone to check on me. "It took a few years before I could have a conversation with anyone but my mother and Dan's head-stone. And that may have only been because I doubted either could hear what I was saying." I give a half-hearted snicker.

Kat grimaces at my remark. But I know she understands.

"Besides, I'm a big girl. I could've called you. I wish I'd been there for you too. But I think Nick is who you needed. I'm so happy for the two of you."

"Thank you. We're still in the honeymoon phase. Can you believe it?

It's coming up on our first anniversary."

The server returns with our drinks and takes our brunch order. Unlike many of the restaurants in the area, The Belleview Café offers brunch seven days a week. We've eaten here so often that we rarely look at the menu.

"How's little Grace?"

Katarina's face lights up like a Christmas tree. "She's wonderful. For a premature baby, she's done remarkably well. I had no idea how much I'd enjoy motherhood until we adopted her." I watch as the corners of her mouth abruptly bend into a frown. "Poppy. You know there are options if you decide you aren't ready to remarry but want to have a child."

"I don't know, Kat. I'm barely coming to terms with living without Dan. I haven't really contemplated children."

"Don't tell anyone, but Nick and I are going through classes to become foster parents."

Her statement catches me off guard. I'd almost forgotten Katarina could no longer have biological children. I'd assumed they would've attempted the use of a surrogate. I'm not sure why, beyond the fact that she and her husband are two of the most attractive people on the planet. Plus, I know Nick could afford it. "That's amazing, Kat. Do you mind my asking why you didn't consider using a surrogate?"

"I don't mind anything you ask, Poppy. I'm an open book." She beams. "We've looked at everything. It's not that we wouldn't consider that route in the future, but neither of us feels the need for our kids to be biological. There are so many children already here who need a good home. I'll be sad to miss the early years, but there are a lot of older boys and girls in foster care. Heck, we met Nick's little brother, Gavin, through the Boys and Girls Club of Virginia mentoring program." Kat makes air quotes as she says little brother. "But their connection was so strong that he's practically a member of our family. So this doesn't feel much different."

I sit back in my seat, trying to absorb all she's said. "You're amazing, my friend. I'm so incredibly proud of you. You deserve your happily ever after."

Kat immediately reaches back across the table, this time grabbing both of my hands. "So. Do. You."

I can't help but look away. We're diving right into the deep end this morning.

"Poppy. You've been through so much. I get it. This wasn't just a spouse losing her partner. You suffered right along with him. You didn't have time to mourn the life you two had together before you had to grieve the heartbreak of losing him."

My sweet soulmate, Daniel Danforth, died at age thirty-one of amyotrophic lateral sclerosis or ALS as it's more commonly known. Many refer to it as Lou Gehrig's disease, after the popular New York Yankees baseball player who died of the disorder at age thirty-seven. ALS is a progressive, debilitating, and ultimately fatal disorder that results in the loss of voluntary motor control. While it's rare to be diagnosed with ALS at such a young age, it can happen.

Stephen Hawkings was diagnosed at age twenty-one but lived with paralysis until his seventies. Sadly, Dan was gone less than four years after his condition was identified. He was only twenty-eight when the early symptoms of stiff muscles, intermittent twitches, and weakness began to occur. My fit, vibrant husband of six years was wheelchair-bound by twenty-nine and by age thirty, was unable to speak or swallow.

Those years were excruciating. I tried to keep a brave face for my loving husband, who never complained. Never shed a tear. He had a nurse with him during the day, and I'd take care of his needs once I returned home from work. During this period, I left my employment at the drugstore and applied to St. Luke's. People's Drug had shifted toward using pharmacists as managers of their stores. The stress was too much, given all that I was dealing with at home. Not to mention, it wasn't what I signed up for when I went to pharmacy school.

But then again, I had no idea what I'd committed to with 'in sickness and in health' either.

Not that it would've changed anything. There was nowhere else I'd be but by Dan's side during that awful ordeal. Even if I felt more like his caregiver than his wife.

Losing Dan was incredibly painful, but I tried to find solace in knowing he was finally at peace. He was no longer this larger-than-life man trapped in a broken shell of a body.

For the first few years, I mourned his absence. The next, I grieved for all of the dreams we'd lost. For the last few years, I've simply felt sorry for myself.

I had it all. I was blessed to meet Dan during my freshman year of university. Other than a brief breakup when he was concerned we were getting serious too quickly, we were together for the remainder of our college years and married not long after graduation. We quickly moved into a swanky townhouse and enjoyed traveling and all the perks of our new salaries. We were living the life.

Dan accepted a job with a well-known retail chain that sold outdoor adventure gear. He worked hard and eventually became a regional sales manager. His job kept him on the road a lot, but that came to an end with the onset of his weakness.

The company was very supportive, but it wasn't feasible for him to continue in his current role selling camping and rock-climbing equipment when he required braces or a walker to get from one side of the store to the other.

Dan and I had talked about children. We wanted to wait until he wasn't on the road as much. But that dream was short-lived when all our attention moved to keeping him well.

There are days I wish we would've tried despite his heavy travel schedule. I might still have a piece of him here with me. Yet, in hindsight, I know there's no way I would've been able to manage both a toddler and Dan's needs.

I can't help wondering what our children might've looked like. Dan was so handsome. With his inky black hair and blue eyes, he drew attention wherever he went. I was proud to be the one he chose. Trying to picture a child walking between us, I wonder. Would our son or daughter have had his dark hair or been blonde, like me?

"You know, you're right. It's been a long, painful process. But I need to rejoin the living. And foster care isn't something I've ever considered before."

"Well, regardless of whether something comes of it, I hope you'll give it some thought. Even if you get qualified to foster, you aren't obligated until you're ready." I watch as Kat tucks into her eggs and realize I've been so distracted over thoughts of yesteryear I've completely missed the server bringing our meals. "Are you doing anything for yourself?"

I reach for my spoon, the yogurt in front of me no longer as appetizing as I'd hoped before this conversation began. "What do you mean? I meditate, go to the gym, yoga classes, swim."

"That's good. But do you do anything fun? Anything that gets you excited?"

"Ha." I laugh sarcastically. It's been a while since I've been excited about anything. "No. Not really."

Katarina puts down her fork. "Poppy. I get it. And there's never any judgment from me. I shunned men and only focused on volunteering and working for years. But you're too young to live every day as a grieving widow. You need to find some way to bring joy back into your life." She picks up her utensils and digs back in. "Have you seen a counselor? For all of the things you're still struggling with?"

I put my spoon down. There's no sense in forcing this meal. My appetite is gone. "I did for a while right after Dan died. But I felt like all I did was cry. It didn't solve much." Heck, I could cry at home for free. Seemed like a waste of time and mascara to keep going back there. "And I tried a grief support group. But the first time a widower asked me if I wanted to grab coffee was the last time I went."

Kat cringes. "My friend, Melanie, is going through something similar right now. I'd connect the two of you, but her situation is still so new." Kat picks up another strawberry, turning it around inquisitively in her fingers. The thing resembles a small apple. It's huge. "It's so hard to know what to say or how to help. I'm trying to give her space, but be in the background if she needs me."

My heart aches for Melanie. The early years are so tough. I'm no longer suffering from the bone-aching pain I initially did. Yet, I still feel numb. It's like I'm trapped in limbo somehow. "That's really all you can do. And pray."

Kat nods before taking a bite of the enormous berry. "You used to love to travel. And didn't you like to do pottery back in the day?"

"Yeah. But I couldn't imagine traveling alone. And I guess I let the pottery get away from me. It's not a bad idea. Finding a class."

"Well, start with that, but I think taking a trip would be good for you. Go somewhere new. Take walks, go to the spa, read, or cry if you need to." All of a sudden, she puts down her half-eaten strawberry and begins to clap. "Ooh, maybe you could have a holiday tryst."

I'd pretend to be shocked, but I've considered as much myself. It's been a long time since I've felt the touch of a man. In the beginning, there was just no desire. Then, I had so much guilt about it. Finally, I was so lonely I drove to the beach for the night and met someone off Tinder at a bar. I was so desperate to feel anything. I just wanted to know I was still alive. But it was a disaster.

I had to be completely intoxicated to have the nerve to sleep with him. Then, once things got hot and heavy, I burst into tears. The guy was so eager to get it on he ignored me and finished the job before slinking out. I think I must've taken twenty showers trying to rid the feeling of disgust from my skin that night.

There have been a couple of other attempts over the years, ones with fewer tears. Yet the experiences felt much like eating something you know is bad for you. Each time, I regretted the decision before the night was over.

"I want you to do me a favor." My head pops up to find Katarina looking intent.

"Um, okay. What?"

She pulls out her cell phone and types something rapidly.

Ding.

Reaching into my purse, I retrieve my phone and notice she's sent me a phone number via text. "Who's this?"

"It's my counselor. I felt the exact same way as you about seeing one. Until I met Dr. Miller. He's done wonders to help me."

I'm not jazzed about seeing another paid professional to listen to me rattle on. But I need to do something. "Sure. It couldn't hurt to try. You'd think after all of this time, I wouldn't still need counseling." I lean my elbow on the table and drop my chin in my hand.

Katarina takes a sip of coffee before giving me a stern look. "There's no deadline for grief, Poppy. Heck, I still see Dr. Miller from time to time. It's a judgment-free zone. A place where a trained professional can help you discuss the things you're struggling with. So you can come up with an objective solution. For me, it's freeing. To have one place where I can get things off my chest without burdening my friends or family."

"I'm sure Nick doesn't think you're a burden."

Kat wipes her mouth with her napkin and places it on the table. A frown appears as she witnesses my untouched food, and I can tell she's figured out I'm no longer interested in eating my meal. "No. I'm lucky. But sometimes, you want to be heard without someone trying to fix things for you. You know?"

Yeah. I do know. Not that I have people standing in line to do that anymore. But it'd be nice to unload my thoughts on someone other than my hard-of-hearing mother or the overwatered fern in my sunroom. I think they're both quite tired of my pitiful mood.

Kat waves toward our server and asks for a to-go container for my meal. "I've got to run." She leans in for a hug. With her heels, she's easily two to three inches taller than I am. "We need to do this more often. But next time, we'll share our achievements and happy moments now that we got the morose stuff out of the way."

"I adore you, Katarina. Thank you. I didn't realize how much I needed this."

"Good. I predict it won't be long before I'll get to hear about your hot date with Dr. Weston."

I immediately push away from her. "What?"

Kat snorts. "Oh, come on. I can dream, can't I?"

Can't we all?

"Not that he'd ever ask. But I'm not dating anyone from work."

"I understand. But if that man asked me out, I think I'd consider giving my two weeks' notice."

CHAPTER FIVE
BROADIE

"Hi, Dr. Weston." I look up from my phone and see Sharon leaning against the nurses' station counter. She's an attractive, albeit overly plastic, blonde with brown eyes and shoulder-length hair. Nothing about her seems natural. Her hair looks over-processed with heavy highlights, and her lips have the inflated appearance of someone who's received an injectable filler. Sharon's worked at St. Luke's as an emergency room nurse for as long as I've been here. I suspect she's probably my age, yet her attempts to look younger do the opposite, in my opinion.

"Hi. Sharon. How are you?" I try to smile in her direction, but it's not genuine. While she's been nothing but professional when I've worked alongside her, I've always had the impression she's holding the door open for more on the chance the right person might venture through it. I don't want to give here any indication that person could be me.

I'm not ignorant of the *Grey's Anatomy* types of relationships that often occur here. I've worked too hard to build a solid reputation to allow that to go up in smoke with an office tryst. Yet, news travels the halls of this hospital like wind to a brush fire. More than a few physicians have gone conspicuously absent due to a rumored affair, only to turn up later at a sister hospital. There's no hard and fast rule about nonfraternization at St.

Luke's unless it's with a direct superior. But it's just not wise to mix business with pleasure.

"Good morning, Dr. Weston," a bright-eyed twenty-something nurse greets from down the hall. Work environment or not, I'd never consider dating someone in their twenties. Hell, my oldest daughter is twenty. Any woman I'm sleeping with needs to be closer to my age than hers.

"Good morning," I reply, ensuring I don't make eye contact with her. But in my determination to avoid her, my eyes land on a familiar blonde-haired, blue-eyed pharmacist instead. I don't get it. I go nearly a decade without laying eyes on her. And now she's everywhere.

Shifting in my seat, I take her in. She's wearing a long emerald green dress under her starched white lab coat. Her hair is down with a bit more curl today than the last few times I've seen her. The doctor and nurse she's speaking with seem to be having a good-humored conversation, as she frequently tilts her head back in laughter.

The sight of her is mesmerizing. That smile is glorious. I drag my tongue along my lower lip, imagining it's the tempting column of her throat.

Get a grip, Broadie. You need to get laid.

Yet, as much as I try to concentrate on anything else, I can't help picturing her sitting across from me, drinking a glass of wine, and sharing humorous tales of our patient encounters through the years. I have no idea why I think she'd be so engaging to share an evening with. She's barely given me the time of day.

"Hi, Dr. Weston."

My eyes nearly roll back in my head. I appreciate the friendly nature of these women but for shit's sake. I stand from the computer stations I've been occupying to find Kat staring at me with a puzzling expression. "Oh, Kat. I'm sorry. I didn't realize it was you."

"That's okay. You seemed preoccupied," she replies with a mischievous grin, tapping her index finger against her jaw as if she's the holder of some fascinating intel. "Do you have a patient down here?"

"No," I answer with a bit of trepidation. "We have a new surgeon joining the practice. I was going to ask Dr. Wilson if I could introduce him to your group at the quarterly meeting."

"Oh." Kat drops her hands down by her sides, appearing perplexed. "Is he single?" There's a glint in her eye I find odd. I've known Katarina for years. First, as the granddaughter of a lovely patient of mine. Then, later, she joined the ER staff as a physician assistant. She's a hard worker, and while she has an easygoing personality, she's always been professional. So, I find this line of questioning quite peculiar.

"Trouble in paradise?" I smirk.

"Ha-ha. No. Things are great with Nick. I was just keeping my eyes peeled for Poppy."

What the hell?

The teasing expression quickly falls from my face at her remark. Over my dead body, am I introducing this guy to Poppy.

I clear my throat. "I'm pretty sure he's married. With kids," I blurt. I have no fucking idea what his marital status is. He's about my age and not a bad-looking guy. I assume he's married. Jarod and Pearl vetted him, as he interviewed during a particularly busy surgical week.

The thought that Katarina is actively trying to hook Poppy up with someone has me seeing red. I have no idea why I'm coming unglued by this. *Am I going through a midlife crisis?* None of this makes any sense.

"Kat, I think your seek and find skills are being requested in fast track." Sharon guffaws in our direction.

Kat's expression goes blank. "Is this of the downtown variety?"

Sharon doesn't answer with words, but her taunting expression says it all. Retrieving foreign objects from private areas is never as entertaining for the provider as it is fodder for their coworkers. But the look on Kat's face is priceless.

"Don't laugh." She points at me. "I don't know which orifice this object landed in when they fell on it." Kat puts air quotes around *fell on it.* That tends to be the most popular excuse for how these things end up where they don't belong. "But if I can't get it out, guess who I'm calling." She laughs as she crosses her arms over her chest.

"May the force be with you." I chuckle. I turn to look for Dr. Wilson as

Kat heads to her newest patient and observe Poppy coming toward me. My heart speeds up a little, and I try to devise something clever to say besides 'hi' when my phone buzzes in my pocket. Once I reach back to grab it, I look up to see Poppy walking through the exit doors without a word.

Frustrated, I bring my phone to my ear and grumble, "Hello."

"Well, hello to you too, Daddy. Having a bad day?"

"Hi, sweetheart. No. I'm fine. How's my girl?"

"Good. I miss you. I feel like we haven't seen you in months."

I can't help but wince, then quickly try to steer away from my history of being an absent parent and give my daughter my full attention. "It has been too long. But then again, your mom's had you jet-setting all over the globe this summer." I glimpse Dr. Wilson down the hall and head in his direction.

"Why didn't you come with us? New Zealand was so much fun."

"I bet it was. It was a busy time here. We had someone already out that week and another who just transferred out of state."

I can hear her harumph across the phone line. "Well, I thought you had seniority there. Besides, you have more money than God. Why don't you take some time off and live a little?"

There's so much wrong with this conversation. First, Lauren has absolutely no appreciation of money. If we aren't careful, this overindulged twenty-year-old will burn through every dime of her trust fund. Second, she needs to understand that a lot of moving pieces are required to keep a surgical practice going. "Lauren, I can't take off whenever I want because I've worked here the longest." And third, I'm growing tired of spending my vacations watching my wife and daughters with the new man of the house.

"I bet you could if you wanted to." Her statement stings. She's probably a lot more on target than she knows. And I'm the selfish bastard who has to live knowing I've continued to choose my career over my family. More specifically, over my children.

Camile and I have been lucky as far as divorced couples go. When we were married, we rarely fought about anything but my job. In retrospect, it's painful to realize how clear I made it that she wasn't the priority in my life. Camile knows my only mistress was the OR. We made it almost ten years before the writing was on the wall, and we filed for divorce.

Two things were clear. I wasn't going to change, and she deserved far better. My daughters were ages seven and five when we split. Luckily, the upside to working all of the time was my children didn't notice much difference until Camile started dating. But the girls are bright and well-adjusted, all due to Camile's parenting, and they've accepted Joel as their new stepdad without missing a beat.

I admit there are times I'm pretty jealous. He's stepped into his ready-made family and spends more time with my girls than I do. But life is about choices, and I have no one to blame but myself. Thankfully, he's been nothing but respectful. At times, he's present when I'm invited to spend time with them, and he gives me some space at others. I dare say I couldn't have hand-picked a better replacement. I try to remind myself of that when I lay my head down at night, all alone in my big empty house.

I've harbored a lot of guilt over my life choices. Yet, there were a lot of things that led up to our split. It wasn't merely my work-life imbalance.

Camile and I met during college. I had a sizable trust fund, so we lived larger than most medical students were capable. I'm sure this added to my attractiveness, as Camile has never been one to settle for anything less than the best.

She grew up with parents who lived a lavish lifestyle. There wasn't a doubt in my mind she'd accept nothing other than the standard she'd grown accustomed. Fortunately, given how well my father and grandfather had invested their income, I could easily afford whatever she wanted. So I never chose to quibble over money.

Once I began my surgical career, I deposited money Camile could draw from and otherwise invested almost every dime. As my practice flourished, I became more aggressive with my investment portfolio. Sure, I splurged on a nice home and a few cars, but I didn't go on lavish trips or shopping sprees. *Who had time? I was always working.*

Over the next ten years, the millions I'd inherited, plus the income from my thriving practice, pushed me into billionaire status. I was grateful my father required a prenup before receiving the inheritance. But Camile and the girls have always been well provided for. There was really no need to argue in court over money. Besides, she was well aware that my guilt over our family's destruction would have me handing over more if needed.

I'm pretty sure Camile was relieved when we split. She had all the money she could want and was free to pursue a normal relationship. I wasn't an easy man to live with. Not so much argumentative or controlling. Yet, I was absent… until I wasn't.

Life as a surgeon is high-stress. I hit the gym daily, eat right, and beyond an occasional cigar or tumbler of scotch, I avoid smoking or drinking. I try to find ways to unwind and have a great group of friends I spend time with who keep me grounded. However, there are times when I just need more. And my ex-wife wasn't a fan.

Camile and I have never had a stellar sex life. In the early days of our marriage, I was getting laid once or twice a week. It was very routine, always in the missionary position, and usually leaving me feeling I might've had a better release with a hand job in the shower. But I was young and had other priorities. It wasn't worth arguing about.

Yet, I found as my stress levels increased, I wasn't satisfied with the usual lackluster vanilla sex. I needed more.

The first time I pulled Camile's hair and smacked her ass, I was worried she'd charge me with assault. I explained that, at times, I needed to be more aggressive. It helped me detach and manage the tension I was feeling. She wasn't keen on this change in our monotonous intimacy but allowed it since it occurred so infrequently. Yet, it was barely more satiating than our run-of-the-mill vanilla sex. Camile was not an active participant and certainly didn't enjoy it. It wasn't particularly pleasurable for either of us, to be honest. I surmised it was merely a feeble attempt, on her part, at keeping our marriage alive.

Once the divorce was final, I vowed not to put another woman through that. There's no sense in becoming involved with a faithful partner at this age when work remains my priority. Choosing my career over a committed relationship is on me.

I come from a long line of workaholics. There's an innate drive to be the best at what I do. I can thank my father and grandfather, rest their souls, for being the same. I'm sure their determination to win at managing their wealth allowed it to grow as it has. It was more than an obsession with money. It was a drive to be the very best at something. However, I need to remember neither of them lived to see eighty. And you can't take the money with you.

Hopefully, I can find some balance before I'm dead and buried. To turn off that channel that's constantly on, striving for more. Because if I use my DNA as a guide, at forty-two, I'm on the downward slope. Until then, my regular girl, Brandee, is available when I need the release. And when I'm stressed, she has no complaint regarding my requirement to be in control. Hell, I tend to think the rougher it is, the more she likes it.

Don't get me wrong. I'm not some dominant asshole with a god complex. I wish I could detach from my job and enjoy the sweet companionship of a woman at the end of each day. But Camile and I weren't wired that way. She enjoyed society galas and lunching with the ladies. I revel in the adrenaline rush of working under the harsh lights of the OR, knowing I can change lives for the better. Camile and I are better off as friends, and we both know it.

Although, it might sting a little less if another man hadn't taken my place so effortlessly.

I haven't completely given up hope that a woman exists who could be my perfect match. Someone who will accept me as I am. Driven and flawed, but with a loving, generous soul beneath it all. Yet, there's no sense in pursuing that if I can't devote the time and attention a healthy relationship deserves. For now, I'll stick to women who respect my limitations and surround myself with my equally imperfect friends.

"Lauren, I'm afraid I need to get back to work. It's not like you to call me in the middle of the day. Is everything okay? Is Lilly all right?"

"Oh, she's fine. All she does is study. I hope she comes out of her shell in college, Dad. She's a senior, but I don't think she's had one date in the last six months."

"Just the way I like it. You two are like night and day. What works for you might not be the same for her." *Thank god.* I've got enough worries about Lauren getting hooked up with the wrong crowd or ending up pregnant. I don't need her introducing her sister to that lifestyle.

"I called because my car wouldn't start this morning. I think I need a new one."

Here we go.

"Lauren, you just bought that car. Maybe you need a new battery."

"I didn't *just* buy this car, Dad. I got it *last* year."

We've created a monster. I need to talk to Camile about reining Lauren in before it's too late. "The car was brand new when we purchased it. There's no reason you can't take it to the shop and have it repaired. You don't need a new car. Your grandfather drove the same truck for a decade." I laugh at the memory. He must've put two new engines in the thing. I didn't understand it at the time, but as my appreciation of money has increased, I get it now. Don't get me wrong, I splurge when the occasion calls for it. I've earned it. But that's the last thing Lauren needs to hear right now.

"Well, that's just dumb. Dad, you have billions. What's a new car to you?"

Looking at my watch, I realize I've spent far too long in this department. And all to arrange introductions to the new surgeon on the block. Now I'm dealing with this nonsense. "I'm sorry, Lauren. The answer is no. Have your mother call me if I need to arrange to tow the car to the Audi dealership." Which is ridiculous in and of itself. Her mother doesn't work. She can make a phone call. "I'll talk to you later."

I disconnect and reach back to rub my tense neck muscles as I head back to the office. Maybe I'll just grab a quick coffee to take back with me. Who knows at this rate if I'll get lunch.

Reaching to swipe my badge to gain entry to the doctors' lounge, my head buried in my phone, I nearly face-plant into the door when it doesn't open. Glancing up, I'm reminded of the renovations and roll my eyes at myself. Coming here is a force of habit. Nothing to do with being overwhelmed by my ridiculous schedule, I inwardly chide.

Sliding my phone into my back pocket, I make my way to the cafeteria, hoping there isn't a long line. That's the main perk of the physicians' lounge. Having a quiet space to eat and a computer station to chart is nice, but the ease of grabbing what I need and getting back to work efficiently is the main appeal.

As luck would have it, the cafeteria doesn't look too congested. But then again, I'm here before the lunch rush. As I reach for a cup of coffee, I notice a cheese danish and think, *what the hell.* The hotline is open, but there's no way I'll have time to consume anything from there before it grows cold. And I'm not tempted by much in this cafeteria. Reheated hot bar food even less.

I grab a bottle of water and a prepared salad from the fridge to avoid returning later in the day. I'm sure I could use that time to catch up on my charting.

My phone buzzes as I move into the cashier's line, and I attempt to juggle my items so I can retrieve it in case Beatrice is alerting me that I'm getting behind on my schedule. To my chagrin, I see Lauren has sent a picture of a shiny red convertible.

Jesus.

Ignoring my spoiled child, I bend forward to return my phone to my back pocket when the most enticing fragrance envelops me. There's no need to confirm the body it's attached to, I know it's her. Unable to stop myself, I close the distance between us, lean into her gorgeous blonde locks, and inhale.

Fuck, she's intoxicating. I can feel my dick start to twitch behind my zipper.

Poppy quickly spins in my direction with a questioning stare.

Smooth, Broadie. Real smooth.

"Sorry. Smelled something and couldn't help myself."

Her eyes pop wide, and evidenced by the frown on her face, I realize I've likely offended her.

"Your scent is irresistible. There was nothing else in here that had my mouth watering, so I knew it had to be you."

What. The. Fuck?

What am I thinking? My game is so bad I could end up in HR for harassment at this rate.

Without a word or reassuring change in her scowl, Poppy spins toward the front of the line and hands the cashier her food as if I'm invisible.

My forehead breaks out into a sweat, but my hands are full, so I stand here looking and feeling like a simp, hoping not to drip perspiration onto the counter once I move forward.

Hell. This woman is my kryptonite.

"Good morning, Dr. Weston," the cheery cashier greets.

I'm relieved for the diversion from my humiliating behavior when I discover I recognize this kind lady. "Good morning, Althea. Looks like I picked the right time to come."

"Yes, sir. It's gotten a bit busier with the doctors' lounge under construction. But it's nice to see you outside of there. You guys are always too busy talking shop to one another to say hello."

Her statement hits me like a two-by-four. That's the very reason I've enjoyed it there. The ability to keep working, only stopping to grab a quick cup of joe or lunch with equally overstressed, work-obsessed colleagues. I'm an asshole. A universally disrespectful asshat.

By all accounts, I'm a nice guy. At least, that's what the reviews always say. And I don't try to put on a show. I want my interactions with my patients to be genuine. Yet I'm not really living. It suddenly hits me that I only take the time to interact with people when it benefits my business or suits me personally.

My grandmother would be appalled. She's probably already disgusted with me for how rarely I visit. She's ninety-nine and lives with a full-time nurse. She's practically deaf and blind, otherwise, I believe her mind is still sharp. That's one more person I need to make it up to. But I'll start with this ever-pleasant dietary worker.

"You know, Althea. You're absolutely right. I apologize for that."

"Oh, I'm not criticizing, Dr. Weston. You've always been so polite to say hello when you could. I know you have more important things to do."

"Certainly not. You've worked here at least as long as I have. You keep us all going, Althea. Your job is very important."

A sweet blush crosses her brown skin, and the interaction causes me to smile brightly at her. This day might be picking up after all.

"Broadie, can I have a moment of your time?"

Or maybe not.

My eyes close at the sound of his voice. Brantly Martin. The administrator whose sole purpose in life is to make mine more stressful. "I'm afraid now isn't a good time, Brantly. I've been detained in the ER longer than I would've liked and have patients waiting in my office." It's a white lie, but he doesn't need to know that. I don't think anyone has been waiting. I take great pains to be punctual.

"I understand. You're an incredibly busy man. I only wanted to remind you that the deadline for appointing a medical director is approaching. Dr. Birmingham will be retiring soon, and we need someone to step in who will move the hospital forward. I feel there are a lot of positive changes that could beneficially impact our facility if you were at the helm. Not to mention, staff recruitment and retention is at an all-time low. I think having you more involved could change this."

I have no idea why he thinks my becoming the medical director would impact staffing. Maybe if the hospital would treat the staff already employed at St. Luke's better than the temporary nurses they keep hiring when the mistreated ones eventually quit, they might be able to retain quality employees.

"I'm not interested in adding to my workload, Brantly. But if I can find a way to contribute something, I'll let you know." I give a halfhearted wave and pick up my pace before he has a chance to come up with anything new.

~

"Sorry for the delay, Beatrice. Do I have many patients waiting?"

"No, Broadie. It's not bad. The nurses have two in exam rooms ready for you. But they haven't been waiting long. One's a gallbladder follow-up who appears to be doing well, and the other is here for an elective breast reduction consult."

"Thank you."

"You seem flustered, dear. Did that old Mr. Martin corner you again?"

My head snaps in her direction, stunned. "Yeah. How'd you know?"

"You always seem stressed when he's been nipping at your heels."

Wow. I don't know if Beatrice is more receptive than I give her credit for or if I'm simply that transparent.

"And he called looking for you." She chuckles.

A laugh escapes. "And here I was starting to think you were a clairvoyant."

"No. You can literally see it on your face when you're stressed. You're always so cordial. But when things are tense, that lovely dimple disappears."

I guess I am transparent.

CHAPTER SIX
POPPY

"Hi, Jasmine."

"Poppy," she greets affectionately. "You here to see your mom?" I notice the kind receptionist looking at her watch. She probably suspects I'm here to voice a complaint or settle a bill. I'm never here at this hour on a weekday.

"Yes. I know I don't usually come this early. I'm working the weekend, so I have the day off. I thought I'd have lunch with Mom."

Her sweet, round face beams back at me. Jasmine has worked at Hanover Haven since Mom first arrived. "Oh, she'll love that. Would you like to eat in the courtyard?"

My mother is deaf as a post. And most likely demented. I know she'll struggle to make out what I'm saying over the clatter of the dining room. "I think the courtyard is a perfect idea."

"No problem at all, dear. Why don't you go surprise her with a visit, and I'll have everything set up at a table in the gazebo in about an hour."

"Thank you, Jasmine. That'll be lovely." I make my way down the cold, sterile hallway until I come to my mother's door. My brother, mother, and I made the painful decision to place her at Hanover Haven while Dan was in his steep decline toward the end.

My brother, Ian, and his wife and kids live several hours away, near Blacksburg, Virginia. He attended Virginia Tech and never wanted to leave. After graduation, he was able to come home to visit regularly. But once he married Rita and the second and third children arrived, his visits became less frequent.

It was understandable. Ian works full time, and the weekends are busy with the kids' sports and church youth activities. Our father had died years ago, and we'd made sure to look in on Mom over the years. In the beginning, this didn't require much. She was a homebody. Our mother had a few friends from church who'd drop by occasionally, but otherwise, she was in the kitchen or her garden.

Yet, as the years ticked by, she became more forgetful, and we worried about her safety living alone. One night, I arrived to find a grease fire in the kitchen. Accidents can happen at any age. Yet the most alarming part was that she was completely oblivious, belting out answers to Steve Harvey's questions on *Family Feud* in the other room as flames licked up the kitchen walls. She had no recollection of placing anything on the stove. I couldn't even identify what she'd been preparing due to the amount of wreckage it caused.

I immediately took her to see her practitioner, expressing concern for Alzheimer's or some other form of dementia. Yet she'd have intermittent spells where she was completely lucid. So it had been difficult to receive a formal diagnosis.

Eventually, she was admitted to the hospital for pneumonia and experienced an episode of Sundowner's while she was there. Mom tolerated the unfamiliar environment during the day, but as night fell, she became increasingly more confused. That occurrence was enough to grant her a dementia diagnosis and allow us to seek placement in a skilled nursing facility where someone had their eyes on her twenty-four-seven.

At times, I feel guilty having placed her here. I'd much rather have her home. Now that Dan is gone, I often reconsider whether she'd be better off at home with me than here. But it'd be a massive undertaking around my job. And I have no guarantee she'd be happier at my place. Plus, there's the risk she might be less safe if there aren't trained professionals to watch her constantly.

"Hi, Mom."

Seated in a wheelchair, my mother is wearing a short-sleeved floral top and light blue pants. Her head is down, and she appears to have fallen asleep as she hasn't moved an inch in response to my greeting. I consider whether I should let her sleep, but my gut tells me that's about all she does anymore.

Knock. Knock.

Nothing. My heart starts to thump in my chest, worried something's wrong. I pound harder on the door before racing to kneel down in front of her. Just as I reach her, my mother's head pops up. "Oh, hello, dear."

My hand flies to my heart and I bite down on my lip to prevent screeching. *Jiminy Christmas.* "Good God, Mom. You scared me half to death." I grimace at my analogy. Probably should avoid using that phrase here.

"Why is that?"

"I was knocking on the door, and you didn't budge."

Taking in my frail mother, my heart squeezes remembering the vivacious woman she once was. When she arrived at Hanover Haven, she was ambulatory. The physical therapist later encouraged her to use a cane for stability, but after they found her frequently walking with it tucked under her arm, they moved to a wheelchair. While she resisted at first, I think her chronic inactivity has caused her muscles to atrophy, and she's given in.

"Oh, I'm sorry, Poppy. My ears aren't what they used to be. What time is it?"

Leaning back on my heels, I exhale a relieved breath. She seems articulate today. Maybe I'm making too much of some of the confusion I've witnessed. "Oh, it's early. I must've caught you during your mid-day nap. I had the day off and thought we could have lunch."

"Oh, that's a wonderful surprise."

As I stand before her, I take a look about the room. Very little changes in her humble abode between visits. A few small books are stacked on her nightstand with a large magnifying glass resting on top of them. Her twin bed is draped in a colorful patchwork quilt she made years ago as opposed to the generic hospital-grade linens covering her roommate Agnes' bed. A small potted plant sits on the bottom shelf of a corner table that's showing evidence of neglect. Walking over to the frail thing, I pluck the plastic stake and read the card.

Happy Mother's Day.
Love,
Dan, Rita, Anne, Henry, and Baxter

Smiling, I return the card to its holder and bring the plant into the bathroom for a little pruning and a drink of water. I can't help wondering if it's had much since he sent it over a month ago. Not sure how I hadn't noticed it until now. "It was nice of Ian to send you this," I shout over the running water. When she doesn't reply, I turn off the tap and question whether I should repeat my statement louder or just let it go.

"How's Dan?"

My feet stop in their tracks, and I stand slack-jawed in the doorway. Why would she ask such a thing? My mother is well aware Dan is dead.

Dementia is a peculiar thing. Some patients may retain long term memory until their disease progresses to the point they can no longer participate in meaningful conversations or activities. Others have inter-mittent confusion. With Mom, the obvious changes present themselves at night. During the day it's difficult to determine if her disorientation is due to her poor hearing or forgetfulness. She's never been confused about the people in her life. And she's certainly never seemed unaware Dan or my father were no longer with us.

"Who?" I ask, dumbfounded.

"Stan," she screeches. "He's the nice old man that lives next door to you with the garden. Right?"

My shoulders relax, and I try to recover from the second scare in ten minutes. "Oh, yes. Stan seems to be fine. His yard is beautiful. I'll have to bring a picture of it the next time I come." I return the potted plant to its home and sit on the edge of Mom's bed. "Do you know what they're serving for lunch today?"

"It's meatloaf. And if you aren't looking to lose a tooth, you may want to reconsider," a familiar voice echoes from the doorway.

"Hi, Agnes. It's good to see you."

"Well, pardon me if I don't return the sentiment. I'd much rather send you a postcard from Fiji." She looks at her watch mockingly. "Surprised to see you. You get laid off from your fancy job?"

"No." I laugh. "And trust me. There's nothing fancy about it. I have to work all weekend, so I have today and Friday off."

"Well, word to the wise. From now on, when you come for lunch, bring it with you. I think they must be short on beds."

I chuckle, almost afraid to ask what she's referring to. "What do you mean?"

"If you didn't lose a tooth on that hockey puck they call meatloaf, you might gag on the boiled Brussels sprouts. Who boils Brussels sprouts? I think they're trying to kill us."

My gaze returns to my mother, who's wearing a noncommittal smile. I recognize it as a pleasantry she gives when she has no idea what's being said around her. Probably just as well.

"Perhaps you'll get lucky, and they'll just make you a salad and some canned peaches."

I giggle. "Yes. Maybe."

"Poppy." My mother's soft hand drops down over mine. "Are you seeing anyone?"

I notice Agnes leaning in like she's awaiting an answer. I should be ready for this question. She asks it often enough, and I'm pretty sure the repetition isn't memory-related, more hopeful inquisition.

"No. I've had a few dates." Lies. "But it's harder to find a match at my age. Not to mention, they have big shoes to fill." I need to let go of the thought I'll ever find someone who makes me feel as I did with Daniel. That qualification is not fair to them or to me. Any future relationship will be different. That's all there is to it.

"Well, you know what they say?" Agnes says as she puts her walker by her chair and takes a seat.

"No. What do they say?" I ask with trepidation.

"Big shoes, big—"

My face heats, and I quickly cough over the end of her response, never knowing what will come out of her mouth.

"Listen to me, Poppy." Agnes waves her arthritis-ridden finger at me. "You have a great opportunity ahead of you. Not many women get the chance to go after Mr. Right once they're old enough to know what they really want. I say you find someone who makes you see stars."

Instinctively, I raise my hand to my cheek to feel the warmth of my blush.

"All jokes aside. You're a beautiful woman. You deserve to be treated that way. Forget the flowers and fancy dinners. Those men are a dime a dozen. You get yourself a real man. One who makes you feel like the sun won't rise without you."

I'm speechless. Agnes is always so witty and sarcastic, I never take much of what she says too seriously. Yet it's like she's speaking to my very soul. That *is* what I want. The fairytale. Perhaps she's been reading the same romance novels I have.

As much as I loved Dan, he was always comfortable. Don't get me wrong, I'd give anything for one more day with him. But our life wasn't full of romance. It was safe. I loved him, and he loved me. That was it. Now I spend my nights with my latest book boyfriend. They're all handsome, swoon worthy characters that leave me breathless in more ways than one. And the best part. A happily ever after is a requirement in romance novels.

So, the hero doesn't die in the end.

"You're absolutely right, Agnes. And once I find one, you'll be the first to know."

∽

"Did you get enough to eat?" I ask, folding my napkin, placing it on the wrought iron table, and wincing when it touches the hot surface. These patio sets are beautiful but not made for the severe heat.

"What?" my mother yells.

"Are you done with your lunch?" I practically scream back at her.

"Yes. It was more than enough." Looking over her plate, I determine she may have had three leaves of lettuce, half of a peach, and likely a table-spoon of cottage cheese. I guess that's about average for her. But given she doesn't burn any calories, she likely doesn't need much more.

"How about you?"

"I had plenty. I was just glad it wasn't the meatloaf," I shout and quickly scan the area to ensure no employees are within earshot. Lifting my glass of water, I take a sip before my mother's next words have me spraying it in my lap.

"You need to start dating, Poppy. If you want to have babies, you need to start dating." She sounds adamant. As if 'enough is enough already.' Yet we haven't had the baby conversation often. I expected it to happen, but when it didn't, I was unclear if she was trying to be careful of my feelings or if dementia caused her to forget to harass me.

"I know. I date."

A thin gray brow lifts in response.

"Okay, not often. But there really aren't that many good prospects out there."

She grows quiet for a minute, and I start to gather our things to return inside when she continues. "How about that Bumble Bee thing?"

My eyes dart about the gazebo on the chance I've misunderstood this conversation, and she's referring to an insect.

"Agnes is forever messaging men on Bumble Bee."

Holy crap. "For real?"

"Yes. She says there are some real lookers."

"Maybe so. But Agnes is in her eighties." I giggle. "Do they know they'd have to drop by Hanover Haven to pick her up?"

"Agnes is a beautiful woman. Those men would be lucky to take her out," my mother scolds, her voice still raised.

"You're right. But I think they might be too old for me."

"Then try a different one. For younger men. You're not getting any younger, Poppy."

"Thanks, Mom." As if I haven't had the same thought myself.

"Your brother is coming for a visit next week," she shouts. "Please try to spend some time with him. You two used to be so close."

Grateful for the change in topic, I grin. "Oh, I'd love to see him. Are Rita and the kids coming?"

"I don't think so. They have camp or something." Mom briefly grows silent before uttering, "I mean what I say, Poppy. Time has a habit of moving on without you. We lost your father before I was ready. But I was far older than you are now. I don't want you to spend your days alone."

I stand, blinking away tears as I gather our trash and place it in the receptacle outside of the gazebo. Grabbing the handles of my mother's wheelchair, we return to her room in silence. I can't say it's comfortable because it's not. Even at my age, her words weigh heavy. I know she's only thinking of me. I'd love to find someone and give her more grandchildren. But I'm not going to settle for a relationship merely to avoid being alone. Unfortunately, things don't always turn out like they're supposed to.

Even if you were lucky enough to live in a house with a white picket fence for a while.

Once I return to Mom's room, I find Agnes in her chair, scrolling on her cell phone, and I shake my head, curious about who she might be messaging. Leaning over Mom's shoulder, I speak directly in her ear, hoping I can avoid shouting. "Do you want to stay in the chair or take a nap?"

"I'd love a nap."

Tucking her in, I park the wheelchair out of the way before returning to kiss her on the head. "I'll try to get back soon."

"I understand, dear. Your job is demanding."

"Well, I'd find yourself a hot doc. Working there on the weekends should come with some perks," Agnes says, her eyes never leaving her phone.

I snicker. "I couldn't do that. Then I'd have to find a job somewhere else. I wouldn't want to work with someone I dated. It complicates things."

Agnes settles her phone in her lap before crossing her arms over her ample bosom. "Poppy, excuses are for people who don't want it bad enough.I want you to answer something quickly without giving your doubts a chance to argue."

Her request makes me a little anxious. But I decide to go all in. "Okay."

"If you'd never met Dan and age wasn't an issue, would you want to be married and have children?"

"Yes." My hand flies to cover my mouth as if I could somehow prevent my inner thoughts from escaping. The speed with which that three-letter word left my mouth shocks me.

"That's what I thought. Then make it happen, girl. If you meet someone at your job, then quit and live a life of leisure like me." An uncharacteristic smile crosses her face, making me giggle. "Find someone gorgeous and have a kid before it's too late. Would be a damn waste of good DNA not to," she goads, running her finger through the air from my head to my toes. I know she means well, but at my age, that could be one more disappointment in the making.

"I think at thirty-eight, my odds aren't very good."

"Well, you might have to put a little more effort into it." Agnes waggles her brows at me and wiggles her hips provocatively.

My hand flies back to my mouth. "Agnes."

"What? You've reached your sexual peak. Enjoy the ride!"

Oh, my god. I glance over my shoulder to verify my mother isn't hearing this. What am I thinking? She usually can't hear anything unless we're shouting.

"And you work in medicine. You know full well there are a lot more options available if you can't have a baby the usual way. Or you could do it like me. Sans man." She laughs.

My eyes widen at this. "Agnes, why did I think you didn't have any kids? How many children do you have?"

"Last count, it was thirty-seven."

Um, what? Okay, maybe I've been concerned about the wrong woman in this room having dementia.

Agnes breaks into laughter at my countenance. "I was a foster mother, dear. After surviving two divorces just to become a widow in my early fifties, I decided to be the love 'em and leave 'em type from then on. But that left a lot of time on my hands. So I took in littles who were in transition. Most didn't stay very long. A lot of parents want newborns. But a few stuck around long enough that I got attached. I was just too old at that point to adopt them. But you could."

"Me?"

"Yes. Why not? I'm only saying there are options. It's time to start living. No more excuses."

"I'm living."

Aren't I?

CHAPTER SEVEN
BROADIE

"Dad!" Lauren waves animatedly from a corner booth at Luigi's. As I head in her direction, I'm shocked to find her sister here with her.

"Lilly. I'm so glad you could make it," I greet, leaning in for a hug from each before sitting across from them.

"She must really miss you to pull herself away from her book," Lauren sneers.

"Well, I'm thrilled to see both of you. Sorry, I'm late."

They instantly give me the same deadpan expression.

"What? I'm punctual."

"It's more that we expect you to cancel than to be late," Lilly says softly.

A voluptuous blonde wearing a skin-tight black mini-skirt and a white button-up approaches. "I have two iced teas and a Pellegrino," she says as she slides the drinks in front of us. "Your girls said they wanted to wait until you arrived before ordering appetizers."

My head falls. Resting my elbows on the table, I lean my face into my palms. I can't believe how I've let them down. It's one thing when it's Camile. She knew what she was signing up for when we got married. But lavish lifestyles or not, it's not fair that they've had an absent father. Or worse, if I've made them feel they aren't important to me.

"Can we have a minute?" Lilly asks.

Looking up, I find the server has left us. "I'm sorry, girls. I've been a really crappy father."

My youngest slides her hand over mine and gives me an apologetic look while her sister keeps her arms crossed over her chest as if she's waiting for me to continue.

"Listen, you'd be proud of me. The hospital administrator is pushing me to take on the medical director position at the hospital, and I told him no. I honestly want to slow down and spend more time with you."

Lilly gives me a soft smile of encouragement while her sister continues to look unphased.

"Of course, working less means we'll probably have to scale back on the spending."

Lauren's arms drop onto the table, and her mouth forms a perfect O. It takes everything in me not to laugh.

"You're one of the richest people on the planet. You could quit work today, and we'd have more money than we know what to do with," she blurts.

"Ah, but something tells me *you'd* know what to do with it." I waggle my finger in her direction. "I don't want you to turn into some obnoxious reality TV star. Money can be dangerous. We're blessed, mainly because of the cunning and generosity of your grandfather and great-grandfather. But I want more for the two of you than to be spoiled trust fund babies."

Lauren lets out an exacerbated sigh. "Mom doesn't work."

"Well, that's your mother's choice. But I know you're capable of great things. I want you to finish college and either work with a charity you are passionate about or start a business. Find a way to make an honest contribution to the world."

Bzzz. Bzzz.

Lauren dives into her purse to retrieve her phone and immediately starts texting a message at the speed of light.

"How's school going, Lilly?"

"Ha." Lauren blurts out. I speculate she's laughing in response to whoever has messaged her until she continues. "Only person I know who volunteered to take summer classes when they didn't have to."

Lilly simply shrugs her shoulders. "It's good. I thought the English Lit course offered by the community college would help me with my SAT scores."

The deadpan look from earlier now returns to Lauren's face as she stares at Lilly. "You have a nearly perfect grade point average."

"That's my girl." I beam, then add, "I'm incredibly proud of both of you, just one applies a little more effort to her studies than her shopping list."

With that, I get the stink eye from my oldest.

"Are you ready to order?" The server asks from beside us.

I pat Lauren's hand to reassure her I'm only teasing when I spot a familiar profile in the mirrored glass behind Lilly's head. Glancing over my shoulder, I find Poppy with a handsome blond about her age. He's sitting next to her at a four-top table, leaning in as if they're having an intense conversation. The muscles along my neck and shoulders tighten, and I force myself to focus on the menu before I give my irritation away.

"Dad?"

"I'm sorry." I look at Lauren to see what I missed.

"She's waiting on your order."

"Can I have the chicken parm, please?" We've eaten here since the girls were young. Not sure why I even picked up the menu except for a diversion.

"What dressing for your salad, Dr. Weston?" My eyes flick up to meet the server in response to the use of my name and find her smiling coyly at me. *Should I know her?*

As she walks away, I observe Lauren silently mocking the server's question.

"What?"

"Oh, she was soooo flirting with you."

"You think? I was trying to figure out if she'd been a patient of mine."

"I hope you didn't do her boob job," Lauren adds.

I should ignore Lauren, but after a few moments, I sneak a peek in the direction of the server. How did I miss those?

I'm a tit man. I appreciate a nice, perky pair. They don't have to be large, but they do have to be natural. And trust me, there is nothing natural about those double Ds. I must've been distracted by the hot blonde and her date if I missed those. Glancing back in Poppy's direction, I notice her companion now has his arm draped over the back of her chair. The muscle in my jaw starts to twitch.

If her husband is dead, and she's still wearing a wedding band, who the hell is this guy?

"You okay, Dad?" Lilly whispers.

"Yeah, of course, sweetie. I'm fine."

"You seem even more preoccupied than usual. Something at work bothering you?"

Lauren's eyes pop up from her phone, and she gives me a wary look.

"No. No. I'm fine. I'm sorry, honey."

"It's that woman over there. Isn't it?" Lilly asks.

I look where Lilly is tilting her chin to make sure we aren't back on the busty waitress and discover she's referring to Poppy. As I glance back at my daughters, I find they're both leaning to the right, trying to catch a better glimpse of her.

"Do you know her?" Lilly asks.

"She works at my hospital."

"So you're not dating her or anything?"

I cough and reach for my Pellegrino. "No. What gave you that idea? She's obviously here on a date."

"She's not into him," Lauren blurts flatly, her eyes back on her phone.

"Why do you say that?" I need to change this conversation, but curiosity is getting the best of me.

"I can tell. It's her body language. He's leaning into her, but she's sitting perfectly straight." Lauren and Lilly again tilt in their seats to take a better look. "I wonder if she's breaking up with him."

Unable to control my snooping, I swiftly look back in their direction to observe them settling the check. Wondering what I missed, I turn to Lauren and Lilly to find them giggling at me. "What?"

Lauren drops her forearms onto the table and blurts, "You like her." Her teeth are about to pop out of her head, she's smiling so big.

"What? No. I barely know her."

"Whatever, Dad. I'm practically majoring in relationship 101."

"I thought I was paying for an interior design degree?" I chuckle. "Besides, I didn't think you were seeing anyone."

Lauren squirms uncomfortably in her seat before changing the topic to her supposed majors. "Well, some of us are multitalented." She laughs. "I can read people. And there's no doubt you like her."

"Have you asked her out?" Lilly interjects.

"No. I just got done telling you we work together. That wouldn't make any sense." I am not discussing my love life with my daughters. *Or lack of it.*

"Why not? You're both adults. It's not like you're two teenagers. If it didn't work out, you wouldn't fight in the hallways like coeds at a rager. If you don't jump on this, you're going to end up all alone. Do you want to die alone?" Lauren asks with complete sincerity.

Lilly is nodding beside her. And they never agree on anything.

"You're being a bit dramatic, don't you think?"

"Oh." The two of them wince simultaneously.

I practically give myself whiplash, turning to see the gentleman kissing her on the cheek, Poppy's arms wrapped tightly around him. My jaw might snap in two due to the tension that's settled there. I can't pull my eyes away. What the heck is it with this woman?

"I still don't think she's into him. You should ask her out," Lauren encourages.

"Not only do we work together, but, from all appearances, she's most likely got a boyfriend. The last thing I need is complicated." Why are we still talking about this?

Lauren shakes her head in disgust. But it's her sister who surprises me.

"Anything can be considered complicated if you just want an excuse to give up. And there's one thing I'm sure you're not. And that's a quitter."

CHAPTER EIGHT
BROADIE

"Hey, Broadie. You looking for Mr. Flynn?"

"The office said he was down here."

"Yeah. He rolled in by ambulance around five this morning. He was complaining of leg pain. He's got a clot extending nearly the entire length of the leg," Dr. Grant explains. "I know we discharge many of these patients home on blood thinners, but he was already supposed to be taking those. I thought I better give you a call."

I've worked with Donovan Grant for years, and thankfully, he has sound clinical judgment. I worry some of the many new hires to the emergency room would have stressed taking his medication and sent him home. "I was worried this could happen. His circulation has been bad for years, but he's so noncompliant with anything we try to do for him. He rarely wears compression stockings, will only walk if he's going to the refrigerator or the bathroom, and he's awful about taking his medicines. The only reason he's made it this long is his wife." I shake my head in disgust. "I hated operating on him. But his hernia worsened. If I didn't act quickly, he'd lose a portion of his bowel."

"Those cases are tough. You're trapped between a rock and a hard place. The surgical site looks good. I think if he's monitored on the blood thinners, he's going to be fine. You did the best you could, given the situation."

Donovan's right. I can't take on the world's problems. I performed the hernia repair without any complications, and we spent more time reviewing his discharge instructions than we usually do. I even ordered home health visits. Do I have to make house calls to ensure he takes his damn blood thinners every day?

I look over his chart briefly before entering his room and am surprised to see he's alone. "Mr. Flynn. Sorry to see you back with us. It appears you have a rather large clot in your leg."

"Yes, sir. That's what Dr. Grant said. Am I going to need to stay in the hospital?"

"We need to ensure you're improving and that there's a plan to prevent this from worsening. We don't want this breaking off and traveling to your lungs. You were already at significant risk, given your medical history. However, decreased mobility following surgery can increase your chances. That's why you need the compression stockings and medication.

"Yes, sir. I'm not good about remembering some things. And I tried, but I couldn't get them damned stockings on. They're too tight. My wife, Louise, is better about that stuff. But her brother died, and she had to go out of town. My son was supposed to come by and help me out 'til she returned, but something must've come up. I didn't want to worry Louise 'bout it when she called. She's under enough pressure right now with the funeral and all."

Scratching the back of my head, I decide to reach out to the case manager to see if we can put this gentleman in short-term rehab until his wife returns. He'll never make it on his own. "When's your wife due back?"

"She should be back by the end of the week."

"Okay. Well, I think it best you stay in the hospital until she returns. So we can make sure you're healing, and she doesn't have any more stress than necessary once she returns. I'll give her a call and explain what's happening."

"Thank you, Dr. Weston. You've always been so good to us. I appreciate your help."

Reaching over, I pat the old guy on the shoulder before leaving the room. Lauren's words taunt me as I make my way back to the office.

Do you want to end up alone? You're going to die all alone.

"Don't forget we've got a date with the Rams tonight," Jarod shouts from down the hall. He's headed to the operating room for the rest of the day while I finish up office patients and head to the wound care clinic.

"I'll meet you at the bar at six," I answer. The VCU Rams aren't my home team, but I enjoy attending their basketball games. Jarod graduated from VCU's medical college while I'm a Harvard alumnus. We haven't been to a game in a while, and after the last few days, I'm looking forward to it. The only thing better to manage my stress would be spending an evening at the club with my friends. *And a good hard fuck.*

"Broadie," Pearl says from the doorway. She's wearing a pensive expression.

"What's up?"

"I'm playing interference for Beatrice."

"Why? What's the matter? Do I have another patient in the ER?"

She grimaces at my tone. I need to rein it in a little. I can tell I'm reaching my breaking point lately. "It might be worse. I have Brantly Martin here to see you."

For fuck's sake. She's right. It is worse. "That guy just can't take no for an answer."

"You can hardly blame him," Pearl says. "No one else in this hospital could turn things around like you can."

Standing from my chair, I meet her in the doorway. "I appreciate the vote of confidence. But I need to find a way to work less, not more. I've got my hands full here. I don't want to take on anything else. I'm the only guy on the payroll with no wife and kids to get home to. It was bad enough before, but the stress of this job is taking a real toll. I'm tired of neglecting my girls. I need to make it clear once and for all, I'm not interested."

Marching down the hall, I attempt to get my ire under control. It's not like him to go so far as to accost me at my office. I'm happy to try and help him in some other capacity. But the medical director position requires more time than I have left to give.

"Brantly, I—"

"Broadie, thank you for your time. I know you're a busy man. I didn't feel comfortable speaking with anyone else about this. Can we talk privately?"

"Sure," I grumble. I extend my arm toward my office and follow him down the hallway. Once there, I shut the door behind me and take a seat. "What's going on, Brantly?"

"It's my wife. She's in the ER. It's her third visit. She gets terrible pain across her upper abdomen, yet each visit when she's evaluated, they can't determine the problem. She's had ultrasounds and CT scans, and everything checks out fine. It's starting to make her feel like she's losing it. On top of that, I'm worried she's in pain and doesn't want to let on for fear she'll go through this all over again. Is there a chance it could still be her gallbladder?"

Scooting forward in my chair, I rub the back of my neck. "I guess there's a possibility. Has she cut out the fat in her diet?"

"Yes. She tried that. She doesn't eat much of anything for days after an attack, then her symptoms ease off gradually. But they always come back."

"She's never had gallstones?"

"No. No abdominal issues, either. She's been taking medication for heartburn and has cut out coffee and tea. She practically lives on dry toast and water."

"I'm not sure what to tell you. I'm happy to look over her tests and see her in the office."

"Could you take a look at her in the emergency room before she's discharged? It would mean a lot to me."

I look down at my watch. This will throw my whole day off. "Sure. Give me a moment to speak with Beatrice, and I'll be down."

"Thank you, Broadie. I'll feel much better knowing you've looked at her."

Brantly exits, appearing relieved before I've even laid hands on his wife. I hope she'll look improved enough to go home. There's no way I'd ask the surgical team to stay late if she's stable.

"Beatrice, there's been a change in plans. Could you offer the afternoon patients to either reschedule or wait for me? I'm heading to the ER, and then I have to make a quick stop at the wound care clinic before coming back."

"Of course. Everything all right?"

"I hope so." But I could sure use a break. Suddenly, it hits me. "Beatrice?"

"Yes."

"You should probably get word to Jarod I'm not going to make the game tonight."

This has been one of the longest days I've had in years. From Mr. Flynn in the emergency room to Mrs. Martin and the mystery of her illusive abdominal pain to arguments in the wound care clinic about proper protocol for treating bed sores. Luckily, Mrs. Martin appeared well enough to be discharged. If we need to schedule the removal of her gallbladder, then so be it. But today is not that day.

Thankfully, my office patients were understanding about the delay. Both of whom stayed to be seen rather than add them to another over-scheduled afternoon. As I scan my desktop calendar, I wonder how I've kept this pace for so many years when my eyes land on the VCU basketball ticket tucked under one corner. And I was really looking forward to that game, too.

Bzzz. Bzzz.

The vibration of my cell phone causes me to jump. The office is otherwise still, given it's now six o'clock and everyone else has gone home for the day.

Looking at the phone, I start to feel a bit better.

"Hi, Brandee."

CHAPTER NINE
BROADIE

"You feeling any better?" Brandee blinks up at me as she bites down on her lower lip.

Not much. But I'll keep that to myself.

Why do I still feel so unsettled and unsatisfied? "Yes, thank you." I button up my shirt as she grins up at me. "Sorry if I was a little rough. It's been a stressful few weeks."

Brandee crawls across the bed toward me, looking at me through her long dark lashes. She reaches up and toys with the buttons of my shirt that I've just fastened. "You sure you have to run off so soon?"

I'm a little surprised by this. We usually have a quick round or two, and it's off 'til the next time. She's a sexy, fun girl. But nothing more. And although I've never paid for her services, there are many who do. You'd think she'd be anxious to return to someone who she could profit from.

Brandee is beautiful, sophisticated, and poised. Any man would be proud to have her on his arm. I'm sure she does well with her escort business. We haven't spoken in detail about the 'extra services' she provides, but my understanding is that for the right price, she'll give them the happy ending they're looking for.

Honestly, I expected there'd be a time where she was no longer available for our impromptu hookups. That she'd be in a committed relation-ship or decide I needed to pay to play. So her behavior tonight surprises me.

"I'm sure there are men waiting in the wings, hoping you'll call them and make their evening," I say, stepping away from the foot of the bed so I can continue to dress without giving her any indication this is going any further tonight.

"Awe, Broadie. Don't you ever get tired of living this way? Wouldn't it be nice to have someone you were compatible with waiting for you each night? Someone who wouldn't complain if you were late or spent all of your time at the office?" she coos.

She's right. I've spent more time contemplating this in the last few weeks than I have my entire adult life. But until the right woman and the right time present themselves, this is what I'm left with. And sadly, Brandee isn't the type of girl I want waiting for me at the end of each day. "I'd be afraid for my own safety if I was the one to take you off of the market." I tease.

I can tell she's gotten my drift that I'm not interested in what she's tossing about when she slumps back down on the bed. Even hurting Brandee causes me some distress, but that's apparently my lot in life—letting all the women in my orbit down.

"Listen." I move closer to her, reaching out to tuck her hair behind her ear. "We've had a good run. You should consider whether you're truly ready to enter into a relationship with someone if you're tired of your business ventures. I'm sure there are any number of wealthy suitors who'd jump through hoops to keep you in the lifestyle you're accustomed." Pulling back and placing my hands in my pockets, I add, "But I'm not your guy, Brandee. I'm not ready to enter into a monogamous relationship with any woman after my divorce. I'm sorry. I don't want to send you mixed signals."

She looks disappointed. But I need to break this off now if she's getting attached. I can find a quick lay at the club if I need one with someone who understands my boundaries.

I met Brandee at the private club I attend with my core group of friends. We've known each other for years and can relate to one another through our focused career goals and massive wealth. Each is a billionaire in his own right, some through family money, while others have earned their way into the top one percent. We try to meet once a month, but it's not always possible.

One of the more mysterious members of our group, elusive billionaire Gianni Black, owns the club and several smaller affiliated establishments like The Rox in Roxbury, Maryland. The Rox provides a more private experience designed for men, and occasionally women, to fulfill their fantasies without needing to interact with other members. Where, in comparison, the sex club where we meet is a full-on social experience.

Our monthly gathering spot is a high roller sex club located just outside the Washington D.C. beltway but close enough to attract any number of wealthy clients. The membership fee is well over two hundred thousand dollars, but the more important criteria is the background check. Every member is vetted through a written application, photos, and an interview process. Security is top-notch. While each of us has our own personal security detail, it's comforting to know each member has had a background check, so we're doubly protected when we are there.

The multistory club provides a venue to relax and enjoy high-quality food, drinks, cigars, and beautiful women. There are several bars, a dance floor, a stage for various shows, and two floors of rooms to grant your every desire. The third floor contains rooms for the exhibitionists and voyeurs to play, while the fourth floor provides an opportunity for private entertaining. This was where I was introduced to Brandee.

One evening, she mentioned she wanted to leave the club to work independently and asked if I'd be interested in continuing to see her. Once it was clear she wasn't looking to add me to her client list, I gave her my number, and we've enjoyed a nice run. We've always been compatible, but it's clear she's looking for more than I can give her now.

"It was worth a shot. We've always gotten on so well."

We've only interacted sexually. There's never been any casual conversation, no dinners or drinks together. Not even a sleepover and morning coffee. I haven't traveled with Brandee. Only sex. If that was truly all it took to get on well, I might be willing to consider more. But I've lived through the heartache of divorce. I don't ever want to go through that again.

As I reach for my phone lying atop my suit jacket in the chair by the door, I notice I've missed several messages. Quickly opening my message app, I see the Billionaire Boys Club Chat we use when we try to make arrangements to meet has blown up.

BBC Group Chat

8:30 P.M.
GIANNI BLACK

We're overdue for a boys' night. I have several new girls to the club you might like to meet. Get your asses down here. Drinks on me. Winky face emoji.

8:35 P.M.
DR. LOVE

I'm there!

8:42 P.M.
BEDROCK

Sorry guys, I have cardiac caths scheduled first thing in the morning. I'll catch you next time.

8:45 P.M.
MAX WILDE

You suck, Derek. I'll meet you guys in two hours.

8:52 P.M.
SLICK WILLY

Oh, I'm so in. Should be there in about an hour.

8:52 P.M.
DR. LOVE

Anyone heard from Broadie?

8:55 P.M.
MAX WILDE

> Broadie, don't pull a Bedrock and bail. Where are you, man?

Perfect timing. Tucking my phone into my back pocket, I walk over to Brandee. "I've gotta run, B." I give her a peck on the top of her head. "Take care of yourself."

"Is this really goodbye?" She pouts.

"I think so. You deserve a lot more than what I can give you. You're smart, young, beautiful. Get yourself a man who'll treat you like you deserve."

I cup her chin and give her one last chaste kiss before exiting the room. Pulling my phone from my pocket, I quickly type into the chat.

BBC Group Chat

8:58 P.M.

BROADIE

> Your timing is on point, G. I'm headed your way.

8:59 P.M.
DR. LOVE

> Yesss. We're long overdue for this.

9:03 P.M.
GIANNI BLACK

> The place is going to be hot tonight. Smoky scotch, Quorum Classic Churchill cigars, Romanoff Black Caviar, beautiful girls that'll get your mouth watering, and a perfectly prepared Japanese Wagyu steak for after you've whet your appetite with the ladies.

9:05 P.M.
SLICK WILLY

Call in sick, Derek! We need you, man.

9:06 P.M.
MAX WILDE

You suck, Bedrock!

9:07 P.M.
BEDROCK

Trust me. I'm painfully aware.

Chuckling at Max and Devon's incessant taunting, I text my driver, Porter, of my plans as well as my head of security, Stu. Gianni runs a tight ship, but you can never be too careful. Being a billionaire comes with a fair amount of risk. So I take him along whenever I'm out of town.

Porter, Stewart Group Chat

9:10 P.M.

BROADIE

Last minute change in plans. We're headed to D.C.

9:11 P.M.
PORTER

Will be at the house waiting, boss. Am I driving you there or taking you to the airport?

9:12 P.M.

BROADIE

Flying. I've earned it.

9:14 P.M.
STEWART

Meet you at Hanover Air Park

9:15 P.M.
PORTER

Trying to arrange a car to meet us in D.C. Just
clarifying what's on the agenda.

9:17 P.M.

BROADIE

We're headed for The Devil's Playground

CHAPTER TEN
BROADIE

"Hell, if you four aren't a sight for sore eyes." I chuckle as I walk into the VIP section of The Devil's Playground. My friends Max, Becket, Devon, and Gianni stand, and we do the usual greeting of bro hugs with slaps on the back before settling in. "I never realized how much I counted on our monthly meet-ups until we missed a couple."

"Yes, three months is way too long. From here on out, unless one of us is either in jail or in the hospital," Gianni pauses, then points to the physicians in the bunch, "as a patient," he clarifies, "we make a deal. Once we hit sixty days without getting your asses here, we call an emergency session."

"Easy for you to say. You practically live here." I laugh.

"Last I heard, you owned a private jet, just like me," Gianni jibes in his thick Italian accent before grabbing my shoulder and giving it a playful shake. I've missed this guy. How I got lucky enough to call this crew my friends, I'll never know.

Gianni Black is an enigma. I'm not sure anyone truly knows where Black's money comes from. He's probably richer than all of us. I have my suspicions he could be somehow tied to some underground family crime organization, but I don't want to let my mind go there. My security detail has attempted to vet him with limited success. Stu's convinced Gianni Black isn't his real name.

Regardless, this man has my allegiance until someone convinces me there's a reason he shouldn't. I've learned in my forty-two years on the planet a lot of your success comes from your mental game. I focus on the positive wherever possible, envision what I want for myself, and go after it. But the biggest key over the years has been listening to my gut. Call it what you will, signs, signals from the universe, but for me it's my barometer for what and who I put my trust in. And it hasn't let me down yet.

"How'd you get here so fast?" I ask Becket.

Becket Ryan lives in the western portion of Richmond, on the other end of town from me. He's a wildly successful Obstetrician Gynecologist at St. Luke's who's worked there for several years, but only after making billions on a patented ground breaking lubrication he invented during medical school. Apparently, it reduces the discomfort older women experience as they approach menopause, allowing them to enjoy intercourse. Many can even achieve an orgasm for the first time in years. Becket definitely did his homework. Who knew this demographic could drive sales of his product into the billions?

I'm shocked he still works, given how successful he's been. But much like me, I think deep down he enjoys his work. His office is littered with photos of all of the babies he's delivered. Becket swears he does it because he'll never have pictures of his own hanging there, but I think he'd make an incredible father one day. Hopefully, that happens once he's gotten his priorities straight, unlike me.

Yet at thirty-six, Becket is a self-proclaimed, lifelong bachelor. He and Slick Willy are the big playboys in our group, hence his nickname, Dr. Love. You'd think the owner of a sex club would be getting all of the action, but Gianni Black has more willpower than one man should be allowed.

"Truth? I was already here. Gianni and I started sounding the call about thirty minutes after I arrived." I bet Becket and Slick Willy spend a lot more time here than the rest of us.

"Fucker," I growl. "You guys could've given us a little more notice than that. Poor Bedrock is missing out.

Derek Hart, or Bedrock, as we refer to him, is a cardiologist. He attended Stanford and Johns Hopkins for his residency and fellowship programs. I believe he may have been introduced to the Devil's Playground while he lived in the D.C. area. He hasn't worked at St. Luke's for very long. I'm pretty sure he was looking for a fresh start after his wife's death when he moved to Hanover.

"You forget it isn't as easy for some of us to break away from the job. We can't just bring our laptop along like Max," I taunt.

"That was your fault for going into medicine. Maybe you should think about that new concierge plan. You know, where you pick your clients, and they have to pay a huge retainer to have access to you."

"That system doesn't work as well for surgery as primary care, dipshit. Unless you live in California, people aren't signing up for multiple surgeries per year."

"Yeah, I don't think I want to make that work for my field. Women typically only come in once a year for a pap smear or to schedule a mammogram. If they need a concierge plan for their gynecological care, I might have to refer them to the health department." Becket shudders. "I don't want to think about what would require enough visits to be worth seeing me at their beck and call unless they're pregnant."

"I don't know what you girls are whining about. G here works more hours than anyone," Devon says. The four of us look out across the brilliant red lighting of the club as scantily clad beauties meander about, some with trays of drinks and others with cigars. Within minutes, we're all bursting out laughing.

William Devon Sly is the oldest among us, but the newest to our group. It was only the five of us for many years. But Gianni introduced us to Dev last year when he moved into the area.

Devon is a unique personality. His wealth is a combination of old and new money. He inherited millions from his family, who own a chain of boutique hotels. His grandfather is British, and the majority of the hotels are located in the UK. Yet, Devon's father went rogue and married an American girl, much to their chagrin.

Dev has used his family's hotel chain as a guide for creating his edgy boutique brand called The Provocateur. I believe he met Gianni when he requested to learn how to build a few private spaces into each hotel to accommodate the more tantalizing palates.

Whatever he's doing, it's working. And while he's probably the biggest rake among us, he's been able to keep his personal life hidden from his professional persona. But as his nickname indicates, he has no problem keeping his dick wet.

"Yeah. G has it rough," Becket chokes out.

Gianni simply sits back in his chair with his hands folded across his chest as he looks proudly over the club. "If you build it, they will come."

"All right, Kevin Costner," I quip.

"Man, I haven't seen *Field of Dreams* in years," Becket adds, reaching for his phone. "Wonder if it's on Netflix?"

"Field of what?" G asks.

"I liked him in *Bull Durham* better," Max interjects.

Maximillian Wilde is the quiet guy in the group. From what I gather, he saves his talking for the ladies, and it's of the dirty variety. Max is a gigolo wannabe trapped in nerd's clothing. He's a self-made billionaire, creating one of the best cyber security firms in the world. Not that you'd know it to look at him. There's no pretension with this one.

Max doesn't dress to impress. He reminds me a lot of my grandfather. He puts a great deal of thought into his purchases, acquiring things that are built to last. I haven't known him long, but he seems like a straight shooter. I don't think this guy will settle down until a smoking hot, equally geeky chick falls into his lap.

After a pause, Gianni asks, "What's *Bull Durham?*"

I snort out a laugh. "It's another baseball flick Kevin Costner starred in, G."

"You Americans and your baseball. You're all late to the party. Calcio is the most popular sport in the world."

Max, Becket, Dev, and I all look at each other in confusion.

"What the fuck is Calcio?" Becket blurts.

"It's soccer, you moron." G scowls.

"I thought they called it Football," Dev adds.

"The British call it fútbol. The Italians call it Calcio. And we all know who the superior country is," G scolds with a stern glance.

"America," Devon and Becket say in unison.

I chuckle as I rub my hands up and down the armrests of the buttery soft, black leather chair and gaze about the club. This place is pure class. Gianni had a vision when he opened the Devil's Playground, and he executed it flawlessly.

Located in an industrial district just outside of Washington, the opulence of the interior of the building is masked by its obscure manufacturing façade. There are a few other nightclubs and restaurants in the area, but this location blends into the background if you aren't sure what to look for. And anonymity is essential with clubs of this nature.

The building's main floor houses multiple bars, group seating, a dance floor, and a stage for entertaining. It's open to a viewing area along the second floor. This floor offers a place for patrons who want to be able to have an actual conversation. I can't begin to imagine the many shrewd business deals that have been completed up there.

The opulent club is well-appointed with plush leather furnishings, decadent lighting, and jaw-dropping artwork. But none of the decor compares to the women. The sultry, seductive sirens of the Devil's Playground are like no other sex club I've attended. Girls from different nationalities—tall, short, curvy, thin, blonde, brunette, or redhead. You name it, and you'll find someone who meets your fancy. While some are strictly here as eye candy, others will gladly entertain in the more private areas of the club. While it's not uncommon for an attractive server to sit on your knee and flirt a bit, this isn't the type of place where you get a fifty-dollar lap dance while your friends hoot and holler.

"I have several new hires making their debut tonight," Gianni says, pointing to the area around the stage. For a minute, I think I recognize one of the girls and lean forward for a closer look, but get distracted when several attractive servers deliver trays of decadent food and drink to our table.

Sitting back, we enjoy our two-finger pours of Macallan and snack on lavish appetizers of caviar, oysters, and black pasta in truffle butter as we anticipate the rest of our evening. The five of us sit in comfortable silence, each undoubtedly appreciating the opportunity to unwind. Strobe lights flicker above the dance floor as patrons grind against one another to the hedonistic, sexy vibe of the music.

Everything about this place is made for sin.

"Cigar, sir?" a gorgeous, scantily clad redhead offers from a silver tray.

"I don't mind if I do, thank you." I reach for a Davidoff and recline back in my seat, watching as Max gives a wink to the server as he declines.

"I'm surprised you're here keeping me company."

"Where else would I be?" Max asks knowingly.

"Upstairs."

"I could say the same to you," he replies.

You'd think I'd be doing just that. While I haven't entertained in any of the private rooms in years, my afternoon with Brandee was lackluster at best. Yet, I can't beat the niggling feeling that regardless of their beauty and expertise, I'd be left as wanting with any of these women. And there's no doubt in my mind why.

I can't stop thinking about Poppy.

"Not into it tonight," I tell him.

"Yeah. I get it. I've got too much on my mind to enjoy it. Wouldn't want to give some poor girl a complex that it was them and not me," he jokes.

We sit quietly, taking in the room for a few minutes. Becket and Dev have gone in search of their late-night entertainment while Gianni returned to work.

"Something's up with you, Broadie. What's going on?"

Fuck. I thought I could play my cards better. "I don't know. Maybe I'm having a midlife crisis or something. You'll be there in a few years." I chuckle. "I'm just starting to find my life is on a loop. Every day is more of the same. I was hoping this diversion would help."

"Maybe you need a trip away."

I snort. "Yeah. I didn't go anywhere this summer. My ex and her husband invited me to join them again this year on their trip to New Zealand. So I could spend time with my daughters. We went to South Africa last year."

"Um, what?"

"It's for my kids."

"It's messed up is what it is. Fuck, thanks for reminding me why I'm never getting married."

"Touché." I take another draw from my cigar, enjoying the aroma. "I don't know. Can't put my finger on it. It just feels like something is missing."

"Something? Or someone?"

My eyes flick to his. This guy is savvy. "No one, really." Taking a sip from my scotch, I focus on the burn, not the odd, unsettled feeling in my chest. "She won't give me the time of day."

Max's face snaps in my direction. "You?" He genuinely looks astonished.

"Yeah, me."

"Where'd you meet her?"

Placing my drink on the glass table in front of us, I prepare for the inquisition. "She's a pharmacist in my hospital."

"I didn't think you dated women you worked with? Or at all, for that matter."

"I don't. But there's just something about her."

"Perhaps she has a similar stance on office romance. One she's more committed to." He chuckles.

I laugh half-heartedly. "Yeah. Maybe."

"Shit, Broadie. You really like this girl."

"She's a woman. Not a girl. And no. I'm merely intrigued."

Max scratches the stubble along his chin. "Think it could be the chase?"

"No. I'm old enough to recognize that by now."

Max leans back in his chair, seeming pensive. "I say you break this down. Do the old pros and cons thing. Because workplace romance can be a bitch." He looks out over the club for a moment before adding, "But after that, if you can't fight this feeling, I say go for it. Could be the universe sending you a sign she's the one."

My eyes connect with his, and the mentalist in me awakens.

You might be on to something, my clever friend. You just might be on to something.

CHAPTER ELEVEN
POPPY

"Ugh. This day has got to get better," I mumble as I reach for a wet paper towel. In my haste to package this bottle of Tincture of Benzoin, I spilled some of the contents on both the pharmacy counter and my lab coat. On the bright side, it should round out the coffee I spilled on my top on the way to work this morning.

Tincture of Benzoin is primarily used for wounds. You only need a small amount. It's a good thing because the copper-colored resin has a strong scent. While it's supposed to smell like warm vanilla, it reminds me more of licorice. *Hope no one's behind me in the cafeteria line today.*

The memory of that afternoon causes my cheeks to flush. No man has ever spoken to me as brazen as he has. I try to remind myself it's just his persona. He's probably flirted with half the women on staff at St. Luke's in the same way.

I have to concede Dr. Weston does have a stellar reputation. If he's been involved in a salacious workplace affair, he's managed to keep it under wraps. Not to mention, the women employed here all flock to him like the maidens in *Cinderella*, hoping their foot is the perfect fit for his proverbial glass slipper.

It isn't that I'm not flattered by his comments. But it's difficult to wrap my head around the possibility they could be genuine. Dr. Broadie Weston is an exceptionally rich, successful surgeon who could have any woman he wanted. If he were going to risk dating in the workplace, you'd think he'd select any of the bevy of young nurses at St. Luke's, not a widow pushing forty.

"Poppy, the ER is on the phone. They say they have a surgeon in the department who's waiting on Versed."

Of course, they do. "Thanks, Abbie. Can you put them on hold, and I'll talk to them?"

"Sure."

"Thanks for holding. This is Poppy."

"Heyyy, Poppy." I recognize his voice immediately. The way Dr. Silver draws out the Heyyy, gives him away. He's a smarmy emergency room physician who I secretly think is a male chauvinist pig. I swear I could have the same conversation with him about a medication shortage or delay as Frank or Marshall, but I've never witnessed him being conde-scending with either of them. "I have a surgeon here waiting to close a wound, but we don't have the medication he's requesting. We ordered it at least ten minutes ago."

Ten whole minutes. I understand it's the emergency room, but we're managing medications for the entire hospital. If it's that urgent, why didn't he call right away? "Could you give me the patient's name and date of birth, Dr. Silver?"

"Oh, how'd you know it was me?"

Most people would've identified themselves. "Lucky guess."

He rattles off the patient's demographics, and I quickly look for the issue. "Ah, I see the problem. It appears the last time this patient had an inpatient procedure, she had a reaction to the Versed." It's clearly listed as an allergy. "I can bring—"

"I don't have time for this. This surgeon has taken it upon himself to keep his office patients waiting so he can come to treat this emergency room patient. Do whatever you need to do to get that medicine here, stat." The line goes silent, and I bite the inside of my cheek to prevent spewing the obscenities I'd like to call that man.

I take a few moments to do some research to ensure the replacement medication is safe for the patient before retrieving it. This isn't the way this is supposed to work. The provider should either correct the order or give me a verbal order for what they want to prevent medication errors from occurring. But there's no way in hell I'm calling him back.

"Do you need me to take that to the ER, Poppy?" My sweet pharmacy technician asks with a bit of a nervous lilt.

"No, Abbie. I've got it." I'd never put her in this situation. "I've got my zone phone. If anyone calls, just forward them to me."

"Okay, Poppy." I've been fortunate enough to work with Abbie for several years. Much like Katarina years ago, she's working as a pharmacy technician to earn money while gaining experience so she can apply to pharmacy school.

Making it to the emergency room in record time, I've barely got both feet through the entry doors when I'm accosted.

"It's about time. I guess I didn't make it clear that this is an emergency. I knew I should've asked for Frank."

What. The. Fuck.

I try to take a calming breath. *Focus on the patient, Poppy.* You can air your grievance to human resources after you leave here. Don't let this asshole cause you to do something you'll regret.

Out of the blue, I see Dr. Weston barreling toward us. Ah, so this must be the hot-head surgeon who's been waiting *not so patiently*. I dig my heels in, hoping to keep my cool until I can escape this department. Yet, when I open my mouth to explain, I'm cut short.

"I'm sorry for the delay, Dr. Silver, but I needed to—"

"I know you aren't about to apologize," Dr. Weston snaps, staring me down.

"I—"

"If you EVER speak to Poppy that way again, I'll have you fired!"

Oh. I wasn't expecting that.

"She's a dedicated, extremely knowledgeable pharmacist, and St. Luke's is lucky to have her. I hope your behavior won't cause her to look elsewhere." Dr. Weston's eyes connect with mine, and I almost quiver.

This is the closest I'll ever be to seeing a mere mortal reenact a scene from one of my romance novels. It's as if a book boyfriend has jumped from the pages and come to life.

He takes a step closer to Dr. Silver, his stance exuding power. Dropping the volume of his voice, he continues, "And it's my understanding that this hospital has a recruitment and retention problem. If this is what our hard-working nurses and techs have to deal with, there's no wonder."

I'm star-struck watching this unfold. I quickly check myself to make sure my mouth is closed. I'm not sure drooling would go over well right now. No wonder this man is considered St. Luke's royalty. His compassion goes far beyond his patients.

Dr. Weston's head tilts upward as if he's noticed something down the hall. "Peck. Are you waiting on something from the pharmacy?"

"Yes. Thank goodness."

"Poppy was nice enough to walk it up here to you," Dr. Weston adds. Is he trying to ensure I'm not, once again, attacked by one of his colleagues?

"Thank you. I was surprised we didn't have it in the department. I looked online, and it's not on national backorder."

"No, sir. This patient has a severe allergy to Versed. That's why the nurse couldn't pull the medication. It's a stopgap to prevent an adverse outcome. When Dr. Silver explained the urgent need for a sedative, I looked for a safe alternative. I'll need to amend the order in the chart and have you or Dr. Silver sign it, but I'm hoping this will work." I extend the sedative to Dr. Peck.

"This will do just fine. Thank you for looking out for me, Poppy. I must've been too rushed to get back to my office and hadn't noticed the allergy."

I can see Dr. Weston glaring down at Dr. Silver out of the corner of my eye. I wouldn't have expected my day to turn around so spectacularly in a million years. "It happens. That's a pretty rare allergy, in my opinion. But that's why the stopgap is in place."

Dr. Peck gives a cordial wave before swiftly walking back in the direction in which he came, and I peer up to find Dr. Weston and Dr. Silver staring each other down like a scene from *West Side Story*. I'd love to stick around and see how this ends, but I think it's best if I head back to the pharmacy and let these two handle this without me.

Broadie

"Hey, Nick. It's been ages since I've seen you. You'd think we'd see each other in the OR more, but lately I keep bumping into your wife here and in the ER." Construction on the physicians' lounge has forced me to reconnect with people in the cafeteria. And surprisingly, these conversations energize me, making my work more productive, not less.

"You're right. I think it's just the way the OR schedule is posted. It's certainly not because Kat and I have been on some luxury vacation." Nick reaches for the container of cream for his coffee.

"Funny you should say that. After hearing so many people mention travel, I realize I'm long overdue for a trip. If I can get my schedule worked out, I might need to give it a little more consideration."

"Word on the street is you might need to schedule that soon."

"Why? Is my number up, and no one told me?" I chuckle.

"In a way, maybe. I thought I'd heard you were a shoo-in for medical director."

Shaking my head, I grab a paper coffee cup and start to fill it with dark roast. "There's no way in hell I'm doing that."

Nick laughs.

"My schedule is so bad I can barely keep up from one day to the next. Why would I add more? You should do it, Nick. You're still young."

"I'm not that much younger than you." He takes a sip of his coffee and winces. "We have an infant at home and are completing the process to foster kids. That's *my* priority."

His statement cuts through me like a knife. I don't know a lot about Nick Barnes beyond what I've experienced through the hospital. We don't hang out in social circles. Hell, I don't really hang out with anyone but my boys at the club anymore. Yet he seems to have a much healthier grasp on what's important than I ever have.

I need to make some fundamental changes. Maybe it *is* a midlife crisis that has me feeling this constant unease. I'm not getting any younger. I don't want to look back on my life with regret.

"That's great. Don't let work take you away from that."

"I'm trying not to. I waited too long for what Kat and I have. But it's like quicksand. Sometimes, you don't see how deep you're getting until it's too late."

"Hey, was that Sebastian Lee I saw with you a moment ago?" I want to be careful not to pry, as the gentleman in question barely resembles the highly sought-after hand surgeon who used to work here. He seemed thinner and walking cautiously with the use of a cane.

Nick reaches up to stroke his scruff looking uneasy. "Yeah. He's got a neurology appointment. He seems to be having more weakness. I'm hoping they can get on top of it quickly." It's clear he's concerned for his friend.

Returning to my office, I replay my conversation with Nick. I'm sure watching his friend give up his career when he was in his prime had to be eye-opening. And they're both younger than I am. If I've learned nothing else from working in medicine all of these years, it's that every day on this planet is a gift. It's time to get out of this quicksand I'm drowning in. It might take something big to turn my life around. But toss me some rope! I'm ready to start living.

My personal Ted Talk has barely finished when I see Poppy coming down the hallway in my direction. *This is a sign. It's got to be a sign.*

"Hi."

"Hi, Dr. Weston. I'm glad to see you."

An uncontrollable smile crosses my face in response to her words. This woman must think I'm losing it.

"I wanted to thank you for what you did the other day. Your compassion for the employees of this hospital is unmatched. What you said to Dr. Silver on my behalf meant a lot to me."

It hits me that she thinks I'm that way with all of the staff. While it's true I'd come to the defense of any employee being mistreated, I doubt I would've handled the situation in quite the Neanderthal manner I did in the emergency room. That was all because of her.

"Poppy, I—" Do I tell her? Reaching back to massage my neck, I try to come up with the right words before she can walk off.

After a short pause where I'm unable to find a quick and engaging reply, she looks down at the floor and then back up at me before saying, "Have a good day." As she starts to walk past me, I begin to panic.

"Go out with me."

CHAPTER TWELVE
POPPY

Oh my gosh. What's going on here?

I enter the dining area to find it's much more populated than usual. There don't appear to be as many people meandering around the salad bar or grill. They're primarily clustered near the floor-to-ceiling windows that look out at the outdoor seating area. While my curiosity is tugging at me, it's a Monday, and my to-do list is a mile long. I really should get my food and get back to work.

I reach for a prepackaged pasta salad and fruit before going in search of my favorite lemonade. There's a loud commotion just beyond the cashiers, where many of the staff are gathered, animatedly talking to one another, arms flailing about in apparent excitement.

"Hi, Althea. Any idea what all of the fuss is about?"

"Lord, Poppy. You haven't heard?"

"Heard what?"

"Evidently, the hospital is getting serious about trying to keep the staff happy. They're doing an enormous giveaway. And the longer you've worked here, the more chances you have of winning. You and I should be getting quite a few." She squeals, lifting her hand in the air, awaiting my high-five.

Well, it's about time they started doing more to keep people feeling satisfied with their jobs. Plenty of competing hospitals are in town to lure people if they don't. For me, it's such a hassle to think about applying somewhere else. You have to go through the application process, the credentialing process, then orientation...

"Poppy?"

"Hmm?"

"You using your ID to pay, or you paying with cash today?"

"Oh, Althea. Sorry. I keep getting lost in my thoughts lately. I hope that's not a sign of something." I grimace.

"If it isn't a man you're lost in, it's probably a sign you need a vacation." Althea points toward the crowd, causing my brows to pinch. What does that mean?

"Thanks, Althea," I say, feeling a bit perplexed. Tucking my wallet back into my lab coat pocket, I grab my things and make my way into the dining area. The staff is all abuzz about whatever is posted along the back wall. I've never seen so many people in the dining area at one time. My interest is definitely piqued.

"Poppy, it's so exciting for you," Kat declares as she comes around the corner. I lean in for a hug, as it's been several weeks since I've seen her.

"What is?" I have to admit, I'm feeling like a kid standing outside of Willie Wonka's Chocolate Factory right now. I just want to find out what this contest is all about.

"Hey, Kat." Turning, I see a gorgeous blonde coming toward us. "It's been ages."

"Hi, Ava. Ava, do you know Poppy?"

"I don't think so. Hi."

"Poppy is one of St. Luke's pharmacists. But I knew her first." Katarina giggles. "She had to put up with me when I worked at the drug store. It was my very first job."

"Put up with you? You were the best pharmacy tech there. I was sorry to see you go. But on to bigger and better things, right?"

"Ava is a PA too. She works with Nick."

"Oh, no way. That's so cool."

"Well, it's not feeling so cool right now."

Kat gives her a worried expression.

"Not because of your darling husband, silly. I can't enter this contest." Ava laughs.

Kat joins her. "Me either."

"Why not?"

"We don't work directly for the hospital like you do. We're contracted employees in the ER."

"Yeah, and I work for the Orthopedic practice. This contest is to help with staff retention. Only full-time employees of St. Luke's are eligible. No temporary workers, locum's hires, or travel nurses."

Wow. I guess that's a clever way to do it. "So, what's the contest? I hadn't known anything was happening until I came to the cafeteria and couldn't get close enough to see what was going on." I point to the overly congested dining area near the back windows.

"I thought I saw a table through the glass as I rounded the corner. The nurses have been taking turns coming up here. I think you have to fill something out to enter and turn it in to human resources."

"You guys are killing me. What's the prize?"

"It's an all-expense paid trip to Jamaica. I think it's for up to four family members," Kat screeches, giving me overexcited jazz hands.

Holy cow. St. Luke's must finally be getting serious about retaining their staff. That's a heck of a lot better than free tickets to the local movie theater.

Ava smiles brightly. This girl is stunning. She's got the most beautiful platinum blonde hair, fair skin, and big blue eyes. "I think they're actually giving away three trips. They said they wanted to try and reward staff from different areas of the hospital."

"What do you mean? Like maybe one for nursing, one for the folks in housekeeping dietary, or maintenance, and another for ancillary staff like physical therapy?"

"And you," Katarina adds excitedly. "From what I hear, they've made it so that you get additional entries for every year you've worked here." She beams at me like I've already won.

"How long have you worked here, Poppy?" Ava asks.

"Eight years."

They both giggle and clap. "I don't know the details. I'm only repeating what I heard some nurses say in the ER. Some of them actually complained it wouldn't be fair to put them in one category because it'd give the other departments an unfair advantage due to the number of nurses working here. I couldn't believe anyone would have the nerve to complain when they're doing something this generous. But then again, they may have just been talking without knowing all the details," Kat says. "Kinda like us." She laughs.

I shake my head. "You can't make everyone happy. I'm just impressed they're going to such lengths to try and show their employees they're worth all of this. It's an expensive gesture."

"From what I overheard on the elevator on the way down from our office, this is the beginning of a new recruitment and retention initiative. So, there may be more things coming. I, for one, am excited to live vicariously through you, Poppy." Ava beams.

"Well, I haven't won anything yet."

"You need to squeeze that little body on up there and get yourself a form, missy. You have a good shot at this." Kat claps.

This seems crazy, but I have at least as much chance as anyone else, right? "Kat, would you hold these for a moment? It might be easier to get through the crowd without holding my lunch."

"Of course, silly. I'm going to let the cashier know these belong to you and pick out something I can take back to the ER. Come grab me when you've wrangled your entry form from them."

"It was so nice meeting you, Poppy. I hope to see you again when you can show me your vacation pictures." Ava grins giving me a quick wave goodbye as she follows Kat toward Althea.

Stepping through several employees chatting over their carry-out containers, I move closer to the table and discover the line isn't long at all. Looking over the nurses' shoulders in front of me, I can see a colorful poster affixed to the glass straight ahead. There are dreamy photos of white sandy beaches, turquoise water, and multiple shots of an oceanfront resort. It must be family-friendly, as there's a picture of the kids' club in the poster's right-hand corner. Wow, this place looks luxurious.

"Good afternoon, Poppy. I haven't seen you in ages."

"Hi, Yvonne. It has been a while." Pointing toward the poster, I can't control my smile. "This is incredible. I can't believe they're doing all of this."

"Not as surprised as we were." Yvonne laughs. She's worked for St. Luke's in human resources for several years. If I'm not mistaken, she transferred here from a sister hospital.

"Do other hospitals do this type of thing?"

"Not that I've ever seen. I've heard of some hospitals in New York trying some outrageous things to keep nurses. The shortage has really affected a lot of facilities. And the administration is committed to rewarding the hard-working staff already here versus paying temporary or travel nurses. I think it's smart."

Nodding, I appreciate that they're doing this for all the staff instead of making this a nursing only contest. Looking at the tropical photos on the poster, I can practically smell salt in the air. It's a nice change from anti-septic. "I'm amazed they're going to this expense."

"Me too. Last year, we pushed a cart around with oranges and butter cookies." She laughs. "So, fill this out and drop it here in this box or the human resources department by the end of the week."

Clutching my entry form against my chest, I nod. "I'll do it. Thank you."

"You're welcome. Good luck, Poppy."

Heading back to await Kat at the cashier's station, I peruse the form. It's an all-expenses-paid vacation to a luxury all-inclusive family resort in Ocho Rios, Jamaica. *Wow. It even includes airfare.* You're allowed to bring up to three guests, specifically immediate family members, for this five-night getaway. Three winners will be chosen from full-time staff who've been employed at St. Luke's Hospital for at least ninety days. You will receive an additional entry for every full year of service.

"What's it say? What's it say?" Kat niggles.

"It's pretty amazing. For the winner anyway."

Kat gives me a puzzled look. "You've worked here eight years. Sure, some folks may've worked here longer, but that's nothing to sneeze at."

"Oh, you're right. I just don't want to get my hopes up. I'm not very lucky." I bite my lip, thinking about how tickled Dan would've been if I'd come home squealing that I'd won something like this.

Kat takes a few steps closer, and I lean in when she lowers her volume. "Trust me. I understand where your mind is. When I lost my second ovary, being single at thirty-five, I didn't imagine I'd ever feel hopeful about anything again. But Dr. Miller taught me I'm more than my circumstances. And now I have a handsome husband, a beautiful daughter, and hopefully more on the way."

Tears come to my eyes as I listen to her. She's right. The days of wallowing in the cards I've been dealt are over. "You're absolutely right." I reach into Kat's arms to retrieve my lunch items. "Now I need to get back to work."

Kat gives me a crooked smile. Unsure if she's gotten through to me.

"So I can fill out this form." I wink.

As I head toward the pharmacy, I admit there's a little extra spring in my step for the first time in a very long while.

Having returned to work, I've accomplished many of the usual Monday tasks and have a break to dive into my lunch. *And that entry form.* As I open my salad and drink, I look over the form. It's pretty straightforward. It asks for name, address, phone number, and email. I eagerly enter an eight next to years of service.

There's a section where the form describes who you're allowed to bring as well as the details of the accommodations. My mouth drops open at the list of things included: All meals, drinks, and use of the various outdoor activities like the pool, water park area, tennis and basketball courts. Many of the water sports are included, such as kayaks, snorkeling, paddle boards, and catamarans. They obviously offer spa services at an extra charge. Cabanas by the pool and beach are available to rent for a fee.

I snicker to myself. *As if.* Simply staying at a resort like this will be luxurious enough.

Tapping my pen along my lower lip, I try to picture it. Lying on a chaise by the ocean, with a Pina Colada in one hand and a romance novel in the other.

"What are you giggling about over there?" Frank asks.

"Oh, nothing." I'm sure everyone on staff at St. Luke's will be dreaming it's them on the beach.

I bring a forkful of pasta salad to my mouth and consider who I'd bring if I won. The form states it's limited to direct family members. There's no way I could handle Mom on a trip like that. We might not survive the flight as poor as her mobility has gotten, not to mention her hearing. *Ugh.* I'd have to call it a day by seven each evening, so she didn't have an outburst like she did in the hospital, confused about where she was.

I could invite my brother, but they have three kids now. Who would he leave home? Deep down, I already know the answer. I'd be going alone. Sipping my lemonade, I ponder whether I could do it. Could I fly to Jamaica by myself and spend five days at a resort surrounded by happy couples and families enjoying the life I want?

The question has me kicking myself again, second-guessing whether I did the right thing, turning Broadie Weston down for a date. Honestly, his question caught me so off guard I wasn't sure what to do. The man is gorgeous. He's a well-respected surgeon who has a heart of gold. Or so it seems. But this job is my lifeline. It's honestly the only thing sustaining me. It forces me to get up and face the day when I'd rather sulk. My job challenges me each day in a brand-new way. I feel accomplished when I can meet a patient's needs.

I can't help replaying Dr. Weston's words, just as I have several times since that fateful day in the ER.

She's a dedicated, extremely knowledgeable pharmacist, and St. Luke's is lucky to have her. I hope your behavior won't cause her to look elsewhere.

I practically swooned when he said, *If you ever speak to Poppy that way again, I'll have you fired!*

That was quintessential book-boyfriend material right there.

Momentarily, I let my mind picture Broadie Weston wearing nothing but a pair of swim trunks and that darned dimple.

"Poppy? Did you hear me?"

Frank's voice startles me back into the here and now. "Oh, sorry. What were you saying?"

"Can you take this soap suds enema to the second floor? Abbie's at lunch, and the nurses on the Ortho floor say they're out."

Well, if that won't bring me back to reality, nothing will.

CHAPTER THIRTEEN
BROADIE

"You made it," Gianni greets me as I approach our usual seating area in DPG.

"Good to be here, G. Can't believe it's been a month already. But I've been looking forward to this all week."

"Come, sit. I'll have one of the girls bring you a scotch. I'm afraid I may be tied up for a bit."

I raise a brow at him, wondering if he means literally or figuratively. It could go either way in a club like this.

"Sadly, it's all business, I'm afraid."

"Broadie. How are you, man?" Derek 'Bedrock' Hart stands and gives me a pat on the back. "It's amazing we work in the same hospital, yet I never see you."

"Agreed. But I guess you're in the cath lab while I'm in the OR."

A striking blonde wearing a slinky gold sequined gown bends down to offer me a two-finger pour of what I'm assuming is top-shelf scotch.

"Thank you."

"You're very welcome." I notice a strong southern drawl. There was a time I'd find this sweet, but looking at her makes me long for another blonde. One who quickly shut me down.

"Where are Devon and Becket?"

"Over there, by the dance floor." I follow Max's finger to find the two sitting side by side, each with a girl on their knee.

"They didn't waste any time," I say. Looking up, I find Gianni has already walked away. I hope everything is okay. Pulling out my cell phone, I text Stu to let him know something's up with Gianni tonight, just to keep him in the loop. I'm not naïve enough to think some shady shit doesn't go down in this place. At least Stu can be one step ahead if something is afoot.

10:20 P.M.
STEWART

On it, boss.

Another beautiful server dips low, carrying a tray of appetizers. Reaching over, I grab a napkin and what looks like a skewer of meatballs.

"Buffalo," Derek says before standing.

"Ah."

I pop a tender morsel into my mouth and moan.

"Good, huh?" Max asks.

It's then I notice Derek has wandered off. "Where'd he head off to?"

"You know, Bedrock. He's probably going to watch until he finds someone he can pound into the wall." We both chuckle. It seems like yesterday when we met Derek here for the first time. He'd lost his wife after a tough battle with leukemia. I think it took him a while before he was ready to begin a relationship with anyone. He confided one night when we were all together here that while he wasn't ready to date, he was quite ready to fuck. *And fuck, he did.*

Apparently, he was in a room next to Becket once he got his groove on. And from what Becket described, Derek gave a whole new meaning to the term pound town. He'd said it sounded like the bed would come through the wall at any moment. And that's a mighty feat, given how much sound-proofing Gianni has put into the place. Poor Becket said he couldn't finish from laughing so hard.

Taking a sip of my scotch, I lean back in my chair and steel my nerves before diving into this uncomfortable conversation.

"Max, how long have we known each other?"

"Uh oh."

"What?"

"You're not like the others, Broadie. Slick Willy or Becket butter me up whenever they need something. But you're a straight shooter. Come out with it."

Scratching the day-old stubble along my chin, I decide to do just that. "I'm hoping you can help me. I need to email someone from an untraceable account."

Max silently raises a brow at me.

"What?"

"Cut the crap. You have Russell Stewart on your team. I'm sure he could manage this. What's this about?"

Stu has helped. I'm afraid to ask how he managed to get that form from HR Poppy completed. Yet, I need Max's expertise to reach out to her about winning. This has to be flawless. And no one can accomplish this like Max can. "I need you to help me email someone that they've won a contest."

The corner of Max's lip curls into an undeniable smirk. "It's that girl. Isn't it?"

Our eyes connect, but I admit nothing. Why should I humiliate myself any more than I already have?

"What'd you do?"

Taking another sip of my scotch, I place the crystal down on the coffee table in front of us and share the details. I explain how I approached Brantly Martin with an offer he couldn't refuse. I advised him that I was in no way interested in taking on the medical director position but instead offered to donate sizeable funds to sponsor three winners on an all-expense paid vacation. The giveaways were intended to boost recruitment and retention at the hospital, as it was sorely needed.

I made keeping my monetary donation anonymous a requirement of my offer. After his assurance that this would be possible, I reminded him that the purpose of this promotion was to get full-time employees excited about working at St. Luke's. Focusing on the opportunities, versus anything negative. That it would be best not to make a big deal about the winners, but instead move on to the next chance for someone new to win. To keep the momentum going. I feel confident about this.

At least, that's what I keep telling myself.

The staff has seemed so much more positive in the last week. And they work hard. They deserve this. I'm well aware I'm a puppet master, trying to find reassurance in my manipulation. But I've replayed the hopeful look on Poppy's face repeatedly. I stealthily watched her walk down the hall from the cafeteria to the elevators after getting her form. That optimistic expression made me feel ten feet tall.

"And all of this is a ruse to what? Get her to take a trip with you?"

Fuck. When he says it like that...

I clear my throat, feeling more than a little ridiculous at admitting this to him. "To go out with me."

Max starts to choke on his Seven and Seven. "Okay, let me get this straight. Renowned surgeon, Dr. Broadie Weston, who could have any chick he wants, needs to con some woman into a date?"

"I can't have anyone I want."

"Name one girl here who'd say no."

I give him a scowl. "It's in their job description."

"Shut the fuck up. You know Gianni's girls are classy, well-educated women. They don't have to go out with anyone they don't want to. They have a choice. And they'd all choose you."

"Well, maybe I prefer someone I have more in common with." I take a much-needed sip of my scotch. "Hell, Max. I can't explain what it is about this woman. I'm not interested in settling down. My career still eats away at ninety percent of my time. I'd like to give the other ten to my girls. They've grown up without me. I have a lot of work to do in the father department. But I have to see this through."

Max strokes the golden scruff along his jaw. "Is it the chase? Since she seems to be the one thing you can't have?"

"I don't think so. I've never had that kind of draw to women, only work. And money." I let out a chuckle. "It's not even about sex with her. Don't get me wrong. I wouldn't turn it down. But there's something intriguing about her. I've never felt it before."

Max snickers. "You going all *The Notebook* on me?"

"What? Hell, no. Maybe I'm excited about the opportunity to get to know her." But she won't even give me a chance.

"Well, this is one expensive first date, my friend."

Tell me about it.

Max leans forward, reaching his arm out to me. "So let me see it. Where's this luxury vacation happening?"

Pulling out my phone, I open my browser and pull up the website for the all-inclusive resort in Jamaica. Handing it over to him, I start to consider whether it's too late to back out. But I saw the way the staff were clamoring around the human resources table for entry forms. The excitement was palpable.

I may not be interested in taking on the role of medical director, but it has nothing to do with a lack of loyalty and admiration for St. Luke's Hospital. That place has been good to me. I've made great memories and a hell of a lot of money there. The very least I can do is make a donation to uplift the staff working there—especially the ones who might not ever have the chance to experience a trip like this. A vacation, I admit, I take for granted.

If I'm going to back out of anything, it needs to be emailing her that she's won.

"It's a family joint?"

"It had to be. One, there wasn't any way I could get away with offering a trip to the staff of the hospital and make it adults only. Two, I have no idea if she has kids."

Max flops back in his chair and gives an almost maniacal laugh. "Shouldn't you have started there?"

"Why? It's of no consequence to me if she has kids."

Max bolts upright, suddenly looking serious. "You told me you didn't want this director's position because you haven't spent enough time with your kids. All parents aren't like you, Broadie. Most of them spend time with their children. I'm glad you're realizing you want to change that now, but you're doing all of this before you know anything about this woman. Whether or not she has children is a very big deal." Max's expression morphs into one of disappointment, as if he's trying to reason with a wayward child. "Say you manage to get a date, and you sleep with her. Are you planning to do all this just to fuck her and run? Is that why her having kids isn't a big deal to you?"

I sit up straighter, feeling like I'm being assaulted. "Hell, no." My jaw clenches in frustration. How did this conversation get so off-track? "Fuck. I don't know what I want."

Dropping my face in my hands, I take a deep breath and try to control the abrupt change in my demeanor. It's not like me to get so defensive. In through my nose, out through my mouth, I repeat the process a few times until I feel my shoulders relax. Looking up, I find Max's expression less accusatory. "I barely know this woman. But something tells me, if she had kids, it wouldn't change a thing. I'd find a way to make it work. That's all."

He's made his point. I've jumped in headfirst and have no idea why. Normally, I'm meticulous about researching anything I'm planning to do. But there was undeniable hesitation from Poppy before she shot me down for a date. I'm certain of it. Once I recovered from the sting of rejection, it was on. There had to be a way to spend time with her. I need a chance to prove we could be good together.

My friend drops his tone as he continues, "Broadie, I'm just saying, if you go into this half-cocked, you may end up with more problems than solutions. Be sure you know what you're doing here so no one gets hurt."

I know he's right. *But this train has already left the station.*

There have only been a few things in my life I've felt innately passionate about. Doing whatever it takes to provide the best surgical care possible to my patients. Living a life my father and grandfather would respect after all they've given me. Being a better father to my children.

And Poppy.

"So, will you help me?"

"I think you're playing with fire, man. What if this all blows up in your face?"

I haven't really considered the consequences. But I can't be any worse off than I am currently, right? I mean, she won't give me the time of day now.

"I'll handle it." There's a chill across my skin as the words tumble from my lips. I pray it's not an omen of what's to come.

Max gives me a look of acceptance. "Okay, what do I need to do?"

CHAPTER FOURTEEN
POPPY

"Poppy. It feels like forever since I've seen you," Mom scolds as I rush into her room. She's right.

Coming in closer, I give her a kiss on the cheek. "Oh, Mom. I'm so sorry. It's been a rough few weeks at work. Several of the pharmacists I work with have taken longer vacations than normal, so I've been working a lot of overtime."

"What?" Mom squawks.

"I've been working overtime. Everyone is on vacation," I shout.

"You're the one that needs the vacation."

Don't I know it.

"How've you been? I've called Jasmine to check on you. I know how difficult it is to talk on the phone with your hearing."

"Everything is good. Just get lonely." A wave of guilt hits me that I haven't been better about coming by. These long days catch up with me, and I feel like all I want to do on my day off is rest. Mom has so many folks around here to socialize with. And activities to participate in. I think I've let that give me a false sense that she's okay without me.

"I'll try to get better about visiting. Hopefully, Frank and Marshall are done with their summer trips."

"Why don't you go somewhere nice, Poppy?"

"Yeah, why don't you go somewhere?" Agnes asks as she hobbles into the room with a walker, a tall, handsome, dark-haired gentleman in navy scrubs by her side. That's odd. She occasionally uses a walker to get around, but not always. Yet I've never known her to need physical therapy.

"I just might," I joke. *Right, Poppy.*

Okay, I admit it. I may have dreamed of the warm sand of Jamaica under my feet a time or two since turning in my entry form nearly a month ago. But it was a nice diversion from my norm, where I work all day, hit the gym, eat dinner alone, and have a long soak in the tub with a book.

The excitement of the staff has waned over the last few weeks. I assume HR has chosen the winners, as the deadline to turn in the entry forms was almost three weeks ago. The buzz around the hospital is that a new opportunity to win something will be coming soon. C'est la vie. It was fun dreaming about it while it lasted.

"Where are you going?" my mother asks with a hopeful glint in her eye. Where on earth does she want me to go?

"I don't know. I was thinking I might go to Blacksburg for a short trip and visit Ian, Rita, and the kids."

"Posh!" Agnes blurts. Her outburst must take her therapist as much by surprise as it has me. He nearly jumps five feet in the air.

"Do you need anything else from me before I go, Ms. Agnes?"

"I don't think I can answer that in mixed company, Ricardo," Agnes says as she fans herself. "But I thank you for the pleasant stroll through Hanover Haven. It's been a while since I had such a pleasant walk with a man."

I roll my eyes, feeling sorry for whatever poor Ricardo likely endured during that walk.

"I'll see you tomorrow," he adds before exiting the room.

Walking around the end of Mom's bed, I take a seat on the edge and look at Agnes. "I didn't realize you were receiving PT. Did something happen?"

"She fell down," my mother yells.

"Tattle tale." Agnes gives Mom the stink eye. "It was nothing. I slipped on the wet bathroom tile and landed on my rump. Nothing got hurt but my pride."

I shake my head, knowing neither my mother's nor Agnes' bones could withstand too hard of a fall on the shower floor without risking a broken hip. "The bathroom is the most dangerous room in the house."

"Our dining room is the most dangerous place in this house." Agnes frowns.

"Do they just have physical therapy coming here as a precaution?"

My mother giggles, drawing my attention. "She said she'd need them to help her get her strength back. I think she just wanted to get Ricardo all to herself."

Agnes merely shrugs.

I laugh. *This woman.*

"Forget Blacksburg. Maybe Ricardo has a brother who can take you away somewhere," Agnes says.

I spend the next few hours puttering around Mom's room, tending to her little plant, and listening to Agnes detail the pros and cons of the men she's stalking on Bumble. *Lord, help them.*

"I can stay a little later if you'd like? Join you for dinner?"

"No, no, Poppy. I'd like a nap before dinner. And you need your rest, too."

"Yes. Save yourself. I heard they were having spam and succotash for dinner." Agnes makes a gagging noise before I turn back to my mother.

Helping her into bed, I give her a hug before promising to do better about visiting from here on out.

Taking a seat in my steamy hot Lexus, I start the engine, buckle my seatbelt, and blast the air conditioner. As I reach to plug my phone into the charger, I notice I have a new text.

2:35 P.M.
KAT

Hey, pretty lady. You doing anything tonight? My sister Rachel is watching Grace, but Nick just got called in to work. Want to meet for dinner?

3:07 P.M.

POPPY

Hi. I'm sorry, I'm just seeing this. Spent the afternoon with Mom. I'd love that. You sure he won't be done in time for dinner? Maybe we should just do drinks.

3:11 P.M.
KAT

He might. He can join us if he wants. But I've learned never to wait if I'm hungry. He could be a while.

3:12 P.M.

POPPY

Okay, great. Where should we meet?

3:13 P.M.
KAT

Let's meet at this new place I just heard about. It's supposed to be really good. I'll text you the directions.

3:15 P.M.

POPPY

Sounds great. I like trying new places. Is six okay?

3:21 P.M.
KAT

Perfect. See you then.

Driving home, I'm excited and grateful for the unexpected plans with Kat for the evening. After checking out the website from the link she sent, it looks like the restaurant where we're meeting is a trendy new farm to table place in the central part of Richmond called SHAGBARK. It's sleek and sophisticated if the pictures are any indication.

Maybe I should dress up a bit. Biting down on my lip, my mind travels to the last time I wore my favorite emerald green dress. I should've been offended by his words, but the swirling sensation in my lower belly had me too distracted. I'd been standing in the cashier's line thinking about what I needed to put on my list for the grocery store when an unfamiliar warmth traveled up my back. I can't say it was unpleasant, but I was so shocked I quickly spun to determine the origin. Who knew those incredible whiskey-colored eyes would be staring down at me?

Your scent is irresistible. There was nothing else in here that had my mouth watering, so I knew it had to be you.

Lord. What is wrong with me?

Parking the car, I head inside my modest abode. Dan and I purchased the one-story ranch after his diagnosis was confirmed. We'd been living in an apartment prior to that, but our residence on the second floor caused him to have difficulty with the stairs early on. A townhouse didn't seem to be an option, as none of them had a first-floor master.

Once we located this neighborhood near the hospital, we knew we'd found the right place. There was a mix of homes ranging from three story lake front homes to single story ranches like ours. We didn't sacrifice the square footage, as the layout is quite spacious. But we were able to have a floor master bedroom and a living area that provided the open floor plan we desperately needed to accommodate his wheelchair and adaptive equipment.

Dropping my purse and keys on the kitchen island, I make my way to the bedroom. Kicking off my shoes, my gaze darts about the room, it hasn't changed much in the years since Dan died. I eventually purchased new bed coverings and tried to brighten up the space to get out of my funk. But quite honestly, it'll always feel like his presence lingers here.

My mother and brother urged me to consider selling. But at the time, I wasn't in the right place for that conversation. I'm still not sure I'm ready, but I'm at least at a point I know I need to consider a future without him. And that might include a new home.

Walking into the closet, my gaze quickly lands on the vibrant green maxi dress. Biting the inside of my cheek, I try not to giggle. It really is absurd how looking at it makes me feel beautiful now. I grab a pair of strappy sandals and some silver and blue jewelry and place everything on the bed before heading into the bathroom to run water for a quick soak before I meet Kat.

Ding.

Darting over to my phone, I verify Kat hasn't messaged to say we should reschedule as Nick is out of surgery earlier than expected. Nope. Just a pesky text about a sale on T-shirts. I knew I shouldn't have clicked that box enabling text messaging when I bought Rita's birthday gift.

Heading back to the bath, I deposit the phone on the chair and start to undress. Maybe I'll put the meditation app on for ten minutes or so while I'm soaking. I used to be pretty good about starting and ending my day that way, but with all of the extra hours at the hospital lately, it's fallen by the wayside.

I reach for my favorite bath oil of eucalyptus and mint and inhale the relaxing scent. I haven't enjoyed such a nice day off in ages. As little as I do beyond work and my mother, I should make more time for dinners with friends. And maybe look into that pottery class I told Kat I'd resume.

Sliding down into the hot water, I carefully reach for my phone and start the meditation app. Thank goodness for these. If there wasn't someone's voice encouraging my mind to "return to the breath," I'm certain I'd fall asleep halfway through. It's feast or famine really. Some days the app works well, and it can train my brain to focus every time it wanders to the fifty things on my to do list. Other days, I consider it a win if I complete the experience without snoring.

As Jason Clarke's soothing voice advises my time is up and to slowly open my eyes, I take another deep inhale and sit up in the tub to try to stretch my muscles. I'll admit, I'm not sure the meditations he narrates are all that relaxing. His voice kinda gets me all hot and bothered. But I tried to keep my eye on the prize, so to speak.

Grabbing my phone, I close the app and decide to quickly check to see if I've received any newsletters from my favorite authors. Sometimes they share sales or new releases. The book I've been reading is okay, but honestly, unless there's some crazy twist I didn't see coming, I'll be happy to try something new. It's not likely that's going to happen in the epilogue, but you never know.

It kind of stinks that I've always been a rule follower. It's nearly impossible for me to stop reading a book I've started, even when it falls flat.

Hmm. What's this?

The subject line says:

Congratulations. You're on your way.

It's probably a scam. The sender is Bedrock Entertainment Corp. Lying back against my bath pillow, I open the email with my finger hovering over the trash icon.

Congratulations, Poppy Danforth. You and up to three immediate family members are headed to Jamaica! St. Luke's Hospital is so grateful for your service to their patients that they're pleased to offer you an all-expense vacation of a lifetime. Five nights and six days at a luxury all-inclusive ocean front resort. We can guarantee you'll enjoy beautiful ocean views from your suite, all you can eat meals and snacks, complementary drinks, and various forms of outdoor entertainment. (The only thing we can't guarantee is the weather.)

We at Bedrock Entertainment are your travel agents for this amazing trip. Once you have decided on the dates for your vacation, please complete the attached contract so we can facilitate the booking of your hotel room, airfare, and transfers to and from the airport.

Holy shit!

Water splashes all about the floor as I attempt to keep my phone from tumbling into the bath. Is this really happening? I'm so overcome with excitement that I can't read the fine print. I pull up the print feature on my phone and send a copy of the email and attachment to my office. I'll get Kat to look over this at dinner. Because I'm so overwhelmed right now, I'm not sure I could trust myself to catch if this is merely a scam. There are too many details that line up with what was on the entry form. It has to be real.

The deep relaxation of my meditation app long gone, I squeal as I kick my feet, adding more water to the tile floor. Taking in the sight, I throw my head back in laughter. Who cares?

I'm going to Jamaica, baby!

Pulling open the heavy glass doors to SHAGBARK, I revel in the gorgeous interior. The dining area has deep brown wood tones on the floor, table-tops adorned in white linen, and chairs with gorgeous, white leather cushions. The lighting is comprised of beautiful clear glass domes, which seem to mirror the stemware on the tables.

"Hi," the hostess greets. "How many?"

"Two," I say, knowing I've arrived a few minutes early. I look around to ensure Kat isn't already seated when two slender arms encircle me from behind.

"Hi, my gorgeous friend."

Spinning to greet Kat with a hug, she immediately pulls back at arm's length. "You look incredible. And it's not just the dress and hair. You're glowing."

I blush, thankful for the compliment.

Leaning in quickly, she whispers, "Did someone get—"

"No!" Swatting her arm, I turn back to the hostess, who's patiently waiting for our shenanigans to stop. "I'm sorry."

"No apologies. Right this way, ladies."

We're escorted past a showstopping long table, which I can only assume they use for larger parties. As we're seated, I see a beautiful auburn-haired girl in her twenties holding a bouquet of sunflowers by the hostess station. A handsome young man enters with several buckets of similar bright yellow flowers. He gives the young woman a sexy wink before following who I suspect must be a manager or owner of the restaurant down a hallway.

"Anyone you know?" Kat asks.

"No. The sunflowers had me mesmerized." I reach for a white linen napkin and drape it into my lap as I continue to take in the beautiful place.

Kat hands me the drink menu. "I'm glad you were okay coming here. Nick will be so disappointed. Hopefully, he can make it before we're done. This place is all about the local farmers, fishermen, and artisans in the area. Those two were probably local growers of some sort."

"Ah, you caught Alex and Tuesday, did ya?" Looking up, I find a hand-some gentleman with a heavy Irish accent dressed in black.

"Who?" I ask.

"The couple at the front. They work with Cygnature Blooms florist. I think Tuesday is thinking of branching out on her own. We've been working with her to supply centerpieces for our tables."

"Oh, I know that florist," Kat interjects. "Nick's bought me flowers from there. They're amazing."

"I'm Rodney. I'll be your server this evening. Could I get you started with a drink?"

I quickly look down at the drink menu and choose a Malbec.

"I think I'll try the Red Veil." Kat beams up at Rodney.

"Good choice, ma'am. I'll get right on these. Here are your dinner menus. Let me know if you have any questions."

"Oh, I have one," I interrupt. "Where does the name come from? SHAGBARK? It's so unique."

The gorgeous Irishman grins. "It comes from a type of hickory tree that grows along the James River." Pointing to the different wood accents about the space, he continues, "They included little touches of Shagbark everywhere."

Rodney steps away after a brief nod, and I lean back in my chair, enjoying this moment with my friend. It's stifling what grief can steal from you. For so many years, I've barely gone through the motions. Merely trying to get through each day without Dan. But there's so much life left to live at thirty-eight. I fight the urge to feel guilty over new expe-riences, knowing he wouldn't want me to wallow alone. It's only dinner. So why do I feel so guilty when I do things, knowing he can't.

A pretty, full-figured brunette arrives at our table with our cocktails.

There's a confidence about her actions that makes her even more attractive. "I have a glass of Malbec from Argentina and a spicy Red Veil. Hope you enjoy."

I look at Katarina's drink with curiosity. I need to be a lot braver with exploring new things. "What's a Red Veil?" I ask as I take a sip of my wine.

"It says it's made of tequila, lime, grapefruit, and simple red pepper. Whatever that is." She giggles. "Since you dressed the part, I thought I'd bring out *my* spicy in my drink tonight."

"Oh, Kat, this place seems fantastic." Opening the menu, I find all of my favorite southern dishes. "I think I'm going to go old school and get the fried green tomatoes with the shrimp and grits. How 'bout you?" I ask, closing my menu.

"I think I'm going to get the summer seafood pasta. But if Nick shows up in time, I might add an oyster appetizer." Kat waggles her brows at me, and I nearly spit out my water. Oh, to have a relationship like the two of them. I admit, even before Dan got sick, he was never terribly romantic. It's not a criticism, just a fact of who we were together. We were friends first, then quickly grew into a couple. I've never had a passionate love affair—long term or otherwise. But I appreciate what we had. Some are never that lucky.

"Kat."

"Yes." She makes a serious face that looks like she's sucking on a lemon. But that could be the drink.

"I have to show you something. I'm trying not to get caught up in it until someone objective looks over it."

Kat's expression turns serious. "What is it?"

Retrieving the printout of the email I received, I hand it over with shaky hands. I practically hold my breath as she begins to read.

"Holy—"

I quickly reach to cover her mouth, as this is too nice a place to be screeching profanity.

"Does this mean what I think it means?"

"I hope so. But I was so excited I wanted you to make sure I wasn't imagining the whole thing."

Kat reads back over the email and then flips the page to check out the copy of the attached form. "Poppy, this looks legit to me." She's beaming as if she just won the lottery. I would know I've been doing the same since the bathtub. "You're doing this, right?"

Covering my straining cheeks with my hands, I nod. "I think so."

Kat dances wildly in her seat just as Rodney approaches.

"The Red Veil too much?"

"No. It's absolutely perfect."

The following morning, I push myself up from the bed and squint at the bright morning light. I only had one glass of wine. So why do I feel like this? Looking at my purse sitting atop the papers I printed for Kat last night, it all comes back to me.

The evening was incredible. Sadly, for Katarina, Nick never made it to the restaurant in time. She said he'd have a lot of making up to do once he met her at their little bungalow in town later that night. Kat had lived there prior to getting married. They now live in a beautiful home on the lake about an hour away, but Nick often stays in town when he's on call.

Yet despite the fun I had with my friend, I had a terribly sleepless night. As excited as I am to venture on this trip to Jamaica, I'm grappling with the continued feelings of guilt over doing something so grand without my husband. I know it's complete nonsense to feel this way. It's the devil doing his due, my mother would say. But I shouldn't keep living like a nun.

Getting up, I decide a fresh pot of coffee, a hot shower, and a day enjoying the things that bring me peace are in order. I've found if I do the things which bring joy, I can often evade the undertow of grief. I'll catch a Barre yoga class, go for a stroll in the park, and maybe even stop by one of my favorite coffee shops for a pick me up.

But as my daily activities are completed, I still feel marred down with shame that I'm considering going on this lavish trip without him. So, I go to talk to the one person I know won't judge me.

Walking up to Dan's headstone, I reach into my pocket for the tissue I'm sure to need. Bending down, I wipe the debris from the area and lay the fresh greenery in front of his marker. "I haven't been here in a while. They've had me doing a lot of overtime this summer. The money's good, even if I don't really need it." *I don't go anywhere.* Plus, Daniel's life insurance is there.

Squatting down to sit beside him, I continue, "I miss you. But I'm struggling, Dan. It's been years without you. Years." The tears start to tumble sooner than I'd expected. "I can't keep living this way." I dab at my eyes and look about the area to ensure I'm all alone.

"I have some news." I sniffle. "I won this incredible giveaway at work. It's an amazing opportunity. I get to go to Jamaica and stay at a luxury resort. I'm a little nervous, going alone. But it's time to do more than just work every day. As much as I wish you could be there with me, it's time I start living again." I leave out that I probably wouldn't turn down the opportunity to have a romantic tryst with a man I'd never see again. But we don't need to go there right now.

My eyes scan the area. For a moment, I feel as if I'm being watched. I often have this awkward suspicion when I'm here, but it's usually just paranoia about crying as if my husband passed away yesterday and not eight years ago. Getting myself together, I try to put a jovial spin on things. "You probably wouldn't have wanted to go to Jamaica anyway. You were more of a mountains kind of guy." I laugh through the remaining tears.

As I push myself up from the ground, I decide then and there I need to give Katarina's counselor a call. She's right. There's no timeline to grief, and I won't beat myself up for it. I'm going to go on this trip and like it, dammit. However, it's probably way past time I talk things over with someone to see if I can move past this. Because I'd like to have a full and happy life. I'd like to consider starting the foster care process and potentially adopt a child one day. I don't want to be held back because of this unhealthy feeling of survivor's guilt.

Lifting my head high, I tell him with an assuredness I didn't know I had, "I'm doing this soon. I want to do this. No. I need to do this, Dan. I'm not really living here. You're probably living more than I am," I choke out. "Watching everything from above. Seeing it all. I'm seeing nothing but this little corner of the world. My job, my mother, our home. It's not enough anymore." I sorely underestimated the amount of tissues I'd need for this visit.

Wiping my eyes on my sleeve, I stomp my feet in disgust. How am I still so full of sadness after all of this time? I was so happy last night. Turning my head to the side, a line from one of my favorite movies comes to mind. When George Bailey realizes he's been given a second chance in *It's a Wonderful Life.*

I want to live again. I want to live again.

As I cross the empty cemetery toward my car, I manage to get my eyes dry enough to feel safe getting behind the wheel. I unlock the car and am about to sit down when I notice a young man. Where had he come from?

I'm sure I'm miscalculating where he's standing. In all the years I've been coming here, I've never really paid that much attention to the poor souls who are buried beside Dan. I'm sure he's visiting them, not my husband. Dan didn't have any family. He'd grown up raised by his grand-mother, who died shortly before I met him.

Sliding onto the hot black leather seat, I quickly turn the ignition and get the air conditioner moving, all the while keeping my eyes trained on the dark-haired boy across the way. He's tall. I guess he could be an adult. It's hard to tell from this angle.

After a few moments, the temperature starts to cool, and I back out of the parking space and head home. I was hoping visiting Dan would bring some relief. Yet, instead, I have the oddest sense of unease. Is it the appearance of the young man? Pushing myself to get back out there and experience life? Or the unknowns about this trip?

Whatever it is. I'm ready for it. I've lived through tougher stuff than this. I'm ready for a fresh start. And what better place to do that than Jamaica?

CHAPTER FIFTEEN
BROADIE

"Hi, Dad."

"Thank you," I tell the hostess as I approach my daughters, currently sitting at a four top table in the Rotunda of this historic Richmond, Virginia landmark. The Rotunda is located at the bottom of the grand staircase of the Jefferson Hotel. The elaborate buffet is just off to the side and contains almost every breakfast and lunch item imaginable.

"What? Am I late again?" I laugh.

"No. We were excited and came early," Lilly says, her cheeks all aglow.

Sitting back in my chair, the memories of this place come flooding back. We used to bring the girls here all the time when they were little and continued the tradition long after the divorce. It was a special time for them. They usually got dressed in something frilly and felt like princesses for the day. We've celebrated any number of birthdays and milestones, like their sweet sixteens, and graduations here.

There's a stately ambiance about The Jefferson Hotel. Its grand staircase has been rumored to have inspired the film *Gone With The Wind*. You definitely feel as if you've been transported back in time when you walk in.

"So, what's the occasion? Our birthdays aren't for months," Lauren says.

"I told you I'm trying to get better about seeing you two. I'm leaving for a business trip soon and wanted to have brunch with you before I left."

Lilly offers a sweet, gracious smile while Lauren looks as if she remains unconvinced. I can't be upset with her hesitancy. I've let them down often enough. It's going to take time to earn their trust.

"So, what are we having?" I ask, rubbing my hands together at the thought of the glorious options. Their champagne Sunday brunch is unmatched in this town, in my opinion. There are the typical southern breakfast delicacies such as their Jefferson's Biscuit Benedict, a spin on the classic eggs benedict, southern comfort French toast, as well as made to order omelets. But I think the ham and ribeye carving stations steal the show.

"I'm just going down the row and filling up." Lilly lets out an excited squeal. She's so slight. Her stomach is never as big as her eyes. And she's not a glutton. She'll usually pick her favorite things and not be wasteful. Her sister, on the other hand, will fill her plate but only peck at the items containing carbs. She has the perfect figure but is very self-conscious about her weight.

"Don't forget to save room for dessert." I chuckle.

"Oh, I won't." Lilly smiles brightly. "There are rows of three-tiered dessert trays over there."

Lauren gives me a sullen pout.

Sliding an arm around her as we make our way to fill our plates, I ask, "What's that look for?"

"If I eat this food, I'm going to gain a dress size, Daddy. Can I use your card to get some new things?"

This kid.

"I'll see what I can do."

∼

It's almost here. The trip to Jamaica is less than two weeks away. Although I enjoy visiting new places once I get there, I don't normally get this excited about travel. There's so much red tape at work to get the time off. Not to mention, knowing what awaits me once I return makes it hard to relax.

Yet the motivation for this trip is entirely different. The time away will let me get caught up on a few things. I can chart remotely, so I'll finally get my backlog of medical records complete. There's a presentation I've been meaning to work on for an educational dinner symposium sponsored by one of the drug reps I've been putting off. However, there's one main item on my agenda.

Her.

I can't help but smile at the thought of finally spending time with Poppy.

Knock. Knock.

As I look toward my study door, I find Stu and quickly usher him in. "Come in, come in. I was thinking about the trip and wanted to tie up some loose ends. Porter should be coming as well."

"Right here, boss." I grin as my driver jogs in behind Stu. These two couldn't look more different. While my head of security, Russell Stewart, is tall and built like an MMA fighter, Andrew Porter is not. However, Porter manages to handle most anything I need. He was hired as a driver, nothing more. We've been together for years, and he hasn't let me down yet.

"Hey, Andrew," Stu greets.

"Take a seat. I know you fellas are probably two steps ahead of me, but I wanted to make sure we were all on the same page. It's been a while since I've done any international travel."

"None since COVID hit," Stu says.

Hearing this triggers my concern. "Do I need to do anything special for that? Test or anything?"

"Nah. Jamaica has lifted all of its restrictions. You're good to go there. I had my office prepare everything you need. The flight plan is booked for your jet. And Porter has taken care of the car you'll be using while you're there. You're all set."

"What about her?"

A barely detectable lift in the corner of Stu's mouth gives him away. He's laughing at me. *Fucker*. Like I give a shit. I'd laugh too if someone I knew told me they were concocting all of this just to get a woman to spend time with him.

"Poppy has her transfer covered through the hotel, sir," Porter says.

"Is she going to be on there with a bunch of people she doesn't know?"

"Not sure. She's traveling alone." I have to fight not letting my contentment with this fact be fodder for the two of them. "But you knew that already."

Nodding, I try to keep this ridiculous conversation as professional as possible. Let's be honest. I'm shocked neither of them has cornered me to ask if I've lost it. Maybe they've already determined I'm having a midlife crisis. "I want someone on her, Stu."

"Already done. We've got several eyes on her in the air and on the ground. Same for you."

I should've expected as much. I take a slow, deep breath before my next question, knowing this could finally push them to ask who this woman is to me.

"Have we paid the resort to block off the rooms near my room and hers?"

"It wasn't easy, but yes. She won't be on the same hallway as you., but most of the floor is vacant. If we'd booked her room too close, she may see you before you're ready," Stu adds.

He's right. I need to slow my roll. I just don't want any drunk fucker coming near her. Even in a swanky, family, all-inclusive resort, there are assholes who could potentially take advantage of women. I inwardly roll my eyes. And this is coming from the guy who's arranged this entire trip to get close to her without her knowledge. But I'd never disrespect her by putting her in a compromising position. I just want a fucking chance. The chemistry between us is intense, tangible. She has to feel it too. Reaching for my scotch, I have to accept the fact that if she's still not interested in anything I have to offer after this trip, I need to let this go.

Even if the very thought of coming home rejected makes me want to throw a temper tantrum Lauren would be proud of.

"The gang's all here," Gianni toasts. "To friends."

"Friends," we all chant.

"I think this is the first time all six of us have been sitting around the same table in months." Derek smiles as he lifts his glass to his lips.

"Well, I wouldn't get too comfortable with that." Max chuckles, looking in Devon's direction. "Slick Willy's already got his eye on his next meal."

Following Devon's line of vision, it appears he's eyeing up a familiar looking brunette from across the room. Her back is turned, but Devon doesn't seem to mind. She has waist length, coffee-colored hair and a shapely ass. I know I've never been up close and personal with this girl. But there's something eerily familiar about her.

"I hear you're headed to Jamaica soon." Gianni nudges my arm.

My head snaps to Max. I thought we were keeping this between us. Rat bastard.

"Yeah, that's why we decided to get together tonight, since it might be a few months before we're all available again," Max quickly adds.

My shoulders relax a bit, realizing he's trying to tell me Mum's The Word. "Yeah. Never been. I'm excited. I need a break."

"Jamaica is beautiful. What part are you going to?" Gianni asks. I notice Derek and Becket have gotten up and moved closer to the railing as they look out about the dance floor and the patrons beneath us. The music has a jazzy vibe about it tonight. Different than the sexy, techno beat playing the last time we were here.

"Ocho Rios."

"Ah. Ochi. I haven't been there in years. Let me know how it was when you get back. Maybe I'll take a trip myself."

"Something tells me G would prefer an adult only resort," Max says under his breath.

My eyes narrow, hoping no one else heard him. I don't need Becket or Derek putting two and two together. My gut feeling tells me they're too busy to get caught up in the St. Luke's drama about contests and whatnot. But I'd rather not find out.

As someone from Gianni's staff approaches, Derek returns, standing next to our table as Becket and Devon head downstairs.

"Devon didn't waste any time," I joke.

"Nah. But Becket thinks he knows the girl. He's going to check her out. I have to admit, she seems familiar to me, too. But his sight is better." Derek laughs and as if on cue, the fine lines of crow's feet appear at the corners of his eyes. Derek isn't that much older than I am. There's the slightest shade of gray at his temples. But my suspicion is, burying your wife might cause you to age a little quicker in the process.

I watch as Gianni follows the staff member, a concerned look etched upon his face. I can only imagine the things he has to deal with here. Despite the thorough application process and vetting of members, there have to be some unscrupulous types who manage to get in. Add to it, some of the high rollers who use his establishment to make illegal deals, and he must stay on edge.

Derek reaches for his scotch then walks closer to where he was a moment ago, likely to get a bird's eye view of the boys down below. That guy keeps his cards close to his chest. He doesn't speak of much except vague commentary on how his work is going, and occasional comments about his daughter, Katie, who's studying abroad. I think with her away, he's had more freedom to meet women. Yet, like the rest of us, he doesn't sound inclined to want to enter into a relationship beyond a physical one.

For all intents and purposes, Derek Hart seems to be as good as they get. He's done a fine job raising his daughter as a single father since his wife became ill. It's a double-edged sword when you have to watch a loved one die as a medical provider. You know too much. There's part of you that thinks you can somehow fix it because of your knowledge or your connections. Yet we're human like everyone else. When there's no magical cure to be found, we bear the guilt of letting them down right along with the pain of losing them.

Poor Derek has that, plus the uncomfortable knowledge that he's a billionaire because of his wife. Her family is old Washington money. They tried to take Derek to court over his inheritance, but their lawyers assured them the case was an unwinnable. Derek's wife had inherited millions from her grandparents at the time of their deaths. She and Derek managed her portfolio well, barely touching the funds over the years. She willed everything to her husband with the understanding that half would go to their daughter one day, and the remaining was to be used for him and the advancement of the Leukemia & Lymphoma Society.

"So. How'd I do?" Max whispers. He's got the cocky grin of a guy who passed an exam with flying colors after finding the answer sheet.

"Bedrock Entertainment?" I ask.

Derek turns to us. "What?"

"Nothing," Max and I answer in unison.

Max chuckles. "I couldn't help myself, man. It was too good."

I shake my head.

"It must've worked, yeah?"

"So far, so good. I'm headed there next week. I'm going to fly down a few days ahead to scope out the place."

Max leans back in his chair. "Really, Broadie? You sound like you're attacking the Pentagon. Please tell me no one is getting kidnapped during this trip."

"No. Not my kink." I laugh. "I'm nervous, man. I've got a lot riding on this."

Max takes a sip of his drink and is suddenly overcome with laughter.

"What's so funny?"

"What are you going to do if, after all of this, she still won't go out with you?"

"Oh, she's going." There's no if's about it. I don't understand this magnetic affect she has on me. But mark my words, after this trip, this girl is going to be putty in my hands. No idea what that entails, but I'm excited to find out.

"You should be asking, what if she figures out you did this?"

"Nah. You were flawless. I've got it from here."

Now I just need to figure out how to make her mine.

CHAPTER SIXTEEN
POPPY

I can't believe it. I keep looking around the airport, waiting for someone to run over and tell me this is all a big mistake. But so far so good. My bags are checked, I've made it through security, and the flight appears to be on time.

"Calling Poppy Danforth to the desk. Poppy Danforth, could you please report to the check-in desk."

I spoke too soon.

My heart starts to race in my chest as I nervously gather my things and head to the counter. Please don't let there be something wrong with my ticket. I would've thought by this point, any issues would've been flagged already. "Hi. I'm Poppy Danforth."

"Ah, Ms. Danforth. Sorry for the interruption. We'll be boarding soon, and there's been a change."

My heart feels like it's in my stomach. Are they bumping me to a later flight? Or a later day?

"You've been upgraded to first class."

What?

"I'm sorry. I must not have heard you correctly."

The attractive agent gives me a wry smile. "Oh, you heard me just fine.

You've been upgraded to first class. If you could hand me your original boarding pass, I'll give you the new one."

Holy crap. This kind of thing never happens to me. "Oh. Of course." Reaching into my purse, my hands shaking, I retrieve the thin slip of paper. "Here you go."

"Have you ever flown first class?" he asks without judgment.

"No. This whole thing is a dream. I won a trip through my job. I haven't done anything like this before."

He stops typing, leans forward, and drops his voice. "I think this is your time to shine, beautiful."

I can feel myself standing a little taller as my grin takes over my face. I'm a little overwhelmed by all of it, to be honest. "Thank you. I'm ready."

He gives me a friendly smile and hands the new documents to me. "We'll be boarding first class passengers soon. When you hear the announcement, come right on up and enjoy every moment of flying the friendly skies on your way to Jamaica." He winks.

I can't help but beam at him. "Thank you. I will."

After hitting the lavatory quickly before the passengers are called to board, I'm barely back in my seat before the announcement is made. Collecting my carry-on luggage, I make my way back to the gate and hand the handsome agent my ticket. My eyes land on his nametag as he scans the slip of paper. "Thank you, Rashaun."

"You're most welcome, Ms. Danforth. Enjoy your trip."

As I head down the gangway, I feel a little zeal of electricity over this start to my journey. Is this the way the billionaire boyfriends from my romance novels travel? Nah. They probably go by private jet. I laugh.

Daniel and I were blessed. We weren't wealthy by any means. But we both had great jobs with limited debt. He'd had a small school loan, which we paid off rather quickly after we were married. My tuition had been paid for by money my father had left in a college fund before he passed away.

We tried to live within our means. We were careful about buying a home we could afford, didn't eat out often, and the vacations we planned were budget friendly. While I drive a Lexus, it's an older model I purchased several years ago from a patient at Hanover Haven. Jasmine said they were looking for someone to take it off of their hands as they no longer felt safe enough to drive. I managed to acquire it for well under Blue Book value. The owner only wanted what was left on the loan. The sale was handled through the patient's attorney, so I'm not one-hundred-percent sure who it belonged to. However, I've always had my suspicions it was Agnes.

"Good morning, miss. May I see your boarding pass?" the pretty flight attendant asks.

"Oh, yes." I extend it to her, and she directs me to my seat.

Wow. I don't fly often, and when I do, I figure I've scored if I get an aisle seat. But these seats are plush, cream-colored leather with blankets wrapped in cellophane lying in wait. "Thank you."

She assists me in placing my carry-on in the overhead bin before I take my seat. "I'll be back once I get the rest of the first-class passengers settled. Would you like a glass of champagne?"

Is she for real? "Um, sure." I mouth 'Oh, my, god.' as she walks away, unsure I believe my luck. Now, if only a scorching hot billionaire would sit down next to me, this trip would be almost perfect.

Lying back in my seat, I can't help but think of the one man who could potentially fit that description. Had I made a colossal mistake turning him down? I've had a hard enough time going to work each day following Dan's death. I don't know if I could handle the anguish of seeing him there if he broke my heart. Which he undoubtedly would. I mean, we have nothing in common.

"Here you go." I look over to see the flight attendant has returned with a flute of champagne. In a glass. No plastic cups here in first class.

"Thank you. Is everyone onboard? I thought it was a full flight, but no one's sitting here."

"The seat was purchased, but it appears they didn't make it."

"Oh." I almost feel disappointed for this person I've never met. Now that I know what they're missing out on. Who knows. Maybe they travel like this all the time and missing this flight is no big deal. "I hope they're okay."

"We'll be taking off shortly. The flight to Jamaica is only about three hours. Plus, there's a time change so you'll gain an hour once you land." Her eyes sparkle beneath her long, dark lashes. I wonder if they have to attend some type of flight attendant makeup training camp? Everyone I've ever met always looks flawless. It's probably in the job description. I shrug, take a sip of my champagne, and giggle. And here I was, hoping I wasn't going to be in a middle seat wedged between a crying baby and someone with body odor.

Pulling out one of several books I've packed, I excitedly open the mafia romance I've had on my shelf for far too long. I'm usually not into mafia books, but 'Taken By My Best Friend' sounds like a great read. And honestly, I need to take a bit of a break from the billionaire romances. I can't help but picture Broadie Weston as the leading man in all of them. This can get awkward when you worry you'll bump into him at work after getting off to thoughts of him between your legs the night before. Heat hits my cheeks at the memory of the last such occasion. I kept imagining how he felt behind me in the cafeteria that day. Except this time, he was naked and buried inside me.

"How are we?"

"Oh." I jump in my seat at the unexpected interruption. "Sorry. My mind was somewhere else."

"It's okay." She giggles. "Mine would be too." I notice she's spotted my book.

"Yeah." I close my eyes, embarrassed. There's no doubt she knows it's a spicy romance. "It's pretty good."

"I'll have to check that one out. I'm reading a Nicholas Sparks book."

I can't help but frown. "I used to read those. But I need a guaranteed happy ending." After what I've endured in real life, I need a happily ever after in my fictional one.

She gives me a kind smile and asks if I'd like anything to eat or drink. "Just a cup of coffee, please."

"Coming right up."

Opening my deep blue blanket, I wrap it around my shoulders and settle back into my seat. Carla, the pretty young attendant, returns moments later with a steamy cup of coffee.

"Here is some cream and sugar if you need them. And hit this bell in a bit and request the cheese plate." She points overhead. "You should try to enjoy every perk available to our first-class travelers while you can."

"Thank you, Carla. I will."

Having thoroughly enjoyed my flight, Carla stops by later to advise we've begun our descent. The relaxed state is immediately replaced with excitement, and I put away the tray table and glance out my window to watch our entry into Jamaica.

Watching the mountainous terrain come into view, I'm disappointed I didn't do more research on the country before my arrival. Hopefully, the driver who transports us from the airport to the resort will have some fun facts.

"Thank you for flying with us. I hope you'll enjoy your stay."

"Oh, I'm sure I will, Carla. Thank you for everything."

I follow the signs to baggage claim to collect my suitcases before heading through to customs. I haven't done a lot of international travel, but this part is always intimidating. Standing in line, I scan the area. There are several older travelers seated in wheelchairs, waiting for someone to take them through. Multiple families are here, some with young children, some older. The parents of the young tots already look exhausted, and it's barely one o'clock. Oh, that's right. It's actually noon. Grinning, I realize that's one more hour in Jamaica today.

"Next." I look up to see the gentleman behind the glass partition waving me forward. I bring my things and hand over my passport as he gets straight to work without so much as a hello. "Who are you here with?"

"No one."

His head snaps up, and he gives me an unnerving stare.

Jeez. Don't judge.

"Where are you going?"

I try to recall the information I typed into the computer for the online Jamaican customs form. I rattle off the name of the resort as he continues to wordlessly type into his computer. I'd already felt odd coming on this trip alone. Now, surrounded by families awaiting the official start of their vacation, I feel even more like a fish out of water. This guy's really not helping.

"Here you go."

Taking my passport, I wonder if we're done.

"Next."

I guess that's a yes.

Moving through the small Kingston airport, I start to feel a little anxiety. What if there's no one here to meet me? Who would I call? What if I go to the wrong place, and they get tired of waiting and leave? But before my head can play any more tricks on itself, a tall, dark-skinned gentleman with a sign that says P. Danforth comes into view.

"Hi. I'm Poppy Danforth," I say excitedly.

"Nice to meet you. I'm Delroy." He reaches for my bag and walks swiftly ahead of me. Picking up my pace to keep up, I reach a white van that looks like it's seen better days. I question if this is the right one, until he opens the back and flings my suitcase inside.

As the back door slides open for me, I discover I'm the only passenger. Climbing in, I buckle my seatbelt and wait for him to get into the driver's seat. It dawns on me that tipping is included at this all-inclusive resort. Does that include him?

"Excuse me. Do you work for the resort?"

"No, ma'am. They hire me to bring guests to and from the airport."

I nod, realizing I'll have to get this man a tip. "How long is the trip?"

"About two hours."

Two hours? I really should've done my homework.

The van rumbles to life, and we lurch forward before he slams on the breaks as two of the children I saw earlier dart in front of the vehicle. Some harsh words are muttered from the front seat, which I assume are Jamaican swear words. Grabbing ahold of the windowsill with one hand and the edge of my seat with the other, I pray the rest of the trip will be less rocky than the start.

About forty minutes later, I feel like I've just completed a heavy workout. This man has swerved to avoid hitting every pothole, and there have been many. It feels like I'm in a real-life version of the video game, *Frogger*.

The town of Kingston sits against a backdrop of mountains. There is blue water to one side and a mix of old and new architecture toward the city center. I try to take in as much as I can while holding on for dear life. As we leave Kingston and head through the mountains, we pass several open-air vehicles with military officers brandishing intimidating rifles.

The driver seems completely unaffected by their presence and turns up a talk show on the radio. It appears to be in English, but it's too low to make out any details. It's basically white noise, adding an additional layer of sensory overload to this trip.

Suddenly, a shiny black vehicle pulls in front of the van, causing the driver to hit the breaks to avoid careening into the back of it. The car slows to a stop in the middle of the road, and a gentleman steps out, walking briskly to the van. I watch, curious, as the driver rolls down the window and speaks animatedly in what I assume is a conversation completely in Jamaican. Moments later, the back doors of the van open, and I watch as my suitcase is removed.

"Hey, what's going—"

The door next to me flies open, startling me. "Come with me," the gentleman dressed in all black directs.

"Where are we going?" I step out of the vehicle and turn to the driver of the van who met me at the airport, but he's already put his shuttle bus in reverse and is pulling around the black town car. My heart is pounding in my chest, fear coursing through my veins. What the heck is happening?

Am I being kidnapped?

My mind is reeling, trying to come up with an escape plan, when the driver opens the door for me. "Please, ma'am."

Realizing my bag is in the back of the car, I determine it's unlikely a kidnapper would stop to get my things and try to get my wits about me. *Breathe, Poppy. Just breathe.*

"I'm sorry. I'm confused. What is happening? Where are we going?"

"My apologies for the mix-up, ma'am. We're going to the resort. You were supposed to receive a luxury transfer instead of the van. I got here as quickly as the error was discovered."

"Oh." I sigh in relief. Completely overwhelmed, I can't think of anything else to say. Sliding into the smooth, leather covered back seat, I find several bottles of water and some tourist information on Jamaica. Boy, this is a change. I'd merely been hoping for a less torturous ride.

"We should have you to the resort in about forty-five minutes."

"Thank you."

Reaching for a water, I chuckle at the label. WATA. Settling into the seat, I glance out the window to my left. I can't quite make out what I'm looking at.

"Aluminum."

"What?"

"It's an aluminum refinery."

"Oh. Thank you."

Over the course of the next thirty minutes, the kind driver points out different Jamaican highlights. Bikes seem to be a big mode of transportation here. I watch curiously as several individuals begin to pedal while carrying stacks of vegetation atop the handlebars.

"What is that they're hauling?"

"Ah, that's sugar cane." We continue to drive until the area becomes more populated with stores and various cement and concrete buildings. "And this is Ochi."

"Ochi?"

"Ocho Rios, ma'am."

We drive through the city center before weaving through to what I assume is the path to the water's edge. There are palm and banana trees lining the roadway, and cars can be found parked along the curb on either side, the owners selling products from their trunks.

We pass several resort hotels and local shops and restaurants before the driver slows and makes a left turn into the gated drive. Sitting forward in excitement, I try to take everything in. There's a gorgeous fountain at the front of the property, tennis courts to the right, and bright turquoise water straight ahead. I'm almost giddy at the sight.

The driver pulls up next to a valet stand and parks. After my door swings wide, a kind man in a white uniform approaches with a warm towel. "Welcome. We're so glad you're here."

I try to take in the swaying palm trees, the festive music in the distance, and the incredible greeting and nearly pinch myself. This place almost reminds me of that show *Fantasy Island* I used to watch with my mother as a child.

The driver hands my bag to the valet and heads back to his car when I remember they don't work for the resort. "Hey, wait." Reaching into my purse, I grab a twenty.

"No, no, ma'am. It's all taken care of. Enjoy your stay."

Wow. If this is the way the next five days is going to go, I'll never want to return to my real life. Maybe the hospital should rethink their strategy for retaining employees.

"If you'll follow me. We'll get you all checked in." The valet escorts me inside, and I'm greeted by a beautiful girl in a deep blue uniform.

"Hi. I'm Shayna. I'll be getting you registered. Please, have a seat." She offers me a welcome beverage after collecting my information, and I lean back, taking in the ocean view out of the back window. The lobby is open and decorated with luxurious settees and chairs made of teal and green fabric. There are pictures of Jamaican landscape wrapped in golden frames hanging on the walls. One counter has bottled water and fresh cookies laid out for guests, while the other has a few computers available for use. Every detail appears well thought out.

"Your room won't be ready for a bit longer. May I show you to one of the restaurants that is serving lunch? Hopefully, by the time you're done, your accommodations will be prepared for you.

"Yes. That would be lovely, Shayna." Grabbing my purse and my carry-on bag, I follow her down the marble staircase until we reach the doors below. As she opens them for me, I'm hit with the smell of sea air coupled with tropical foliage. It's a dream. *A fantasy.* I giggle.

Shayna turns to look at me.

"I'm sorry. I'm just so in awe of everything. It reminds me of something from a television show or a movie."

"Yes. It's beautiful here. And they did actually film a James Bond movie not too far from us." She continues walking past an array of round tables which appear to be set up for an event of some kind. "There are multiple restaurants on the property. If you have the app downloaded on your phone, you'll be able to find their hours and a copy of the menu."

"Do I need reservations?"

"No, no. Only for a candlelight dinner on the beach."

As nice as that sounds, I don't plan on doing *that* alone.

"Here you go. Enjoy your lunch. Take your time, and I'll try to put a rush on your room."

"Thank you, Shayna."

After checking in with the hostess, I'm escorted to a small table with views of the pool and the ocean. There is festive music playing and ceiling fans circle overhead. While it's quite warm, it only serves to immerse me into vacation mode.

The hostess advises she'll bring the Margarita I've ordered shortly, but that I can help myself to the buffet. I stand and walk over to the various rows of food, and my mouth falls open. Rows and rows of decadent options. Various forms of rice, jerk chicken, and grilled vegetables are located on the first table I encounter. Looking around, I find a bread station, fruit and cheese, salad with a variety of toppings, and pita chips and an assortment of dips. They even have a grill where they'll make your burger to order.

Filling my plate with Jamaican specialties, I turn and find a row of desserts. Ah, tempting, but no. I think I'll have to be careful eating like this every day, or I won't fit into any of my clothes by the time I return home.

I find my table and notice a frosty frozen drink is waiting for me. Now this is the life. I tuck into my food, eating slowly to fully enjoy the experience. Looking closer, I discover there's a bar built into the pool with multiple tile barstools surrounding it, allowing swimmers to order their next libation without leaving the water. A resort employee is leading some type of game at the front of the pool while parents pull small children behind them on floats at the opposite end.

Taking a bite of my chicken, I'm relieved to find it flavorful without burning a hole through my tongue. I wasn't sure my palate could handle jerk chicken.

"Can I get you anything?" a server asks.

"No. I'm in heaven." I smile. "I'm just excited the jerk chicken wasn't as spicy as I'd read about."

"Oh, that's just here on the resort, ma'am. You try it at a restaurant off of our property, and it might be a much different experience." He grins. "Are you enjoying your stay?"

"Very much. But I literally just got here. Haven't even checked into my room yet."

"Welcome. Is it your first trip to Jamaica?"

"Yes. I'm thrilled to be here. It's been on my bucket list for years."

"Good, good. Well, enjoy yourself. Let us know if you need anything."

The friendly, attentive server walks off, leaving me with an ear-to-ear grin. This place is absolutely incredible. It would've been one thing if the hospital had offered to put us up at a chain hotel along the waterfront. But this is amazing.

As I continue my meal, I have the oddest sense someone is watching me. Looking about the dining area, I don't see anyone out of the ordinary. The staff is so overly attentive, I'm sure that's all it is—watching in order to anticipate your every need, that and being at this phenomenal resort all alone. I feel as if I stick out like a sore thumb. But I'm not letting those fears get to me this week.

After finishing my amazing meal, I casually stroll back to the front desk to see if my room is ready. Again, that odd feeling returns. Yet, there's no one that seems out of place. There are a few men dressed in black that look as if they do security for the resort, but otherwise, nothing seems amiss.

"Hi, Shayna. Lunch was simply incredible. By any chance is my room ready?"

"Oh, yes. We put a rush on it. Let me escort you there."

Shayna takes me to the elevator, pointing out various amenities along the way. We walk to the end of a corridor, and it strikes me that there's no sound. I've seen no other people, not even room service trays or dishes outside of any of the rooms. Their housekeeping staff must be top notch.

"Here we are." Shayna opens the door and waves me in to one of the most luxurious rooms I've ever seen. It's like something from one of those life of the rich and famous travel shows. The room is appointed in rich mahogany wood furniture. The massive king size bed is covered in an inviting white duvet. There's a lower level to the room, with a comfy couch and table, perfect for reading. But the showstopper is the ocean-front balcony. I push open the glass doors and inhale the sea air.

"This is unbelievable, Shayna."

"I'm so glad you like it." She has to hear this a lot. "The mini fridge is fully stocked with water, juice, and soda, and a bar menu is beside the coffee station. Please fill it out, letting us know your wine or beer preferences.

I turn to her, my mouth ajar.

She giggles. "Your keys are on the counter. Please feel free to contact me at the front desk if there's anything at all you need. Your butler should stop by each evening to restock the fridge."

"My what?"

"Your butler, ma'am."

Plopping down on the end of the bed, I'm starting to wonder if this really is a dream.

"You are staying in one of our top-of-the-line suites." She smiles. "Your bag is already in the closet. I'll let you get settled."

I stand in complete disbelief as Shayna exits the room. Now I'm sure of it.

I'm never going to want to leave.

CHAPTER SEVENTEEN
BROADIE

"Has she made it here, okay?" I've tried to keep my mind occupied on my work, but it's impossible. About two hours ago, I went to Stu's suite to inquire whether Poppy had arrived at the Kingston airport and found he had a car trailing her van. As I kept my eyes trained on the monitor, it was like watching a tin can bounce down a barely paved street. There was no way I was putting her through a two-hour ride in that thing.

Porter and Stu quickly jumped into action, sending a town car to meet her. Initially, they'd encouraged sticking with the normal transportation hired by the hotel, but I couldn't stand it any longer.

You're going to have to be careful. If you upgrade too many things, she's going to get suspicious. Stu had said. Porter and Stu both recommended I lay low today, and I fear they might be right. I'm too anxious and would likely blow my cover. So now that she's here, I'll bide my time before making my presence known. Then any future spoiling she receives, she'll know comes directly from me.

"Is she all checked in?"

"Yes, sir," Porter answers. I can practically feel his eye roll from here. "Go have a drink, Dr. Weston. Everything's fine."

In the short time I've been at the resort, I've probably had more to drink than I've had in the last two months. Between the hot weather, the relaxed atmosphere, and the fact the drinks are all included, they seem to be offered up to guests at a fevered pace. Luckily, alcohol has never been a vice. I enjoy a good scotch or a glass of wine, but when I'm stressed and need an escape, it's usually the gym or a good hard fuck that do the trick.

"I think I'll hit the gym, Porter. Then I might grab an early dinner and finish the rest of these charts."

Porter shakes his head. "Just what I'd be doing on vacation."

Again, he's right. But I have a hard time letting go of my responsibilities long enough to truly relax. Add to it I've set this ruse into motion, and I'm not entirely sure I can pull this off. Working may offer the distraction I need so I don't do something crazy. *Not that I can think of much that can top this.*

"I hear you. I'm going to try to relax. I'm not planning to leave the resort tonight. Why don't you go enjoy yourself?"

"You don't have to ask me twice."

I laugh as Porter scurries out the door.

Might as well hit the gym. Otherwise, my curiosity will get the best of me, and I'll start hunting for her all over this place.

Room service, a glass of wine, and the heavy workout at the gym should've relaxed me, yet I'm still wired. I can't even focus on work.

Grabbing my sunglasses and a baseball cap, I make my way to the main area of the resort. I have no idea what I'm doing. I'll just get a drink at the bar. I just need to burn off some of this nervous energy.

The layout of the property has been well thought out. There are little alcoves dotted with brightly colored tropical plants that lure you off the main path toward the restaurants, bars, and pool. After pulling my hat down and dipping my head at passersby, I decide to stick to the less traveled trails in case I come upon Poppy.

As I walk up to an open-air bar with a view of the main restaurant and pool, I dart inside and ask for a gin and tonic before taking a seat in the corner. A small garden like area separates the bar from the pool, but from this vantage point, I can enjoy both the ocean, the poolside nightly entertainment, as well as the comings and goings of the resort guests. The sun sets early here, but the pool area is well lit. I've found over the last few evenings that the reflection of the moonlight over the water's surface to be undeniably relaxing.

The bartender delivers my drink and I settle back in my chair, trying to enjoy the environment. Maybe I'm just not built to relax. I have to acknowledge that being caught in the fray is where I seem to thrive—even if it's exhausting.

There were occasions when the girls were small that I was able to unwind and lie on the floor to play with them. But it was usually after a long, stressful day. We took family vacations. But I preferred to rent a beach house, whereas Camile wanted to travel somewhere exotic. It took a few years to figure out that the beach house made it easier to stay in touch with the office and my accountant. *And keep working.*

Camile caught on to this quicker than I did. I'd assumed she enjoyed the vacations in over-the-top destinations because she was used to such a lavish lifestyle. That may have played a part in where she chose to go, but ultimately, those trips forced me to detach. While most healthy people revel in the weeklong break from the chaos, it only made me edgy.

I'm not a total control freak. There's no doubt I can spend more time with my girls and pull back from the pace I've grown accustomed. It's just a matter of breaking the cycle. When I graduated from my surgical fellowship, I couldn't wait to put my years of education to work and start building my practice. It's grown beyond anything I could've imagined.

While my father and grandfather earned their millions in business, I've always been drawn to medicine. My grandmother had been a nurse back in her day. Perhaps the many hours I was in her care rubbed off on me.

Dad had tried to talk me out of going to medical school. *It's long hours and strife for little reward,* he'd said. Yet I'd grown up watching him be beholden to the mighty dollar. He was a good man but a slave to success.

My grandfather, while disappointed I wouldn't take over the family business, was more supportive of my choices. I'm sure dear old Dad is having the last laugh now, watching me work every bit as hard as he did. The difference is, hopefully, I'm learning before it's too late. In the wise words of my oldest daughter, *I have more money than I know what to do with.* Now I simply need to find a way to scale back my efforts at work to allow for a more fulfilling and meaningful life. Which is proving difficult since my brain seems to think the only way to feel satisfied is with a scalpel in my hand.

A warm breeze flows through the bar, bringing an electricity with it. The evening's entertainment hasn't changed, nor have there been any shrieks from children in the pool area. Visibly, the area seems unchanged. But I feel it before I see it.

See her.

Sitting up in my chair, I instinctively pull my cap down lower and take her in. Wearing a long, flowy yellow sundress, Poppy strolls across the pool deck, her blonde locks dancing in the wind. She's wearing heeled sandals, carrying a cocktail of some sort. And a book. I love that she reads. Picturing her in a tiny pair of pajamas, curled up on the couch with her book as she occasionally gazes out over the azure water below makes my dick stir. Who knew I was into bookish women?

I watch as she lowers herself onto a chaise, places her book in her lap, and takes a sip of her red and white frozen drink. There's a contented smile on her face that warms my heart. It's been a rare occasion to see her laugh or smile at the hospital. If nothing else comes of this giveaway charade, at least I've given her this. *Okay, who am I kidding? I want a lot more to come of this.*

I don't know much about her personal life beyond what Jarod and Stu have shared. Her husband died about eight years ago. She lives alone. She has a brother in Blacksburg with a wife and kids. Her mother resides in a local long term care facility. And, as I learned the hard way, she doesn't appear to date anyone from the hospital.

Poppy slides off her shoes, and I watch as her feet dance to the beat. The resort entertainment for the evening includes a dance troop who perform acrobatics to the distinctly Jamaican music. Whether poolside, seated at the open-air restaurant, or in the water, all eyes appear to be on them.

But mine.

"Can I get you another?" a staff member asks, pointing to my empty glass.

I start to say no, but then reconsider. This is the best entertainment I've had in ages. I might as well enjoy myself.

"Sure. But can I try one of those red and white frozen concoctions everyone's drinking?"

"A Miami Vice? Sure. Coming right up."

I can't recall the last time I drank a frozen drink of any kind. But I'm curious to know what Poppy's sipping on.

As if on cue, she lifts the straw to her mouth and takes another sip. As she puts her drink on the table beside her, I watch as her tongue darts out to lick her lips and feel my cock jump in my pants. *Hell. I might need to dump the damn cocktail in my lap if this keeps up.*

The server brings my cheesy, overflowing red and white layered frozen cocktail and deposits it beside me. I take a sip, and my tongue is hit with a frosty sugary sensation. It's essentially a combination of a straw-berry Daiquiri and a Pina Colada. I turn to look behind the bar and notice both are readily available from slush machines. I can't help but chuckle. I'm sure it's not bad for relaxing by the pool on a hot summer day, but I'll stick to my scotch.

Turning back around, I see red. And it's not the drink. Some tall, ripped asshat wearing nothing but his swim trunks and tattoos is standing beside Poppy's chair.

Who the hell is this fucker?

I shouldn't be surprised. Poppy is beautiful. And as she's sitting there all alone, why wouldn't someone try? But if anyone is getting a shot at a holiday tryst with her, it's me.

Continuing to watch their interaction, I sense she's uncomfortable. Does she do one-night stands? Is this guy her type? One thing's for sure, he doesn't work for St. Luke's. I made sure none of the other winners would be here this week.

Poppy sits forward, grabbing her sandals and stands. *What the hell? Is she going somewhere with him?* She just met him, for fuck's sake. Unless they met earlier in the day? Stroking the two-day growth of beard I've amassed, my eyes narrow.

She's not into him. I can see it written all over her face. From my vantage point, it appears she's attempting to give him a polite but curt brush off before walking away. But the guy isn't taking the hint and continues trailing along beside her as if he's not taking no for an answer.

Getting up from my seat, my protective instincts are kicking in to overdrive. While this loser is smiling down at her, Poppy's lips are pressed in a thin line, as if forcing herself to remain cordial. I grab ahold of the seat back as I watch them walk down a dimly lit path back to the main resort.

Giving a safe distance, I cautiously follow along behind them. Until I see him put his hand on her lower back and my restraint snaps like a fallen twig beneath my feet. Without a second thought, my pace hastens. I've almost reached them when I'm struck from the side, landing in a bed of Hibiscus underneath something large.

"What the—"

A large hand clamps over my mouth, and my eyes fly wide until I see my assailant.

"What the hell, Stu?" My voice is muffled beneath his large palm.

"Shhh," he instructs as he sets me free.

Turning my head, I discover Poppy and her companion are gone. I start to bolt upright when Stu pushes me back down onto the ground.

Glancing from side to side, he gives me the stare down. "For a brilliant surgeon, you're one dumb fucker. We didn't go to all of this trouble just to have you blow it right out of the gate."

Shit. He's right.

"I can't sit by and watch some—"

Stu's large hand lands on my shoulder. "We've got it covered, boss." He reaches for my arm, pulling me up to my feet just as I see the tat covered gym rat that was with Poppy earlier, stroll past us.

"Sorry, man." I say to Stu.

We both walk silently up the remainder of the cement pathway to the doors to the hotel, Stu in front of me to ensure Poppy isn't anywhere in sight. As we walk onto the elevator, it hits me.

I've lost my fucking mind.

"Look. I don't entirely understand what's going on. But we've worked together for a while now. From what I can gather, you've used a lot of time, money, and resources for a chance with this woman. Regardless of what I said earlier, you're the most intelligent man I know."

My head drops at his words. There's nothing smart about any of this. It's like some love-struck teenager has overtaken my mind. *And I'm not even in love.*

"Women can make you do some crazy shit." Stu's large hand pats me on the shoulder, and I shake my head at my employee and confidant. "I've been there."

"Really?" I ask skeptically.

He chuckles. "Well, nothing like this. But, yeah."

It dawns on me how little I really know about Russell Stewart. "Did it work out for you?"

"Been married for twelve years," he answers with a proud grin.

I knew he was married but assumed he had an ordinary relationship with a domestic goddess who stayed busy with her own life, accustomed to his absence. Not a woman who could bring this tree trunk of a man to his knees.

"Took a lot of convincing to get her to go out with me. I'd known her growing up. I didn't have a good reputation back then. Got myself into a lot of spats. She's a simple girl and didn't want any part of it. But somehow, my heart knew before my head did. She's the love of my life. So, I had to prove it to her."

"Thanks, man. For everything. I hope I figure all of this out soon. And that you're still speaking to me when it's all over."

"Nah. You're good. Just be careful. Secrets have a way of coming out."

Rubbing the back of my neck, I've already contemplated this. "I know. I'll tell her, eventually."

I just want the chance to figure out what this hold is she has over me first.

CHAPTER EIGHTEEN
POPPY

"Good morning, Ms. Danforth. Are you enjoying your stay with us?"

My eyes flick up from my book to see Shayna. "Oh, yes. Immensely."

The corner of her mouth lifts in a grin as her eyes land on the sexy image on the cover of my romance novel. I know a lot of people prefer to read on their kindle or buy books that don't give away what they're reading, but I love the feel and smell of a book in my hand. And if I'm being honest, a hot guy looking back at me from the cover does more to entice me to purchase a book than the book's description.

Plus, I'm on vacation, dammit. I'll read what I want.

"It looks good," she says. *It or him*, I wonder.

"So far. I just started it this morning." I giggle. "I tore through the last one.

"Ah. I like a good book too. I never seem to find the time."

My smile falters a bit, realizing all I seem to have is time. I really do need to find some type of art class when I get home.

"I'll let you get back to your book."

Putting my novel down, I push my chair back and stand. "I'm actually headed back to my room. Now that my breakfast is over, I think I'll change and spend some time by the pool." Looking over the area, I'm shocked to find the majority of the chaise lounges are already spoken for.

Shayna must note my pout. "It's all right. Here, give me your things. I'll grab a towel and place them over there." I follow her finger to find a lone lounge chair under an umbrella by one of the cabanas available for rent. "You go change, and it'll be waiting for you when you get back."

My eyes narrow, attempting to read the sign sitting on the lounge chair. "Are you sure, Shayna? It looks like it belongs to whomever has rented the cabana for the day."

"I'm sure. That guest has rented it for the entire week, but I've yet to see him there. Don't you worry. If there's any problem, I'll take care of it." She winks.

"Okay." I reach for my key card and head to my room. Why must I be such a rule follower? Shayna works here. If she says it's okay, that should be enough for me.

As I stroll back to my room, my mind goes back to my childhood. While my mother was easygoing in her parenting, my father had been a strict disciplinarian. I didn't get into much trouble growing up. But I admit I was likely too afraid of the consequences to do otherwise.

Reaching my room, I swipe the key and walk inside, already trying to figure out which bathing suit I'll wear. I hadn't been shopping for new clothes in ages. Knowing I was going away to a private beach vacation gave me courage to purchase some items I wouldn't normally wear if I thought I might bump into someone I knew.

Pulling open the dresser drawer, my hand immediately goes to the aqua blue bikini. I quickly change and slide into the wedges I purchased to go with them. Turning from side to side, I admire how the sandals make my legs look long and lean. Grabbing the ridiculous sun hat the clerk encouraged me to buy, I place it on my head and bite my lip when I see myself in the mirror. *Not bad, Poppy. Not bad.*

I can practically hear Madonna's "Vogue" playing as I walk out of my room. I lift my chin and embrace my inner diva. I've never been this girl, dressed to impress. I was happier to be on my husband's arm in a pair of sweats than to consider wearing an outfit that would put the spotlight on me—especially dressed in something worthy of a runway. Dan never seemed all that interested in what I wore. Yet, I never took offense by this. Maybe we were simply comfortable enough with one another that it felt unnecessary. So, as Madonna might say, don't just stand there, Poppy. Let's get to it. Because today, I'm dressing for me.

The warm Jamaican breeze hits me as soon as I reach the outdoors. It feels as if the temperature has increased ten degrees in the short time I was in my room. Shrugging my shoulders at myself, I giggle. Who cares? I'm in Jamaica, *man*. I inwardly pronounce man as if I'm a native and laugh again.

As I come around the corner of the pool deck, I spot my things. Shayna even went so far as to grab a bottle of water for me. I feel my feet wobble beneath the tall heels as I walk. Between the slick tile at the pool's edge and my lack of experience with these treacherous shoes, it dawns on me I should've worn them around the house before leaving in order to break them in.

This thought has barely left my mind, when I feel my feet fly out from beneath me. My arms thrash in all directions as I go catapulting to the ground. However, instead of striking the surface of the ceramic tile, I land in the pool with a loud shriek.

"Well, hello."

Barely able to acknowledge the deep rumble against my cheek due to the splashing of water and the sound of my pulse racing in my ears, I blink rapidly in an attempt to figure out what just happened. Discovering I've landed in a muscular pair of arms, I prepare myself to push away from the overzealous man who had a hard time accepting 'no' last night. Then I see him.

Him!

"Am I dreaming?" I ask.

"You dream about me?" His facial expression has morphed from one of delight to complete seriousness.

Broadie Weston. *The* Dr. Broadie Weston. St. Luke's royalty and the man of my dirty dreams is here in the flesh. *I think.*

Moving my hand from around his neck, I place the pad of my index finger into the space where his dimple usually resides. His smile widens, and I feel that familiar indention deepen beneath my touch.

"It is you," I say in complete shock. As much as I appreciate him saving me from an even more embarrassing fate had he not caught me, I push away, confused. "What are you doing here?"

Broadie clears his throat. "I'm attending a conference."

I picture the brochures I receive on a regular basis, offering continuing education credits at amazing destinations all over the world. This never seemed like a viable option for me. But I'm sure with unlimited funds, it is for him. It dawns on me that this resort likely caters to medical providers, hence the giveaways.

Looking around, I await some gorgeous young woman to approach, wondering why her man is so close to me. "Are you here with your family?" I ask, treading water in my attempt to reach the side of the pool. I hope I haven't completely destroyed my new shoes. But it's probably safer I not wear them down here again.

"No. My daughters just got back from New Zealand with their mother. I came here alone."

I'm not sure what's happening to my body, as his statement stirs something low in my belly. My gaze flicks to his, and the heat in his eyes has me blushing. I glance toward the stairs but find they're at the other end of the pool.

"Here." Broadie's hands wrap around my waist, and he hoists me onto the pool's edge with ease. I lift one leg, then the other, as I remove my waterlogged wedges. There's no escaping the fact they're ruined beyond repair.

"I'm sorry about your shoes, Poppy."

"I should've known better than to think I could prance around like some supermodel in these things. I'm used to flip flops." I laugh, embarrassed. Looking back toward him, I catch the moment his eyes flick from my chest to my mouth and blush. Peering down, I find my nipples are firm peaks, pushing against the thin blue fabric of my bikini. Glancing back at him, there's an undeniable current floating between us. *You better get out of this pool before you're electrocuted, Poppy.*

"Thank you. For catching me. Now that I'm completely mortified, I'll just head over to my lounger." I say self-consciously.

"Don't be embarrassed. It was the highlight of my day." He grins. His tan skin and dark hair glisten in the sun, as his light brown eyes smile up at me through dark, wet lashes.

Getting to my feet, I give him a shy smile, carry my useless shoes over to the chaise, and sit down. As I dry off, I can see Broadie diving under the water out of the corner of my eye. He may still be submerged, yet there's no doubt what floats beneath. His arms felt like bands of steel as he held me tight to his chest. A very warm, muscular chest, covered in a light smattering of hair. Okay, change the channel, Poppy, or you'll never get your body under control.

Taking a sip of my water, I remember my sunscreen is in my pool bag. With my fair skin, it wouldn't take long in this Jamaican sun to burn to a crisp. Once I'm completely dry, I reach into my bag and retrieve my sun block. I apply a liberal amount to my face and neck before rubbing it into my arms and legs.

"Everything okay, miss?" a resort staff member asks.

Is he referring to my fall earlier. I'm sure everyone here got a big laugh out of that. "Yes, thank you."

"Can I get you a drink?"

"Not right now. The water is fine, thanks."

I apply more lotion to my neck, chest, and abdomen as he walks away. The festive music has changed from a Jamaican vibe to more like the American music I've found on cruise ships and at pools back home. The tunes have a fun rhythm that make you want to dance or sing along. While I'd normally be lying back on my chair, eyes closed, tapping my toes to the beat, I admit having Broadie here has me feeling more conspicuous.

Reaching behind me, I try to apply my lotion when I notice the sun disappear and quickly look up to see if a storm cloud has moved in. I admit I haven't been paying any attention to the weather forecast. It seems to rain for about an hour each day here, much like I find it does in the late afternoon when I visit Florida. Plus, there's nothing I can do about it anyway. So why worry?

"Can I help you with that?"

Turns out my storm cloud is one tall, handsome drink of water. The very thought of having his hands on my body could be the death of me.

"I—"

"You're so fair skinned, Poppy. You don't want to burn."

Ugh. He's right. I'd managed yesterday, but only because it was so late in the day by the time I made it to the pool the sun was probably less intense. Scooting forward, I lift the lotion up toward him and shield my eyes. Whether it's from the sun or those eyes that are doing weird things to my belly right now, I haven't decided. "Thank you."

The chaise dips as he sits himself down behind me. The feel of him so close is making my skin feel electric. Or is it the sheer anticipation of feeling his strong, gifted hands all over my back. Whichever it is, I'm well aware it's not coming from the sun. The moment his hands hit my naked back, I jolt.

"Sorry. Is it cold?" His deep voice caresses my ear, and I nearly swoon.

"No. It just startled me for a second." *Good grief, Poppy. Get it together.* But the feel of his warm hands gliding against my skin is doing anything but relaxing me. I feel myself tense as I discover all Broadie Weston has to do is rub sunscreen on my back, and I'm getting wet. I try to distract myself from what he's doing to me. "So, has your conference ended or not begun?"

He immediately stops the rhythmic movement against my skin. "Oh, you caught me." His laugh sounds as if it carries an element of shame. "I played hooky today."

"So how long are you here?" Gah. That sounded as if I was coming on to him.

"I'm here for four more days." Jeez. Really? That's some coincidence.

"You're so tense," he jokes as he playfully massages my shoulders with the sunblock.

Irritated that he's able to have this effect on me, I turn and grab the lotion from him. "Thanks," I say, hoping he'll take the hint he can go now.

"I'm sorry. I didn't mean to upset you."

Grrr. Now I feel like a witch. I'm not prepared for what this man does to me. It was bad enough alone in my room at night. Having to touch myself to relax enough to get to sleep. And now the star of my fantasies is right behind me. *I mean, for god's sake.*

"You didn't upset me." Now, I'm embarrassed. he's been nothing but nice to me. "You make me nervous." I whisper.

All of a sudden, I feel his body move flush against mine. "Me? Why?" His warm breath tickles my ear.

My eyes close at the nearness of him, before a fine sheen of goose-bumps appears, mortifying me further. I simply shrug, not knowing how to answer him without making my body's responses to him even more obvious. I've never known a man who could turn me on this way.

"Would it be okay to ask you to return the favor?"

"What?" I ask shocked, my mind still fixated on how aroused he makes me.

"I can't reach either." He taps the lotion that's now sitting by my side.

"Sure." *What is happening here?*

"Switch?" he asks, standing from his spot behind me. For the first time, I let my eyes feast on his nearly perfect form. He's tone without being overly muscular, his abs are well defined and covered under gorgeous, bronzed skin. As my eyes meet his, there's a question lingering there.

Oh, yeah. Switch seats, Poppy.

Hopping up from my spot, I move to the back of the chaise as he sits in front of me. I squirt the lotion into my hand and rub my palms together. Hoping he doesn't notice the tremble in my touch, I place my hands on his shoulders and glide the sunblock over his beautiful back. The muscles dance underneath my touch, causing my breath to catch in my throat. Holy crap. If rubbing sunblock onto his back is doing this to me, I'm afraid to think what sleeping with this man might be like.

"There," I say, patting his back awkwardly, informing him I'm done.

"Thanks." He winks, sending another electric current straight to my lady parts. This man is dangerous. Too dangerous. If he was some rando I'd met here, it might be different. But I still have to work at the same hospital as him once I leave here.

Broadie stands, turns, and walks back toward the pool, where he takes a seat on the edge momentarily before jumping back in.

Grabbing my book, I attempt to return to my earlier passage, but find I have to reread the same sentence over and over, given I have one eye on the page and the other on the pool. *Okay, so on the doctor in the pool.*

I've managed to settle my attention back on my book as I discover I've reached a rather spicy scene. I thought I'd become overheated by the summer sun, yet it may be this—

"Good book?"

Alarmed at my current overly heated state, I slam it closed. "Yes. Thank you." Now I'm annoyed. Glancing up at him, there's a glint in his eye. There's no judgment, just a sexy smile. I slide off of my chair and stand.

"Leaving?"

"I need to cool off a bit." He doesn't need to know why. As I enter the pool, I welcome the relief the cool water brings. I dive beneath the surface and swim to the other end of the pool, where a waterfall splashes cool mist across my skin. The pool bar is congested with guests awaiting their turn at receiving a refreshing libation. As tempting as it is to join them, I'm afraid I'm no match for the combination of the Jamaican sun and alcohol. I'd likely fall asleep before dinner or lose my balance and make a fool of myself.

Oh yeah, I've already done that.

As I swim back to where my lounger is located, I realize Broadie is dressed, with his things in hand. Giving me a curt wave, he walks away from the pool area. Has he decided to attend his meeting after all?

And why, if I wanted to get some space between us, do I suddenly feel so disappointed?

∼

Toweling my delicate skin after my shower, I apply some aloe before putting on my sundress. Despite the liberal use of sunscreen, a rosy glow is present along my nose and shoulders. The pretty floral dress is sleeve-less, but still causes irritation as it grazes my sensitive flesh.

After doing my hair in loose waves, I reach for some simple jewelry. Once I've finished, I apply a little lip gloss and mascara before heading out. I could kick myself for the thought, but I'm almost hoping I bump into Broadie again.

I don't know what it is about him. Okay, I know exactly what it is. He's smart, gorgeous, and charismatic. And he makes me feel desired. But is that his game? How he comes on to the women he's attracted to?

The biggest obstacle with agreeing to go out with him isn't even the fact we work together. Broadie Weston isn't someone you date once and walk away from unscathed. I'm sure of it. It would be my luck to finally feel a spark again, just to have the rug pulled out from under me. It's safer to keep my defenses up.

Between the large lunch and the full day in the sun, I'm not very hungry. I think I'd just like a glass of wine and maybe some fruit or cheese. I grab my key card and my purse and make my way downstairs.

Entering the lounge, I note there aren't many people here tonight. Strange, given how many people were at the pool today. Sitting at the bar, I take out my phone to check the app for the various evening's activities. Who am I kidding? I won't last long enough for all of that.

"Hi. What can I get you?"

"Hi. Can I have a glass of Pinot Grigio? And do you have a bar menu? Anything besides burgers and fries?"

The bartender returns with a small card listing the various options.

"Oh, this is perfect. Can I have the charcuterie board?"

"Coming right up."

I glance back down at my phone, flipping through the evening's activi-ties, when I feel him.

"Hi. May I join you?"

My pulse picks up at his proximity. "Yes, of course."

Broadie's dressed in a pair of dark jeans and a white button down. He's as handsome as ever, but I'd put money on the fact his scent is the most intoxicating thing in this bar. It's a rich blend of citrus and spice with a hint of musk. As if everything about him doesn't scream sexy man, this cologne is the exclamation mark.

"Here you go, miss." The bartender slides my wine and the large board covered in dried meats, cheeses, olives, grapes, nuts and figs as well as a variety of sliced bread and crackers in front of me.

Peering down at the platter, I nearly gasp. "Thank you. This is gorgeous." I pop an olive into my mouth.

"Enjoy. Can I get you something, sir?"

Noticing Broadie hasn't answered, I gaze in his direction and find him watching me. My mouth, specifically.

"I'll have what she's having," he answers. His eyes not straying from mine. Hell, this man.

"The wine and cheese, sir?"

Dropping my hand over his, I stop him. "Oh, Broadie. I'll never eat all of this."

His eyes briefly land on my hand before answering, "Thank you. That'd be nice. Just the wine then."

I quickly bring my hand back to my glass, so he doesn't think this is more than two acquaintances who happen to be in the same place at the same time. Or perhaps, so I don't start to let myself consider there could be anything more.

"Do you mind if I ask you something personal?" he asks.

"Sure." I pop a grape into my mouth before taking a sip of my wine.

"Are you seeing anyone?"

Nearly choking on my grape, I have to carefully swallow it down. His question has completely thrown me off kilter. "No."

"But you won't have dinner with me?"

The server approaches and places Broadie's wine in front of him. As he walks away, I turn to Broadie. "Can I be honest?"

"Please."

"I'd love to go out with you." A magical smile crosses his face, and I almost stop there. He's so handsome. And whether this is some game or not, it feels pretty darn amazing that he's looking at me with such hopeful exuberance. "But we work together. I just don't think it's a good idea."

He looks away, but not before I notice how his expression has fallen. God. I wish a fortune teller was one of the activities scheduled. I'd love to go out with this man. Yet, I'm not prepared for another heartbreak.

Looking into my glass, I decide to put it all out there. "My husband died about eight years ago. He had ALS." I notice the audible intake of air from beside me. "It was so incredibly painful. To watch the man I loved falling deeper and deeper into an abyss I knew he'd never return from." I trail my finger around the bottom of my wine glass, hoping to stifle the tears. I refuse to cry anymore. "It's taken me a long, long time to heal. I think Kat was right when she said I had to grieve not only him, but the years leading up to his death." I take a sip of my wine and try to push forward. "I've tried to date, but my heart hasn't been in it. Until now." My eyes flick to his, and I try to be as honest as I can. "But I'm worried it's still a bit tattered. I'm fearful of putting myself out there."

Broadie takes a sip of his wine but remains silent.

"Can I ask you something?"

"Anything."

"Are you dating?" I reach for a crusty piece of bread and nibble on the end, trying to focus on anything but how anxious I feel being this honest. "What happened with your ex-wife?"

Broadie takes a deep breath as if he's about to dive into deep water. "I'm not dating. Haven't dated since before I was married."

I lift a brow in disbelief.

"It's the truth. I don't date for the very reason I got divorced. My career has always come first. It's humiliating to admit that fact. My ex-wife knew the score when we got married. But it still didn't make it right." He takes another sip of his wine and turns so he's facing me. "I have a lot of guilt over it. Especially that I wasn't the father I should've been to my girls. I'm trying to make up for it because they deserve better."

He turns away from me momentarily, as if he's deep in thought, before spinning back around to look me straight in the eye. "Poppy, I can't guarantee what happens tomorrow, if I'm being honest. Until I feel confident that I can treat a woman as an equal partner, I can't commit to anything more. But I really am working on it."

Having barely touched the food in front of me, I select one last Kalamata olive. This deep conversation has caused me to completely lose my appetite. "Do you want any more?"

Broadie shakes his head.

I wave to the server. "Can I take this back to my room?"

"Of course, I'll get it packaged for you."

"Thank you for being honest with me." I detect a slight flinch at my words, but I'm sure it's because he knows where this is going. Placing my hand on his forearm, I continue, "I think you're an amazing man. And I'm flattered you asked me out. But until you're ready for more, it's too big of a gamble for me."

Broadie's head drops. "I understand."

Gathering my leftover snacks, I lean in and give him a kiss on the cheek. "I've enjoyed getting to know you a little better." When he doesn't look at me, I take it as my cue to leave.

I barely make it two steps before I'm spun around, his strong hand wrapping around the nape of my neck, pulling me into him as his mouth devours mine. The plastic container starts to wobble, but Broadie is quick to grab it from me and place it on the bar. My hands slide up to the back of his neck, pulling at the ends of his hair as he tilts my head, deepening the kiss. Holy crap, in my entire life, no one has ever kissed me with as much passion. No one.

As his tongue slips between my lips, I feel his hand press to my lower back, pulling me closer. There's no denying he's hard. And if the firm press of him into my belly is any indication, this man is big.

It's not until a throat clears behind us that I remember we're still in the middle of a very public place. As I pull back, my lips swollen from the delectable assault, all I can think is that I want more. Who wouldn't want more of this? Yet, he just said he couldn't make any promises. Could I handle him passing me in the cafeteria like this never happened?

He trails his thumb over my lower lip, his eyes as hungry for more as mine are. "Sorry. I needed to know."

"Know what?"

"If you tasted like more."

CHAPTER NINETEEN
BROADIE

What am I doing? Really. What am I doing?

I must've jacked off all night long to the memory of that kiss. She'd just finished explaining why we couldn't go out. She was worried I'd hurt her. *The guy she'd thanked for being honest with her.* The guy who's been lying to her about everything.

What is wrong with me? How am I intelligent enough to graduate from Harvard and manage a million-dollar surgical practice, but lose my wife and kids and potentially the chance at a relationship with a woman who makes me feel like I could have it all? Am I this messed up?

I wasn't the product of a bad home. My parents and grandparents loved each other. They treated each other with respect. Sure, they worked themselves into an early grave, but I never witnessed any indication the women in my life felt mistreated. So, what's wrong with me that I've allowed my career to take over my life?

Walking over to the dining table, I grab a cup and pour hot coffee from the carafe. I'll keep the breakfast items covered by the silver dome until after my shower. This presidential suite is mammoth. There are three bedrooms, a dining area, and even a room with bunk beds and gaming stations. *Like I need that.*

Walking to the balcony, I open the door and sprawl out on the lounge chair. I try to picture what it might be like, having a new family. I'm only forty-two. If I want a second chance, it's not beyond reason that it could happen. But I've barely scratched the surface with getting my relationship back on track with my girls. They'd need to know they were a priority before I ever considered adding anyone else into the mix.

I take another sip of the rich, dark roast coffee when my mind harkens back to the evening my daughters saw Poppy with her date. *Wait.* Poppy said she wasn't seeing anyone. So, who was that guy? My girls had been right. She wasn't into him, whoever he was.

What's more, they were goading me to ask Poppy out. They want me to find love. *Love?* I almost choke on my morning joe. The way those two romanticize everything, they probably did mean love. Here I'd be happy simply to have a relatively normal, healthy relationship with a woman.

I admit, until Poppy came along, the idea never even crossed my mind. But there's something about her that makes me feel as if she holds all of the answers. I've never wanted to try with anyone like I do with her. Not even Camile.

Hopping up from my chair, I put down my coffee and head to the shower. I only have a few more days here. Up until that kiss last night, I contemplated packing it in and considering anything with Poppy Danforth to be dead in the water. But that kiss changed everything.

There's no way I can let her go without giving this a shot.

Showered and shaved and ready to greet the day, it hits me that I need to lie low until after lunch. I already told her I'd played hooky yesterday. I need to act like I'm really here for a conference. Looking up to the sky, I pray karma won't be a bitch once we return home. Even if I deserve it.

I'm not the lying type. I've never manipulated anyone, man or woman, for my own personal gain. But I had to see this through. Find out if there could be something between us. Walking away simply wasn't an option. I just have to pray if things work out for us, that somehow she'll forgive me.

Deciding to use the downtime to work on my presentation, I grab my laptop and bring it out onto the deck with me. I've barely begun when I spot a beautiful blonde in the distance. My eyes must be deceiving me because although I'm certain it's her, she's holding the hand of a little boy with dark hair who must be three or four. I watch as she squats down at eye level and speaks to him. Instantly, she's pulling him in for a hug and lifting him into her arms. I know he's not hers. Stu verified that not only did she come alone, but that she has no children. Hell, I saw her arriving all alone in that rickety van.

I'm left to assume he's lost. But it's not her compassion that has me fixated on the two of them. It's watching her caring for a child. The sight is stirring something primal in me. What kind of crazy caribou do they have here in Jamaica? Is there ganja in this stuff?

That's got to be it. I've gone from not wanting a relationship with any woman to picturing children with Poppy. I have to have been drugged. No kiss causes a man to go off the deep end like this.

But that's the way it's been with Poppy all along. Nothing about our connection makes sense. It's as if I had no other choice. I had to do what-ever was necessary in order to see if this was real.

Looking down at my watch, I shake my head. I have at least two more hours before I can go in search of her. In the past, I would've ignored everyone with me in exchange for the opportunity to work. Yet, this woman has me watching the clock like a kid on the last day of school.

I stroll down the walkway, hands in my pockets, hoping to easily find Poppy. I'd eaten a hearty breakfast in my room, so have no plans to eat lunch. But the main dining room is located next to most of the hotel's activities. If she's spending time by the pool or enjoying the buffet, I should spot her here. If not, I'll take a stroll along the beach and see if I can locate her.

As if a genie has granted my wish, I find Poppy standing nearly twenty feet in front of me at the excursions desk.

Leaning over her shoulder as she peers over the list of offsite activities in the area, I whisper, "Find anything interesting?"

She jumps, nearly colliding with my jaw.

"I'm sorry, Poppy." I laugh.

She spins toward me, her hand outstretched over her heart. "Oh, my, god. You scared me."

"We going somewhere fun?"

Her expression morphs from shock to playfulness. "You done for the day?"

"Why? Is that your way of asking me to come along?" *Please say yes.*

"Sure. Why not?"

I think my smile could rival the light given off by the moon last night.

"Oh my gosh. You're so cute right now."

I chuckle. "Did you just call me cute?"

Poppy turns back around to the Island Route attendant behind the counter. "Do you have any availability this late in the day for the Jamaican Bobsled excursion?"

"Are you serious?"

"What? You wanted to go on the cannabis tour?" She giggles.

Unable to help myself, I wrap my arms around her, resting my chin on her shoulder. "Please tell me this is a go."

The attendant waves a packet of tickets at me. "It's a go."

Poppy looks over her shoulder, her big blue eyes connecting with mine, and I swear there's more to this than playful teasing when she says, "We're a go, Dr. Weston."

A hopeful lump becomes lodged in my throat as I stand here holding her. *Please don't let me fuck this up.*

The attendant interrupts our moment asking for pesky details in exchange for the tickets. "Do you need anything before you head out?

"I don't think so. I have sunscreen in my bag," Poppy advises, like we do this all the time. I can't get the damn smile off of my face.

"If you'll wait right here, we have a few more guests joining us. We'll head out in the next ten to fifteen minutes."

Poppy turns to face me. Her sun-kissed skin is all aglow. For a moment, I'm tempted to ask her who the little boy was from earlier, but I'd only give myself away. How could I be in a conference and simultaneously watching her off of my balcony?

She reaches into her purse and retrieves a hair tie, which she wraps around her soft, blonde locks. I can't help but admire the soft skin along her throat as she arches her neck to secure her hair. I want to trail my tongue from her collarbone to her ear, but that might be pushing it.

"Please tell me you've never done this."

I laugh out loud. "I've definitely never done this."

"Good. I like knowing we're both out on a limb here." There's probably no better phrase to describe my relationship with her. *Out on a limb.*

The driver arrives, and we're escorted to the front of the resort, where the van awaits. Thank fuck it's in better shape than that thing Poppy rode in from the airport. The six of us climb in and get settled as we make the fifteen-minute ride to the Mystic Mountain Bobsled. We're told we'll first have the opportunity to ride the Sky Explorer over Mystic Mountain and the coast before boarding the Bobsled ride.

I'm dying to put my arm around Poppy on the way there. Bury my face in her hair and trail kisses along the soft skin at the back of her ear. But I'm trying to stay focused. This unexpected trip has already exceeded my expectations for today. I don't want to push my luck and ruin this.

In no time at all, we're driving up the steep incline to the mountain. A guide greets us and takes us to check-in before escorting us to the Sky Explorer. It's basically like riding a ski lift, except this one takes you through the tropical rain foliage.

As the lift breeches the palm trees and rainforest, the turquoise waters of the Caribbean 700 feet below us come into view. Poppy lets out a gasp as she grabs my hand, her mouth ajar at the stunning view below. But I can barely pull my eyes away from the stunning view in front of me. She's breathtaking. So open and real. Closing my eyes, I try to sketch this into my memory for later. This whole trip will have been worth it for just this moment.

As the Sky Explorer ride returns to where we began, we exit the chair lift and make our way to the Bobsled ride. The green and yellow vehicles of the rollercoaster are modeled after the cars used by the 1988 Jamaican Olympic Bobsled team. We are each assigned our own small vehicle. Poppy seems eager to go first.

"You sure this thing is safe, Pop?" I ask as she buckles in. The thing looks as if it is barely attached to the metal tracks below. Looking down at her, I'm met with the most glorious smile. Hell, if I've got to die, at least I'll have that vision in my head when I go.

I chuckle at her squeal as the car starts its descent. Following her lead, I squeeze myself into this little coaster and buckle up. Suddenly, the thing takes off, flying through the air as if I'm hurtling to my death. I've never been a big fan of rollercoasters. But I was jumping at the chance to try something new with her. Yet, no matter how hard I attempt to stomp on the breaks, this thing feels like at any moment it could fly off the rails like something from a *Bugs Bunny & Road Runner* cartoon.

As my sled finally comes to a halt, I spot Poppy clapping and jumping up and down, her ponytail bouncing behind her. It takes physical force to push myself out of the car after that adrenalin rush.

"Oh my gosh. That was awesome," she shrieks, flinging her arms around me.

No, this is awesome. I'd ride it ten times if I knew this was waiting for me at the end.

"Thank you for coming with me. I was afraid to admit how nervous I was. I never do anything like this. Like, ever."

My heart is pounding, but I honestly can't tell if it's from the ride or her. Her cheeks are rosy from her excited state. What I'd give to cup them in my hands and kiss her. But I don't know that I'll be able to stop the next time I do.

Reaching for her hand, I pull her along beside me as we walk back to the van. I've never felt anything this natural in my life. It's like the universe hand plucked this woman just for me. There's no wonder I haven't been able to stop thinking of her since the moment I laid eyes on her.

Poppy Danforth is mine. I'm certain of it.

As we walk into the main lobby of the hotel, I pull her into me. "Please say you'll have dinner with me?"

"Hmm. Okay. Just this once." I know she's being playful, but I can't help but frown at her reply. I watch as she places the pad of her index finger to where my dimple normally sits as I smile at her. She teases the space until I chuckle.

"There it is." She giggles.

"Is five o'clock, okay?"

"Yes. Where'd you have in mind?"

"How about Neptunes? The seafood restaurant. Have you eaten there yet?"

"Oh, I've wanted to go there. That's perfect."

Heading to my room, there's no need to coax my dimple out now. It might be permanently indented there.

∿

"Oh, I love this place," Poppy says. She's wearing a teal blue halter dress with an open back. The color brings out her eyes. But the exposed skin of her back is toying with my dick. I want to spend the evening trailing my fingertips up and down the gentle slope of her spine. This woman is a goddess. I honestly don't think she has any idea how beautiful she is. In fact, that might be one of her most alluring features.

"I cannot believe you did this." Poppy twists from side to side, modeling her new shoes. "How on earth did you manage to find these? And they fit perfectly."

"I had some help." Boy, is that an understatement. It took more trouble than she'll ever know to get those replacement shoes here. Two days, a lot of money, and a lot of phone calls. But to see how happy they make her, it was worth every bit of effort.

She walks closer, sliding her arm through mine. "Do you know what you want? I was so hungry I looked at the menu from the app after I got out of the shower." She laughs. "I think Mystic Mountain worked up an appetite."

Staring at this radiant creature, all I want to eat is her. Okay, surf and turf and then her.

I order a bottle of wine, and we casually sip, chat, and laugh until our meals arrive. To see this stunner of a woman cutting into a steak does things to me. She's so genuine. No pretending to be something she thinks a man would want her to be. Women should eat what they want. Fuck the 'I'll just have a salad bullshit.'

Leaning in my direction, Poppy lowers her voice. "Have you looked over there?"

"Where?"

"Right beside us." She tilts her head in the direction of the poor, run down cinderblock home surrounded by kids. *And chickens.* "My first day here, I went down to the beach. Way over there." She points to the eastern most end of the resort property with her steak knife. "This woman kept calling, *Hey Mammi.* Jamaican people live in squalor next to these huge resort properties. So, they pull out anything they can find to sell to the guests who come here. I gave her twenty dollars for a picture of Bob Marley." Poppy laughs. "Not sure what I'm gonna do with that."

It's then I wonder if the child from earlier was a resort guest or had managed to come over from their home next door. "I wonder if the kids ever sneak over and go to the pool."

"Oh, I doubt it. The resort wouldn't want to allow that to become a habit. I mean, they have a business to run."

Hmm. He must've been a guest.

Finishing our meals, we decide to take a stroll on the beach before heading to the bar for a nightcap. Rolling up my pants, I kick off my shoes and place them with hers on a lounger before reaching for her hand and enjoying the ocean together.

I want to tell her how much I've enjoyed this, but I know she's already nervous about the future. I don't want to dig this hole any deeper.

Returning to the chaise, I sit down and pull her into my lap. "This is nice," I say, burying my face in her windblown hair. *Okay, I tried to keep my hands off. But hell. She's irresistible.*

"Yes. I think this may have been a perfect day."

Walking into the lounge, I'm surprised to find it more raucous than our last visit. There are guests drinking and laughing at the bar, and several others are on the dance floor. All of the booths seem to be occupied, so we take a seat at the bar.

"What can I get you two?"

"I'll have a frozen Margarita, please."

"And I'll have a scotch on the rocks."

The music is loud. Much like you'd expect in a dance club. It's more of a vacation, party vibe versus the dance music I find at the Devil's Playground. This thought has me wondering what Poppy would think of the place. Would she be scandalized to know I go there? Would she believe I haven't slept with anyone there in years? Would she ever take a walk on the wild side and join me?

The bartender returns with our drinks, and we sip and laugh over the day's events. I can't remember feeling this happy. It's ridiculous. I haven't thought about work once. Hell, I had to force myself to try and get some work done until I could seek her out earlier today.

Before I know it, Poppy has finished her drink and is bouncing on her bar stool to the music. The bartender slides another in place of her empty glass, and I chuckle as she picks up the new one completely unaware.

The song changes and "Give Me Everything" by Pitbull starts to play. "Oh, I love this one," Poppy says. Now, I'm not a dancer. But if this woman is grabbing my hand and pulling me along behind her onto the dancefloor, then a dancer I will be.

We gyrate to the thumping base along with the other sweaty bodies around us. All of us smiling and laughing. She looks more happy and free than I've ever seen her. Well, except for at the bottom of that Bobsled ride, maybe. She's swinging her arms back and forth over her head as Pitbull and Ne-Yo sing about how they can't promise tomorrow but to give them everything for one night. She sings along with the words as if it's an invitation, so I join in, almost unable to sing along because of the unrelenting grin on my face.

Poppy spins around, and I slide my arms around her waist. As her tight ass rocks against my cock, it's getting increasingly more difficult to hide my hardening dick. She feels so good swaying back and forth against me. I could stay like this with my arms wrapped tightly around her, and my cock nestled between the glorious globes of her ass as she rubs against me all night. My lack of control around her is downright humiliating. Embarrassing or not, I couldn't have planned this night better.

Poppy suddenly places both palms flat against my white shirt, looking up at me. "I'm toast, Broadie. I need to call it a night."

"Okay, Pop."

"I like it when you call me that," she says with a dreamy look upon her face.

Unable to control myself, I bend down and place a chaste kiss on her lips.

"Oh my gosh. You two are the most beautiful couple I've ever seen," a staff member coos. "You should do promo pics for the resort. Could I—"

"No!" I interject.

Immediately, Poppy's exuberant face falls. *Shit.*

"Sorry, not interested."

"That's okay," the kind woman apologizes.

As I attempt to take Poppy's hand, she pulls away. Fuck. I've ruined this incredible night with my outburst. But how the hell would I explain *that* to anyone? After a few more steps, I grab her arm, pulling her to me. "Poppy, I'm falling for you. But until tonight, you wouldn't even go out with me. I'd need to at least tell my girls I was dating someone before I risk our pictures turning up on social media." She grows quiet. "Not to mention someone at St. Luke's seeing them. It would only be a matter of time before the rumor mill got going. Don't you think we should figure out what's happening between us before others start speculating?" This has her attention.

"Oh. I hadn't thought about that."

We casually walk back to her hotel room in companionable silence. I feel a little better that I may have salvaged my blunder from earlier. As we reach her door, I can't help praying she'll invite me in.

Poppy pulls out her key card and looks up at me. My brows pinch as I take her in. She seems unfocused.

Hiccup. "Do you want to come in?"

Hell yes. But, fuck. Not like this. "I do. But not when you've had too much to drink."

The corners of her pouty mouth turn down into a frown. "I thought you might want to kiss me again."

"Oh, I do. But I need you to be fully aware when I kiss you here." I point to her lips. "And here." I point to her neck. "And here." I trail my finger down to her collarbone. "And here." Moving lower still, I tease the top of her exposed breasts. Fuck, I want to untie that halter top and cup her sweet tits.

"And here." Dropping my finger down lower, I reach under her dress to glide it along the center of her warm, wet panties, eliciting a moan of delight as her head falls back, her eyes closing in her aroused state. Sliding it back and forth, I revel in her ecstasy as she grips my arms firmly in her hands, rocking her wet pussy over my finger. "So needy."

With this, her eyes spring wide.

"Off you go." Before I change my mind. "Can you manage?"

"What if I said no?" *Hiccup.*

"Good night, Poppy." I place my hands in my pockets and head the short distance to my room once I know she's inside. As much as I want her, I'm not taking advantage of her. *Well, anymore than I already have by planning this whole charade.* I need to know she wants me every bit as much as I want her.

Tempting little minx.

It's my last day here. This week has flown by. I've stayed in touch with the office, so I haven't had to share where I am. But I honestly can't remember the last time I was away this long without devoting time to my work. I'm going to be buried when I return. I should spend the morning catching up on emails, but despite my second cup of coffee, I can't focus. On anything but Poppy, that is.

At any rate, I need to gather my things so I'm ready to head out bright and early tomorrow. I have an early flight, and even though my private jet is parked at the Ian Fleming Airport, less than an hour away, international travel is tricky. I'll need to be prepared.

I wish I could have Poppy fly home with me, but that could potentially open a whole new can of worms. At least I know she'll be more comfortable on the drive back to Kingston than she was on her way here. I've made sure she has access to the VIP lounge at the airport. And, of course, upgraded her seats to first class. Hell, it might cause undue suspicion, but if she can't return with me, that's the very least I can do to make sure she's comfortable.

After finishing my emails, I hit the gym, shower, and ask Porter to drive me to the adult only sister resort to this location. It beats hiding out in my room pretending to attend a conference. I'm curious to see how different the two properties are. If I'm ever able to come back, I'd love the chance to really unwind.

Like a normal person.

Of course, I can't help but imagine Poppy there by my side. Strolling along the white sandy beaches, lounging in a private cabana, or actually staying in a secluded over the water bungalow. Do they even have those in Jamaica?

Who am I kidding? I could stay almost anywhere with her and be happy. I'm almost certain of it. Not that I would. Once I don't have to pretend I'm somewhere under false pretenses, there's no need to settle for anything but the best. Let's just hope once she finds out what I've done, I'll still have that chance.

Returning to the resort, I decide to grab my things and head to the pool cabana I've rented. Might as well. I've had it all week and not used it once. Maybe I'll convince Poppy to head down to the beach and go snorkeling. Yet, as I enter the main lobby, I notice her standing at the registration counter with her bags beside her. What the fuck?

"Hey."

She turns to me, eyes red. *What the hell?* Is this because of last night? Jesus, has she already figured out why I'm here? Why we're both here?

"Pop, what's going on? Are you okay?"

She shakes her head, a tear spilling from her eye. "My brother called. My mom might have had a stroke. He doesn't know much yet, but he said she's in the hospital."

"Our hospital?"

"Yes." She sniffles.

"When did you find out?"

"About an hour ago. I don't have international cell service. My brother had to reach me through the hotel. I'm kind of a mess. I'm trying to see if there's any way I can catch an earlier flight, but you have to be there three hours early for international flights, and the airport is two hours away..." She starts to choke on her sobs, and I pull her into me.

"Shhh. Shhh. Don't worry about any of that. I'll get you home."

"But how? You don't leave until tomorrow."

"Do you think I'd stay here when you're going through this? Come on." I take her hand, pulling her over to a settee before grabbing my phone. "Porter, could you come to the lobby and assist Ms. Danforth with her bags? And there's been a change of plans. We'll need to get back to Hanover as soon as possible. Can you and Stu take care of everything?"

"Yes, sir. Are you packed?"

"Almost. It won't take me long."

"I'll get right on it."

Disconnecting the call, I wrap my arms around Poppy and kiss her on the top of her head. "Listen, try not to get too upset. It's always worse when you don't know what's happening. But we'll be headed home soon."

I can feel her nod underneath my chin. I start to reach for my phone to see if I can find someone at the hospital who can update Poppy, but how will I explain this to anyone? Why we're both here.

"Do you mind coming back to my room with me? I can try and find out where she is, and you can use my phone to talk to the nurse while I finish packing."

"Oh, Broadie. Thank you. That would make me feel much better."

"Come on."

Moments later, I open the door to my room and usher her inside. I don't miss the look of shock on her face when she takes it all in.

"Wow. And here I thought my room was ridiculous. Who knew places like this were even a thing?" She meanders about the space, and I get nervous, wondering if there's anything incriminating here. "And right down the hall from mine."

Shit.

"Here, let me get the hospital on the phone for you." Pulling out my phone, I call St. Luke's main number. "Hi, this is Broadie Weston. Could I have the nurses' station for…" covering the receiver, I ask, "Poppy. What's your mother's name?"

"Oh, it's Sara. Sara England."

I give the operator Sara's name, and once connected with the appropriate nurses' station, I immediately hand the phone off to Poppy while I head to the bathroom to finish collecting my things. I try to give her some privacy, but I can't help being concerned.

When I return to the room, she's already off the phone, her face buried in her hands. I toss my toiletry bag onto the bed and wrap my arms around her. "Oh, babe. I'm sorry. What can I do?"

"No. You're already doing so much. I feel terrible troubling you this way. The nurse said it was likely a mini stroke, as her symptoms have already resolved. I feel terrible that you've gone to all of this trouble."

Holding her back so she can plainly see my face, I push her tousled hair behind her ears. "Are you kidding? You need to be there. It's your mother, Poppy. It wouldn't matter if she'd sprained her ankle. If you want to go back, we're going back."

She immediately buries her face in my neck, and I think to myself, this is so much bigger than some magnetic attraction. Seeing her hurting is tearing me up inside. I'm falling hard for this beauty, and I don't need anything else to convince me.

There's no doubt in my mind, this woman belongs to me.

CHAPTER TWENTY
POPPY

"Mom," I practically shout from the door as I enter her room. Oh, who am I kidding? I always shout, or she won't hear a lick. But this is different. "Thank God. You look good. How are you feeling?"

"Calm down, Poppy. I'm fine. I can't believe you cut your trip short on account of me."

"Are you serious? I came straight from the airport." Now that I think of it, I'm not sure how I'm getting home. When Broadie's driver pulled up in front of the hospital, I simply kissed Broadie on the cheek, thanked both of them, and ran. Heck, I think my bags are still in his car. I drop my face into my hands. I'm a wreck.

Knock. Knock.

My head springs up, and I see none other than Dr. created from heaven above Weston, standing in the doorway. Relief washes over me like an afternoon shower on a hot summer's day.

"Can I come in?"

"Oh, of course. Mom. This is Dr. Weston. He's a surgeon here. This wonderful man made all of the arrangements to get me to you," I gush.

My mother's eyes are gleaming, staring at Broadie as if she got the last slice of chocolate pie. "Come over here, son. Let me get a good look at you."

Oh, Lord.

Broadie seems to take it all in stride, casually walking over and sitting on the other side of the bed, close to her. He takes her hand in his and says loudly and clearly, "It's a pleasure to meet you, Ms. England." Hell, his affection for my mother is almost as much of a turn on as his affection for me.

"Oh, my. The pleasure is all mine, Dr. Weston. Thank you for getting my Poppy here. I think you two are the best medicine a mother could ask for."

Several days later, surrounded by piles of laundry, I try to get ready for my return to work. Mom's back at Hanover Haven, looking better than ever. If that was a mini stroke, you'd never know it. I'd laugh if it wasn't so scary.

Honestly, I think meeting Broadie has done wonders for her. The man has that effect on people, not just me. It's no wonder his patients all go on and on about him.

She's barely been back in her room twenty-four hours, but he's sent a floral arrangement to her and a big bouquet to me. I know he's being thoughtful, but if this doesn't work out with us, I'm going to be devastated. How can you not fall hard for someone like him?

Folding another T-shirt, I place it on top of the stack. I miss him. I know I want to take this slow. And by all accounts he does too. Other than the flowers, I've not heard from him.

He's made it very clear there are no promises for the future. His career has always been his priority. Plus, he was very honest about his need to be a better father. The last thing he needs is some old broad getting clingy.

But I still miss him. Those blissful moments with him on that trip were ones I'll never forget. Even when I was crushed that my mother chose that very time to have a serious medical emergency, he comforted me on the plane until I fell asleep in his embrace.

Bzzz. Bzzz.

Reaching for my phone, I smile when I see Kat's name. "Hi."

"You're back. How was everything?" Holy cow, if that isn't a loaded question.

"How much time do you have?"

"Oh gosh, Poppy. Please tell me that's a good thing."

"It is." I giggle. "What's your schedule like? I have to go back to work tomorrow, and I'm trying to get caught up with all of the laundry." Normally, I'd have started this as soon as I returned, but all of my attention has been on my mother.

"I'm off today. Can you meet for a glass of wine? I want all the deets, girl."

It hits me that she's an hour away. "Are you at the lake?"

"Yes, but we could meet at the Saude Creek Vineyard. It's halfway between us."

"Oh, I've always wanted to go there."

"It's great. It needs some work. But it's a sweet little place. Sebastian Lee's brother, Sam, manages it."

My heart twists thinking of Dr. Lee. I didn't know him well, but I was sorry to hear he had to give up his practice. "That sounds perfect, Kat. I'll see you at four. Is that okay?"

"You got it."

"Oh, Poppy. Jamaica looks good on you." Katarina pulls me in for a hug.

"Thank you. I'm so glad you encouraged me to go. It was the best thing that's happened in so long." Let's just say it. It's probably the best thing that's happened in over a decade.

Kat takes my hand and pulls me along behind her as we enter the doors to the Saude Creek vineyard. It's a rustic appearing place. There's a central bar area made of wood that I suspect is used as a tasting station. It looks as if it's seen better days, honestly. There are several windows which allow a lot of natural light, but the interior is clearly dated. "I know it looks a bit rough around the edges, but the patio is what sold me. I think Sam started there but plans to renovate the entire place in stages."

Re-examining the place with a fresh perspective, I see where it has a lot of potential. I watch as Kat approaches the sommelier behind the counter. I can't make out what they're saying, but assume she's asked if we can sit outside when we're escorted to the patio.

This area is beautiful. It's rustic but has purpose. There are tables and chairs made of wood with greenery surrounding the area. There are no other patrons here at the moment, so we take a spot under a large umbrella and order two glasses of wine and a cheese plate.

"I see why you like it here."

"It's cute. It's missing some of the ambiance from when Nick and I last came here. But I think Sam has been struggling with the place. Hopefully, he'll get things turned around. So, tell me about you. I want to hear everything." Resting her elbows on the table, Kat drops her chin into her palms.

"It was amazing. The resort was beautiful, and the Jamaican people were all so friendly. I only took in a little bit of the island, from the airport to the resort. The rest of the time, I enjoyed everything included at the property."

"Why not? It was all-inclusive, right?"

The sommelier from earlier delivers our wine and slides the charcuterie board in front of us, and my mind goes back to the one I enjoyed in the bar. This one is missing something.

Or someone.

"I had one of these on the trip." I giggle.

"Oh."

"It was nicer."

Kat scrunches up her nose. "This doesn't look that bad. But I told you, Sam is trying to work on some things."

I laugh as I pop an olive into my mouth and reach for a hazelnut. "It wasn't the food that was better. It was the company."

"Hey!"

"No. That came out all wrong." I guffaw. "The last time I had one of these was with Broadie Weston." I bite my lower lip and wait for her response.

"Shut the front door. What?"

I'm giggling so hard I need to dab at the corners of my eyes. "Kat, it was like something out of a movie. I still can't believe the coincidence. It was my first full day there, and I was dressed like Elle Woods in *Legally Blonde* when I slipped on the tile at the pool and landed in Broadie's arms in the water."

"Holy shit, Poppy. For real?"

"Yes! I swear I thought I was dreaming." I laugh as I recall the serious expression on his face when he said, *"You dream about me?"*

"Did anything happen?" she asks, her brows waggling at me.

"No. Well, we kissed once."

"Please tell me that man kisses as good as he looks like he would."

I simply nod.

"Oh, my, god. I can't believe it. Are you going to start seeing him?"

"Kat. Is that really smart? I really want to. But this is the kinda guy that would make it so I never wanted to date again if it didn't work out. Jeez, it's taken me eight years to date after Dan."

Kat takes a sip of her wine, a bite of cheese, and then looks contemplatively out into space. She drums her fingers on the table. "I feel like Dr. Miller would say life is nothing without taking chances."

"Oh, I have an appointment with him on Thursday."

Kat instantly sits up. "That's perfect. Oh, I think this is going to be great, Poppy."

"I also signed up for a pottery class that starts next week. Getting involved in something that interests me is long overdue. Having the class to focus on will keep my mind from being idle. If it's going to happen, it's important to me that we take this slow. It'd be way too easy to get caught up in him."

"I could see that," Kat says in a dreamy voice. "What are the odds? That he'd be there at the same time as you?"

"Yeah. I've thought about that too. But he was there for a medical conference. Maybe those types of resorts are on a list or something." I reach for a piece of crusty bread and dip it in the well of olive oil.

"Never thought of that. You're probably right." Kat mimics my actions with a sliver of bread. "Have you heard from him since you got back?"

Shaking my head, trying to swallow, I reach for my glass. Taking a sip, I continue, "Gosh, I forgot to tell you. So I got an urgent message from Ian that my mother had been hospitalized with a stroke. I was so upset that Broadie flew me back right away in his jet."

Kat starts to choke on her wine, and I reach over to pat her back. "You forgot to mention you flew back on his private jet!"

My head flies back in laughter. This girl is so animated. "Sorry. There was a lot going on with this trip."

"No shit." She chuckles. "What was it like?"

I have to stop and think. I was so worked up about Mom, I honestly didn't take the time to really put it to memory. "I don't know, like what you'd expect. All leather and cream interior. Fancy dressed flight attendants that look like they just left the set of *America's Next Top Model*."

Kat leans in and whispers, "And you didn't decide to join the mile high club?" She's dead serious.

"Did you miss the part where I said we were flying back because my mother had a stroke?"

"Oh gosh, Poppy. I'm so sorry. I got distracted by private jet. Is she okay?"

I laugh. "She's fine. They think she might've had a mini stroke. But once she laid eyes on Broadie, she was as alert as I've ever seen her. Now he's all she can talk about."

Kat pops a grape into her mouth, her eyes as wide as saucers. "He came to see her?"

"Yeah. Even sent her flowers."

"Holy crap, Poppy. If you don't marry him, I will."

"Uh, won't Nick be a little offended?"

She giggles. "You're right. Plus, I was there that day."

Looking down, I notice we've devoured this charcuterie board. "Hmm? What day?"

"When he pretended to make small talk with me so he could talk to you."

I cover my mouth and laugh.

"He wasn't undressing *me* with his eyes. It was all you."

~

"Have a seat, Ms. Danforth. Dr. Miller will be with you shortly."

"Thank you."

Sitting down on a beautiful deep green chair across from an imposing mahogany desk, I pat my hands over my knees in nervous anticipation. I'm not sure why I'm so anxious about this. I've seen several counselors following Dan's death. Looking back, I probably should've sought them out sooner. My grief started the day his diagnosis was official. But I couldn't justify letting anything pull me away from his side.

The door behind me swings open, and I instinctively stand to greet the doctor Kat has gone on and on about. And then I see his face. *Holy crap.* He's a dead ringer for Matthew McConaughey. I quickly snap my mouth shut as he extends his hand to me.

"Sorry to keep you waiting, Ms. Danforth. Gilbert Miller. Happy to meet you."

I'm sure I can't be the only person who sees this.

"Please, sit down. Tell me how I can be of help." He unbuttons his jacket and takes a seat. But as opposing as the desk is, he seems nothing but warm and endearing.

"Katarina Kelly… Oh, well, Katarina Barnes now, recommended you."

"Oh. That's nice. She's a nice lady."

Inwardly, I chuckle. Kat's so silly, it's hard to refer to her as a lady. "Yes. Well, she encouraged me to speak with you. I've seen a few other counselors in the past, but the experiences weren't very helpful. So I discontinued going."

"I take it you're still having the same issues?"

"Yes. And no. I've gotten better, but it's taken a very long time, and to be honest, I'm still struggling more than I think I should after all of these years."

He sits quietly with his hands steepled together, assumably waiting for me to continue. When I don't jump in quick enough, he adds, "There's no time limit on healing, Ms. Danforth."

"Poppy," I correct. "Please, call me Poppy."

We both sit momentarily staring at one another. Well, this is awkward. I finally decide to dive in. "My husband, Daniel, died eight years ago of ALS. The years leading up to his death were only marginally less painful."

"If you don't mind my asking, how long did you have with him after his diagnosis?"

"Three years." I look away. The agonizing memories from long ago that always seem to lurk beneath the surface are still there, waiting to pull me under. "It took years to grieve losing him. Longer still, to come to terms with all we went through together before he was gone." I reach for a tissue, just in case. "Don't get me wrong, he wasn't perfect. I think I grieved a version of him I'd created. Anyone who has to endure losing the control of their muscles, speech, ability to eat... well, they deserve to be elevated to superhero status in my book." This may not make a bit of sense to him or anyone else. But it's how I feel about it. Watching these incredible people trapped in their own bodies. It's amazing they don't all want to give up.

"I understand why you'd feel that way. It's a pain no one could truly appreciate except for your husband and those in his life that had to experience his debilitation."

His words make me feel validated. The years of grief weren't unusual. They were necessary. "I'm finally at a place where I want to live again. But the survivor's guilt can be stifling."

My gaze drops down to the tissue clutched in my hands. While it's a bit mangled from my nervous energy, it's not damp. I have to acknowledge that after all these years, I really have healed more than I've given myself credit for.

"Have you met someone?"

"Yes." I can't fight the smile that comes to my face. "But it's complicated."

He shakes his head before grinning at me. "It always is. That's life, Poppy. Perhaps it's simply the people I meet in this line of work that has me jaded. But in my humble opinion, you have to be willing to step in some crap to get to the other side of the yard." He stops for a moment, as if gathering his thoughts before looking directly at me. "The trials and tribulations of our lives make the wins that much sweeter. You don't always see that when you're in the thick of it." He places his hands down flat on the desk in front of him and leans forward. "And it doesn't matter how long it takes. There's no race to the finish line. It's all part of the process. But I think you already know that."

He's right. It's taken a long time to learn. But he's right. If I'd tried to rush the grief process, I might've ended up trapped in a marriage I wasn't emotionally ready for. I needed the time to find me underneath the rubble of my loss.

"So, why are you here today? I can't give you permission to date. Only you can do that. But I can encourage you to trust your instincts. If, after all of this time, you've found someone who might be a good match, keep the lines of communication open. Tell him if you're feeling sad about experiencing feelings for someone other than your husband. If he doesn't understand that, I think you've found your answer about moving forward with him."

Holy crap. Kat's right. This guy is exactly what I needed.

"It appears I'm farther ahead than I thought I was."

"Now isn't that refreshing." His lips curl into a gorgeous smile, and it's like being told you are moving up a grade.

An unattractive laugh tears from my very soul. "I can't believe it."

"Poppy. I can't guarantee you won't face hurt and disappointment in your attempts to get back out there. People, by nature, are flawed. But you seem to be a bright, grounded woman. I think your intuition will protect you. Just be careful not to revert backward. Don't let every heartbreak or setback be about your husband. It's easy to crawl back to that place when you're hurting. It's comfortable. You've spent a long time there."

"I hadn't thought of that. I'll try to keep that in mind."

Dr. Miller stands from his chair and walks over to where I'm seated. As I rise to my full height, he places his hand on my shoulder. "I think you've already done the work. But I'm here if you get stumped on something or simply need a sounding board."

I'm so relieved. I should've done this years ago. "Thank you. I'll take you up on that."

"Hi. I wanted to come by and see you." I look about, as is my routine, verifying I'm alone. Taking a deep breath, I push on.

"It's important to me that you know I'll always love you." *Good grief, Poppy. Don't be so dramatic.* I realize I can have these conversations in the privacy of my own home. But somehow, I feel closer to him here. Discussing important things in this special place gives me closure.

"I met a new counselor today. He said I've come farther than I've given myself credit for." Stepping closer, I place my hand on Daniel's headstone. "What I'm trying to say is, I think I might be ready to get back out there, Dan."

My mind plays tricks on me when it comes to my husband. I want to know he's still involved in my life. That he celebrates the good things, while sending celestial hugs when I'm down. But there are some things I'd prefer he wasn't a witness to.

"It's tricky, the thought of being with another man. But it's part of life. Please don't think I love you less." A fat tear splashes onto the debris in front of his granite marker. Where the heck was that earlier when I was prepared?

I have to admit, I feel guilty for some of the thoughts I've had with Broadie. What I feel with him is different than what I felt with Dan. But I think Dr. Miller is right. That's life. It's messy and complicated. It doesn't diminish what Dan and I had, simply because it's different.

Reaching into my pocket, I pull out the pretty shell I brought back from Jamaica. It's an odd appearing thing full of tiny pinpoint holes. Yet despite its flawed appearance, it's still whole. It's as if Mother Nature created this glorious, stippled appearance as a result of the life it's led. Bouncing along the ocean floor. Beauty from pain so to speak.

"I hope you can be happy for me. I'm nervous about starting the next chapter in my life. But I want to live again, Dan. It's time."

Placing a kiss to my fingertips before transferring it to his headstone, I walk back to my car, feeling as if a new chapter in my life has officially begun. Opening my car door, I sit down and decide to find something happy from my playlist. Maybe I'll pull up that Pitbull song from the bar that night. No, that'll only get me turned on.

As I back out of the parking space and exit the cemetery, I notice a flash of movement in my rear-view mirror. Gently tapping my breaks, I gasp.

It's him again—that young man. And this time, I'm certain he's standing at Daniel's headstone because he's holding that imperfectly perfect shell.

CHAPTER TWENTY-ONE
BROADIE

"Beatrice, could you let Jarod know I have to take my patient back to the OR? And ask him if there's a chance he could see any of my patients so I don't have to inconvenience them by moving them to another day."

My schedule has been packed twice as deep as usual since I've been back. It's to be expected I'd have to see more patients than normal to get caught up. The trip to Jamaica wasn't planned several months ahead like most of my time away. Thus, I couldn't make arrangements for one of my partners to evaluate them. They picked up enough slack for me while I was gone.

Normally, I can hit the ground running and quickly get things back on track. But my mind isn't on my job. *It's on her.*

While I've been tempted to reach out to Poppy, I don't want to set up false expectations that I'm going to be that guy. The kind who calls every day, just to say hi. There's so much to do, and now patients are checking in with post-operative infections that need to be addressed. We've only been back a week, and that quicksand Nick Barnes described is already trying to pull me under.

Luckily, I managed to get another set of flowers delivered to Poppy and her mother. Tuesday, my main contact at Cygnature Blooms, is going to think I'm off my rocker if I keep this up. But if I can't take the time to connect with Poppy in person or by phone, this is the next best thing. Plus, I'm hoping to get a little helping hand from Sara with the most recent delivery.

I look up to see Beatrice standing in my doorway, a dejected expression marring her otherwise cheerful disposition. "What's the matter, Beatrice? Ready to send me back to Jamaica yet?"

"Only if I get to tag along." She laughs. "Jarod said he'd try to squeeze a couple of your patients in, but he has a Little League game to get to right after work."

My head falls. That's right. I remember last year he had two days a week he needed to be out of the door by four-thirty. "It's okay, B. I'll find some way to work them in. Even if I have to come in early and work through lunch."

"I thought you already did that."

Touché, Beatrice. Touché.

~

"I'm heading out, Dr. Weston. You sure you can manage these last three patients?"

"Yes, Beatrice. I've got it."

"Okay, just let them know I'll call them in the morning with their next appointments and anything you've ordered."

"Thanks, B. See you in the morning."

I stand to go and evaluate the last three patients of the day before heading to the hospital to round on my admitted patients when I realize I have a new message. Opening the app, my heart skips at her name. Until I read her message.

5:30 P.M.
POPPY
We need to talk.

Shit. Nothing ever goes well after those four words. Has something happened? Has someone asked about her trip that's informed her something is amiss? It could be about her mother's condition, but can't imagine she'd open that conversation like that.

My mind is reeling. How am I supposed to concentrate on my patients with that hanging in the air? I have a gut feeling responding will only delay me further. Thus, I pick myself up and head toward the incredibly understanding people waiting in my exam rooms. Hopefully, I can use the time to steady myself for whatever it is we need to *talk* about.

It's six-fifteen, the last patient of the day is gone, and the doors to the office are locked. I take a deep breath as I pull out my cell phone and hit Poppy's contact number. Whatever happens, Broadie, just take a second to think before you respond.

6:16 P.M.

BROADIE

Hi, Pop. Sorry it took me a while to message you back. I've been drowning in patients and wanted to give you the attention you deserved. Is this an okay time to talk?

She doesn't respond, and I assume she's with her mother or otherwise occupied and try to stay focused on what's left on my plate before I can knock off for the day.

6:20 P.M.
POPPY

I'm finishing up some things here at work. Are you still here?

6:21 P.M.

BROADIE

Yes. Will be for at least another hour or two. Haven't started rounding on my inpatients yet.

6:25 P.M.
POPPY

> Any chance I could meet you in the parking lot for
> a few minutes around 7?

Jesus. I'm sweating like a banshee here. That's thirty-five minutes from
now. At this rate, I'll have to change my shirt, or she'll wonder where the
storm I got caught in went. Is this what an anxiety attack feels like?

6:26 P.M.

BROADIE

> Sure. Where are you parked?

6:30 P.M.
POPPY

> Not that you've ever been there, but in employee
> parking. It's across the street from the physicians'
> parking.

I knew where it was. *Or I thought I did.*

6:31 P.M.

BROADIE

> See you soon.

Tucking my phone into my suit pocket, I head to the general surgery
floor to see if I can manage to round on a few patients before I meet her.
Okay, let's be real. I'll be lucky to focus on one before I'm waiting for her
to walk out the door.

As luck would have it, one of my patients was with their case manager.
It sounded as if she was making arrangements for rehab placement after
discharge. So, I'll stop by and see them later tonight or first thing in the
morning. Plus, I can always review the patient's chart from my laptop at
home later. Jenny was on duty when I saw Mr. Rexrode. I can always
reach out to her if the progress notes in the computer aren't clear since
I've already seen each of the folks on my list once today.

Right now, there's only one thing on my agenda.

As I reach the exit door to the parking area, I take a fortifying breath and hope I'm not going to get my ass handed to me as the remaining day-shift employees leave for their cars. I've barely taken two steps onto the asphalt when I see her.

Poppy stands by a black Lexus, wearing a deep blue silky sleeveless blouse, white linen pants, and sexy blue heels as her hair softly swirls about in the wind. Even though I'm worried my house of cards is about to come tumbling down on me, I can't help but smile. *She's so fucking beautiful.*

The closer I get, the more anxious I become. How has this woman turned the tables on my life? I answer to no one. Not even my mother or grandmother. But if this pretty pharmacist dares to turn me away, I'm likely to get on my knees to beg her forgiveness in the middle of this damned parking lot.

"Hi." My voice cracks. *Fuck, Broadie. Man up.*

"Hi." She crosses her arms over her chest, the action making me swallow hard. "I think we need to have a talk about your underhanded behavior. Do you have no boundaries?"

I stand there like a statue, my hands buried in my pants pockets to prevent them from shaking. Is this how all of this ends? All of that trouble, and I barely got a shot with her.

"I have it on good authority that you sent another set of flowers to my mother. And apparently, a note on one bouquet was requesting another date with yours truly."

Thank fuck. I nearly blurt my relief out loud. I'd completely forgotten about sending those. Arching a brow at her, I ask, "How do you know that bouquet wasn't your mother's?"

Poppy giggles, and it's taking every ounce of willpower not to pull her into my arms right here for all to see. "Didn't realize you were into older women."

"Oh, I am. Especially if it will get me in her daughter's good graces."

"Well, you'll love Agnes, then. Heck, you may have chatted with her on Bumble."

"Excuse me?"

Poppy laughs. "Agnes is Mom's roommate. She's probably who opened your card and read it loud enough anyone within a one-hundred-foot vicinity could hear."

"Is she some sort of attention hog?"

"Probably. But given anyone reading to my mother has to shout, it only stands to reason the entire wing would've heard it."

This woman. Even standing here talking to her about her hard of hearing mother with a roommate that rivals Blanche from *Golden Girls*, she's hands down the very best part of my day. We both stand here smiling at one another for a moment before she breaks the silence.

"It was manipulative, and you know it. There's no way I can turn you down now." She again crosses her arms, the act pushing her perky tits so they spill into the V-neck of her blouse. "I didn't know you had it in you to act that way."

Guilt colors my vision, but I try to make light of it to spare this little slice of heaven that's shined on my otherwise dreary day. "You have no idea the lengths I'll go to get you to go out with me."

It's her turn to smirk at me. "Well, it worked, Dr. Weston. I'd love to go out with you."

My resolve breaks, and I step a little closer. "Really?"

"Yes. When were you thinking? I figured when I hadn't heard from you that your schedule was ridiculously busy. And I know you need to reconnect with your kids too."

Damn. A normal father would've thought of that. Guess what I'm doing on the way home.

"Returning to everyday life has been chaotic, as I assumed it would be. But it's harder to concentrate on my work when I'm constantly daydreaming about this stunner I met on vacation." A pretty red blush stains her tanned cheeks, competing with her sexy lips for my attention. "Please tell me your weekend is free. I can't wait to see you again."

She seems shocked at my admission. Hell, she's not as shocked as I am that I'm putting it all out there. It's probably because I'm so relieved she didn't confront me with my misdeeds. The nervous energy I was holding onto is now spilling out like endless rain into a paper cup. Okay, I'm paraphrasing from a line written by John Lennon when he was writing songs with the Beatles. But it fits.

"No."

There's no hiding my disappointment. My face falls.

"Oh my god. You *are* cute. I meant I've got plans with a hot surgeon."

Fuck, I want to kiss her. "Can I pick you up around four?"

"Yes." She blushes. "But only under one condition."

"What's that?"

"From now on, if you want to ask me out, you don't do it through Mom or Agnes."

"Deal." I grin.

Now, if only I can get through the next four days without being distracted by thoughts of her.

3:10 p.m. I remove my watch and adjust the dials. How is it only 3:10? It feels like this day has dragged on. I'm sure it has nothing to do with the fact I've looked at the clock one hundred times today. I'm tempted to have Porter drive me to her place and wait down the road so I can be at her door at four-thirty on the dot.

I'd already been wishing time would fly by more quickly when Poppy sent a text on Thursday, asking if we could bump our date back thirty minutes. She'd signed up for an art class and wanted to have time to get home and clean up. As much as I didn't want to delay our date a minute more, her message was perfect timing.

Poppy sharing that she was excited about returning to pottery gave me an idea. There was a new art exhibit at the Virginia Museum of Fine Arts I'd seen in the news recently. Maybe a visit would help get her creative juices flowing.

"You ready to head out soon, sir?" Porter asks from the doorway. I've yet to have a real conversation with him about everything that happened on the trip. Let's hope he doesn't think this midlife crisis is here to stay.

"Porter?"

"Yes, sir?"

"Thank you."

"Um. You're welcome. But that's my job, sir."

Rubbing the back of my neck, I decide to go all in. "Yes, but setting a trap for poor Poppy wasn't. I'm going to confess when the time is right."

"I think that's a good idea. She's a nice lady." He grows quiet. "Can I ask you something?"

"Of course."

"You don't think she would've come around, eventually?"

I've questioned this myself. Was I merely impatient to have my chance with her? "After spending time with her, I'm not sure she would have. She went through a lot, losing her husband. She was his caretaker as much as his wife. He died young due to Lou Gehrig's disease. I can't imagine how hard that was for her. I'm sure she's been trying to protect herself from any further heartache. Add to it that we work together, and I'm not certain I would've had a chance otherwise." At least, that's how I'm justifying my actions.

Pulling in front of Poppy's home, I exit the car and button up my jacket before walking to her front steps. I consider ditching my suit jacket due to the August heat, but my thoughts come to a halt when the door opens, and I see her. She's wearing a form-fitting champagne-pink dress, held up by tiny spaghetti straps.

Does anyone at St. Luke's know what this goddess is hiding under her lab coat?

Her beautiful blonde hair is styled in waves that tease her tan shoulders. My eyes travel the length of her until I land on her heels. Her toenails, painted a champagne- pink hue to complement her dress, peek at me from the opening of her nude-colored stilettos. It's fitting we're headed to the museum. She's a fucking work of art.

"Hi."

"Hi." My voice crackles as she comes closer. I'm overcome by this woman. It's not simply her beauty. But watching her bloom. Every time I see her, she shares something new and unexpected with me—whether it's her thoughts, her desires, her heart, her beauty, or her pain. "Poppy, you're stunning."

"Awe, you make me feel like *Pretty Woman*." She giggles.

"Julia Roberts has nothing on you, Pop."

She reaches for my lapels and pulls me into her, placing a chaste kiss to my cheek.

"You ready?"

"Yes. So, what do you have planned for this date exactly?"

"I plan to do all I can to impress you."

"We'll see." She smirks.

Opening the door for her, she slides into the back seat of the town car. After rounding the rear of the vehicle, I join her. "Porter, this is Poppy. Poppy, this is Andrew Porter. I don't think I introduced you before. We've been together for a long time. If you need anything, he's your man."

"Thank you, sir. Nice to meet you, Poppy." As Porter pulls off, I take Poppy's hand in mine. Bringing her wrist to my lips, I give her a gentle peck. The fragrance she's wearing reminds me of the day in the cafeteria when I lost control, and I chuckle.

"What's so funny?"

"It sounds creepy. But I like the way you smell."

Poppy's cheeks turn the sweetest shade of pink. "I have to admit something."

Uh oh. "Go on."

"As appalled as I seemed the day you said that to me, I've replayed it in my head about one hundred times."

Turning to her, I bury my face in her blonde locks, nuzzling her neck. "Thank god. Because I don't think I'm going to be able to help myself today. Do you have any idea how much restraint I've had to use around you so far?"

I notice a shy smile cross her face before she turns to look out the window. My gut tells me she hasn't heard compliments nearly enough. Is this just since her husband died? Or has she been waiting to be adored for even longer?

"So, you aren't letting me in on where we're going?"

"No big fancy surprises really. I just wanted the evening to be all about you."

Poppy's brows pinch together as if she's unsure what that means.

"No *Pretty Woman* stuff. I'll save taking you to shop and model clothes for me for another time." I laugh, trailing my finger along the satiny contours of her dress as it caresses her curves. "Besides. It appears you don't need any help from me."

"Why, thank you. I'm glad you like it." She giggles. "I can't explain it, Broadie. But that trip did wonders to boost my confidence."

This statement makes me feel proud. That I unknowingly gave that to her. Although it will be little consolation if she ever figures out what I did. It's my turn to look out the window, my guilt causing me unease. I only need a few more dates with her. Once she gets to know me, I'll confess everything.

And pray she'll forgive me.

"We're here, sir." Porter pulls up at the Virginia Museum of Fine Arts, and I hop out to escort Poppy inside.

I watch as she looks toward the door. "Wow. I wasn't expecting this."

"In honor of starting your art class, thought this could provide some inspiration."

Sliding her arm through mine, she looks up at me adoringly with those big blue eyes. The sight almost takes my breath away. I already know there will be nothing inside this museum that can hold a candle to Poppy Danforth.

"I haven't come here in so long," she says.

We get our tickets and decide to roam for a while to take in as many of the exhibits as we can until dinner. However, there is a new one that I have a sneaking suspicion she'll love.

Poppy is drawn to a photography gallery where I find a display on the Art of Advertisement depicting posters from the late 19th century. "These are fascinating," I utter to no one in particular. Poppy is examining a colorful poster depicting the Morning Journal from 1895.

"They are," an attractive woman to my left replies with a sultry grin.

"Do you happen to know where the Kintsugi exhibit is located? I'm excited to show my girlfriend."

Girlfriend?

What the hell? Don't get ahead of yourself, Broadie. In my haste to let this woman know I'm not available for small talk unless it's with Poppy, I inadvertently put a label on us.

"No," she says, her response flat.

I turn to see Poppy coming in my direction and smile widely at her. Taking her hand, we meander through the different sculptural exhibits before migrating to a large collection of paintings. Then, as I turn the corner, I see it. Poppy steps beside me, and she audibly gasps.

"Oh, Broadie. I can't believe it. This is my favorite." She covers her mouth with her hands, seeming to almost become emotional at the collection. "How did you know?"

"I can't explain it, really. I saw a piece on the news about Kintsugi. They said it was coming here for a short time, and I immediately thought of you. It's not what I think of when I picture pottery. In my head, I picture Demi Moore in *Ghost*." I chuckle. "But as I understand it, Kintsugi is the Japanese art of repairing broken pottery by mending the fragmented pieces with gold or silver. To make the cracked portion part of the art, rather than hiding it."

Poppy's hand flies to her heart. "That's it exactly. But what about it made you think about me?"

"When I was making small talk about your hobbies on the jet, trying to distract you from worrying about your mother's condition, your spirits seemed to lift as you mentioned wanting to reignite your love of pottery. That it was therapeutic for you. Then, I saw the piece on the news. They highlighted an artist who was taking broken bowls that had been passed down through generations and mending them with beautiful gold lacquer. Incorporating the broken pieces into the art as a whole made it that much more beautiful. I have a feeling caring for your husband did that for you."

Poppy comes closer, and I see tears in her eyes. *Fuck, Broadie. Why'd you have to go and bring up her dead husband, you moron?* But before I can apologize, she cups my face with her hands and kisses me. And this is no chaste kiss. My arms slide around her waist, and I take what she's offering.

"Thank you."

"You're welcome."

We spend the rest of our time here in this one exhibit. I can see her cataloging her favorite pieces in her mind. I couldn't have hoped for a better way to begin our date.

"These are so beautiful. I have so many ideas now."

"Good."

"You know, you could come with me."

"To an art class? Pop, you know I love you, but there's no way in hell I'd go to an art class. I've barely done anything in years but work. That would drive me insane."

Poppy is staring at me with her mouth hanging open.

"What?"

"Did you just say I love you?"

Shit. It was a figure of speech. "Poppy, I—"

"Oh my god. You should see your face right now. I'm kidding." She snorts.

"Well, keep laughing like that, princess, and I'm sure it's just a matter of time before I'm madly in love."

"Ha ha."

"I almost didn't hear your snort over my stomach growling. Are you ready for dinner?"

She slides an arm around my waist and smiles up at me. "Yes. I'm starving."

We casually make our way back to the front of the museum. Spotting Porter parked by the curb, I give him a wave before he jumps into action. Pulling the car around, he parks long enough for me to let her settle in. As I come around to join her, she places her hand over mine.

"Broadie, I hope you don't think you have to take me somewhere ultra-fancy for dinner. I mean, if that's what you like, I'm fine with it. But your money doesn't really do it for me."

"Ah. So, it's my dick then."

Her mouth falls open before she shakes her head at me. "I make a decent living and have Dan's life insurance and savings if I need it. Not that I've touched it. I don't need a lot of things."

"Well, I'm glad to hear you feel that way." I laugh. She'll understand once she sees where I'm taking her for dinner. Lifting her knuckles to my lips, I give them a tender kiss. "I like that about you. And my dad and grandad would have *really* liked you." I laugh. "They were that way."

Porter pulls up to the curb next to our dinner stop. In a strip mall. Carena's Jamaican Grille.

Poppy bounces in her chair. "Oh, this is perfect."

I smile with pride. This dating thing isn't so bad after all.

Escorting Poppy inside, we're shown to a small table and provided menus. Poppy laughs, pointing to the label, DA MENU. After placing our orders for a beer and a rum cocktail, Poppy and I decide to try the conch fritters. As we continue reminiscing about our trip to Jamaica, Poppy orders the jerk chicken, asking if they can serve hers mild, while I order the Appleton Rum glazed ribs. They're supposed to be coated in a dark rum and guava barbecue sauce. It will be a mess, but I can't resist.

We laugh and eat Jamaican food with our fingers from a strip mall restaurant, trying not to ruin my suit jacket or her hot little dress. I'm sure the sight of us right now is laughable.

"Is there anything else I can get you?" the server with the Jamaican accent asks us.

"No. I'm stuffed," Poppy says. "I want to rub my belly, but after I stole one of your ribs, I'd just end up with that sauce all over me."

"We'll try that later," I whisper. Finishing my last rib, I catch her mouth fly open at my remark from the corner of my eye. "I'm going to go wash up before we head to our next stop."

"Next stop?" she asks as she wipes her mouth.

"You'll see. It's not Rodeo Drive, but I still want to take you shopping." I start to walk off when I notice something and step closer. Bending down, I drag my tongue along the corner of her mouth and moan. "You missed a spot." I wink.

Who knew holding hands would be so distracting? As we snuggle into one another in the back seat of the town car, I am drawn to her like a moth to a flame. No matter how dangerous this could be, getting drawn into her world when I have priorities I haven't sorted. Time and time again, I prove I have no control.

Leaning my head back, I realize Porter is slowing down. As the car comes to a stop, I bury my nose in her hair. "Ready to go shopping?"

Poppy gives me a curious stare until Porter opens the door for her, and she realizes we're at a Barnes & Noble bookstore.

"There are some other quirky little independent book shops in the area, but I wasn't sure they'd have what you're looking for." I waggle my brows.

"Stop!" she shouts, seemingly embarrassed.

Pulling her into me, I whisper, "I cannot tell you what a turn on it is to me that you read. Specifically, that you enjoy reading romance."

She pulls back to look at me, surprised.

"It's sexy as fuck." I mouth. Leaning back in, I add, "I want you to get all hot and bothered so you have no other choice…"

She cocks a brow at me, waiting for me to finish my statement. "Then to let me take care of you."

After walking inside, I let her have some privacy. I don't need to make her uncomfortable. I want her to pick the books that speak to her. Heading to the suspense section of the store, I check out the new releases. I admit, it's been a very long time since I was able to sit down with a good book.

After about an hour, I go in search of Poppy and find her holding two books.

"Only two?"

"That's for this week." She laughs. "I'll be back here by Friday night."

"Please, Pop. Get whatever you want." I pull her in for a hug, so happy with how my night has gone, I can barely get enough of her. "I'd build you a library if you wanted. A place you could go to whenever you wanted to escape for a while."

"Okay, can I take it back?"

"What?" Is she going to get a few more?

"What I said earlier?"

My brows lift in confusion.

"Maybe I do need a lot of things." She giggles as she points at the shelves behind her.

As we pull up to my home, I discover it's late. Caught up in Poppy's spell, I've totally lost track of time. She's been thumbing through her new purchases, I assume deciding which she'll dive into first.

I tell Porter to wait in the car and walk around to Poppy's door.

She steps out and stares wide-eyed.

"You okay?"

"Um, yeah." She stammers. "This is... I thought we..."

"Poppy?"

"Yes."

"Stay with me?"

CHAPTER TWENTY-TWO
POPPY

Walking up the slate steps of his palatial home, Broadie holds my hand tightly as he guides me inside. I'm speechless. I expected his home would be something out of this world but seeing it in person is another thing entirely.

His home isn't the four-story brick mansion I was picturing. Its design is more of a craftsman-style but on a mammoth scale. The home appears to be three stories, in a steel blue color with gray and black accents and wood trim. There's an attached three-car garage plus what appears to be an unattached one of similar design perpendicular to it. The home sits on what looks like several acres of well-landscaped grounds.

As the door closes behind us, I try to take in the first floor. It's quite open, with a study to the right, the main seating area located centrally, and a dining room on the left. Again, it's impressive, but not in an ostentatious way. The furnishings are luxurious but not flamboyant.

"You okay?" he asks as he comes to stand behind me, cocooning me in his embrace.

Trying to think quickly on my feet so I don't look like a simp, I reply, "Yeah, just surprised."

"By what?"

"That you'd bring me here. All the hot, rich guys I read about don't want women knowing where they live."

"You think I'm hot?"

"That's the part you zoned in on?"

"Poppy, I don't bring women here. But you're different. I want you to know where I live." Broadie gives me a sweet kiss on the shell of my ear, rocking me back and forth. I'd love to know how I'm different, but I'm so overwhelmed right now I can't even go there. "You want a quick tour?"

Heck, yes.

He slides off his suit jacket and drapes it over the back of a beautiful wing chair in the foyer before taking my hand. Broadie points at the study before leading me through the dining area. He actually has one of those Butler pantries that has a wet bar and counter space located between the kitchen and the dining room. The kitchen is bright and airy. It has a large marble island in the center surrounded by stainless steel appliances and cabinets, which are white on the top and a gray-blue color on the bottom. I love that the home appears to be tastefully decorated, not overly masculine.

All of a sudden, I feel Broadie's finger push my chin up.

"Sorry. I didn't realize I was drooling." I laugh. "And all of this is just for you?"

"Pretty much. I think of this as my girls' home too. But they don't come here much. We usually meet out for dinner or something."

I can't help frowning at this. "Because of your job?"

He shrugs. "Could be. But I think they simply prefer it there."

Looking at him blankly, I'm not sure how to respond.

"If you think this house is big, you should see my ex-wife's."

I spin to face him, my brows pinched, rather surprised by the comment. *Had she won it in an ugly divorce settlement?*

"She kept the house after the divorce. It's the only home the girls have ever known. I don't need all that. Hell, I don't need all of this. But it was a good investment, and I needed someplace where I could get to and from work easily."

I nod as I look about the place, trying to take it all in. I notice through the glass doors at the back of the home that there's a large pool and outdoor entertaining area. "Your home is stunning, Broadie."

Pulling me against him, he gives me a chaste kiss. "It is now."

My nerves may be getting the best of me. I place my trembling hands on his chest and take a deep breath. *God, I want this. I want him. But...* "Are you sure this is a good idea?"

"What?"

"Us?"

He scoops me up, depositing me on the kitchen counter before boxing me in with his arms. "Poppy, I'm nervous too. I haven't dated since before I was married. I can already guarantee I'm going to make mistakes." He stops briefly, his eyes dropping to the floor as if he's deep in thought. "But even though I'm worried I'm going to let you down, I want this." His gaze flicks back up to meet mine. "I can't adequately explain how much I want this."

I reach out to caress his cheek. "Can we take this slow?"

"Poppyyyyy," he moans.

"No. Not that." I giggle. "I meant I don't want to be the talk of St. Luke's." Abruptly my heart clenches, as my voice takes on a more somber tone. "Plus, if it doesn't work out, there won't be as many prying eyes."

Broadie leans in for another peck, this one on the cheek. "Of course. I'm happy to be your dirty little secret, baby." He winks. His playfulness is exactly what I need right now. I don't want to consider the what ifs. I want to stop time... stay in this moment. I never want this magical night with him to end.

Broadie lightly places his fingertips along the inside of my thighs and spreads my legs so that he can move between them. Leaning in for a deeper kiss, he darts his tongue into my mouth as his hands trail up and down the outsides of my thighs. Goosebumps scatter over my skin, eager to experience every touch.

Wrapping my arms around him, I dig my hands into his brown hair as he pushes himself against me. There's no mistaking he's hard as he grinds his hips against my overheated center. One strap of my dress floats down my shoulder, and he takes this as an invitation for more.

Broadie's eyes remain on mine as if silently asking permission as he peels the front of my dress down to expose my right breast. The nipple is pebbled, and he doesn't waste a moment licking the tip before he begins to suckle from it. He buries his face between my breasts, his stubble electrifying the sensitive flesh, before he moves to lick and suck the other nipple. He seems to revel in this moment, squeezing, fondling, and sucking. I barely notice that his other hand has moved to the apex of my thighs and is toying with the seam of my panties. It's only been a few glorious minutes, and I'm already embarrassingly wet.

"I want to see all of you, beautiful. May I?" Again, his eyes seem to be pleading.

"Yes."

I've barely finished uttering my approval before he's gliding my panties down my legs. Broadie pushes me back to lie against the countertop and takes a good, long look at what lies before him. Dragging his tongue across his lower lip as he examines me, I can't help but squirm. I start to turn away when he lowers his head, runs his nose along my center, and inhales. My head lulls to the side. I've never felt so desired in my life.

"This pretty pussy is all mine." In an instant, his tongue is swiping through my folds, and his fingers are teasing my sensitive clit.

"Oh god," I belt.

It's as if my words have struck a match. His face is buried in my core, his tongue teasing my opening while his talented fingers run circles over my swollen flesh. He abruptly thrusts a finger inside as he repeatedly teases my clit with the tip of his tongue. The pressure beyond perfect.

Holy crap. He's barely... it's only been...

"Broadie!"

His mouth replaces his finger, giving my clit a firm suck as I come apart. My entire body convulses. It's quick, but powerful.

Jeez. Really?

A few moments later, I can sense he's hovering above me. But I can't open my eyes. I'm so humiliated.

"Pop, look at me. What's the matter?"

My hands fly up to cover my face. "I'm so mortified."

"Why?" His voice drips with concern.

"*Why*? I've been dreaming in vivid detail about what it would be like to spend the night with you, and now it's over in approximately three and a half seconds."

Broadie chuckles. "Who said it's over?"

I push myself up onto my elbows. "I'm not the kind of girl that has multiples."

A brow lifts as he stares down at me. "Challenge accepted." Broadie lowers his head back down and starts to devour me. I can count on one hand how many times I've received oral sex in my life. And until tonight, none of them memorable. Yet this man is diving in for seconds like I'm his favorite meal. My hands slide into his hair as he continues to bury his face into my core. His tongue is nothing short of magical. That combined with the friction from his five o'clock shadow, and he's well on his way to proving there's no task to great for the likes of him. While the build-up feels more gradual this time, it's no less intense when I feel him slide a finger inside me. And then another.

"Oh god. Please," I cry out.

Broadie picks up the pace, rhythmically rocking his talented fingers inside and curling them to hit a spot I didn't know existed. It doesn't take long before that familiar sensation returns. I can't believe it. I can't, I can't… "Broadie!"

"That's it. Come on my face." With that, he swiftly withdraws his fingers and buries his tongue inside me. It only takes a little friction from the flick of his thumb against my clit to make me detonate.

Digging my fingers into his hair, I start to thrash. I've never felt anything this intense in my life. As the waves of euphoria start to ease, I realize I've probably just made this man bald. Releasing my grip on his hair, he slowly moves over me.

"Is it okay if I carry you to my room? I want you completely naked and in my bed."

"Yes." It's pitiful that is the only word I'm capable of right now. Anything he wants. *Yes*.

Scooping me up, Broadie lifts me into his arms before carefully walking to the stairs. I leave one arm locked around his neck but drop the other down so I can wrap my hand around his bicep. He's perfect. Not overly muscular, but tall and ripped. I never got the opportunity when he was holding me in the pool to actually touch his body. I was still in total shock seeing him there. But I'm quite excited for naked time with this Adonis.

His room is gorgeous. I was expecting it to be dark and uber-masculine. Instead, there are warm wood tones to the four-poster bed and dresser, but the fabrics are all in a creamy white. It resembles a high-end luxury hotel. As he drops me onto the edge of the bed, I find my ability to investigate further is quickly thwarted once I see him unbuttoning his shirt.

Scooting further back, I bite down on my lip. I should probably remove my dress the rest of the way, but I'm completely distracted by the show happening in front of me.

"Slide that gorgeous dress off, baby. Lie back on the bed and let me finally see if my dreams are anywhere close to the real thing."

I blush. He's already seen all of me, just not the full picture. I stand and lower the top of the dress and shimmy out of it before bending to reach for my shoes.

"Those peek-a-boo heels have been driving me fucking crazy all night. Lie down and let me take them off of you, Pop. I don't want to miss out on one thing I've pictured in my head."

Knowing he's fantasized about me... this man has had dirty thoughts about me... well, it's doing all sorts of things to me right now. I know he's probably a cad. I'm not stupid. He may not have made dating a priority before, but I'm sure he's had sex with plenty of women. I don't know what's different about me. Yet he hasn't felt like a player. Every moment with him has felt genuine. So I'm not going to let self-doubt destroy the most amazing sexual night of my life.

Getting situated on his bed, I quickly turn to watch him disrobe the remaining items he's wearing when I see he's already moved to the end of the bed. Standing in nothing but black boxer briefs, my mouth waters as he glides his hand up and down the hard length nestled in the tight fabric.

"Fuck, you're beautiful, Poppy."

I suddenly feel vulnerable in this state. Lifting my hands, I cover my breasts but attempt to massage them, hoping he won't think less of me.

"No, no. Those are all for me," he chastises playfully.

I drop my hands, hopeful he'll join me so I don't continue feeling like I'm on display. However, any awkwardness I'm feeling immediately vanishes when he lowers his boxers, and the most incredible cock I've ever seen bounces free. He's not scary big, but longer and thicker than I've been with. I can't look away. It's perfect. He's perfect.

His muscular hand warps around the base, and he begins to tug on it, a bead of precum glistening from the smooth mushroom head. I've never been one who enjoyed giving blow jobs before, but all I can think about is wrapping my mouth around it.

Without waiting for an invitation, I crawl down to the end of the bed and look up at him. "Please?"

"Oh, fuck. I'm not sure I'm going to last with those puffy red lips around my dick." He continues to stroke himself, and I'm starting to become more aroused than before he made a meal of me. *What sorcery is this?*

"Please?"

He gives a curt nod, and I eagerly bend down to lick his tip. A hiss escapes him before I wrap my mouth around him and take him in as far as I can.

"Holy fuck." Broadie's hands are in my hair. His grip is firm but not painful. But the sounds he makes as I bob up and down on him are filling me with pride. "Baby, I need to be inside you. I don't want to come in your mouth." He backs away, and before I can comprehend what's happening, he scoops me up and carries me to the side of the bed.

Dropping me to my feet, he gives my butt cheek a playful slap before asking me to turn around. "Up on all fours, Poppy."

My limbs are shaking as I climb onto the bed. I hear him open a drawer before looking over my shoulder to watch him roll a condom onto his thick, veiny cock. Suddenly, butterflies are swirling in my belly in anticipation of this. How is this possible after the two orgasms he already gave me? I read about this stuff in books, but I've never experienced anything like it. I was always grateful to have one. I dare say, even that hasn't happened in years.

His hands lightly caress my ass before one dips down between my legs. "Hell, you're soaked, sweet girl. Is all of this for me?" His fingers glide back and forth through my swollen, delicate skin, and I practically sway my hips side to side in answer. He's turned me into an animal.

"Yes."

With that, he wastes no time pushing forward. The stretch of my body around his causes an intense burn, and I feel myself clamp down. Sensing my distress, he curls his body over mine and places a hand over where we're joined. "You feel so fucking good, Pop. Like you were made for me." His uneven breath caresses my neck as his fingers dance circles over my sensitive skin. After a few moments like this I start to relax. I can feel him inch forward, a little at a time, until he's completely seated.

I start to wonder if something is wrong, as he hasn't moved a muscle since his body became flush with mine. His hand has moved from the apex of my thighs to my hips. I'm so turned on right now, the anticipation making me quiver. I contemplate turning to look at him when he slides nearly all the way out and then slams back into me.

"Oh god," I cry out.

His grip on my hips grows tighter. "I've never felt anything so fucking good in my life, Pop. I'm going to get a little rough. I need you to tell me if it's too much."

The only thing screaming in my head right now is, *yes! Please, yes!* I nod, encouraging him to give me more, and he does just that.

The pounding starts slow and rhythmically, but the pace picks up, and I've never imagined anything could feel so good. I just need friction. I'm tempted to lie down so I can slide my hand down to touch myself as he thrusts into me, but I don't have to think about it any longer when he places his hand in the center of my back and pushes me into the bed.

Lying on top of me, his magical fingers are back on my clit as his legs spread me wider, his cock hammering into me. As if this wasn't erotic enough, the unintelligible sounds he's making above me are like ear porn.

"Fuck, that sweet pussy... you're going to make me fucking come... I need you to... oh, fuck, Poppy... listen to how wet you are, taking my fat dick like a good girl... come on my cock, baby."

A familiar buzz starts to vibrate in my belly, and I know another one is close. I dig my fingers into the covers and hold on, certain this will be the strongest orgasm of my life. I just hope I stay conscious for the whole thing because I'm in complete sensory overload right now.

"Oh, Broadie," I yell as my climax takes over, my body beginning to quake.

"That's it. Scream out my name when you come," he commands as the pummeling reaches a fevered pitch.

"Broadie!" I feel like I've been hit with a thunderclap of sensation. "Oh god." White spots cloud my vision as my pulse pounds in my ears.

I've barely come down from the waves of this orgasm when I'm flipped onto my back. Broadie crawls over top of me, trying to kiss me, but I can barely breathe. Large hands slide under my shoulders, pulling me farther across this king-sized amusement park. "I need to see you. You're so beautiful, baby." I'd laugh if I wasn't so out of it right now. I must look like a mannequin that fell onto the store floor overnight, all sprawled out, unable to speak, with my focus unclear.

Broadie places kisses along the column of my throat and my collarbone before dropping his mouth to suck on my nipples once again. I bet that would feel good if the post-orgasmic high I'm still clinging to hadn't made me practically numb. He slides his cock back inside me, his mouth still on my breasts.

"These tits. They're perfect," he mutters between sucks. "I need one more from you, Poppy."

One more what?

"I can't. I... and even if I could, I won't be able to walk."

He slams into me before reaching for my wrists and pulling them over my head as he starts rocking into me. "You don't need to walk anywhere." Thrust, thrust, thrust. "I'll carry you wherever you need to go." There's no chuckle or playful undertone to his words. He actually means it. Well, I don't think it's physically possible to have another. *I can barely feel my lower half.*

As if sensing another challenge, he sits up, draping my legs over his shoulders, and drives himself deeper into me. His head drops back as he hits my inner walls, the sight of him coming undone actually stirring something awake again. *What the hell kind of sexual superpowers does this man have?*

Holding my leg against his chest with one hand, his other returns to my clit. All the while, his hips are undulating like an Olympic hula-hoop champion. "Fuck. I'm going to come so hard." He pants, his thumb flicking over my swollen bundle of nerves like a guitar player. I knew this surgeon would have magical fingers, but good lord.

Broadie looks down at me, and I can tell the moment the wheels come off. His pace picks up, and the force with which he ruts into me becomes more powerful. He drops my legs, enveloping my body with his as he fucks me within an inch of my life. "I need another one. Give it to me, Poppy." He grunts.

I start to tell him to let go, that it simply isn't physically possible, when the friction of his pelvis against my clit as he drives into me causes my legs to shake. *There's no way.*

"That's it. That sweet pink pussy is begging for me to fill it."

And that's all it takes. I don't know which is his most lethal weapon, his talented hands, his impressive cock, or that deliciously dirty mouth. I can't even find words at this point to moan anything. My eyes roll back in my head, and it's all I can do to hold on to consciousness for a few more moments.

"Open your eyes," he barks.

My lids spring wide. I can see him floating above me, but I feel like I'm under anesthesia.

"Fuck. Fuck. Fuck," he chants as his hard, sweaty body thrashes into me.

I can tell the moment he's reached his final destination, as he stills, his exhales shuddering above me. Luckily, as my bodily functions start returning to normal, I'm able to see a look of pure rapture on his face that nearly brings tears to my eyes. That I could make anyone look like that. Feel like that. Much less, this amazing man.

Broadie

Overwhelmed with emotions I wasn't expecting to feel, I drop a tender kiss on Poppy's forehead before withdrawing and heading for the bathroom. Quickly disposing of the condom, I turn on the faucet to wash my hands and catch a glimpse of the man in the mirror. I barely recognize him. Staring, I can see a contentment in his eyes that's new. This realization combined with the way I feel after spending the evening with Poppy is unnerving.

This woman is nothing short of amazing. Poppy took everything I had to give, never once seeming alarmed at my words or recoiling when things got rough. I never felt as if I was taking my pleasure from her, but instead that she was giving herself to me. Her satisfaction was palpable.

And it's not just the sex. Sure, it might be the endorphins talking right now, but the entire evening was incredible. There wasn't a moment I thought about work or any of the stressors that normally occupy my thoughts. Poppy steals all of my attention. But in a good way. Not in a needy, demanding way as I suspected another relationship would bring. An odd sensation stirs in my chest.

Could I have finally found someone suited to all of the sides of me?

Shutting off the water, I realize this woman could be a real turning point. I need to embrace this second chance. Because I might just be able to have it all with her. The career, the financial success, love, and family. With her, a balanced life feels possible.

I've accomplished things in my life most people couldn't dream of. Some through hard work and determination, and the rest through believing in myself, the great power of manifesting what I want in my life, and maybe a little luck.

Yet, as hard as I tried, for years now, I've struggled to feel whole. There was always something missing. What good was the all-consuming career and riches if, at the end of the day, you were all alone? My friends were as driven as I was, so spending a few hours every couple of months was as much as I could hope to expect. My interactions with women were shallow, merely physical connections. My family lived with another man who could commit to them. And my only confidants were on my payroll.

Then this mysterious woman walked into my one-dimensional world and brought a light I've never known. It was as if I felt it before I'd even met her. Like a gift from the man upstairs. I can't squander this chance. But I need to take this slow so I don't scare her. Hell, *I'm* already alarmed at how I'm feeling. I don't want to risk pushing her away if she feels smothered. But I have to see where this goes. Because the thought of a world without her now is terrifying.

I walk back to bed, finding Poppy lying on her back, one arm thrown over her head, her eyes closed, and her golden hair splayed over her pillow. Sliding carefully under the sheets, I try not to wake her when her eyes fly open.

"I'm sorry, Pop. Go back to sleep, baby."

"I wasn't asleep." Her voice sounds odd. Almost distant. And she's not smiling. My heart drops.

Reaching across her, I stroke her cheek. "Are you okay?"

"I don't know."

Swallowing hard, I pray I haven't hurt her. Or worse, caused her to have any guilt about being so physical with me. It's clear she still holds a deep love and commitment to her husband. "Did I hurt you?"

"No," she blurts. "No. I just can't believe…"

Holding my breath, I try to give her space to say whatever is on her mind. Even if it's hard to hear.

"If that's what sex is supposed to be like, I've been doing it all wrong."

There's no holding back. I pull her beautiful body into my arms, a sense of inner peace that's eluded me for so long washing over me as this sweet woman snuggles against my chest. I let out a relieved chuckle. "I was worried I'd hurt you." Poppy pulls back, the most angelic look on her face, as she dips the pad of her index finger into my dimple. The action never ceases to make me smile harder. "I want to make you feel good."

"No worries there." She giggles.

Tracing a heart onto her chest, I say, "No. I mean here."

Rising with the sun, I carefully slide out of bed so I don't wake Poppy. I've never woken up with a woman in this house. It should feel alien to me. But everything about this moment feels right.

I start to go in search of coffee before hitting the shower when I notice my phone has several new messages. Taking it with me, I head to the kitchen to grab my morning dark roast. Dropping the pod into my Keurig, I open my phone messaging app while anticipating the familiar aroma that signals my day has officially begun.

> 5:30 A.M.
> JAROD
>
> Hey, man. I'm on call, but one of your patients is being admitted. Looks like they may need to go back to surgery. I've started them on two antibiotics. But you might want to take a look. I'll send you their info on the private server.

Dammit. I don't know why this is so surprising. It's been my entire existence. I spend many a day off in that hospital, either being on call or due to situations such as this. As much as I'd like to take up my new balanced life right this very moment, I have an obligation to my patients to ensure a good outcome.

Grabbing my coffee, I head to the bathroom to quickly shower and change until I stop in my tracks, trying to think of a way to keep Poppy here until I return. Then it hits me. My dirty obsession with imagining her curled up in a sleep set, reading her books, had me spending an hour online several weeks ago. I was saving it for a special moment. Yet, no time like the present.

I walk into my closet and reach up to seize the pink and black Agent Provocateur bag containing the little pink silk camisole and sleep shorts I'd ordered for her. Grasping the handles of the adjacent bag from the

bookstore, I pull down the beautiful hardcover copy of Pride and Preju-
dice I found. It was a striking version of the classic with gold foil lettering
embossed into a dark matte background.

Bringing the gifts out to the kitchen island, I walk to my study in order
to retrieve a pen and paper.

Poppy,

I'm headed to the hospital to check on a patient. I
didn't want to wake you but also didn't want you to
think you weren't a priority.
I understand if you need to head home. I've left a
card with Porter's number. He'll take you wherever
you need to go.

But on the chance you'll stay, please help yourself to
coffee. There are breakfast items in the pantry and
fridge. I got distracted during our tour and never
introduced you to the library. It's just past my
office. Help yourself to anything that interests you. I
left a little something I admit I've fantasized about
seeing you in. Picturing you reading in it has given
me many pleasant nights' sleep.
Thank you for one of the best nights of my life.

Yours,
Broadie

Walking in the door from the garage, I have to acknowledge I'm nervous. Did she stay? I could've messaged Porter asking if he'd dropped her off. But honestly, I didn't want anything disrupting the satisfied bubble I'd been living in. I'm going to be really fucking disappointed if she's gone.

Holding my breath, I walk into my bedroom to find Poppy lying on her belly, her chin resting in the palm of her hand as she reads her new book. She's wearing the pink and black sleep set, slowly kicking her legs back and forth behind her as she's deep in thought. The delectable globes of her ass are taunting me from the silky bottoms, causing my dick to stir.

"Hi." Her greeting interrupts my salacious thoughts, catching me by surprise. She flashes a sweet smile at me from the bed, and my day is made.

"I'm not sure that outfit was the best choice."

Her smile quickly fades as she rolls on her side. "You don't like? I thought I looked cute in it." She pouts.

"Yes. But you're going to look much better out of it."

CHAPTER TWENTY-THREE
POPPY

"Poppy!"

Turning my head, I spot Kat making her way toward me. "Hey, how are you?"

"I'm good." My cheeks heat at the thought of sharing my date with her.

She gives me a quizzical look. "I have a funny feeling I'm behind on something. When can we meet up again?" She giggles.

"I'm off tomorrow. Then I'm back for the next three days since it's my weekend to work."

"Tomorrow it is, then. Can you come to the lake?"

I clap my hands at the thought. "Oh, Kat. I'd love to."

"Yay! Now I have something to focus on besides these cranky pants patients I've had all day. Is it a full moon or something?"

Shaking my head at her, I appreciate my limited patient contact during times like those. "I've got to get back. I can't wait to see you tomorrow, Kat."

Making my way back to the pharmacy, I catch the movement of someone in the corner of my eye and see Broadie, dressed in his lab coat, talking to the hospital administrator. He doesn't look happy. Realizing my stride has decelerated, I head in the direction of the stairwell, so I'm not caught gawking.

I can't imagine the amount of stress he must have to deal with on the daily. While my job isn't easy, for the most part, I only have to show up and do my usual tasks. Well, that and put up with grouchy doctors who are impatient when I can't read their minds about the medications they need. But it's rare I'm pushed to do more than provide clinical education on medications. Broadie is constantly being sought after to help lead the hospital forward, in addition to his taxing surgical responsibilities.

As I make it back to the inpatient pharmacy and return to my tasks, my mind wanders to the handsome surgeon. It's been over a month since our night together. We've met once for coffee, but otherwise, our schedules haven't aligned. Or he's not interested in more. I have to at least consider it's a possibility.

He's a busy man, but he's managed to text me something sweet each day. Even if it's just a hello or have a nice morning. As much as I miss spending time with him, it's probably better I try to avoid getting too attached. But I can't fight the feeling that if I were to allow myself to fall, he's the one I'd want to catch me.

"Oh, Kat. This place," I gush. Her serene lake house literally feels like something from a Thomas Kinkade painting. The beautiful wooden home sits on a lush green hill overlooking the water below, surrounded by beautiful trees and a gentle slope to the dock.

"I know. It's our little piece of heaven. There's a bit of a breeze off the lake today, do you want to eat on the screen porch?"

"That sounds great. Where's Grace?"

Kat reaches for a pitcher of tea and motions for me to follow. "I just put her down before you got here. If she gets up while we're still talking, Nick should be back by then."

I turn to her, confused. "Back? Is he off today?"

"Yes. He's on call this weekend. He took our friend, Huggie, out on the boat."

"You have a friend named Huggie?" I giggle.

"Well, his name is George Hughes, but we all call him Huggie."

We sit down at her table, set with the prettiest vintage mismatched pieces and water goblets. She pours some tea before placing the blown glass pitcher in the center of the table next to a vase of peonies.

"This is beautiful, Kat."

"I'm glad you like it. We're far enough out that it's not often I get to entertain. So, I wanted to pull out all of the fun stuff." She laughs.

Reaching for my glass, Kat pushes the pretty ceramic sugar bowl my way, and I shake my head as I drink mine unsweetened. "How's everything with you and Nick?"

"It's great." She snickers. "But you know good and well, I didn't coax you to join me today to talk about me. I want the scoop, Poppy." She uncovers a pasta salad and places a serving spoon inside.

"Not much to tell," I reply, scooping a helping of the chilled salad on my plate. The smile I'm trying to tamp down must give my fib away.

"I see that." Kat laughs. "Now, spill it."

"I finally went out with Broadie."

She sits blinking at me like a dog waiting patiently on a bone.

"And it was the best night of my life."

"What?" She gasps. "And I'm just hearing about this?"

I laugh. "Oh, Kat. It was amazing. I'm afraid nothing will ever top it." I grimace at the statement. I'm sure this thought must be on repeat in my mind, whether I want to admit it or not. "He took me to the museum before we went to dinner. Then he took me shopping."

Kat's mouth drops open.

"Okay, wait. Before you go thinking this was something from the Richard Gere playbook, our dinner was in a strip mall restaurant. And shopping wasn't on Rodeo Drive. It was in a bookstore."

Kat cups her cheeks, hanging on my every word.

"It was so thoughtful. He'd gone out of his way to make sure the entire evening included things he knew were special to me. It never felt flashy or over the top, like he was trying to impress me. He was so kind and attentive."

"And?"

I put a forkful of pasta into my mouth. "And, what?"

Kat puts both hands flat on the table in front of her. "I'm patiently waiting for the good stuff."

My cheeks immediately heat, and a broad smile crosses her face.

"I said it was the best night of my life."

Katarina does a silent jig in her chair before looking back at me. "So, you two are an item?"

"What? No."

Watching Kat's expression is the equivalent of observing someone getting the air let out of their tires. "It was a hookup?" She belts out. "That seems odd. Did he go to all of that trouble of wooing you like that to get laid?"

"I don't think so." I laugh. "The date was a little over a month ago. We've met for coffee once. And he's sent texts to tell me he's thinking of me. But I knew what his life was like. It's the very reason his marriage fell apart. I'm trying not to get carried away or push for more."

Kat slumps back in her seat, her arms crossing over her chest as if she's digesting what I've shared.

"Kat, I'm fine. Please don't worry. Eat."

"But, Poppy. I don't want this man to use you. I think the world of Dr. Weston. But I only know what I've seen at work. Maybe I was wrong about him."

I take another forkful. I'm not sure why she seems to be getting so upset. Sure, I'd love to see him more. But this is all new. And the man is incredibly busy. He's trying to rebuild a relationship with his daughters. That's his priority. I'm happy to see him when he's as attentive as he was on our date. Not to mention, I probably needed time for my body to recover from the sexathon that night before opening the door for another.

"I think you're making too much of this. I don't want to dive headfirst into a relationship with a man who admits he's had a hard time balancing his life. Plus, there's always the chance we could burn bright and then fizzle out if it's too much, too soon." I take a sip of my tea, hoping I'm convincing myself as much as Kat with this speech. "Besides, I've started seeing Dr. Miller and returned to an art class. Between that, work, and my mother, I don't know how much time I have for a hot and heavy relationship."

Kat picks up her fork, and I think I've finally gotten through to her when she lays it back down with a look of concern. Oh, good grief.

"What's the matter? Please don't be worried." Reaching across the table, I take her hand. "I don't have any reason to doubt him."

Kat pulls away, her earlier look of concern turning to one of distress.

Do I?

"Poppy. I don't know how to say this." My pasta salad suddenly feels as if it wants to come back up and join our conversation. "I heard something yesterday. I don't believe it. But it worries me that if there's a chance it could be true... well, I don't want you to get hurt."

Putting down my fork, I grip the table. "Kat, you're scaring me."

"Please don't be. It's probably just the rumor mill. You know how these things get started. If there's any truth in it at all, it gets lost the more people who get involved."

"What things?"

Katarina takes a visible inhale. "I overheard one of the ER nurses gossiping to a few others that..."

God, she's killing me here.

"That Dr. Weston frequents sex clubs for women," she blurts before closing her eyes as if afraid to witness my reaction. We both sit quietly, me trying to imagine the man I know in that capacity. Kat opens one eye, her face contorted as if in pain.

"How would she know that?"

"Apparently, she works there." My mouth drops open. "I wouldn't put any stock in anything Ashton says, Poppy. I think she's a complete attention hog. Everything she says is exaggerated."

My hand drops to my stomach. I wasn't expecting anything like this. It'd be one thing if someone heard a rumor about him with a nurse or getting back with his ex-wife. But this? "If she still works there, can't she get fired for sharing information like this? I'd think they have contracts to protect clients' privacy at places like that?" At least they all do in my romance novels.

"I'd think so, too."

"Did she say what the place was called?"

"Yeah. I admit I hung around far longer than I should have, trying to gather any intel I could. She said it's called the Devil's Playground. But I tried to research it on the internet and couldn't find anything."

Dropping my face into my hands, I try to wrap my head around this. Broadie seemed to be so up-front with me about everything. But I can't help but wonder after that night with him. Broadie Weston is a sex god. There's no other way to put it. I honestly had no idea a man who could give me multiple orgasms existed, much less four.

"You okay?" Kat whispers across the table.

"I don't know."

"Let's just say he is a member there. That doesn't necessarily mean he's into some weird kink or anything. Or that he's been there since you."

I'd agree with her if I wasn't already considering the fact that I've barely seen him since our one night together.

"Kat. I'm scared."

"I know, sweetie. Me too. But we need to figure out how to handle this. Because it wouldn't be fair to ruin what you've found with him over a rumor."

"What rumor?" a male voice asks.

My gaze pops up to see Kat's husband, Nick, and a very attractive man about their age at his side.

Kat reaches for my hand, giving it a squeeze. "Poppy, this is Huggie. Huggie, my friend, Poppy."

"Hi. Sounds like we walked in on something intense. Should I go?" Huggie asks as he reaches for a glass and begins to pour himself some tea.

"Poppy. I think we should tell them. See what they recommend."

I can feel the color drain from my face at the thought of hearing any confirmation this could be true. Not to mention, sharing all of my dirty laundry with these men.

Kat nods as if asking permission to share.

Giving her an eye roll before nodding my approval, I drop my forehead onto the table in utter misery.

"There's a rumor going around the ER. About one of the doctors at St. Luke's. A doctor Poppy's just started seeing."

Nick pulls up a chair beside his wife, appearing to be all ears.

Looking up at Huggie, she continues, "Poppy hasn't dated since her husband died. And this doctor has come on hot and heavy. But she hasn't seen much of him since their first sleepover."

"Oh, shoot me now," I groan.

I feel a hand rub my back at my utterance and look up to see Nick giving me a concerned look.

"We were just wondering if there's any way short of confronting him to find out if the rumors are true."

"What rumors?" Nick asks.

"That Dr. Weston goes to sex clubs for women."

Huggie begins to choke on his drink as simultaneously, Nick's eyes go wide.

"Didn't see that one coming, huh?" Kat grimaces.

"Would that be a deal breaker?" Huggie asks seriously.

"Um, are you kidding?" I ask him. "I don't want to start a relationship with a man who's sleeping with other women, much less at a sex club."

Huggie's expression is odd.

Why would anyone think that would be okay? I mean, if that's what he's into, that's fine. *Okay, it's not fine. I don't want that to be what he's into.* But then why initiate anything with me? Is this all a game to him?

"Maybe that was before."

Kat and Nick turn to look at their friend before returning to peer at me, neither agreeing nor disagreeing with the possibility.

I guess I can't judge him for what happened before. Unless he was into some kink I'd be weirded out by. But how would I ask him about this? I mean, this isn't the type of question you'd find in a 'getting to know your date' manual.

"I wish there was a way to know for sure. Because this situation is bigger than I'm prepared to live with. At least without having some answers."

"You know…" Kat says, tapping her finger against her chin.

"Uh oh," Nick interjects. "The last time you had that look, poor Bella ended up dancing on stage at Daddy Rabbits for amateur night."

Uh, what?

"I'm just saying. If we could somehow get into the Devil's Playground and see what the deal is… it might make you feel a lot more comfortable with the situation. I mean, maybe it's just a place he goes for drinks."

Nick raises a brow at her like Kat has officially lost her mind. "Aren't there less scandalous places to have a drink?"

"I've been to a private club before. It wasn't that scandalous," Kat argues.

"A private sex club?" Nick prods.

Kat throws her palm in Nick's face as if silently telling him 'talk to the hand, buddy.'

"I agree with Kat. These places may offer the opportunity for more, but everyone who goes there isn't looking for some kinky hookup."

All three of us look at Huggie curiously. Is he trying to make me feel better?

"So, say you could get in there, Poppy. What if you saw Broadie getting a lap dance? Would that be all you need to stop seeing him?" Huggie asks.

I sit back in my chair. Broadie and I have never had the monogamy conversation. I don't have any right to assume he's only with me. But he knew my past. And he was honest about his. Why would he pursue anything with me if he still wanted to hook up with women in a sex club?

"Honestly, Nick, I think it would. I realize we haven't had that discussion. But I'm thirty-eight years old. I've lived enough heartache in my short time on the planet that I don't need to be involved with someone who's interested in playing games."

"That's fair," he says without any judgement.

Kat giggles. *Did I miss something?*

"What's so funny?" I ask.

Her face is almost red, she's laughing so hard. "I can't believe the main thought going through my head right now is that it's a shame Nick didn't have a membership before we were together. I mean, color me intrigued!"

Nick pulls his goofy wife into his side and buries his face in her hair, whispering loud enough for all of us to hear. "I can take care of that for you if you'd like, Mrs. Barnes." This only causes her to laugh more.

"I don't think so. But I wouldn't mind going, just to see what all the fuss is about. Do you think Sebastian has a membership?"

"Trust me, Sebastian, didn't need a sex club to get his rocks off."

I watch the two of them laughing while my heart is dying inside. I was really falling for this guy. Kat must notice my dejected expression.

"Oh, I'm sorry, Poppy." She reaches for my hand. "I didn't mean to make this worse. I wish I knew someone who could get us in so we could give you the answers you're looking for."

"Uh, hmm."

All eyes are now on Huggie.

"I can get you in."

CHAPTER TWENTY-FOUR
BROADIE

"Roxanne, get Broadie another scotch, please."

"Yes, Mr. Black."

"Thanks, G. What's going on? This didn't feel like the usual boys' night when you summoned us." I notice Becket and Derek wearing a concerned expression and sit up in my seat. "Did something happen?"

"I don't think so, but I'm a bit worried," Becket says, taking a pull from his beer. "Remember that chick that Derek and I were watching the last time we were here? I swore I recognized her from somewhere. I thought it was from here, but I'd remember sleeping with a girl that tall." He tilts the amber bottle back once more. "With heels, she's almost my height. I tend to like them shorter and curvier. Derek hasn't hooked up with her either, but had the same feeling of déjà vu."

My eyes flick to Derek, and I notice this is more than trying to put a name to a face. He looks alarmed. "Well, you know I haven't slept with her. I haven't been with anyone here in years." I blurt.

Roxanne returns with my drink and I accept it eagerly.

"What difference does it make that you can't place her? Gianni screens all of his girls and has them sign an NDA."

"I know, I know. But I'm worried it could still blow up in our faces," Derek says.

"What could?"

"I'm pretty sure that girl works at St. Luke's, Broadie."

Instantly, the scotch feels like acid in my throat. "What?"

"I don't recognize her from labor and delivery. But once Derek got a good look at her, he's pretty sure she works in the float pool," Becket says.

Immediately feeling alarmed, my eyes connect with Derek. "I had the same niggling feeling as Becket. Then, a few days ago, I was on call and a patient came through the ER having a heart attack. She was one of the nurses pushing the stretcher to the cath lab. It was when we arrived upstairs that she pulled her hair tie loose and her long dark hair fell down her back that my hair stood on end."

My blood runs cold. "Ashton?"

"Yeah. You know her?"

"No. Not really. I know she's worked in the ER and the general surgery floor when they've been short. She hasn't worked for St. Luke's for very long." Running my hand through my hair, I huff. "Something about her has always rubbed me the wrong way."

"Look," Becket interrupts. "I know none of us are into crazy kink. But this place is our private haven. I don't need a bunch of lies getting spread about us. You know as well as I do rumors spread like a fungus in that hospital. Our professional reputations could be at stake."

This is bad.

"Who is this girl?" G asks. "I don't have an Ashton working here."

Becket pulls out his phone. "Here, this is her Instagram feed." He scrolls for a few minutes before handing his phone over to Gianni.

"I knew it."

"What?" the three of us ask simultaneously.

"That's Anjolina." Gianni rolls his eyes. "I knew her name was fake. From what I recall, her background check didn't show any red flags. I think she was fucking one of the bouncers. He'd vouched for her, saying he'd worked with her at another club. But nothing about it sat right with me."

"What the fuck are we going to do?" Becket asks.

"Don't worry. I'll have my guys let her know in no uncertain terms that she'll be taken to court for breach of the nondisclosure agreement if we find out she's been talking. There's no way I'm keeping her here. It's not worth the risk. I'll let her go for falsifying her application. We would've never hired anyone affiliated with your hospital."

"Won't that cause her to be more likely to lash out?" Derek asks.

"My guys can be very persuasive. Silly little girl. She doesn't know who she's dealing with."

Reaching back to massage my neck, I try to ignore the pictures in my head. The hospital administrator asking for my quiet resignation so as not to bring negative press to the hospital. The news getting word of this. My patients. My daughters. *Poppy.*

"Max, any chance you could get some anonymous email to the hospital expressing dissatisfaction with her care? I'd had my concerns about her unprofessional conduct. I'm just kicking myself I didn't act on it before." Derek asks.

Max rubs his hands together as if embarking on an exciting mission. "I'm on it. Emails are my specialty." He winks at me, and I want to punch him in the junk.

Bzzz. Bzzz.

Completely keyed up by this new conundrum, I nearly jump from my seat at the vibration of my phone. Realizing it's Stu, I quickly answer, "Hello?"

"Hey, boss. Thought you might want to know. Your girl is out on a double date."

Jumping from my seat, I cover my left ear with my hand to make sure I've heard him correctly. "What did you say?"

"Poppy appears to be out on a date. The guy has his arm around her, and they have another couple with them."

What the fuck?

"Are you sure?"

"No. Not entirely. But nothing about this makes sense."

"What do you mean?"

Stu starts to laugh. "She's wearing a red wig and dressed like she works here."

My mouth goes dry. "What do you mean *here?*"

"Apparently her date's a member. She just walked into DPG with three people. Dressed like she's planning to entertain here later."

"You've got to be fucking kidding me."

"Nope. You might've met your match with this one." He chuckles. "I can't make this shit up."

As I hang up the call with Stu, I scan the room but come up empty. Could Poppy really be dating someone else? And of all places, why is she here? Is he someone who wants to take her for a walk on the wild side? None of this matches the girl I know. Especially the inexperienced one I slept with.

How could she have gone from not dating for years to juggling multiple men? Maybe our night together caused a sexual awakening in her. But if that's the case, why wouldn't she have asked me to bring her here?

I take the steps, deciding to roam each floor of the club until I find her. *I need answers.*

It takes about ten minutes to locate her and her companions. But less than one to recognize Kat and Nick. He has his back to me, and Katarina is wearing a long blonde wig, but I know it's them. I observe them from the safety of a dark alcove, as they both point and gawk at various things like kids on a field trip. It's clear this is their first time at DPG. They aren't members here.

Poppy's wearing a slinky little black number and gold stilettos. The short red wig is styled like a bob. She's hot as fuck. If I get to the bottom of this, I'm taking that saucy little redhead over my knee.

My gaze falls on the gentleman standing next to Poppy with his hand on her lower back, and now I'm seeing a whole different kind of red. I briefly contemplate confronting them, when I see Annaliese walking over to where Poppy and her acquaintance are standing. She pulls the gentleman in for a brief hug before he introduces Poppy. Annaliese has a very animated conversation with Poppy, pointing up and down as if describing the layout of the club. Are they applying to become members here?

I consider asking Gianni what he knows when I notice Annaliese walking away with Poppy's chum on her arm. *What is that about?*

From what I recall, Annaliese manages The Rox. It's a smaller club suited for prearranged hookups or specialty kink. While the Devil's Playground is a social club, The Rox is designed for anonymity.

I've only visited once. I'd met Brandee at DPG several years ago, but we had done no more than flirt initially. Until one night when it was clear we both wanted more. Yet, instead of checking into a nearby hotel, she provided the address for The Rox. Turns out, she was living there at the time. She'd had a high-rolling regular who put her up there, hoping to ensure her availability whenever he was in town. Worked for me. I may have met a few women at this club back in the day, but I never had sex with them here. This place was merely foreplay.

Lurking in the shadows, I keep a safe distance between us as I watch Poppy ascend the stairs. Is she curious about what goes on here? Is it purely happenstance that she's here?

Or is she looking for me?

I watch as she peers over the railing from the second floor onto the dance floor below. Poppy seems to be inspecting the area beneath her with great intensity. She *is* looking for me. I just know it.

Staying put, I find her wandering about the second floor, scrutinizing every corner until she comes up empty and heads for the stairs.

That little minx has no idea what she's in for. I hover a little closer, still blending in with my surroundings in order to keep a watch over her. There's no way I'm letting any man here take his shot, thinking she either works here *or came to play.*

The third floor of the Devil's Playground is a voyeur's dream. There are multiple rooms with two-way mirrors designed to let exhibitionists explore their sexual fantasies while allowing onlookers to anonymously enjoy the show.

Each night brings unique entertainment. Whether it's a couples first time having sex for an audience or multiples who like to push the envelope, getting off on shocking the viewers on the other side of the glass.

Sure, I enjoy watching. But usually, only if I'm with someone who wants to leave for a hotel afterward. And I haven't made time for that in years. Up until Poppy stole all of my thoughts, I met Brandee when I needed a quick release. Nothing more. But the idea of watching Poppy's reaction to what she finds has me wound up.

The viewing window of the first room has only a few onlookers. There are two men who appear heavily into bondage. One is wearing leather chaps and bent over a table, while the other is slapping his ass with a whip. Poppy doesn't stand among the viewers long, instead continuing down the hallway.

I follow the sexy siren in a red wig to the next room, where a woman stands as a man buries his face between her thighs. This holds her attention only a few minutes longer before she moves on to the next room.

The third room has a king-size bed in the center of the space. It appears there are two women and one man fondling each other. It's difficult to make out exactly what is happening as they remain partially covered under the red satin sheets.

In my experience, the farther back you venture into these rooms, the more twisted the games can become. Is she merely checking it all out? Or does she think she might find what or who she's looking for here?

It's the next room that seems to grab Poppy's attention more than the rest. As I move closer, the couple comes into view. The young blonde is blindfolded, with her arms tied behind her back. She's seated on the end of the bed, fully naked. The gentleman with her appears older. He's gently stroking her skin as he whispers into her ear. The blonde's nipples are tightly peaked as he caresses her breasts.

All of a sudden, he places his hands on her thighs, pushing them open wide for all to see. It's clear, even from here, she's turned on. Her pussy is bare, swollen, and glistening. I watch Poppy's face intently as she takes them in. Something about this scenario seems to do it for her, as she steps a little closer to the glass.

My eyes continually flicking over to Poppy, I watch the performers as he steps aside, allowing another blonde to walk into the room. The gentleman continues to whisper into his blindfolded partner's ear, just before turning her head and lining it up with his rigid dick. Cupping her face, he slowly fucks her mouth as the other blonde woman kneels down between her legs and begins to lick her pussy.

Unable to hold back any longer, I move in behind Poppy. "Like what you see, beautiful." I feel her jump in front of me. Is it the realization someone is watching her, or does she know it's me?

I'm a little surprised when she doesn't move as I come closer. "Do you like to watch?"

"Yes," she whispers. A hint of shame tainting her speech.

"Would you like to have others watch you?"

Poppy quickly shakes her head no.

"Good."

With this, she cranes her neck to see me.

"Because I'm not interested in sharing."

"Broadie, I—"

"No, ma'am. I'm not sure why you're here. But, for now, keep your eyes on the show." I place my hands on her hips, pulling her ass snug against my cock. Watching her here has me hard as a rock.

She gives a slight gasp as my fingers reach under her dress, grazing the seam of her panties. Her head starts to shift from side to side as her back becomes rigid. "Don't worry about anyone else, Pop. They're not watching you. They're watching them."

My finger slips into her panties, finding her warm and soaking wet.

"Fuck, you feel good," I moan.

Poppy's breathing quickens as the gentleman in the viewing window withdraws his cock from the blindfolded woman's lips and moves to switch places with the blonde between her legs. The blonde moves to sit beside her, stroking her tits before bending down to suck and lick each of them as the man thrusts his dick into her waiting pussy.

Poppy is practically grinding her ass into me as I tease her wet, swollen flesh. Reaching around her, I run circles around her clit as I drive two fingers of my other hand into her.

"Broadie," she groans.

"I want you to come for me."

Suddenly, the male pulls his companion's legs up over his shoulders, slamming wildly into her, and Poppy's body starts to convulse.

"That's it. Such a good girl, Pop."

Within moments, she falls weakly against me, and I bend to scoop her up, taking her somewhere we can sit down.

"You okay?"

She doesn't answer me, merely buries her face in my neck.

"What are you doing here, Poppy?"

"Looking for you."

"Me?" I try to play innocent. "Why were you looking for me?"

"I'd heard a rumor you came here for sex. I needed to see for myself."

Fuck!.

"You heard wrong, baby. I come to DPG to meet my friends. That's all. My friend owns this club. I haven't been interested in anything sexual here in years. And when I was, I didn't have sex at the club. It was a pick-up place. No different than meeting a woman in a bar. Just more private." I push a lock of hair behind her ear.

She gives me a guilty look.

"Why didn't you just ask me?"

"I wasn't sure how. We'd never talked about exclusivity. I didn't want to come off accusatory. But I knew if you were sleeping with other women, it would be a deal breaker for me."

"There's no one else I want but you. No one. This place served its purpose when I needed it. Now it's simply a private place to meet my friends. Or it was."

"I'm sorry, Broadie."

"You have nothing to apologize for. We should've talked about this before you were forced to consider I wanted something different. I'm sorry you had to take things into your own hands now that rumors are spreading."

She lifts her hand to my face, stroking my hair. The act feels so natural, as if she's done it for years.

I start to mimic her actions but lift the strands of her wig, arching a brow.

Poppy giggles. "How did you know it was me?"

"I'd know you anywhere." I laugh. "But my security spotted you."

She shifts in my lap, alarm on her face, and I realize I better at least let her know this much. "I've had my security department keep an eye on you."

"You what?"

Here we go. "Poppy, I'm sorry. I'm a wealthy man. With that wealth comes risk. And

Sometimes, the people at the greatest risk are those who mean enough to me to have bargaining power."

She remains silent, eyes wide, appearing stunned.

"I have them assigned to me, my daughters, and you."

"I mean that much to you?" she practically whispers.

"Yes. I know this is new. And we haven't had the opportunity to develop a relationship the normal way. But get one thing straight. You're mine. And no one touches what's mine."

Holding my breath, I prepare for her to push back on my power play. Yet I'm greeted with a shy smile. As if she's proud to claim the role.

"Are we good, Poppy?"

"Yes."

I can't put this off any longer. "Who's the guy?"

"Who?"

"The guy who got you in here. Because I know Nick and Kat aren't members."

"Jeez. You're good. You recognized them, too?"

"Those two are hard to miss." I laugh. "Who. Is. He?" I accentuate each word.

"I don't really know him, Broadie, honestly. His name is George. He's a friend of theirs. I only met him today at their house."

She seems sincere. I make a mental note to have Stu look into him. But for now, I reach for my phone, sending a text to Stu and Porter, asking them to get the jet ready.

"Good. Because there's the matter of this hair, these shoes, and this fucking dress to contend with."

CHAPTER TWENTY-FIVE
POPPY

"Is there anything I can get the two of you, sir?" the pretty flight attendant asks.

"No, thank you, Brenda."

"Broadie, is there any way I can get word to Kat and Nick that I'm headed back home with you? I don't want them to worry. But my phone is in my purse, which is in Kat's car."

Broadie unbuckles and stands from his seat, reaching his hand out for mine. "It's already handled, baby. My security guy took care of it."

Taking his lead, I stand and follow along behind him as he escorts me through a doorway at the back of the jet. *Holy crap, there's a bedroom back here?* The room is floor-to-ceiling cream, with a bed against the back wall decorated in a lush navy and white duvet.

"Come here."

I move to sit on the edge of the bed beside him. I'm nervous and a bit overwhelmed at being back on this jet with him. The last time, I was too upset about Mom's condition to really take it all in. It's still difficult to comprehend I'm dating a man with this kind of money. Not that I ever considered that attractive. I was happy with Dan. I'd admittedly stereotyped wealthy men into an arrogant, elitist category. Yet, I'd never met anyone like Broadie.

"I'm sorry I haven't tried harder to make time for you since we returned from Jamaica. That night with you... it was one of the best nights of my life, Poppy. I replay it often." He reaches for my hand. "Being away made my schedule an uphill climb for a while. I'm getting caught up, but administration is pestering me, and now I have to deal with these rumors."

"Please don't." I hold up my hand to stop him from apologizing. "I know how busy you are. I'm trying to focus on my art class and getting back into the things that bring me joy. It's probably better we don't spend too much time together anyway."

Lifting my legs and draping them across his lap, he stills. "And why is that?"

I'm a little caught off guard by the question. *Isn't it obvious?* "Well, in case it doesn't work out."

Broadie's brows pinch together. "I'm working to get my life in order so I can spend as much time with you as possible. Trust me, Pop. This *is* working out." He leans in, dropping a kiss on my forehead. "There's nothing I want more."

I can't fight my grin. "It probably wouldn't matter anyway." I laugh.

"What wouldn't?"

"How much time I spent with you." I tease the area where his dimple usually resides, hoping to coax it out. "I think about you all the time."

That sexy smile returns, bringing that flirtatious indentation with it. *Jeez.* Am I falling for him or just hypnotized by that smile?

"Poppy?" he asks as he leans forward, dragging his tongue along the hollow of my neck.

"Yes?"

"You know this is more than physical between us, right?"

"Yes." I bite my lip to keep from squealing like a fangirl at a BTS K-pop concert.

"Can I fuck you on this bed?"

My legs instantly quiver. There's no need to answer, my eager expression must be all he needs.

Running his hand up and down my thigh, I groan at the feeling of his mouth on my skin. "I might get a little rough with you. Is that okay?" *Kiss.* "That outfit has had me hard for hours."

"Broadie?"

"Yeah, Pop." *Kiss.*

"Do you go to that club because… well… are there things that women do there that you like?"

He immediately pulls away, looking serious. "I don't want you to be uncomfortable that I go there, Poppy. DPG is where I meet my friends. Nothing more." He pauses as if fighting an internal battle over how much to share. "There was a time…"

Broadie runs his hand down his face, seemingly uncomfortable. Sitting up, he says, "I don't deal well with stress. While I haven't dated anyone since my divorce, I still fuck. Albeit not as often as you might think." He turns away as he finishes his thought. He needn't be embarrassed. He's a healthy man with a normal appetite for sex. I'm not judging him.

He hastily turns and grabs both of my hands in his. "Pop, I get a little out of control when stress pushes me to my breaking point. While I've stayed away from relationships because I couldn't commit to giving someone the time and attention they deserve, I also didn't want my needs to create added tension. I probably shouldn't share this, but it caused a real rift in my marriage. I don't think it was why Camile wanted out, but it certainly didn't help."

Broadie looks down at his feet. "Typically, women who spend time in clubs like DPG are accustomed to rough sex. It relaxes me to have that control when everything else in my life feels as if it's spinning out of it. It's a physical release, nothing more. There's no BDSM or group kink," he reassures. "I haven't been with a woman there in ages. I want more. I want you." His eyes drop as if he's ashamed. "But I don't want to hurt you. I just—"

"I want to be what you need." Swallowing hard, I can feel my heart rate speed up. I'm still trying to digest his words. While he didn't have to, I'm grateful for his admission.

Leaning forward, the brush of his lips over mine causes me to tremble.

He moves his mouth to the shell of my ear. "Lean over the end of the bed for me, Pop."

Getting to my feet, my legs shake beneath me like a newborn foal. I lie face down on the bed, instantly feeling him pull my wrists behind me. I'm unsure what he's using, but it's silky smooth against my skin. Like I suspect his tie might feel. He then lifts a pillow off the bed. It's hard to see what he's doing in this position. The pillow abruptly flies over me to the head of the bed before my eyes are covered by a cloth that I suspect is the folded pillowcase.

"Jesus. You're the hottest thing I've ever seen."

I should be nervous. He just finished saying he gets a little out of control and plans to be rough with me. But after the last night I spent with him, all I'm feeling is eager.

Cool air hits my backside as Broadie unexpectedly lifts my skirt. A low growl escapes him before I feel his fingers tugging at the sides of my panties. The anticipation is making me squirm against the bed. He's not the only one who's replayed our night together.

As my panties pass over my feet, I lie motionless, curious as to what's happening behind me, until I feel his hands on my ass, spreading my butt cheeks wide. Holy cow, this man is filthy. How did I go from vanilla sex to no sex, to I've only read about this in my spicy books sex?

"Oh, god." I squeal into the mattress as his tongue drags from my clit to my asshole. The sensation hasn't even sunk in completely before I feel the thwack of his palm against my ass.

"That's for making me hard all night."

Thwack.

"That's for spying on me instead of warning me about the rumor you heard."

Thwack.

"That's for getting wet watching another man earlier."

"No!" I yell into the mattress.

Broadie immediately stops what he's doing and leans over me. "Did I hurt you? Do you want me to stop?"

"No. I'm not hurt. But you have it all wrong. I was getting wet pretending it was you."

His warm breath tickles my ear as his large palm caresses my stinging flesh. "Oh, that's my good girl. Who's the only man who's allowed to slide their cock in this pretty pussy?" he asks as his fingers graze my wet center.

I've barely been able to achieve one orgasm during sex with anyone else but him. And now I'm about to climax just listening to this man's dirty talk. "You. Only you."

"That's right." I can feel him rubbing circles over my tender ass cheek and prepare myself for another slap when all of a sudden, his fingers slide inside me.

My body is no longer under my control. It's as if my hips are rising to meet him with each glide of his hand.

"Your greedy pussy is begging for my cock, isn't it, Pop?"

"Yes. Please?"

He quickly withdraws his hand and drives his beautiful dick into me. "Fuck, yes." He groans. It's as if he's read my mind.

Without easing into it, he immediately starts pounding into me. Every now and then, he grabs ahold of my bound wrists and tugs as he rotates his hips and returns to pummeling into my swollen flesh. "You feel too damn good, baby. I'm not going to be able to last."

Me either. I would've never thought I'd be able to orgasm like this. But with my hands bound, my eyes covered, and the friction beneath me, I'm hanging by a thread.

"Poppy…" He shifts above me, lifting me up to place a pillow beneath my hips. I can feel his skin flush against my back as he rams into me from a slightly different angle. Each thrust hitting a spot that's quickly sending me over the edge.

"Broadie, Broadie…" My orgasm crashes into me, white lights dancing behind my closed lids.

The erotic grunts above me signal his orgasm is cresting as well. He stills, his shuddered breaths staccato against my ear.

Knock, Knock.

"Yes?" Broadie belts out.

"We've begun our descent, sir."

Sliding the makeshift blindfold from my eyes and freeing my wrists, he chuckles as he rests his hand across his sweat-covered chest. "So have we."

Broadie retrieves a wet washcloth to clean me up after hastily returning from the washroom. Giving my behind a playful swat, he encourages me to stand. He smirks as he reaches up to toy with the red strands of my wig.

"I think we might need to save this outfit for later."

CHAPTER TWENTY-SIX
POPPY

"There you are. I'll forgive you for not coming to see me in so long if you tell me it's because you've been with that handsome doctor," my mother yells as I enter her room.

I start to defend myself when she catches my smile.

"You have been with him!" She claps.

"It's not anything serious, Mom. Don't get ahead of yourself."

A loud commotion has me spinning on my heels. "What the hell are you waiting for, Poppy? Someone better to come along to get serious about?" Agnes asks as she tries to get control of the walker she just slammed into the doorway.

I giggle. "Do you need a license to use that thing?"

"Ha ha. You laugh all you want. At the rate you're going, you could end up living here before you land a man."

I shake my head at her. If she'd said that to me a week ago, I might have been tempted to go after Broadie more aggressively. But Kat's idea to go to that club and find out what he was really doing there ended up being gold. Not only did I have an incredibly hot night with Broadie, but he shared a little more of his past with me. I really feel like I can trust him. Even if I wish we could spend a little more time together.

"Well, if you haven't been hot and heavy with Dr. Dreamboat, what've you been doing?" Agnes interrogates.

"If you must know, I've been going to yoga, doing meditation, and returned to taking pottery classes."

"Boooring," Agnes groans. "What are you, a hundred and two?" She slumps into her chair, the walker nearly falling to the ground. "Youth is wasted on the wrong people."

"Wasn't that a line from *It's a Wonderful Life?*" I laugh.

"Just as true today as it was in the forties." She huffs.

I shuffle around the room, straightening the papers stacked on Mom's nightstand, when I notice something odd. Picking up the greeting card, I find it has a floral design on the front and *Hope you're having a nice day, Broadie*, is inscribed on the blank page inside. "What is this?"

"It's a card," Mom yells before leaning to look past me at Agnes. Her brows raised, as if questioning my sanity. "Are you feeling all right, dear?"

"Yes, I know it's a card, Mother. But I'm just surprised. Since when is Broadie sending you greeting cards?"

"Why not? Maybe she's his plan B," Agnes snaps.

Oh, for goodness sake.

"He's a nice boy, Poppy. Don't let him get away."

I flash my mother a reassuring smile before moving to give that poor, neglected plant a drink. The very last thing I want to do is let him get away. *But, trust me, Mom. He's not a boy. He's all man.*

I leave Mom's skilled nursing facility and decide to have a total 'me day.' I'll go to yoga before my art class begins and maybe hit my favorite coffee shop on the way home. Anything to try and keep my mind occupied with pleasant things. And off of him. I can't spend every day pining over him. He's a busy man.

I walked into the Barre Yoga studio with my head held high. I was going to crush this and leave feeling invigorated. But halfway through, it was all I could do to remain conscious. This class felt hotter, and the stretch more brutal than the ones I've attended in the past. Either I accidentally ended up in an advanced class, or I'm more out of shape than I thought.

After a cold shower and a rest on a teak bench wrapped in a towel, I at least feel like I have enough energy to collapse in my car. *When did I get this old?* Even after trying to wake up with the cool spray of the water, my body still feels overheated and exhausted. I think I might have to get an iced coffee before my art class. I'll never tolerate anything hot.

Is this what I have to look forward to? Am I perimenopausal? *Don't think about it, Poppy.* A 'me day' is supposed to be a good thing. Contemplating my fertility is definitely not on that list.

Walking into my favorite café, I order my drink and take a seat at a corner table by the window. Thankfully, I still have an hour before my pottery class begins, and it's not far from here. I'm excited to push myself today.

A small triangular crack had developed in my last piece after it was heated in the kiln. I was so disappointed as I'd worked diligently on it before that. But then my mind drifted to the Kintsugi exhibit at the museum the night of that incredible date with Broadie. I'd learned that Kintsugi was the Japanese term for golden joinery. The art of repairing broken pottery by mending the area with a powder mixed with gold, silver, or sometimes platinum. Maybe I could try something like that this afternoon. Create something beautiful to highlight that crack versus painstakingly cover it.

Taking a sip of my drink, I can't help but reflect on this. The Japanese philosophy of wabi-sabi, I'd read, embraces the flaws. It regards cracks or imperfections as valuable moments in history. It accepts change as fate. And isn't that how we should approach life? The things with which we have no control.

My mind's reverie is suddenly halted as my eyes flick across the street to a familiar figure. *It's him.*

As if I'm on autopilot, I rise from my seat, grab my drink and my purse, and make haste for my car, all the while keeping my eyes trained on him. Maybe that Barre Yoga class fried my brain. Why I'm chasing this young man is beyond me. Yet, it feels necessary, as if this third time seeing him is the charm. I want answers.

Starting my car, I idle as I watch him on his phone in his vehicle. He definitely looks more like a boy than a man. Before I can contemplate this further, his car pulls out from where it's parallel parked along the curb.

Trying to keep my distance, I follow along behind him. I feel like there should be theme music from an old *Starsky & Hutch* police show. Those two were always trailing someone. But what sense is there in a thirty-eight-year-old pharmacist turning private eye? I have no idea.

I haven't been able to shake why seeing this young man in the cemetery has rattled me. Why does he keep coming there? Who is he visiting? A grandparent? I've noticed some family members leave trinkets, note cards, and such by their loved ones' graves. But there would be nothing of value to pillage from Dan's. I shudder even contemplating that's why he might be there. Is it simple curiosity? Why someone as young as Dan may have died?

As I continue following along behind him, I try to let other cars slip between us, so he doesn't realize he's being tailed. Okay, so maybe I have been watching too many crime shows. But now that I've finally decided to know more, it no longer feels optional. I want some answers.

It only takes a few more blocks before I realize he's leading me right to Dan. Does he know I'm behind him? Is this some sort of trick? Working on my hunch that he's headed to my husband's grave, I pull back. Losing sight of him momentarily, I park under a large oak tree to the far right of Dan's headstone. Carefully stepping out of my car, I slowly make my way in that direction when I see him. I guess I'll be saving my broken vase until next week. I'll never make it to art class now.

Coming closer, he appears to be over six feet tall with dark hair. He's wearing jeans and a beat-up cotton T-shirt. Standing motionless in front of Dan's headstone with his hands in his pockets, I take a few steps more when I step on a branch.

The young man's head snaps in my direction, his bright blue gaze locked on mine. His face is expressionless.

"Hi." My voice is low. The crack a telltale sign of my nervousness.

"Hi." His voice sounds much more relaxed, in control.

"I've seen you here before."

The young man doesn't answer, just continues to watch me as I approach.

"I'm Poppy. Dan's wife."

"I thought you might be," he responds.

What? I have to swallow down the lump in my throat.

"I'm Gavin." He turns back to look at the headstone, and my head spins. *That's it?*

I take a few steps closer. "Nice to meet you, Gavin." Why am I so nervous? He's just a boy. "Did you know my husband?"

"Yes."

Wow. And here I thought Dan and I shared everything. Had he mentored him somehow, and I hadn't retained the information as being important? Or perhaps Gavin was an avid rock climber and had met him at the store where Daniel worked before he became so weak.

"I feel bad," I say. Gavin's head turns back, giving me his full attention. "I don't recall him mentioning you."

Gavin's eyes drop, and there's the slightest change in his expression. As if these words have somehow offended him, but he doesn't want to let on.

"I'm sorry. I don't mean to upset you. I'm sure he didn't tell me everything." I try to laugh, but it comes out half-hearted. *For I really thought he did tell me everything.*

"It's okay. I'm not upset."

Taking in a fortifying breath, I decide to go all in. "If you don't mind my asking, who was Dan to you?"

Gavin looks at me warily as if he's unsure whether or not to answer.

"He's my father."

CHAPTER TWENTY-SEVEN
POPPY

"Poppy?"

My eyes open, and I see a very worried young man staring down at me.

"What happened?"

"You fainted."

What? Placing my hands on the cool grass, I try to sit up as this kind young man places a hand on my shoulder.

"I wouldn't get up too quickly. I tried to catch you, but it all happened so fast."

My mind instantly goes to how weak I felt after my shower. That yoga class must have really done a number on me. And then it all comes flying back to me.

He's my father.

Peering over at him, I analyze him with a fresh perspective. This incredibly attractive young man has features that are unnervingly similar to my husband's. His eyes are a similar blue, though even more vibrant than Dan's. Yet, it could be that my memory of Dan's eyes is tainted by the constant pain I saw in them at the end. Gavin has a similar build. And while his hair color is brown, like Dan's, it's much darker. But maybe everything about my husband felt somehow muted in the end.

"Are you okay?"

"I don't know." Physically, I'm fine. I think. But otherwise, none of this feels real. It's as if I'm trapped in some sort of nightmare.

"Should I call for an ambulance?" He seems nervous. Lord, I must've scared the crap out of him.

"No, no. I'm fine. I'm so sorry. I don't know what came over me."

Gavin reaches behind his neck, massaging the muscles there with an almost humorous expression on his face. "Well, I'm pretty sure it was me."

Instinctively, I reach over to touch his arm. As overwhelmed and confused as I am by his earlier statement, there's nothing about this boy that makes me feel threatened. I'm certain he's just confused.

Jumping to his feet, he reaches for my hand. "You sure you're okay?"

"Yes. I think so." I look at my watch. It's 2:15 p.m. "Do you have anywhere you need to be right now?"

"Not really. Why?"

"Is there any way we can go somewhere and talk? I'm not sure I should risk staying out in this heat any longer. But I need answers."

Gavin looks at me as if he's now carrying the weight of the world on his shoulders. "Yeah. I guess I could do that. But is it okay if I drive? I'm not sure you should get behind the wheel of a car just yet."

"That's fair. If you have air conditioning, we could probably talk there."

The corner of his mouth lifts. "I do." He leads the way, even going so far as to open the car door for me. Once inside, he starts the engine and cranks up the AC. "Here." He reaches beside him and opens a bottle of water. "Drink this. It's still cold."

"Oh, I don't want to—"

He shoots me a glare, and it hits me that I don't want to do anything to cause him to leave before I can get more information from him. I quickly take the bottle from him and take a few sips. Dropping my head back against the headrest, I close my eyes and try to think of the best way to proceed. Until I simply blurt, "Why would you think Daniel is your father?"

After a few moments of silence, I turn to look at Gavin. He has his hands on the steering wheel, deep in thought. "Well, because he told me so." He rubs his hand through his unruly hair. "Not in so many words. I can't remember the early years very well. He didn't visit often, but he'd come once every few months. And I only ever knew him as Dad."

My coffee from earlier feels like it's churning in my stomach. There's no way this could be true. He has to be mistaken. "Are you sure you have the right headstone, Gavin? I mean, maybe you're thinking of someone else. My Dan didn't have any kids."

"I'm fairly certain it's his. Unless there were two Daniel Danforths that died young."

Quickly grabbing the water, I suck down almost half of the remaining contents. I have to be dehydrated. Overheated. Something. There has to be a logical explanation for this. None of this makes any sense.

"I wasn't sure if you knew about us."

My head snaps to him. The word *us* feeling like it's set off an alarm.

"I can tell you're upset. Are you sure about this?" Gavin asks, looking concerned. Why doesn't he seem dismayed by my appearance? But then again, if he's known about me all of this time, he's had time to come to terms with it.

"I'm sorry, Gavin. None of this feels real right now. You seem sincere. But I can't fathom how anything you're saying could be true."

Scratching the back of his head, he pushes forward. "You're a pharmacist. Right? And he was a salesman, before he got sick. You live in Hanover and have been married for a long time. Well, were married for a long time."

My mouth goes dry, despite the water.

"You never had kids. He traveled too much or something." He stops and looks out the windshield. "His favorite food was meatloaf. Who likes meatloaf?"

My hand flies to my throat. How would he know that?

"I don't want to upset you. You seem like a nice lady."

The reality of this situation starts to smother me like a dark cloud. Tears tumble down my cheeks, and I have to look away. How is this possible? The man I knew and devoted the majority of my adult life to, both before and after his death, was a liar.

The glove compartment flies open, the sound making me jump.

"Here." Several napkins with the MacDonald's logo on them are thrust in my lap as my tears turn into full-blown sobs. "Shit. I should've never told you."

"No. Someone should've told me years ago," I wail. This poor kid. I need to get myself together and get in my car. None of this is on him. Yet, I'm afraid to walk away, even if this is more than I can handle right now. I need to know. "I'm sssorry." I stammer.

"It's okay," he says. His voice sounding uneasy.

"I just need a minute." *Or a thousand.*

Gavin sits quietly as I try to get my blubbering under control. I guess his patience reminds me of Dan, also. Yet I don't want to consider any positive qualities that man possessed. I'm so fucking upset right now. Sure, I have no proof any of what he's telling me is true. But deep down, what possible reason could he have to lie?

"Do you mind starting at the beginning, Gavin? When was the first time you remember meeting your father?"

He turns in his seat to face me, leaning against his door. "I don't really know. I was pretty young. It's always been my mom and me. We never sat down and had some long conversation about my dad. He didn't visit all that often. When he did, it was short. We'd play catch or eat dinner. I think once we went to a movie. But I knew early on he had another family."

I take another drink of water, wishing it was something much stronger. Sitting still, I try to keep my tears from resuming and hope he'll continue.

"It wasn't until I was like ten that I finally asked my mom why he didn't come around anymore. I thought maybe he'd just gotten tired of us and decided to focus on his real family."

I chastise myself as the tears start to trickle down my cheeks again. But these aren't only for me. This poor kid. If this scenario is real, even though Dan had been steadily lying to me, he'd made his son feel unworthy. My head drops back again, wondering who in the hell I was married to. How could anyone I loved as I had him behave in such a way?

"Mom told me he'd gotten sick. That was why he'd stopped visiting. I was almost eleven when she said he wouldn't be coming back. And why." Gavin peers out the windshield in the direction of Dan's headstone. "It wasn't until this year I pushed for answers. I graduated high school and thought I'd better start figuring out what to do with my life. My mother has never had a plan for herself. Or us. She's always worked odd jobs. Some in not so great places. So I guess..." He scratches his head. "Oh, I don't know. I'm not sure why I thought he could help me sort it all out."

It dawns on me that Gavin must have his important conversations with Dan here also.

My head is spinning. I'm completely overwhelmed, but there's so much more I want to know. Even if I'm afraid to hear the answers. "Had your mom and dad been married a long time ago?" It didn't make sense that it could be a possibility. But there were more than enough two-timing men living double lives on Dateline that it had me considering it. Heck, after meeting Gavin, nothing seems all that farfetched anymore.

"No."

"Do you live here? In Hanover?" Had his, what... mistress... and her son... had they lived here under my nose all along, and I had no clue?

"Yes. We've moved around a bit. But have always lived in Hanover."

A sniffle escapes before I can contain it. How is this happening? Out of the blue, it hits me. I try to do the math. When Gavin was born, we would've still been in college. I would've been nineteen or twenty, and Dan almost a year older. "Do you know how they met?"

Gavin shakes his head. "No, not really. From what I gather, I think it could've been anything. A one-night stand. A short-lived relationship. But there was me... so." He rubs his chin before continuing. "I love my mom. She could've aborted me or given me away. And, trust me, there were times I wondered if I wouldn't have been better off if she did. Life wasn't easy growing up. She worked odd jobs to pay the bills. Most of them in bars. She brought plenty of men back to our place. That was fun."

My gaze immediately goes to him, his expression one of disgust.

"I think my dad gave her some money to help with me. But who knows for sure? We never talked about that kind of stuff. It could be it just felt easier back then because I was too young to notice how bad things were."

It's taking everything in me not to open this car door and hurl. How had my fairytale life been such a fabrication? While I lived blissfully unaware of my husband's cheating and lies, this poor kid had to endure growing up this way.

My whole life, I've felt loved and cared for. With my parents and brother growing up. And even more so married to Dan. Why hadn't he done the right thing? Was he concerned I'd leave? Was he ashamed of conceiving a child with her? Or had he actually been the complete and utter asshat I'm currently judging him to be, thinking he could get away with this?

Because he did get away with this!

"Gavin." Lifting the damp napkin to my nose, I wipe away the continued evidence of my distress. "I'm so sorry you had to grow up that way. No one deserves that."

"It's okay. It's all I knew. Sure, it sucked, and I wouldn't want to wish it on my worst enemy, but it's over now." He looks down at his joined hands, and a small smile curls his lips. "Good people came into my life when I needed it. Things have changed for the better because of them. My mom is still a hot mess, but I've decided family isn't blood. It's the people who treat you that way. Who want you in their life because they care. Not because they're obligated."

I'm a mess. That this amazing young man could've turned out so grounded despite his circumstances. I need to focus on that and not how completely betrayed I feel right now. But I'm so overwhelmed I can't see straight.

"Can I drive you home?" Gavin asks, looking concerned. "I don't think you should try to drive after all of this."

"Yeah. You're probably right. Are you sure you don't mind? I mean, you were nice enough to sit with me, and then sharing all of this had to be uncomfortable for you. I don't want to keep troubling you."

"It's no trouble. I didn't have anywhere I had to be."

"I could take an Uber."

He shakes his head. "I really don't mind. And to be honest, it would make me feel better to see you home safely. I've wondered what it would be like. If I ever met you. And now that I've made you cry... well, I'd feel better if I could get you home okay."

This young man. If Daniel Danforth had any redeeming qualities that were passed on to this boy... well, I can't say it would be this. Gavin seems honest and caring. The polar opposite of the words I'd use to describe my deceitful dead husband. "Thank you. Let me grab my purse from my car."

Several hours later, after multiple sobs in the tub, shower, and bed, I still can't wrap my head around everything. My heart aches like a bad tooth. The throbbing is both agonizing and unrelenting. Thankfully, I have tomorrow off.

Walking to the bathroom, I reach for another tissue when I catch myself in the mirror. I look like I've been beaten with a stick. My face is swollen, my eyes bloodshot. All the cool compresses and eye creams in the world won't fix this by Monday. I begin to sniffle again. I never miss work. Even when I'm sick. But I deserve some time to face this head-on before trying to explain to everyone I know that nothing is wrong.

I reach for my phone and send Marshall a text, letting him know I'm not well and will need a few days off. It's a white lie, but not far from the truth. I'm *not* well. I begin to sob again. How are there still tears?

Barely completing my text, I head to the kitchen to put on another pot of tea when the phone dances across the counter.

It's Kat. "Hello?"

"Hey, Poppy. I felt bad I hadn't reached out to you to see how you were after you left the club. When Dr. Weston's security detail told us you were flying back to Hanover on his jet, we assumed things were good." She giggles.

"Yeah. Everything was fine." I cover the receiver as a sniffle escapes.

"You sick? You don't sound like yourself."

"It's probably allergies."

The line goes quiet. "Poppy?"

"Yeah?"

"You suck at lying. Did something happen between you and Broadie?"

I wipe my tears, wondering how much to divulge. "No. No. We're fine. I haven't heard much from him since last weekend beyond a few texts. But that's how things seem to go with him."

"Are you sure you're okay with that? You sound upset."

Plopping down on my couch, I release a jagged exhale. "I just got some bad news. It has nothing to do with him."

"Poppy. What is it? Is it your mom?"

The tears pick up. There's no way I can share any of this with her over the phone. Kat will likely never be able to understand what I'm saying over my sobs. "Mom's fine. I just can't talk about it on the phone."

Kat grows quiet for a moment, and I wonder if I've lost the connection. "Poppy, I'm coming to get you."

"What? No."

"You sound awful. And I don't want you there alone. Do you have to work tomorrow?"

"No."

"Okay. Pack an overnight bag. If there's one thing about this house, it will bring you peace. You tell me as much or as little as you want, but you're not staying huddled up by yourself in that house anymore. I've kicked myself for years for not being a better friend after Dan died. Don't suffer there alone."

She's right. Not about not being a better friend. But the last place I need to be right now is here. Constantly reminded of his painful deception in the place where I gave up everything to care for him. Day in and day out, took care of his every need. All the while, he hid his double life from me.

"I'll be there to get you in an hour. Okay?"

"Okay," I whimper into the phone. Hanging up, I drop my face in my hands. Please, Lord. Let her be right. Please. Let me find some peace.

~

Sitting across the kitchen table from Kat, I feel hollow. She looks as stunned as I felt listening to Gavin share everything with me earlier.

We'd traveled the distance from my home to hers in silence. I wasn't ready to dive in. Plus, seeing little Grace kicking her legs in her car seat made it difficult to concentrate. Her daughter was so full of smiles and exuberance, it was an odd juxtaposition to how I was feeling.

Once Grace was down for her nap, I slowly warmed up to commencing the conversation. I had to stop on occasion, overcome with grief. But my sweet friend took my hand and tried to offer comfort, even in her shocked state.

"First, I think you should call Dr. Miller on Monday because this is way beyond my pay grade."

A sarcastic chuckle escapes me. "I get it." She's probably right, if I ever needed someone like Dr. Miller to help, it would be now.

"I'm struggling to wrap my head around all of it, Kat. It doesn't feel real."

"I know. I wasn't married to him, and I'm flabbergasted. I can't imagine what you're feeling right now." She takes a sip of water. "God, Poppy. I was so envious. I thought you had it all—a great job, a great guy, traveling everywhere. Then, when Dan got sick, I felt terrible for being jealous. For all you were enduring to care for this brave man." Kat pauses. "Don't get me wrong, I'd never wish ALS or anything like it on anyone. But to think you were the sole breadwinner, rushing home to send the nurse away so you could care for him. And all the while, he was keeping this from you."

Looking out the window toward the lake below, I feel numb. So lost in what is real versus the version of life that was spun for me. "I have more questions than answers right now. But the one person who can give me what I need…" I bite the inside of my cheek, hoping to prevent the return of more tears. He had every opportunity to share this with me. He chose not to. For years and years, he thought lying was the answer.

"Poppy. I'm simply playing devil's advocate here. But are you sure this young man is on the level?"

"What possible reason could he have to visit Dan's grave and tell me all of this? He looked as if the very act of sharing this story was painful for him. He even drove me home."

Kat grows quiet. "But that's just it. Could this be some setup? Like he's trying to convince you that he's Dan's long-lost son so he can get access to his life insurance or retirement somehow?"

Clearly, after everything I've learned in the last twenty-four hours, it's not a stretch to think I may be naïve. Yet, I never once felt suspicious about anything he'd said.

"Like, now he knows where you live. What if—"

The front door bursts open, and Nick unexpectedly comes through. "Hey, hope you've got room at the table for one more tonight. Look who called and wanted to come by."

Kat looks up and smiles. "Hey, Gavin."

"Gavin?" I blurt, jumping to my feet.

"Poppy?"

"How do you two know each other?" Nick asks.

Glancing down at Kat, I give her a knowing stare.

"No way," Kat says, covering her mouth.

"You told her?" Gavin asks.

"Told who what?" Nick's face is a mask of confusion.

"Pull up a chair, dear. Do we have a story to tell you."

Several hours later, long after our conversation, dinner is complete and Kat and I are putting the last of the dishes away, I finally let out an exhale. There's no doubt. What Gavin shared has to be true. This kid is the real deal. Who knew the people he claimed had taken him under their wing when he needed it had been Nick, and later his wife.

Kat reaches for the baby monitor, turning up the volume as Nick puts Grace down for the night. "I'm telling you. Hearing this is like ear porn." Kat giggles. "There's nothing hotter than listening to a man put his child to bed."

I give her an insincere smile. I'm happy for the two of them. Unfortunately, the timing stinks.

"Oh, Poppy. I didn't think about Dan and Gavin."

"Don't, Kat. From all Gavin shared before he called it a night, it didn't sound like they had that kind of relationship."

Kat places a serving spoon into the dishwasher. "It almost feels like Gavin thought the relationship was forced, as if Dan was only going through the motions."

"I just can't figure out why Dan wouldn't have told me. From doing the math, I'm assuming he must have gotten Gavin's mother pregnant around the time of our brief break up my freshman year. Technically, he wasn't cheating if that's the case."

"Why did the two of you break up? Another girl?"

Rinsing off a serving bowl before placing it in the dishwasher, I shake my head. "No. At least, I didn't think so. He told me he was feeling overwhelmed. That things had gotten serious so quickly with us, and he was worried we needed to take a step back, focus on school, and make sure this was what we wanted." I never once contemplated he might be sleeping with other women back then. I was more jealous of his heavy course load. "But it was barely a few months, and he was back saying he was more certain than ever how he felt and that I was the girl he was going to marry."

"Do you think he had any idea she was pregnant when he came back?"

I turn to look at her, deadpan. "I'm not sure of much of anything anymore, Kat. This whole thing is a mystery to me." Taking a sponge to the kitchen counter, I add, "For all I know, she didn't tell him until years later. I mean, did they have time to date during that short period of time? Or was it a one-time hookup? Because if it was the latter, she might not have known how to get in touch with him."

Kat abruptly stops what she's doing and puts her hands on the counter. The last time she had this look on her face, I was about to try on wigs to sneak into a sex club.

"Why am I worried about what's about to come out of your mouth?"

"Just hear me out, Poppy. Shelly's not dead."

"Who?"

"Gavin's mom. Maybe you should talk to her."

The room feels as if it's starting to spin. I may have finally hit my limit on shocks to the system today. Finding a kitchen chair, I plop into it.

Kat rushes over. "Oh god. Are you okay? You look pale."

"I'm all right. I think I might just need to call it a night."

"Oh, Poppy. I'm sorry. I only mentioned it because I think she's your only hope for getting any real answers."

Nodding, I drop my face into my hands. How is this possible? How do I believe anything now? When everything I thought I knew was a lie?

CHAPTER TWENTY-EIGHT
BROADIE

"Dammit."

"What's the matter, Broadie? Stocks drop, and you could end up a lowly millionaire?" Jarod teases.

"Shut up, smartass."

Again, I've called and left messages for Poppy with no return call. Is she mad because I haven't been able to spend time with her after returning home from the club that night? I've sent morning texts and planned to meet for drinks to see if we could compare schedules to go out again.

As much as I've been tempted to call and ask her to come over, I don't ever want her assuming this is only about sex for me. She means too much to me to send those kinds of signals. Hopefully, if she ever finds out I've tried to look in on her mother, she'll realize it's more. Not that I send flowers and cards to Sara to get to Poppy. But her mother is the center of Poppy's universe. It tore me up to see her so distraught when she got word Sara was being hospitalized. I only wanted to be there for both of them. Maybe it was a step too far.

Hell, it wouldn't be the first time I did that.

"Brantly getting after you about the director's position again?"

"No, no."

Jarod drops down into the chair across from my desk. This guy has it all figured out. A beautiful wife and kids, a reasonably priced home in the burbs, and cuts his days short to attend Little League.

So, why is this so hard for me?

"What's going on, man? You haven't seemed like yourself. You got back from your trip and looked better than I'd seen you in years. Fuck. You almost looked relaxed."

Memories of that trip come flooding back, making me smile. God, I pray I'm not left with memories. That I haven't screwed this up with her beyond repair.

"Truth?"

Jarod arches a brow. "It'd be nice."

"I've started dating someone." I rub the stubble along my jaw. "But I've only really had one date with her. And now she's not returning my calls."

"Damn. That bad already? You really do suck at relationships."

Leaning forward, I run my hand down my face. "Why is this so much harder than my job?"

Jarod chuckles. "Most of your patients are under anesthesia. There's a far less chance of a disagreement."

Looking out my office window, I consider this. "Maybe. But we don't really fight. She's almost too understanding."

"And that's a bad thing?"

"Only so much as I don't want her to walk away because she's had enough before I have the opportunity to fix it."

Jarod leans forward in his chair, as if he's about to divulge state secrets. "Here's a thought. Don't let it get that far."

"I know, I know. But it's hard shifting gears. I haven't dated in a decade. And now that I want to, I'm struggling to balance work, my girls, and Poppy."

Jarod's eyes spring wide. "Poppy Danforth?"

I freeze. *Why did I let her name leave my lips?*

"Our Poppy?"

I tense. "No. My Poppy."

Jesus, I've really done it now.

Jarod starts to laugh. "You dumb fucker. The one person on the planet who managed to get her to give them the time of day, and you've already blown it? This isn't the kind of woman you treat like a casual date. If things are going slow, it should be because it was *her* choice. Not yours. Fuck, if she'd given me the chance, there'd be no doubt I was interested. Because there are plenty waiting in the wings who are."

My back stiffens. *Like fuck they are.* But he's right. I've come too far to lose her now.

"Have you sent her flowers?"

Does her mother and her crazy roommate count? "Not recently."

"Does she know you really care about her?"

Leaning back in my chair, I let my head lull backward. Visions of my hand slapping her perky little ass come to mind. "Probably not."

"Well, I'd fix that. Because I can see you care. But women don't like to have to question it. Especially if she's into romance. They already set a high bar."

Fuck.

~

"Dr. Weston?"

"Oh, thanks for coming by, Stu." I wave him into my study. "Take a seat."

"You said there was something you needed."

"There are a couple of things, yes. I wanted to know if you have any more information on the Ashton situation."

"Yes. As a matter of fact, she was let go from her float pool contract with St. Luke's and their sister hospitals as of this week."

Had Ashton actually been a hard-working nurse like her peers, I might've found a way to let Gianni handle her and the NDA she broke. From what Poppy shared, Katarina had overheard Ashton spreading rumors about me in the ER. In retrospect, she seemed to do more gossiping than patient care. It was Ashton divulging private information that caused them to sneak into the club that night. That alone was enough reason for me to want her out of our hospital. And the Devil's Playground. But time was of the essence. We needed to contain her before any more derogatory information was leaked amongst the hospital staff.

Max, Becket, and Derek uncovered a fair amount of dissatisfaction with Ashton's job performance from fellow nurses annoyed with her poor work ethic. Add to it, she had no problem blabbing that she made more money than her peers because she was part of the float pool. Float pool nurses are chosen because they have excellent clinical experience and are willing to work in whatever hospital or department has a need, versus being assigned to a permanent location. Questions started to arise about how Ashton, of all people, managed to land her job.

"So was there enough negative feedback received by the hospital that they were forced to terminate?"

He chuckles. "Not exactly. As it turns out, Ashton doesn't know when to shut up. After all of our work trying to give the hospital cause to fire her, someone anonymously came forward saying they knew Ashton had been hired into the float pool after sucking off an administrator at a sister hospital with enough clout to make the transfer happen. This led to both of their dismissals."

"Nice." I chuckle.

Gianni had already assured me that not only was she persona non grata at DPG but that his legal team came after Ashton hard enough he didn't suspect there'd be any further problem with her.

I take a deep breath. I cannot believe it's come to this. "So, the second thing. It's about Poppy. I haven't seen her at work lately. And when I called the pharmacy, she wasn't in. I know it's farfetched, but I wanted to make sure you guys had seen her and everything was okay." I almost roll my eyes at my damn self. I can't stick security on her simply because she isn't interested in spending time with me.

"Yeah, she hasn't been at work all week."

Alarmed, I sit up taller in my chair. "Is she sick?"

Stu gives me a look. "I'm not sure, boss. She spent the weekend with the couple she went to DPG with. There was another guy there too."

"Must be that friend of Kat and Nick's that got them into the club."

"No. He was younger. Almost looked like he could've been her kid."

Okay, now I'm really confused. Stu is top-notch at what he does. But I'm certain Poppy doesn't have children. *Aren't I?* I mean, she would've brought that up when I spoke about my girls. Right? "Poppy doesn't have kids."

"You're right. Nothing I've researched says differently. But he appeared quite a bit younger."

Reclining back in my chair, I cross my arms behind my head. "Have you seen her with him since that time?"

"No. But we haven't seen much of her. I don't think she's left her house."

Maybe she *is* sick. Part of me wants to go by and check on her. But how would I explain that I know she's been home all week? Her not answering my calls wouldn't explain that. And while she knows I have security watching her for protection, I don't want her becoming irate when she discovers I've gone a step too far and used them to determine her whereabouts.

Hell, Jarod is right. I really do suck at relationships.

∾

Knock, knock, knock.

Nothing.

Knock, knock, knock.

Her car is parked in the driveway. Maybe she's out with someone? I feel like a chump, standing on her doorstep holding flowers and a large container of freshly squeezed lemonade. I start to turn toward the car when the door opens. My face lights up, knowing it's her—until I see her face.

"Poppy, what's wrong?" Her face is swollen, her eyes red. "Is your mother okay?"

"Yes. She's fine." She doesn't elaborate. Doesn't invite me in.

"You haven't been taking my calls. I got worried."

"Don't be. I'll be okay."

This hurts. It feels as if she's plunging a sharp object into my chest. I wouldn't have noticed if someone had done that six months ago. Yet, now, I'm hooked on this woman. And she's shutting me out. "Baby, talk to me."

"No."

Shit. Is it already too late? Jarod was right. I blew this. After everything, I blew my one chance.

"Please. I'm sorry I haven't been here for you."

"It's okay, Broadie. I never asked you to be. I knew where we stood."

Perhaps she should fill me in. Because I thought things were okay.

"Poppy, I—"

"Look. I never asked for more than you were ready to give me. I respected where you were. I'm not upset about it. It was new for us."

"Was?"

Poppy's lips come together in a thin line. "I only meant, I'm in a bad place right now. I need time to sort it out. Alone."

I'm not sure what to say. I don't like this. It's bad enough when things at work force me to feel as if I have no control. But somehow, this is worse.

"Can I just come in and hold you for a minute?"

Her face starts to turn red. She's pissed. "Why is it when you don't have time to see me, busy with work or your friends at the club, that's okay? But if I want space, the same courtesy isn't offered?"

The sweet, poised woman I've come to know now resembles a cauldron about to blow. But she's right. I'm a selfish bastard. The very reason I'd avoided dating was so I didn't treat someone as I'm treating her now. Like her needs are less important than my own.

"You're right. Here." I hold out the flowers and lemonade. If I have to take them back with me, it'll make leaving that much harder. And I really do want her to have them. They weren't bribes. "I'm sorry, Poppy. I'll go."

As she takes the gifts from me, I can see a slight shift in her mood. Her expression isn't quite so stabby. I should feel relieved, but I don't. And not because of anything she's said or done. This is on me.

If I'd tried harder, she'd likely let me in. Not into her home but into her heart. Because I can see how badly she's hurting. This sensation is new. This hollow ache in my chest isn't because she won't allow me to fix her. I acknowledge that's my nature, both in and out of the operating room. But this is different. I had the chance to show her I could be the person who put her above all else. That I could be her safe place to fall.

And I blew it.

CHAPTER TWENTY-NINE
POPPY

"Poppy, it's good to see you."

"Thank you, Dr. Miller. I appreciate you fitting me in."

"I'm glad we could. Tell me what brings you here." His face reflects my anguish. I'm glad this isn't the first time I'm seeing him. He's established the fact he knows what he's doing here. I can relax and empty my worries onto his desk, knowing he's trained to give me the very best advice. Then, ultimately, it's up to me what I do with it.

"I guess I'll just dive right in." I clear my throat, willing myself to stay strong. I'm tired of sniveling. And my face hurts. "I'd noticed a young man loitering around my husband's headstone at the cemetery."

Dr. Miller shifts uncomfortably in his seat. I raise my hand, sensing where his mind has gone.

"He didn't hurt me."

His face instantly relaxes.

"Not physically, anyway. He claims to be my dead husband's son."

Dr. Miller sits quietly with his hands steepled together like he did in the past when he wanted me to continue. So, I do.

"As best I can tell, it appears my husband fathered this child during a breakup we'd had in college. At least, that's the way I calculate the timing.

But instead of letting me know what happened, he continued to be in this child's life, while leaving me completely in the dark. The young man says when he was a boy, Dan would visit every few months. But this stopped abruptly around the time Dan became wheelchair-bound."

"Wow. That's quite the revelation. Do you believe this young man?"

"I have no reason not to."

Dr. Miller nods. "While I'm here to help you deal with the emotional aspects of uncovering such information, I still recommend you get a DNA test. I think enough has been hidden that you should encourage him to at least confirm it once and for all. If nothing more than to protect yourself."

"From what?"

"If you were unaware of a son, there might also be some monetary provision set aside by your husband you know nothing about. Or this boy may simply feel he's entitled to something."

"You're probably right. I'll look into that." I pause before adding, "I can't explain it, Dr. Miller. My inclination after all of this is to not believe anything anyone says. Yet, I believe this young man. And I don't think he's looking for anything but answers. And, as it turns out, he has good references."

"I don't understand."

"He's a friend of Kat and Nick Barnes. Nick has known him for years. He was assigned as his 'big brother' with the Big Brothers, Big Sisters organization. Now that he's eighteen, they consider him family."

"Small world."

"Well, that's Hanover for you." I give a cynical chuckle. "Small towns." I shrug.

"It appears to me that you're handling this quite well."

"Ha!" I shake my head. "Looks can be deceiving. I think I've cried long enough I'm numb to a lot of it now, which is how I handled losing my husband. Given that took me nearly eight years to come to terms with, I thought it best I see you this time."

Dr. Miller gives me a Hollywood-worthy Matthew McConaughey smile. Jeez, could they be related? I can't believe Katarina never asked him. I mean, I wouldn't put it past her.

"I appreciate this is a lot to learn about your spouse. Especially when he's no longer available to answer the questions you have."

Wiggling my finger at him, my conversation with Katarina comes to mind. "Well, according to Kat, there's one other person who could provide the answers I need."

"That's certainly an option if you feel that strongly about your questions. But at what cost? I warn you to consider this before meeting with her. Your husband has been gone for years. Do you want to open the door to questions you might not want to know the answers to?"

He's right. There's nothing in me that believes he was engaging in an affair with Gavin's mother. Physical or otherwise. And Gavin never expressed that Dan's visits were anything more than brief moments spent with his son. Nothing else. But it's clear I can't trust what we had. Meeting her might open Pandora's box. Have me questioning things that are no longer relevant.

"What is the main emotion you've felt since being confronted with this, Poppy?"

"Fear."

"Not anger?"

"Sure, I'm angry. But that feels like a wasted emotion. The main person I'm angry with is gone. What he stole, I'll never get back."

"And that is?"

"Trust. How am I supposed to believe anyone now?"

Dr. Miller grows quiet, those steepled hands beneath his chin causing him to seem all-knowing. "Tell me this. If he'd told you while he was still alive, would it have changed anything? Lessened the betrayal?"

"It depends. If he'd told me early on, it might have. But it's the years of hiding it that make me feel this way. This young man is an adult now. Regardless of whether I could've been involved in his son's life, Dan ruined my ability to trust someone."

Dr. Miller shakes his head. "I concede, what he did was wrong. Selfish. Cowardly. But no one can take away your ability to trust. That's on you. Sure, it may be more difficult now that you've experienced betrayal of this magnitude. But trust and forgiveness don't have to be a life sentence. Make it a choice."

Biting my lip, I know he's right. If I want to live a healthy, happy life, I need to find a way to move on from this. I'm not certain I can forgive Dan for the lies. But I can try to accept things for what they are. It doesn't mean everyone in my life will treat me with such duplicity.

"What have you been doing since we last spoke?"

"What do you mean?"

"You left here with a spring in your step. Ready to take on the world."

Reflecting on that visit, he's right. I was so proud of how far I'd come. How I'd managed my grief. Feeling more than a little miffed at my current situation, I consider that had I learned this news years ago, it may have made me angry enough to push past my sorrow. I could have rejoined the living years sooner. But then again, I may have been too bitter to trust again. Who knows?

"I'm kind of dating someone. But I'm not sure how that's going anymore. After I learned of Dan's double life, I pushed him away."

"You are both adults. What you are going through isn't easy. As I said before, if after discussing things with him openly, he can't understand your needs, you'll have your answer. But I hope you have something else to focus on besides the men in your past and present."

"I do. I've gotten back into art. I missed my last few classes, but I'm more determined than ever to dive in."

Dr. Miller stands from his desk, signaling our time together has come to a close. "What type of art? Painting, sculpture, photography?"

"It's pottery. More specifically, kintsugi."

"Ah, embracing the flawed or imperfect."

"Yes." I clap. Unbelievable. Not only did I not cry the whole time I was here, but I'm leaving excited about something. This man's a genius. "Thank you, Dr. Miller. I don't know how you do it. But I feel so much better after seeing you."

"You give me too much credit, Poppy." He winks, and I can't control my blush. *Matthew McConaughey just winked at me.*

Driving home from Dr. Miller's office, I notice a familiar intersection, and a thought comes to mind. If I recall correctly, he said he wanted me to know where he lived. I giggle.

I can't believe I'm doing this. A week ago, I swore I was done with men. So why is this surgeon getting under my skin?

As I turn down the street lined with impressive homes built on gated multi-acre lots, my stomach is doing backflips. It's been several weeks since I turned Broadie away from my doorstep. He was sweet to bring flowers and attentive to notice I enjoyed lemonade. But I was feeling manipulated.

I'm no longer going to tolerate relationships where I must accept whatever they're willing to give. This needs to be a fifty-fifty partnership. In Broadie's defense, this is an area he's trying to work on. But he needs to know that if he wants space, it works both ways.

Parking my car in the driveway, I can feel my pulse thrumming in my neck. I doubt he's even home at 4:00 p.m. on a Thursday.

I walk up the steps, take a deep breath, and close my eyes.

Here goes nothing.

CHAPTER THIRTY
BROADIE

"I'll let you know when I'm ready to head out, Porter."

"And you want to drive, not fly?"

"It sounds like there will be a lengthy delay waiting to take off. I just want to get out of here."

"You've got it, sir."

Knock, knock.

"Who the fuck is that?" I grumble. This day has been shit. Okay, the last few weeks have been shit. I can't take it anymore.

The patient our wound care team had so diligently fought to heal had to suffer an amputation when, despite their efforts, the infection continued to spread. Brantly Martin and his incessant whining about that medical director position. I've already told him no, for fuck's sake. Now he seems to be intentionally creating meetings and distractions from my workday. My daughters never seem to have time to see me when I'm available. Can't they see I'm trying here?

But deep down, the problem is me. I'm pissed that I have no control over the things that are most important to me. It's annoying when things occur at work that could've gone better. It's frustrating when I attempt to make time to spend with my family, and it's not convenient. But my job and my kids aren't going anywhere.

Poppy. Now that's another matter entirely.

I don't like that I had the chance to go all in, as Jarod put it. And when I was too late, she called me on it. It felt like I was being punished. There's no fighting it. I want her. Not just physically. I want a healthy relationship with her. But the lack of control I'm feeling is maddening. If I can't find a way to ease this chaos swirling around me, I'm afraid I'll become unhinged.

The days of calling a willing female to let me quiet the storm are over if I ever want a monogamous relationship with a woman. And I'd never want to hurt Poppy. But maybe what I need is beyond the pale. Perhaps I'm wired in such a way that I was right to avoid relationships.

Swinging open the front door, I notice Poppy jump in response to my ire. What is she doing here?

On the one hand, she's the perfect medicine. No one makes me feel like she does. But on the other, she's too big a risk. If I hurt her, I may lose any chance at a future with her. *Jesus. What the hell is wrong with me?* I'm forty-two and feel like a defective monster.

"This isn't a good time, Poppy."

Her face falls. I have no idea why she's here. Maybe she thought it would be easier to make a clean break in person. Yet she doesn't appear solemn and serious as I'd expect she'd look if she was here to that end. She has on a pale yellow blouse paired with a short blue skirt. She's wearing the wedge sandals I bought for her in Jamaica, the little silver anklet around her left leg arousing my dick as I picture it over my shoulder. *Shit.*

"I wanted to say I was sorry for the way I pushed you away. I needed some space. It wasn't about you."

Turning away from her, I'm growing increasingly uncomfortable. I've fallen so hard for this woman. But we can't seem to get on the same page. Okay, so maybe I've met my match because she won't accept whatever page I choose to give her.

Suddenly, I feel her soft hand on my wrist. Fuck. I want to pull her into me. Close this door to the rest of the world. But I'm too far gone. Too angry that I can manage a successful surgical practice and billions of dollars worth of investments but can't figure out how to let someone in.

Poppy takes a step closer. "Can we talk? Just for a minute?"

"I'm heading out. It's not a good idea that we talk when I'm like this."

"Where are you going?" Her tone carries a bite to it.

My gaze snaps to hers, confirming her suspicions. "Meeting the guys for a drink."

"Ah. So, it's okay if you're with them when you're like this?" She uses her fingers to make air quotes around 'like this.' "I guess I misunderstood what was happening here." She waves her finger back and forth between the two of us.

"Poppy. I don't want to hurt you."

"But that's exactly what you're doing. You hand me scraps and then withhold when you should be talking to me." The weight of her statement causes me to wonder if this isn't something more. She thrusts her finger into my chest, startling me. "Am I not worth it? Am I only useful for a good lay when you're in the right mood?"

"Hell no, Pop. You're all I want. I don't want to physically hurt you. Because I'm more than a little off the chains right now."

She comes closer, standing tall and proud. "I thought you wanted to be with me."

"I do," I practically plead. "But when things get too much, this is how I've had to deal with it." Shit. I don't even know what I'm planning to do once I get there. Maybe drink until I can't see straight. "I'd never touch another woman. Hell, I don't think I could get off with anyone but you. You're all I want."

"Then we better learn how to handle when things get too much."

Fuck. I'm falling so hard for this woman, I worry I'll never recover. "I don't think you know what you're asking for."

Bzzz. Bzzz.

I pull the phone to my ear. "Hello?"

"You need more time, boss?"

Poppy is close enough, I'm sure she's hearing every word of this conversation. But she's right. We need to stop this dance. If there's a chance for us, we need to take it. Talk about limits. Agree to be equals. Make time for one another. I'm not willing to walk away because I haven't learned how to make her a priority. "There's been a change of plans, Porter. Can you let Stu know I'll be staying home tonight?"

"Yes, sir. Anything else you need from me before I sign off for the night?"

"No. I have everything I need." My eyes bore into her.

Poppy places her hands flat on my chest. Her ruby-red lips pulling me to her like a magnet. "Take what you need, Dr. Weston."

CHAPTER THIRTY-ONE
POPPY

Broadie's expression turns dark. What is wrong with me that I find this more exciting than frightening? "On your knees, Poppy."

Holy cow. I had no idea I was walking into this an hour ago. But yes, please. Dropping onto the floor in front of him, I almost laugh. Is the door even closed?

"If, at any time, I'm hurting you, or it gets to be too much, tell me to stop."

"I don't even get to pick a safe word? Like orangutang or something?"

His right brow tents, and he gives me a smirk. He may be acting like Mr. Alpha, but that flirty dimple tells me there's still a playful side here. "Orangutang? That's the best you could come up with?"

"I thought it was better than baboon."

"Are you trying to get that pretty little ass red?"

"Oh, don't tease."

Out of the blue, there's a sparkle in his eye as he gazes down at me. I can't explain it. But I immediately know we're going to be okay. It's as if he's sending me a signal that my willingness to try to give him what he needs is enough. That I'm enough.

Broadie steps forward, grabbing my hair and yanking my chin to look up at him. "Hands behind your back. Don't speak. Do as you're told. And if you're a good girl, I might let you come."

I clamp my lips together, gulping down the lump in my throat. He can be worried all he wants. But there's no doubt in my mind that he'd never hurt me. His demons are internal. His inner war over letting an equal into his unbalanced life. Beyond that, in these moments, I've never felt safer.

"Eyes down, baby girl."

Jeez, he might make me come just using these pet names.

He moves behind me, and I hear what sounds like a code being typed into a pad. I didn't pay that much attention to the security when I was here before. I was too enraptured by him and his thoughtfulness.

My head is yanked back by my hair, while another hand wraps around my throat. "I want to feel those soft ruby-red lips sliding up and down my cock. But if I tell you to stop, you stop. Do you understand?"

"Yes, sir," I purr. This girl doesn't read spicy books for nothing. This is a freaking dream come true.

He lets go of my head and comes to stand in front of me. His thick, veiny dick in his hand. I swear my lady bits have their own pulse right now. Just the sight of him with his talented fingers wrapped around that impressive cock has me drooling. *Everywhere.*

"Open," he barks.

I drop my mouth open as wide as I can. My tongue practically curling in anticipation. A hiss escapes him as the soft tip of his dick glides into my mouth. There's no inching his way in, he holds my head still as he drives in until he hits the back of my throat. My eyes immediately water, and my gag reflex kicks in. *That's gotta be hella sexy.*

"Fuck, yes, baby." He trails his thumb around my lips as he pushes back into my throat. "You're taking my cock like a good girl."

Well, maybe it is.

As his dick slides in and out of my mouth, I try to hold my jaw open wide and breathe through my nose. He's a lot to take. But the sensation of his heavy cock as it moves over my tongue combined with his dirty words… well, there might be an embarrassingly large wet spot on this floor when I get up.

Broadie has my hair in his fists, fucking my face, and I'd give anything to touch myself right now. Abruptly, he stops, and I wonder what's happening but try to stay still.

He withdraws from me, lifts me up by my throat, and brings me to the kitchen island, where he swiftly bends me over before ripping my panties down.

Thwack.

"Oh!" I can't control my whimper. The unexpected slap has my legs quivering.

I can feel his warm breath hit the shell of my ear as he bends over me. "You think I wouldn't notice you squirming? Trying to rub those pretty thighs together for relief?"

Thwack.

"No one but me is making that pussy wet. You understand me?"

Overwhelmed, I'm unsure if I'm allowed to speak so I simply nod vigorously.

Cool air hits my skin as he steps away from me. I want desperately to watch what he's doing, but if the slaps to my backside keep up at this rate, I'll never be able to sit down.

"Oh, that ass. Do you have any idea how much I want to fuck that pretty little ass?"

Slap or no slap, I look over my shoulder in alarm. I never contemplated he would go there. I thought he merely meant he was going to be rough. Yet, I completely lose all concern over being initiated into that club when my eyes land on his hands. One hand is cupping his balls, while the other is stroking his cock, all while his eyes are feasting on my backside. Holy hell, this man.

Fighting the desire to squirm again, I try to face forward and keep my trembling limbs under control.

A few moments go by without feeling his touch, and it's almost unnerving. What is he doing?

Broadie's hand wraps around my throat, pulling my head back as I feel him tease my opening with the head of his cock. It's taking all of my willpower not to back onto him. He's making me crazy. Is this what he meant? He was going to torture me by making me wait for it?

All of a sudden, he slams into me and stills. I appreciate the brief moment of hesitation as my body attempts to accommodate the invasion. It doesn't last long before he's pounding into me. The more forceful the thrust, the tighter the hold on my throat. It's not tight enough to make me lightheaded or fear for my ability to breathe. Yet it's a constant reminder of who's in charge. And boy, do I like it.

Thwack.

"Oh," I cry. I wasn't expecting that. But the sting of the strike of his palm combined with the rapid battering of my swollen flesh is making me come unglued. If he was that aggressive about squirming, what will he do if I can't hold out until he gives me permission?

Before I can contemplate the possibilities, he pulls out and spins me around. Lifting my top over my shoulders, he quickly unsnaps my bra and throws it to the side before squeezing my breasts together, taking turns sucking from each one. Jeez, I'm almost euphoric. It's like an out-of-body experience watching this man take what he wants.

Scooping me up into his arms, he carries me over to the sofa. As he tosses me down, I scoot back to make room. For what, I have no idea.

Broadie bends down, pulling my skirt from my hips so I'm completely bare to him. He stands beside the couch, still wearing his shirt, his pants unzipped, and his stiff cock exposed. When did he put the condom on? I watch intently as he begins to undress, devouring me with hungry eyes.

Once he's naked, he climbs over top of me, straddling my chest. My eyes are wide in anticipation when he leans forward and repeatedly pushes his hard dick between my breasts. Good lord, this man is an animal. I had no idea this kind of thing happened in real life.

"You want to come, baby?"

Again, although I'd prefer to shout it from the rooftops, I nod.

He stands, pulls me up, and directs me to sit on his lap. I'm a little nervous about this position, given his size. But I follow his lead.

"You're shaking. You scared, little one?"

I want to tell him no but also ask if he can keep calling me that.

Shaking my head, I climb on top and hold onto his shoulders as I start to lower myself. But he places his hands on my hips and slams me down onto his rigid length, practically knocking the wind out of me.

"It's okay, Pop," he whispers as he caresses my ass with his hands. "Rock back and forth if you need to."

Doing as he says, I can feel the moment when my inner walls relax. But the friction against my swollen skin as I sway to and fro is so good. I don't want to stop.

"Up and down, baby. I need you to slide up and down on me." He pants.

Putting added weight on my knees, I do as I'm told and am rewarded with the pad of a finger circling my swollen clit. I throw my head back in complete ecstasy, his tongue licking the underside of my breast before sucking a nipple into his mouth.

There's no way I'm going to be able to wait for him to give me permission. I'm so wet, this orgasm is only moments away from happening. Will it make him mad? Will all my efforts to give him what he wants be in vain?

Unable to stop myself, the pace with which I'm riding him picks up.

"That's it, Pop. Fuck me." He grabs my hands from his shoulders, pulling them behind my back, encircling my wrists as he continues to nip and suck at my nipples. I can feel myself tighten around him. "Oh, shit, that's it." Restraining my wrists with one hand, he moves the other in front of me, his thumb thrumming against my sex, and I know my orgasm is happening with or without his say so. "Come all over my cock, baby."

I let out a scream as my orgasm tears through me.

Broadie lets go of my arms and lifts me up from him far enough he can buck his hips wildly into me. "Fuck. Oh, fuck, Pop." I can feel him shudder inside me as he pulls me back down on top of him. The combination of his heavy breathing and the sexy swearing he's chanting beneath me could practically get me going all over again. But I'm not sure my legs could go another round.

Or my ass.

I lie still for a moment, expecting his sweet words of praise. Yet instead, he lifts me off of him and walks away without looking back. *What the heck?*

After a few moments, I gather my clothes and dress. I'm not sure what the protocol is for this kind of thing. I wanted him to take what he needed, but I'd hoped when his release came, he'd be back to the kind, affectionate man I remembered. Is this behavior part of the rough sex? Being dismissed?

'Cause I'm not a fan.

About twenty minutes later, I've had enough and decide to go in search of him. As I reach his doorway, I find him sitting on the edge of his bed, freshly showered. He's leaning forward, elbows on his knees, with his face buried in his hands.

"Broadie?" I ask cautiously.

He peers up at me, stunned. "You stayed?"

"I didn't realize I'd been dismissed." My tone is curt. "Do you want me to go?"

"No!" He gives me an apologetic look, those whiskey eyes holding more emotion than I can decipher. "I'm sorry, Poppy. I'm..."

"What?"

He drops his head, unable to make eye contact with me. "I'm so ashamed. The way I've treated you. You deserve so much more. What's wrong with me? I'm crazy about you, but I keep giving you one reason after another to walk away." My heart aches watching him. He looks anguished.

Coming closer, I take a seat before reaching over to stroke his stubbled jaw.

"You deserve someone who'll cherish you. Protect you. Not pounce on you like an animal."

Pushing my thumb into the space where I know that dimple should be, I whisper, "But that's the part I liked."

His head snaps up, his eyes full of hope.

"You weren't that rough. Were you holding back because it was me?"

"No. You were perfect." He drops down to the floor, burying his forehead into my lap. "You're everything I want. You said to take what I needed. But this isn't who I want to be with you. This controlling asshole who takes and takes. I'm generally a happy, well-adjusted man. My life may not be well balanced, but I'm usually even-tempered." He pauses for a moment, rocking his head in my lap from side to side. "But sometimes, all of the stress and lack of control catch up to me. It's how I've learned to cope. But I don't want to detach anymore. I want to handle the pressure before it impacts you."

Running my fingers through his damp hair, I pray we've reached a turning point somehow. "I'm here when you're stressed. Bring your tension to me. I know you'd never hurt me. We all handle things in our own way. I'd much rather know we're there for one another than worry you need to detach from your troubles with something or someone else. Don't run away and drown your worries in a bottle of scotch or a meaningless one night stand. Share it with me."

Broadie looks up, an odd mix of relief and optimism swimming in his eyes. "Please don't ever leave me."

I feel a warmth bloom in my chest. Feeling embolden I say, "I think we should be done with giving each other space. We're good together. Can I see more of you?"

"Yes. I want that too, Pop. No more promises. I'm making changes. You and my girls are my priority."

"I'd love to meet them one day."

His smile could light the whole house. "They were the ones who encouraged me to ask you out."

"What? How'd they know anything about me?"

You were at Luigi's a few months ago with some guy. They saw that I couldn't stop staring at you." He chuckles. "They swore you weren't into him. My oldest, Lauren, thinks she's a professional matchmaker."

I shuffle through my memories, trying to recall the night in question. "Oh, that was my brother." I laugh.

Broadie buries his face back into my lap. "No other woman could bring me to my knees, Poppy. I'll do anything to make this work."

"Well, I can handle anything you can dish out. So long as it doesn't involve cheating or lies."

CHAPTER THIRTY-TWO
POPPY

BZZZ. BZZZ.

"Hello." I giggle.

"Good morning." Broadie's sexy voice comes across the line, and I wish I could snuggle up with him.

"What? No text this morning?"

"I couldn't wait to hear your voice. I miss you."

"It's been two days."

"That's forty-eight hours."

"I knew you'd be good at math."

"No, seriously. I need to see you. There's something I want to talk to you about."

I wave at Abbie who's entered the pharmacy, giving me a curious smile in response to the dreamy one I must be wearing right now. "Oh, yeah? This sounds serious," I tease.

"It is. I've been trying to approach the subject for months, but it was never the right time. I wanted to tell you the other night, but things were too heavy. But I can't put it off any longer."

"Now I'm nervous. Should I be worried?"

The line grows quiet. I assume he's been interrupted by someone at work, but admittedly, I'm a little anxious by this discussion.

"What time can you come over?"

"Is eight okay? I'm working 'til seven tonight."

"Yes. I'll see you then."

"Bye."

Hanging up the call, I reach for a patient medication sticker as Abbie comes closer. "Nice to see you with such a big smile on your face." She beams.

"Yeah. I kinda like it too."

Bzzz. Bzzz.

Pulling my cell phone from my lab coat pocket, I notice a new message.

> 8:15 A.M.
> BROADIE
> Is it eight yet?

I giggle and put my phone away. Hoping I'll be able to concentrate the rest of the day.

"Poppy, can you run this down to the ER? They're all out of rabies vaccine."

"Sure. No problem, Frank."

As I arrive at the ER, there's a commotion inside. I move out of the way as a gurney rolls by with an EMT actively doing CPR. Richard, one of the pharmacists assigned to the ER, follows the gurney along with a nurse who is pushing the code cart. Watching the lifeless body on the stretcher immediately causes me to think of Dan. He never received CPR, as given his condition, he chose to have do not resuscitate orders if anything were to happen to him. Yet, I'll never forget the moment they said he no longer had a pulse. The internal war within me was screaming to give him one more chance, as if CPR would fix all of the other issues.

It's so hard to let go. And even though I'm angry with him now for not trusting me enough to share his secret, my heart still aches when I think about that sad day.

"Poppy."

I look to the left and find Ava coming toward me. "Thank you for bringing that down. I have a man who got bitten by a stray dog. It actually crushed his finger. I wanted to get his first dose of rabies prophylaxis started."

"Oh, of course. Here you go. Is Kat working today?"

"Yes. I think she ran to get something from the cafeteria."

"If you see her, will you tell her I said hi?"

"Sure. Catch you later, Poppy." She waves as she walks swiftly back down the hall.

As the doors swing open, and I see grilled cheese and fries on Katarina's plate, my stomach literally growls. "Oh, that looks good. I haven't gotten anything from the grill in so long."

Kat gives me a flat smile. I wonder what that's about.

"Poppy, it's probably not that—"

"Kat, can you give us a hand?" one of the triage nurses yells beside a patient who appears to be bleeding all over the floor.

"Sure, be right there." Kat darts over to the nurses' lounge and places her food inside before running back out. "See you, Poppy."

"Bye. Good luck," I mutter, happy to return to the safety of my quiet pharmacy.

As I make my way down the hall, the smell of freshly baked bread wafts from the cafeteria, prompting me to look at my watch. Well, it is 11:45. I admit it. I'm weak. The memory of Kat's cheesy sandwich and fries is too tempting. Might as well save myself a trip and grab lunch while I'm here.

As I reach the dining area, I notice a few people congregated around the floor-to-ceiling glass windows that overlook the atrium and outdoor seating areas. Coming closer, I turn to see what has their attention and freeze.

Three large posters are taped to the glass. My eyes jump from one to the next. *Wait a minute. What?*

Stepping closer, as if my eyes have deceived me, I find each colorful poster contains a picture of a happy family. Three happy families. Three happy families who won trips to Jamaica from St. Luke's.

I'm confused. If there are three of them posted, and no one from the hospital contacted me directly about winning a trip...

"Poppy?"

Spinning on my heel, I come face to face with a very wary Broadie Weston.

"I can explain."

No. He didn't.

I've been had.

CHAPTER THIRTY-THREE
POPPY

"Poppy, please," he begs, practically chasing me down the hall.

I'm so pissed off I can't even look at him.

"Please, wait." He reaches for my arm, and I swat it away.

"You really should go, Broadie. You wouldn't want to air your dirty laundry where everyone can hear. I mean, you have an image to protect."

"Stop."

I halt, turning to face him, not caring who's in earshot. "What would all of these people think? Huh? If they knew the lengths you went to. Just to get to little old me." I hurl the last word at him before I hastily walk toward the safety of my department. The hell with lunch. I feel like I could throw up.

"Wait." He grabs for my arm again, and I step away.

"I said no lies. I put up with everything else. All I said was don't lie to me."

All of sudden, I'm whirled around and pushed through a set of doors. It isn't until I'm able to gather my senses that I realize he's pushed me into the chapel.

"Poppy. I'm sorry. I kept trying to find a way to tell you. But there was never a good time. I was going to tell you on the last day of the trip. But you needed to get back to your mom. Then there were others, but I'd managed to get out of the doghouse about something else and wanted the smoke to clear."

"Are you really trying to make excuses for this? You sent me an email saying I'd won. You pretended the whole time we were together it was merely a coincidence. And you kept on lying once we returned home." I cross my arms over my chest, wondering what the hell is wrong with me that these are the men I'm attracted to.

"I just wanted a chance. One chance to prove how good we could be together."

"But the chance was built on lies. And not just one or two little white lies. This was full-on manipulation!" I screech before I remember where I am. Heck, God should understand what I'm feeling better than anyone.

"Poppy, I—"

"Sit down."

"What?"

"For a smart guy, you better listen up. Sit. Down." I point to the pew beside me, and he quickly takes a seat.

"You want to know why I pulled away from you and needed space?" I don't wait for him to answer. "Because I found out my deceitful husband had a child with another woman. And hid it from me for years!" I stop for a moment, looking away, hoping to calm the rage I'm feeling before someone calls security on us.

"I still don't know all of the details. But apparently, he managed to knock up some woman while we were in college, proceeded to marry me without sharing any of the details, and then withheld his having a child while he continued to visit them. The entire length of our marriage," I say louder than necessary. "I only found out when I saw the boy visiting Dan's grave."

Shaking my head, trying to hold back my tears, I can tell Broadie is in complete shock. "What a laugh they must've had at my expense. Right here in the same town, all of those years. I thought he was off earning sales on the road. But he was playing catch with his kid. Then coming home to me, acting as if nothing ever happened."

"Poppy—"

I swiftly throw my hand up, halting him from joining this conversation.

"It took years, but I'd finally healed from losing the man I'd devoted my life to. The man I fed, bathed, dressed, and helped go to the bathroom because he could no longer do it on his own. I gave him everything. And yet, there was never a right time to tell me what he'd done."

I see the moment he gets it, and Broadie's head drops. "I went to counseling. Told him I was afraid I'd never be able to trust another man. But he convinced me that trust is a choice. I shouldn't let the sins of one man ruin my chances at a happy life."

Broadie glances up, looking defeated.

"Ha! The jokes on me."

Broadie buries his face in his hands.

"I spent years devoted to a man who betrayed me. Only to allow another one to manipulate me in the most egregious way. How dare you!"

Walking toward the doors to the chapel, I stop long enough to turn back to him and make one last thing very clear.

"This is over."

CHAPTER THIRTY-FOUR
POPPY

I stretch across the bed, my face buried in my pillow, feeling for the box of Kleenex. Patting all around, I come up empty. "Grrr…"

Lifting my weary head, I see it just out of arm's reach. Leaning in that direction, I grab a corner of the box and manage to pull it to me, only to find it empty. Flopping face-first back into my soggy pillow, I wince at the sensation as I have an epiphany.

Pushing myself up on my elbow, I flip my pillow over and collapse back in. There. That's better.

I'd managed two days before I could have a day off to wallow in this. And wallow I have. But I'm entitled. And I'm getting this out of my system before I head back to work, darn it. There's no way I'm letting him see me like this. He's stolen enough from me. Or should I say, bought? He's not entitled to my tears.

So, for now, I listen to Billie Eilish singing "What Was I Made For?" on an endless loop.

Trying to find a silver lining to this experience, I focus on what I've learned:

1. Never trust a man.
2. Keep this to yourself, or Kat or Agnes might have you on a Tinder date before the day is over.
3. Don't listen to Billie Eilish when you're depressed.
4. If you're ever, in any way, tempted by a sexy smile, refer back to number one.

CHAPTER THIRTY-FIVE
POPPY

"Poppy. You have another delivery!" Abbie yells from the front of the pharmacy.

"You take it."

"You don't even want to see this one?" She pauses. "Wow, this one is stunning, Poppy."

"Don't care." Of course, it is. If you can't get what you want honestly, you maneuver and buy your way in. I'm not letting this man get to me.

Even if I can't stop thinking about him.

Sensing a presence behind me as I compound a medication in the sterile hood, I look over my shoulder to find Abbie leaning against the door frame. She's grasping a monochrome bouquet of some of the prettiest white flowers imaginable. Roses, anemones, and ranunculus, peonies, and hydrangeas tied tightly within a satin bow.

"Are you going to tell me what's going on?"

"Nope."

"C'mon, Poppy. My life is so dull. I work here, go to class, and then take care of my baby brother while I spend my evenings buried in chemistry books. Let me live through you a little."

"Trust me, Abbie. My life isn't how it seems." My task complete, I package it for the patient and walk to the sink to wash my hands. There was a time, even I thought I had it all. Yet my life was all smoke and mirrors. "It always looks greener in someone else's yard."

"Heck, Poppy. I don't even have a yard. Literally." She chuckles. "But I think I'd settle for a bad boyfriend after this draught."

"I'd rather be alone," I snap.

She comes closer, sans flowers. "But someone cares enough to keep sending you those." Abbie points behind her. It's been almost a month of these nonstop deliveries. I haven't disclosed who they're from, instead calling the volunteers to come pick them up and deliver them to some of the patients without visitors.

"I've discovered there's a fine line between the words care and control."

Abbie climbs onto a stool, appearing to mull over my words. "Did he cheat?"

"No." I reach into my pocket, finding a small tube of hand lotion. "But I'm a strong, independent woman. I don't need any man manipulating me."

Abbie logs into the computer where she's seated. "I guess." She grows quiet. "I just don't want to end up all alone like my mother. She works all the time to take care of my brother and me. And then goes to sleep alone, only to do it all over again the next day; for years, that's been her life."

Turning to her, I reach over and rub her arm. "Did your mother and father go through a bad divorce?"

"No. My dad died when I was sixteen. He had lung cancer. Never smoked a day in his life but died of lung cancer."

"I'm so sorry, Abbie."

"Yeah. Me too. He was the best." Her voice quivers a bit with her reflection of him. "But my mother has decided she's had her chance at love. But she's not even forty yet."

I get it. I'd almost joined that club. I'd given up on men. There was no one in my mind that could ever measure up to how contented I felt with Dan. Look how that turned out. Dan let me down, keeping his double life a secret from me. Then Broadie comes along and gives me hope.

He made me feel confident. I felt more alive than I ever had before. I took chances, lived in the moment, and gave myself permission to explore physical intimacy without shame. My lips turn down into a deep frown, realizing it was all built on lies. He went to extraordinary lengths to get what he wanted.

"You'd really prefer to spend the rest of your days alone than try to find love again?"

Her question breaks through my torturous thoughts. It's unnerving because she's right. I do want to find love again. I'd given up on happily ever after—until him. I'd never been that happy. Not even with Dan. Yet, I refuse to teach any man that it's okay to treat me that way.

"I don't think anyone prefers to live that way, Abbie. But finding one partner with whom you share love, trust, and respect is hard enough. Two is near impossible." She doesn't need to know I'd mistakenly given my trust to both of them. That's my cross to bear.

Abbie shrugs her shoulders before hopping off her stool to collect the medications she needs to deliver. "All I know, if I had someone as mad about me as you do, I'd find a way to make that work."

~

"Poppy, wait up."

Holding the door open to the outdoor dining area, I see Kat running toward me. "What are you doing here?"

Kat's dressed in street clothes instead of her usual scrubs. "I wanted to bring Nick lunch. We got distracted last night, and I didn't have a chance to pack a lunch for him." She waggles her brows at me.

"Oh my gosh, Katarina. You really are living your best life." The words barely leave my lips before a hollow ache fills my chest.

So were you, Poppy. So were you.

"Well, it must be love if I'll drive an hour to bring him tuna fish casserole." She giggles.

I shake my head at my vivacious friend. "Did you get to see him after all of that?"

"Barely. I got one kiss, an ass slap, and a see ya later," she says, rolling her eyes.

Oh how the tables have turned. I hate to admit how jealous I am of what the two of them have found together. Digging into my sad-looking salad, I try to focus on my meal and not on the empty feeling inside. Apparently, my acting sucks because Kat wraps her hand over mine.

"I know you don't have long for lunch. And I don't want to upset you at work. But talk to me, Poppy."

"There's nothing to say."

Kat reaches over and steals a thin slice of carrot from my plate. "There's plenty to say. He was in love with you."

"You've lost it. He wanted something he couldn't have. I'd turned him down, so he manipulated me into getting his way. Mission accomplished."

Kat leans back in her chair, crossing her arms over her chest. "I didn't realize you were so easily swayed."

"What does that mean?"

She leans in, looking me straight in the eyes. "The Poppy I know wouldn't have put on a red wig and a pair of fuck me heels to sneak into a sex club and learn about the man she was falling for unless *she* was in control of her feelings. No man can engineer that. Broadie may have gotten the ball rolling, but what you had with him was the real deal. And you know it."

Putting my fork down, I turn away from her and rapidly blink away tears. It did feel real. Nothing makes sense to me anymore.

"Poppy," Kat tries to comfort me. "Are you sure it has to be this way?"

"Yes. How do I forgive what he did? Especially after everything I've learned Dan did. How do I trust anyone after what these two have pulled?"

"Well, you can't compare what Broadie did to Dan. You were married to him for years. He was lying about where he was and who he was with."

Wiping my mouth with my napkin, I start to get defensive. "Broadie lied too."

"But he did it because he was nuts about you. And you wouldn't give him a chance. Sure, he's a spoiled rich kid who used his power to get what he wants. And he wants you."

Looking past Kat, I watch hospital staff grabbing their meals and chatting as if they haven't got a care in the world, while I mourn, again. Except this one is different. I didn't lose a spouse to a fatal medical condition. I lost the dream of what could be. For a brief moment in time, a man made me feel special and adored. Made me believe I deserved more.

"Do you think you would've actually given him a chance if he hadn't done what he did?"

"Yes," I snap, feeling oversensitive. "Maybe." *Be honest, Poppy. No.*

Kat gives me a skeptical look. "Look past his sin for a minute, Poppy. It has to feel nice that a man like that would go to such lengths for you."

She's right. There've been many nights I've almost reached for my phone, wanting to reason away his misdeeds. "It's all a game to men like that. I was a challenge. Nothing more. And I folded like a cheap deck of cards."

Kat shakes her head, looking disappointed. "You're wrong. He's crazy about you. He's sent enough flowers to open a Cygnature Blooms satellite location at St. Luke's." She pauses. "And I can barely look at him."

"What?"

"Poppy, the first few days, when I passed him in the hall…" She turns away, her eyes watery. "It broke my heart. He looked so sad."

That hollow ache in my chest roars back to life until I realize she's using past tense. "Well, apparently, he's recovered."

"Why do you say that?"

"You said he *looked* so sad."

"Poppy, that's because he hasn't been here. No one has seen him in weeks."

Shifting in my seat, alarm bells start to go off. "That doesn't make sense, Kat. That man lives for his career. He'd never take extended time off unless it was something bad."

She shoots me a serious look. "I don't want to mislead you. Neither Nick nor I have spoken with him. But any of the consults placed when he's been on call have been returned by Jarod or one of the other surgeons. I've worked a bunch lately covering last-minute vacations before the summer ends. And I haven't seen him in probably three weeks."

I have to swallow hard past the lump in my throat. Closing the lid on my salad, I know there's no point in trying to eat.

"He's a good man, Poppy. He made a mistake."

I simply nod. There's no way I can get caught up in my feelings and go back to work.

Kat stands from her seat. "Don't impose a harsher punishment because of what Dan did. Granting someone grace is a choice. And the way I see it, his crime was falling for you."

"Hi. It's taken me a while to face you after everything I've learned." Twisting my tissue in my hands, I continue. "Gavin is a good boy. Well, man, now." I squat down beside Dan's headstone. This time, it isn't to feel closer but rather to speak softly and feel less conspicuous.

"It's sad what we missed out on. I would've liked to have seen him grow up." A tear trickles down my cheek. I can't believe this is what I'm jealous of. Not that he created a child with someone else. But that they had the opportunity to experience this kind, young man's life. While they kept me in the dark.

"I'm pretty fucking mad at you. That you thought so little of me that I wasn't worth the truth." As the bitter words fall from my lips, my conversation with Kat comes back to me. *But he did it because he was nuts about you. And you wouldn't give him a chance. Sure, he's a spoiled rich kid who used his power to get what he wants. And he wants you.*

"You've made it hard to trust anyone, now." *Even myself.* "Everyone makes mistakes. But what you did was huge. And for what gain? He could've been my only chance at being involved in a child's life. I'm thirty-eight. I've spent years mourning you. You stole that from me too!"

Covering my face, I begin to weep. Every time I think I'm done grieving, there's something else that churns up my feelings of loss. But this isn't for Dan. And I know it. I was so close to having a second chance at love.

A hand lands on my shoulder, and I jump.

"Gavin," I sniffle. "How much did you hear?" This unbelievably kind young man squats down, wrapping me in his arms.

"Enough."

CHAPTER THIRTY-SIX
BROADIE

Sitting in this dark club, strobe lights flashing, I feel completely detached from the world around me. My eyes bounce amongst Derek, Max, Becket, Devon, and Gianni as they stare back at me from around the table.

"I want to know how we're just finding out about all of this," Dev says.

Becket slaps Derek on the arm. "And we work with her."

"I've never actually met her," Derek says, rubbing his forearm.

"She's hot."

I flash Becket a menacing glare.

"Am I wrong?"

Ignoring his comments, I turn my gaze away from him only to land on Gianni. "I don't buy it."

"What?" I ask.

"That you pulled all of that off on your own." Gianni rubs the dark hair along his jaw as his eyes fall upon Max.

One by one, each of the guys look in his direction.

"Fuck."

"Really, Max? You aided and abetted this fool?" Dev asks. "And you couldn't talk him out of this?"

"No. And I didn't want to. He was in love with her."

"No, I wasn't."

All five of my friends return their judgmental stares my way. "Not then, anyway."

"Broadie? For real?" Becket chimes in. "What are you going to do?"

"Nothing I can do."

"Bullshit," G interjects. "You're one of the most accomplished men I know. There's got to be something."

"No." I can't pretend around these guys. If I truly want help, I need to come clean. "I'm a fixer. It's what I do. But I'm not sure I can fix this." What a mess I've made of everything. "I've tried flowers. And begging. She won't return my calls." I look into my scotch glass. Looking for answers there will only make things worse. "I'm not going to risk pushing her away for good."

"He's right." All heads turn to Derek. "From what I've heard about Poppy, she's a smart woman. And now you tell us she devoted her life to a man who betrayed her." Derek's gaze locks on mine, and I can tell he's feeling uncomfortable about what's coming next. "I think it's easy to try and make things happen when we have the kind of resources we do. But this woman won't want flowers or gifts to let you back in. She wants integrity. You need to find a way to show her she's a priority."

"But how do I do that? I've wracked my brain trying to figure it out."

"Start with you."

"What does that mean?" I notice Becket, Max, Dev, and Gianni's faces bounce from Derek to me, back and forth, as if they're watching Nadal and Federer lob a ball back and forth.

"Can I be frank?"

"C'mon, Derek. Of course."

"You said it yourself. Your ex-wife and kids are growing up in the house you used to live in, creating memories with another man. All while you work yourself into the ground and take vacations in their spare room."

"Ouch," Becket blurts.

"And then you move mountains to get a chance with Poppy, and what have you done to change things? Nothing."

"You don't know that."

"Oh, yeah. How were you making her feel like she mattered? What's different? How many times have you taken her out?"

"I—"

"And you aren't allowed to count the time she came here spying on you."

Hanging my head, I accept defeat. I'd been excited to say three, conveniently leaving out that one was a coffee date and the other the night she came here. *I am ridiculous.*

Leaning forward, I let out a heavy exhale.

"C'mon, bro. Stop beating yourself up. It's hard to change a routine you've adopted for ten to fifteen years. But it's not too late. If you really love this girl." Max says.

"Max is right. Create new habits. Set some boundaries," Dev encourages.

"Join a yoga class and start meditating on what you want," Becket adds. Our heads all spin in his direction. "What? I'm a flexible, zen motherfucker."

"He's right. Focus on you and your girls. And I bet the universe will give you another chance," Devon says.

Running my hand through my hair, I try to hold onto their votes of confidence.

Derek slaps me on the back. "I think this could be the best thing that ever happened to you."

I toss him a glare.

"Honestly, Broadie. You've worked your whole life healing other people. It's time you focused on yourself. It's not going to be easy. But once you've embraced a balanced life, and the people you care about know where they stand, that's when you'll really feel like a rich man."

"Dad!" Lauren waves from the table in the corner.

I walk in their direction, finding smiles on Lilly, Lauren, and Camile's faces. I wasn't expecting to see my ex here. "Hey, girls. You look good. Thanks for inviting me to dinner."

Lilly pats the chair next to hers, and I give her and Lauren kisses on the cheek before settling in.

"You're on time," Lauren announces.

"I told you I'm working on that."

"So, what've you been up to, Broadie? It feels like forever since I've seen you." Camile leans in and gives me a peck on the cheek.

"That's a hard question to answer."

All three of them give me curious glances in response to my statement. "I'm finally trying to change my life. So, I'd like to say I've been up to a lot less." I chuckle.

Lilly grabs my hand, giving me a proud smile. "You've got this, Dad." *This kid.*

"Who is she?"

"What?"

"She must be some woman to finally have you going to such lengths," Camile says. But her tone isn't snide. She seems happy for me.

My daughters seem to almost bounce in their seats, their expressions hopeful.

"I'm not seeing anyone," I announce.

All of a sudden, a flash of blue darts past me. I quickly turn to see Poppy rushing from Luigi's, a young, dark-haired male rushing after her. *What the fuck?*

"I'll be right back," I toss over my shoulder as I chase them into the parking lot. Yet, Poppy is too quick for me. I don't see her anywhere.

"Hey," I call to the boy in ripped jeans and a faded polo shirt. Jogging in his direction, I just want to know she's okay. "Is Poppy with you?"

"What's it to you?"

"I only wanted to make sure she's okay."

"She will be." I'm not sure what to make of this.

"Who are you?"

"Just an honest Joe." He sneers.

Hell. He knows about me. What I did. It's then I notice Poppy sitting in her car in the last row of parking spaces. I start to make my way there when this kid jumps in front of me.

"I don't think so."

"I only want to make sure she's all right. I didn't realize she was in the restaurant until I saw her run out."

"That was obvious."

Now I'm getting pissed off. "What does that mean?"

"Let's see, from where she sat, it looked like you were out for dinner with your family."

"So?"

His brows nearly meet his hairline. "Are you that dumb? This poor woman finds out her dead husband has a son. That he spent their whole marriage playing part-time dad with me and my mother once a month. Only to watch her lying, scheming ex-boyfriend hanging out with his."

My eyes flick back over to Poppy's car, but she's gone. "It isn't like that. I was meeting my daughters for dinner. I had no idea their mother was coming. We've managed to remain friends for the girls' sake. She's remarried."

Why am I arguing with this kid in the middle of a parking lot? He clearly means something to Poppy. I need to walk away, say my good-nights to the girls, and head home before I get myself in trouble. Turning to do just that, I stop, unable to help myself. "The only woman I care about, besides my daughters, is Poppy."

Gathering what's left of my dignity, I walk back into the restaurant, plop down in my seat, and drop my head in utter frustration. The closest I've been to her in over a month, and she runs out of a restaurant because of me.

"Dad?" Poor Lilly sounds upset.

I reach over and grab her hand. "It's okay, honey."

"Is that the woman from the last time we were here?" Lauren asks.

My gaze darts to Camile, who's taking this in with rapt attention.

"Wait. Were you two a thing?" Lauren asks excitedly.

"The primary word in that phrase is were." I've officially lost my mind. Why am I telling them any of this?

Camile grins.

"What?"

She rubs her nails across her chest in a show of triumph. "I love it when I'm right."

I turn to look out the front window, as if it could save me from this awkward conversation.

"You love her!" Lilly declares.

"Stop," I beg.

"But you do," Lauren chimes in.

"Doesn't matter. I blew it."

"Oh, Daddy." Lilly looks as if she might cry.

I reach for her hand, giving it a comforting squeeze. Letting go, I play with my silverware for a moment, trying to figure out a way to salvage this night. "Girls. I'm not really in the mood for dinner anymore. Would you mind if we reschedule?"

Glancing up, I'm met with three pitiful faces.

"I'm sorry."

"Don't be sorry," Camile says. "We understand."

I stand from my seat, bend to plant a kiss on each of my daughters' heads, and leave. Making my way to the car, I'm tempted to drive to her house. Beg for her to talk to me. However, Devon's words come back to me like a mantra.

Focus on you and your girls. And I bet the universe will give you another chance.

CHAPTER THIRTY-SEVEN
BROADIE

"That looks wonderful."

My eyes slowly move from the object in front of me to the overly kind woman by my side. "You don't have to say that." I laugh.

"I know I don't. I'm honestly impressed. You have great attention to detail."

Who knew a surgeon's hands could come in handy for something like this?

"It's essential with this type of piece."

Pulling back to get a fresh perspective, I smile. I still think the little dish looks like a kindergartener constructed it, but the painting has turned out better than I expected. If you'd told me a few months ago that I'd be spending my Saturday mornings in a pottery class, I'd have sworn you were high.

It took some convincing to bring the instructor to my home for private lessons. But I couldn't risk bumping into Poppy. I'd never want her to think anything I was doing was for secondary gain.

I was intrigued by the Japanese artwork we enjoyed at the Virginia Museum of Fine Arts on our date. Art is subjective. My mind works on a very objective level. If you give me a blank canvas, I'm lost as to where to start. Using the philosophy of creating art from the broken gave me some-thing I could relate to. Not only as a surgeon but a man who's lost his way over the last twenty years.

"The golden lines of the mended portions of your pottery seem almost perfectly placed," the instructor commends.

"They do. It worked out better than if I'd broken it myself." I chuckle. I'd been so careful with the clay piece. The first few had fallen apart on the potter's wheel. Then I handed this one off to her to bake in the kiln, and somehow, it developed cracks in several spots. She suspects I overworked those areas.

The story of my life.

I look around the room covered in protective cloth. I'd turned my office into an art space. I was rarely in here, using my study more frequently. The only other option was my library, but I couldn't help picturing Poppy reading in there. So that wasn't an option. Plus, this room gets a lot of natural light.

It's ridiculous how happy it's made me, knowing this room exists. The thought of bringing Poppy here, if she were to ever come back to my home, fills me with pride. And if she doesn't, I'll have to accept that the universe has other plans for me. That thought still causes dread. But if I repeat it often enough, maybe one day, I'll believe it.

Dipping the tip of my paintbrush into the bright green paint, I care-fully decorate one of the broken areas, now mended with gold powder.

"Dr. Weston. You have visitors."

"Thanks, Porter. Send them back." Placing my paintbrush down, I grin. "Susan, I apologize ahead of time for the commotion."

"What?"

"No way!" Lauren squeals.

"What? I asked if you wanted to take an art class with me?"

"I can't believe you did all this," Lilly chimes in, jumping up and down.

Hell, I should've done this years ago. "Susan, these are my daughters. Why don't you see what they'd like to create?"

Lilly walks over to where I'm sitting, her hand resting on my shoulder with a look of contentment I honestly can't recall. "I'm so proud of you,

Dad." She places a peck on my cheek before scurrying over to examine all of her options.

You did good, Broadie. You did good.

"Good morning, sunshine."

"Good morning, Daddy."

"Want me to make you some French toast?"

Lilly stops dead in her tracks. "Are you serious?"

"Sure. We might need to go somewhere to eat something that isn't burnt afterward. But how hard could French toast be?"

Lauren shuffles into the kitchen, looking like she barely slept.

"Dad just offered to make French toast," Lilly tells her.

"I didn't say it would be good." I laugh. I can't remember the last time my girls spent the night here. It's been years. But they were having so much fun playing in the art room that we ordered pizza and stayed up half the night.

"Dad?"

"Yeah, baby?"

"Have you talked to your girl?" Lilly asks.

My face falls before I can stop it. Plastering a reassuring smile back on my face, I answer her honestly. "No, honey. I made a big mistake. And I hope you two never let a man treat you the way I treated Poppy."

Lauren's suddenly wide awake. "Did you cheat, Dad?"

"No, no. I'm not that kind of guy. But I lied to her."

Lilly brings her coffee over to where I'm sitting, curling up by my feet. "What did you do?" she asks, blowing across her cup.

I rub my neck, wondering how much to disclose. "She was the first woman since your mother I was interested in having a relationship with. But she turned me down. I can't explain it, but I just had a feeling we'd be good together. That was right before you girls saw her at Luigi's that night with her brother."

Lauren sits on the ottoman, holding her coffee in both hands, listening attentively.

"I don't want to go into detail. But I basically tricked her into dating me."

The two of them tilt their heads in confusion.

"I manipulated the situation, so we were at the same place at the same time. It was wrong."

Lauren looks bewildered. "But she liked you too, right?"

"I think so. But there's no room for deceit in a healthy relationship. I tried to justify what I did. But it was wrong. Plain and simple."

"You don't think she'll ever forgive you?"

This conversation is going to require another cup of coffee. "I hoped she would. But it doesn't look that way." I place my mug under the Keurig and press the start button. "Look. If a boy had lied to you and didn't come clean about it until he got caught, I wouldn't want you with someone like that."

Noticing the room has grown quiet, I look up to see the two of them staring at one another. I love these girls. "Please, don't worry about me. It was a lesson I needed. I'm grateful she shut me down. If not, I'd probably still be working seven days a week instead of spending my Sunday morning with you two."

"I love you, Dad," Lilly says, her eyes full of tears.

Pulling her in for a hug, I try to get this morning back to a more jovial conversation. "Awe, baby. Don't be sad for me. Things work out as they're supposed to. Now let's see if I can make breakfast without the fire department paying us a visit."

Lauren smiles mischievously at me. I don't even want to know what that's about.

Poppy

Bzzz, Bzzz.

Clutching my towel, I race for the phone. I quickly hit the speaker button once I see her face on the screen. "Hi, Mom. I'm running a little late, but I'll be there in about an hour." My Saturday mornings have gotten busier with my weekly yoga, my art class, grocery shopping, and visits to Hanover Haven to see Mom. Then this morning, everything changed when I got a call from Gavin asking if I wanted to meet for brunch. It threw off my schedule, but was worth it.

"Poppy, that's why I'm calling. The place is on quarantine," she shouts.

"For what?"

"The flu. It's torn through the place. They're not letting any visitors in until they get this under control. It's a good idea. I don't want you getting sick."

Me? "What about you?"

"They won't let me leave, dear."

I giggle. "No. I understand that. But I don't want you or Agnes to get sick."

"We'll be fine. I'm getting my meals delivered to my room, and Agnes says she's too mean to get sick."

I laugh. "What?"

"She says it boosts her immunity. Germs are scared of her."

"Okay. Please let me know if anything changes."

"I will. I love you, Pop."

My hand flies to my heart. *Pop*. She never calls me that.

"I love you too, Mom." Disconnecting the call, I place the phone down on the counter so I can put on some clothes. I barely know what to do with myself now that my afternoon is free.

Walking into the kitchen, I decide to put on a pot of tea. Maybe I'll dive into a new book. It's then I recall the delivery I found on my porch last night. I head to my office and see the book mail delivered from Amazon yesterday. As much as I enjoy reading on my Kindle or listening to Audible, there's just something about a book in your hand.

Lifting the brown packaging, my eyes drop to the papers lying underneath. Dan's life insurance. I've avoided using much of it, deciding instead to live off my own salary and save this for a rainy day. But after meeting Gavin, knowing he's Dan's son, it feels wrong keeping this to myself.

I've become quite attached to this young man. I'm aware he has a mother. I have no interest in stepping on her toes. Yet I feel oddly protective of him. Knowing Nick has mentored him gives me some peace that he has a strong male presence in his life. But I feel as if part of this money belongs to him. Dan likely didn't make arrangements because he was worried I'd find out about Gavin. Yet the days of letting my husband's secrets and lies get in the way of doing the right thing are over.

Knock, knock.

That's odd. Who could that be? I run my fingers through my still-damp hair and head to the door. Swinging it open, I expect to find an Amazon delivery driver but stop in shock when I see who it is.

"Hi."

"Hi. I'm sorry if we're intruding. Is there any way we could come in?"

"Of course. Please," I say, waving them in. It took me a moment to collect myself after opening the door. But I recognize these beautiful girls from Luigi's with Broadie.

"Thank you," the younger one says.

These girls are absolutely gorgeous. But so was their mother. The older one has dark blonde hair and a perfect figure. She's dressed in what looks like designer everything. Her younger sister is thin, with light blonde hair, and a more timid disposition.

"I'm Lauren, and this is Lilly."

"It's nice to meet you." And it is. Even if I don't understand why they're here. Is this some ploy on his part to get back into my good graces? Seems oddly timed, as he stopped sending me flowers, cards, and gifts weeks ago.

"My dad doesn't know we're here," Lauren reassures me.

"We're worried about him," Lilly adds. This makes my heart squeeze.

"Where are my manners? Please come sit down. Can I get either of you anything?"

"No," they say in unison, sitting down carefully on the couch.

Taking a seat across from them, I try to calm my nerves. "Why are you worried about him? Is he okay?"

The two of them look at one another before the older girl starts to speak. "I've never seen him like this. He's so sad."

My heart hurts for them. They look so concerned.

"He told us what he did," Lilly says.

Wow. Really? "I'm surprised he shared that with you."

"He said he'd manipulated you and felt terrible about it. That he wanted us to learn from his mistakes." Lauren says.

"Because he never wanted to see us hurt by trusting the wrong man," Lilly adds.

"He made a mistake. But I hate seeing what this is doing to him. And I feel like it's all my fault." Lauren says, looking pained.

Her statement catches me off guard, and I scoot forward in my haste to reassure her. "How on earth could it be your fault?"

"Because I pushed him to ask you out." Lauren sniffles.

Unable to stop myself, I grab the box of tissues from my coffee table and come to sit between them. "I don't understand."

Lauren sighs. "We saw the way he was looking at you. At Luigi's. I've wanted to see my dad happy for so long. And he's never looked at anyone the way he looked at you. But now he's hurting. And maybe you are too. I should've left things alone."

"Lauren, that's not on you. We're adults. Responsible for our own actions. Please don't put that on yourself."

"He's come such a long way since meeting you." I turn to Lilly, unsure of what she means. "Is there no way you could forgive him?"

"I'm not sure what you mean."

Lilly gives a slight smile. "He's cut back at work. He meets us for dinner a lot more now."

This makes me smile. I know how important reconnecting with his kids was to him.

"He even invited us to an art class," Lauren interjects.

"What?" I recall the time I asked Broadie to join me for a class and he said it wasn't possible. He even joked that he "loved me" but couldn't miss work to take an art class.

"He said he needed something healthy to focus on. So, he wasn't tempted to bury himself in his job to forget his troubles."

Lilly reaches into her oversized purse and pulls out two small white boxes, each tied with a pink bow. She hands the larger box over to me.

"What's this?"

Lauren laughs. "Ha. I'm not really sure. He's proud of it, but I can't really figure it out. It looks like he messed up and tried to put it back together again."

"Why are you giving this to me?"

"I'm certain he made it for you," Lilly says. "After seeing what was in this other box."

My curiosity is killing me. I untie the satin bow and lift the lid. As I peer inside, my eyes fill with tears. He's created kintsugi.

"Please don't be upset. He tried really hard on it," Lauren pleads.

"Oh, I'm not upset. I'm shocked." My finger trails along the golden veining where the broken pieces are now melded together. I trace the symbols contained within the triangular spaces of each broken piece, unsure if I can identify them. "These look like shoes."

"Oh, yeah. You're right." Lauren smiles.

"I'm not sure what this is," I say, examining the green, yellow, and black oval. "This looks like a book."

"Oh, it is. You're good." Lilly giggles. She holds out the other box. "I think this might help."

Having no idea what she means, I tug on the ribbon and lift the lid off of the shallow square box to reveal a charm bracelet.

Once I identify a few of the charms, my tears spill down my cheeks. There's a pair of shoes, like the damaged ones he bought for me in Jamaica. I see a stack of three books, Jane Austen's name inscribed on the spines. A margarita glass makes me smile. But then I find the little bobsled and gasp. How on earth did he find a charm like that?

"What is it?" Lauren asks.

"It's a bobsled. I made him ride one when we were in Jamaica."

The girls turn to one another. "He hates rollercoasters."

"Oh, girls. I'm sorry." I reach for a tissue, practically sobbing in front of them.

"Oh, Poppy. We didn't come here to upset you." Lilly sniffles. "We wanted you to know how important you are to him. He's really trying to be a better man."

"And father," Lauren adds. "And it's because of you."

Grasping two more tissues, I try to sop up the mess. "Thank you. It means a lot that you'd bring this to me. I'd hug you, but I'd get you all wet."

Both girls immediately wrap their arms around me, and I can't explain the feeling. It's as if I've known these two for years.

"Are you sure your dad won't be upset when he finds out these are missing?"

The girls look silently at one another. "We didn't think that far ahead," Lilly admits.

Then it dawns on me. "How did you know where to find me?"

"Stu," Lauren says.

"Who?"

"Russell Stewart. Dad's security guy."

I look at them, baffled.

"He was tired of seeing Dad moping around too. When we came to him, he gladly gave us your address."

"Do you know where your dad is?" I ask, dabbing at my eyes.

The girls' faces shine in their enthusiasm. The younger of the two, sporting a dimple similar to her father's blurts, "He's at home."

CHAPTER THIRTY-EIGHT
BROADIE

Pushing myself out of the pool, I reach for a towel and head inside. Summer is gone, and now fall is upon us. The temperatures have started to drop in the evening. Thank heavens the pool is heated. I admit, I've not taken the time to enjoy it much over the years, preferring a quick workout downstairs in my gym. But I've come to appreciate it now that I'm embracing more downtime. I've come to appreciate a lot of things.

Walking into my kitchen, I grab a bottle of water from the fridge. I've always considered myself the grateful sort. It's part of why I worked so hard to prove to my family I'm deserving of my acquired wealth. That I've worked every bit as hard as my father and grandfather, even if in a different field. Lifting my bottle in a silent toast, I pray they'll be prouder still of the man I've become.

I head toward the stairs to take a quick shower before reaching out to Becket and Derek to see if they want to grab dinner and drinks when I hear a knock at the door. Pausing, I contemplate whether I should text Stu before answering, but then consider it could be the girls.

Opening the front door, my mouth falls ajar. The very last person I expected to see is standing in front of me. Her eyes fall to my chest, and her cheeks instantly blush.

"Oh, I'm sorry, Pop. Come in. I'll run and grab a shirt."

I close the door behind her before heading for my room. "Make yourself comfortable. I'll be right back." Taking the steps two at a time, I quickly grab a shirt from my closet and change into a pair of gray sweatpants. My heart is racing. And it's not from my workout.

I dart into the bathroom and run some gel through my wet hair. God. This woman turns me into a teenage boy every time I see her.

Jogging down the stairs, I find her perched on the couch. I don't want to get my hopes up. Yet, I'd get back on my knees again if only she'd stay.

"Can I get you anything?"

"No. I'm fine."

Coming closer, it appears her eyes are puffy. Has she been crying? "Poppy, is something wrong? Is your mom okay?"

She shakes her head and laughs. *Laughs.* "No. Everything is fine. At least, I hope so."

I know I should probably give her some space. Sit across from her while she explains why she's here. But I'm just too fucking weak.

Lowering myself to sit on the couch beside her, I take her in. Her sweet smile, those beautiful red lips, and blue eyes I could drown in.

"God, I've missed you."

A blush stains her cheeks, and I realize I've said that out loud.

"Sorry."

"I've missed you too."

My heart rate starts to quicken, and I worry I might have to call Derek for a whole different reason if this keeps up. I'm not sure my heart can stand being rejected again.

"Pop, I'm almost afraid to ask. But why are you here?"

She turns, reaching for her purse. *Damn. Is she going to return my cards?* She retrieves a white box, lifting the lid to reveal my vase.

"How'd you get that?"

"It was delivered this morning," she says, lifting it up high enough that my eyes land on the charm bracelet she's wearing. *What the—*

"Poppy. I had no idea they'd send you that. Please don't think I did this to influence your forgiveness," I blurt.

"I don't." She scoots a little closer. "Your daughters are wonderful, Broadie. They came to see me and brought these." She blinks a few times before looking up at me. "You should be so proud."

"I am." I'm baffled by all of this. What did they say to her?

"Not just of them."

"What do you mean?"

"They told me everything. How you confessed what you did, warning them away from anyone who'd mistreat them. That you've cut back at work. And then this." Her eyes fill with tears. "It's genuinely the most beautiful thing I've ever seen." She sniffles as big, fat tears course down her cheeks.

"Baby, don't cry. I don't ever want to see you cry again." I reach up, swiping away the droplets with my thumbs. "I hate that I hurt you. I know I don't deserve your forgiveness. Not after what I did."

"Forgiveness is a choice. One I hope is granted to me if I ever fall short. I don't like what you did. And if you ever lie to me again, I'll cut your balls off in your sleep. But I'm choosing to appreciate why you did it."

"Because I'm fucking nuts about you?"

"Well, you've got the nuts part right." She reaches over, placing the pad of her thumb in the deep indentation residing in my cheek. There's no need to coax that sucker out. My face hurts from smiling so hard. "You're going to blind me with that smile." She giggles.

"I love you. I'm so crazy in love with you. I think I felt it the very first time I saw you."

"Okay, don't start getting creepy on me." She laughs.

Jeez. Maybe I am nuts.

Poppy cups my cheeks with her hands, pulling my face close to hers. "I love you too." Leaning forward, she traces her tongue along the seam of my mouth before covering my lips with hers. Who knew how much this workaholic curmudgeon needed to hear those beautiful words?

"Poppy, can we make a fresh start?"

"No."

CHAPTER THIRTY-NINE
BROADIE

"No?" I thought things were finally falling into place, and now I feel like the rug just got yanked out from under me.

"No." Poppy crosses her arms over her chest defiantly. "I made the choice to forgive you, Broadie. However, that doesn't mean I plan to forget. I wasn't sure I'd ever get past this. And if it weren't for your daughters showing me how much you've changed, I'm not sure I would have."

Hell. I might have to buy those two new cars after all.

"I want this to work. But if you ever lie to me again, we're done. Remember that if I ever ask too many questions, it's because I'm having trust issues. I'm not going to be so naïve in the future."

Pulling her close, I try to convey my sincerity. "I swear I'll never keep anything from you again, Pop. Never. Unless it's about a gift or a surprise for your birthday." This is met with a glare. "Okay, okay, I hear you. I'm not a dishonest guy. Only impatient." Thinking back, I still can't believe the lengths I went to. Not that I'd take it back. Those moments with Poppy were some of the best of my life. "I've never acted that way with anyone else. Deep down, I knew from the moment I saw you that you were mine. I was desperate."

"Whatever." I see the change in her expression as her eyes return to my little vase. "When did you start taking art classes? I thought you said you'd never be able to do that. Sit in an art class with all the work that had to be done."

I stand up, pulling her with me. "A little over a month ago. I needed to find something to focus on besides my job. And you. I was a fucking mess when you said we were over." I pull her hand to my lips, kissing her knuckles. "Taking classes made me feel closer to you."

"That's sweet." She grins. "Where are you taking me?"

"I want to show you something."

Poppy stops in her tracks. "I don't even get dinner first?"

"Huh?" I turn to her and find her eyes on my sweatpants.

"Ha ha. I'll save that for later. I was going to show you something else, dirty girl."

We resume walking until we reach the art room. It's a mess after the way the girls and I left it the other night. But she'll get the gist of it.

"No way."

"Ha, that's what my daughters said when they saw it. Excuse the mess—"

Poppy throws herself at me, arms clutched around the back of my neck, as her lips crash onto mine. And for the first time, in a long time, I feel whole again.

Poppy

After a tour of the art room, Broadie leads me down the hall to his library. I'm completely in love.

He has gorgeous floor-to-ceiling shelving stacked with beautifully bound books. There are a few non-fiction books, but the rest are a mix of fictional classics, suspense, who done its, and romance.

Stained mahogany shelves line the cream-colored walls, bringing an added richness to the space. While cozy easy chairs flank the wood-burning fireplace along the opposite wall. Oh, to curl up in this room by the fire's warmth with a cup of tea and a good book. Who would ever want to leave?

Stepping onto the wooden ladder on wheels attached to the tall bookshelves, I run my hands over the spines of the classic Jane Austen hardbacks. Jingling my bracelet, the charm depicting the little stack of Austen's books glimmers in the overhead light.

"Where did you find such unique charms, Broadie?"

He peers up at me from the David Baldacci book he's holding. "I had them custom-made."

"You did? Where?"

"My buddy, Gianni, helped me."

Gianni? *Isn't he...* "The guy that owns the sex club?" I'm baffled by this.

"G's a man of many talents. Now he's one book you shouldn't judge by its cover." He smirks.

Sliding off the ladder, I reach for a foil-embossed hardcover by Charlotte Bronte. I can't believe I've never read *Jane Eyre*. "I'd love to hear all the tales of your billionaire boys club, Dr. Weston. I bet they'd keep me on the edge of my seat." I chuckle.

"The six of us are quite a collection." Placing his book down, he wraps his arms around me. "Can you stay?"

"Do you think that's a good idea? Rushing back into things?"

His dimple disappears with the determined expression on his face. "In what way did we ever rush? Well, I know how I rushed... but once we spent time together and realized what I knew all along, how did we rush?"

He's right. We barely saw one another once we returned. "Well, that's because someone was working seven days a week."

I expect him to make excuses, but instead, he holds me tighter. "You've taught me the error of my ways, Pop. Never again. You, Lauren, and Lilly. You're my priority now." He drops his forehead to mine. Closing my eyes, I revel in the feel of his openness. And I honestly believe him.

Broadie heats up a mouthwatering meal of salmon and grilled vegetables his private chef had prepared for him, and we spend the rest of the evening catching up on the things that have transpired while we were apart. He tells tales of Lauren and Lilly's shenanigans, and I meet his stories tit for tat with those of my mother and Agnes.

As we lie on a chaise lounge on his lanai, I decide to share my thoughts on Gavin. I tell him how fond of him I've become and that I'd found him when he'd been searching for answers. We lamented the fact Gavin had to grow up this way. Barely knowing his father, then losing him so young.

"I'm so thrilled Nick was matched with him in that Big Brothers, Big Sisters program. He's been such a great role model for him. I think he and his dad have given Gavin something to strive for."

"I'm glad. You don't realize how lucky you are in life to have family until people like Gavin remind you how quickly all that can be taken away."

I run my hand over Broadie's chest, nervous to share what's been on my mind lately. "I want to take a portion of Dan's life insurance and put it in a trust for Gavin. For college."

Broadie shifts beneath me. "You sure, Pop?"

"Yes. He's Dan's son. Part of that money should go to him."

He strokes his hand through my hair. "Don't get upset with me. But I think you should talk to a lawyer. Find out what they recommend."

"You're right. Why would I be upset with you for saying that?"

He's quiet for a moment. "I think there's still a lot you don't know about their situation. What you want to do is very generous. Yet, it could cause trouble if you don't have the trust clearly stipulated. Say he doesn't want to go to college. Or his mother wants to lay claim."

I hadn't thought about that.

"And you might want to get a paternity test. I don't doubt what he's told you. But legally, it's probably best you do everything by the book."

Unsure where they're coming from, I'm suddenly rattled by the thoughts swimming in my head. Having Gavin in my life has made me feel maternal. Had Dan chosen to include me in their lives, I would've been his stepmother. "Have you ever considered the possibility of having more kids?" My voice is meek as the question sneaks out of my mouth. What's the old adage? Don't ask the question if you don't want to hear the answer. "Never mind. I shouldn't have asked that."

"Why not?" He twists so we're facing each other on this narrow lounger. "You can ask me anything." Tucking my hair behind my ear, he smiles down at me. "If you'd asked me a year ago, I'd have laughed you right off of this chair."

"And now?"

"You offering?"

My brows pinch. *What is he asking?*

"You want me to put a baby in here, Pop?"

I bite my lip. "Maybe one day."

Leaning in, he nuzzles my neck. "I'm forty-two, baby. One day might need to come sooner versus later." He chuckles.

Same.

"Seriously, Broadie. I'd still love the chance to have children. But it's not a deal breaker for me. Before you came along, I hadn't ruled out fostering children or adopting one as a single parent."

"I missed out on so much with my girls." His expression looks so grim. "I'm open to whatever possibilities the future has in store. So long as you're here with me."

His hand drifts down to my belly, a strange expression crossing his face. "You know, you're right. I don't want to rush into things with you. Not these kinds of things, anyway. I want to spend time together, you and me. Learn all of your secrets. What makes you happy. And if we have the chance to create a family when the time is right, I'll be the luckiest guy on earth."

My heart is swelling in my chest. I'm so in love with this man.

"Come on." Broadie stands from the lounge chair and pulls me up beside him.

"Where are we going?"

He pulls me along behind him, making his way for the stairs. "To practice."

"What? You just said—"

"We want to be ready when the time comes, right?"

Following along behind him, I stiffen. I'm not sure I'm ready for him to take charge just yet. Not after all that's happened between us. I let go of his hand, standing tall in the doorway.

I can tell he senses my hesitancy when he turns to face me. "Poppy?"

It's now or never. Use your voice, Poppy.

Stepping closer, he pleads, "Let me make it up to you, Pop. Let me show you how sorry I am." His voice is sincere.

"On your knees, Dr. Weston."

His eyes bulge, shocked at my request. However, he quickly complies.

I start to tell him, don't speak. But who am I kidding? I love that dirty mouth of his. So instead, I add, "And if you're a good boy, I might let you come."

CHAPTER FORTY
POPPY

Stretching my arms overhead, I blink my eyes open to greet the day. Has the last twenty-four hours been a dream?

As I turn to Broadie's side of the bed, I find he's not there. Springing up, it feels like déjà vu. Has he gone to work? As much as I loved the gift of Agent Provocateur and a romance classic, I'd honestly prefer he kept me company. Not Mr. Darcy.

"Good morning, sunshine."

My head snaps in the direction of his cheerful voice, and I find one hot, shirtless surgeon carrying a breakfast tray.

I am dreaming!

He deposits the tray on the bed beside me and leans in to place a chaste kiss on my temple. "I'm still learning what you like. Coffee or tea?" I hadn't noticed there was one of each. "And I don't know how you like your eggs, so I brought yogurt, croissants, and fruit."

Cupping his cheeks, I pull him toward me for a peck. "This is amazing. I'm not picky. I like just about everything. But coffee is a must." Lifting the mug to my lips, I sip it carefully. "I save tea for when I'm reading."

"Good to know."

"How about you?"

"I like coffee and a brisk workout in the morning. Then I shower and eat before heading in to work."

I can't prevent my frown.

"Turn that frown upside down. I'm off today."

I nearly spill the coffee and tea onto the bed with my glee. "Really?"

"Yes." He chuckles, and that hypnotizing dimple comes out to play. "What do you want to do today?"

"Everything. And nothing. It was so nice relaxing here with you last night. I feel like I've gotten to enjoy a whole new side of you I didn't know existed."

"It didn't. Until you." Broadie feeds me a grape. "I have an idea. Why don't we visit Sara and Agnes today?"

"Oh, you're so cute. But we can't. Hanover Haven is on quarantine. The flu is running rampant in the place. So, they're trying to keep everyone in their rooms."

I watch as he scratches the delicious scruff along his jawline. It's thicker than usual. "I have an idea." He practically jumps from the bed and darts out the bedroom door. Wow. He's as limber as a cat. I tear a piece of buttery croissant and pop it into my mouth.

Broadie saunters back into the room with his phone to his ear, now wearing a T-shirt with his pajama bottoms, and I frown. He must catch my reaction as the dimple pops with his smile. "Lauren? It's not that early. Oh, come on. Wake your sister and come over here."

I can practically hear her groaning from here. She doesn't strike me as someone who rises at dawn on a weekend.

"Poppy and I need your help with something." My head snaps up in time to catch him winking at me. "Yes. She's here."

"Oh. My. God! Lilly!" Broadie pulls the phone away from his ear and laughs.

He crawls back onto the bed with me, and I run my hand down his sexy face, saying, "What are you up to?"

"Oh, it's on. It's going to be a great day." With that, he pops a mandarin orange slice into his mouth before hitting a few buttons on his phone.

"Hi, Tuesday? I'm going to need your help with a really big order today."

Giggling bursts through the phone.

"I need about two hundred balloons. Can you manage to have them blown up with ribbons tied to them by lunchtime?"

What is this man doing?

"Perfect. If you could deliver them to Hanover Haven by noon? We'll meet you there. Thanks, Tuesday."

"Who is Tuesday, and what on earth are you doing?"

"We're going to give them the best medicine money can buy today," Broadie says, bopping me on my nose. "Now, you better hurry. If you don't get in the shower, my daughters are going to get an eye full when they come flying in here."

Darting out of the bed, I make quick work of getting cleaned up. Once I return, I find him speaking with Porter at the base of the steps. What's that about, I wonder.

Broadie catches me in his periphery and turns, motioning for me to join them.

"All the other stuff you asked for is on the way."

"Thanks, Porter. Send the girls in when they get here. We should be ready to leave by eleven- thirty."

"Got it, boss."

As his driver exits the front door, I come closer. Wrapping my arm around his waist, I lean into him. There are bags and bags of grocery items on the kitchen island. "Will you please tell me what's going on?"

"What you said bothered me. Can you imagine anything worse than being quarantined in a nursing home? They're already called shut-ins. Because they require help and can't go anywhere. Now they can't have visitors or even leave their rooms. We have to do something, Pop."

This sweet man.

"What's your plan?"

He walks over to inspect the bags, dumping out little juice bottles, Hershey's Kisses, and tissue packets.

"The calvary is here!" Lauren shouts from behind me. I spin on my heel just in time to catch them rushing toward me and engulfing me in a big hug.

"Jeez. I see how I rate," Broadie says behind me.

The girls giggle and swarm their father. "What's going on?"

"Poppy's mom lives at Hanover Haven. And they're on quarantine because so many residents have the flu. I thought we could do something nice and cheer them up."

"Oh, fun." Lilly bounces from foot to foot, clapping at the idea.

"We're going to make some care packages and deliver them with their lunches. I need you to help put these tissues, Hugs, and juices in a little gift bag and come up with something cute to write on each one."

"I love that!" Lauren says. "Let's take these gift bags into the art room and decorate them. We can fill them afterward." She and Lilly dash down the hall, their arms full of bags.

Reaching for Broadie's arm, I give him a gentle squeeze. "This is so incredibly thoughtful. But you know they aren't going to let us in."

"Oh, they'll let us in." Spoken like a true billionaire.

Several hours later, we arrive at Hanover Haven with the gift bags packed and ready to go. A large Cygnature Blooms delivery van is parked by the curb.

"Oh, I'm so excited," Lauren gushes.

"Me too!" her sister chimes in.

Turning to Broadie, I put my hands on my hips. "So how is this going to happen? With the quarantine in place?"

He holds up a finger. "So little faith." He chuckles before walking over to Porter.

My gaze lands on his two beautiful girls. They're simply radiant standing in the midday sun. Yet, I have no doubt this isn't the UV rays. It's all him.

Broadie comes back to us, his arms laden in bright yellow garb. *Wait? Is that?* "All right, everyone. Time to suit up."

"Are those gowns from St. Luke's?" These look suspiciously similar to the isolation gowns we wear when entering a patient's room who is under contact precautions, to both protect us, but also prevent the spread of germs.

"Yep." He laughs, reaching into his pocket to retrieve several sets of gloves. "And once you have these on, I'll help you with your headgear."

Porter brings over surgical caps, N95 masks, and face shields.

"I look like a big banana." Lilly giggles.

"This way, we're protected, and so are they. There's no reason for anyone to worry," Broadie adds. It appears he's thought of everything. Almost.

"Broadie, I appreciate what you're doing. But those gifts are full of sugar. I'm sure some of these poor residents have dietary restrictions."

"That's where we come in." A soft voice lilts from behind me. I turn to see the beautiful auburn-haired girl from SHAGBARK the night I met Kat for dinner. "Hi, I'm Tuesday. Thank you so much for letting me be a part of this, Dr. Weston."

"You were the first person I thought of when coming up with this plan." He grins down at her. She's holding dozens of long-stemmed Gerber daisies. They're bright and beautiful, just like the florist carrying them. "We'll consider the area just outside of the front doors ground zero. If you can help gather the gift bags, balloons, and flowers we'll need for each wing, we'll hit them one at a time."

"Of course. Oh, to see the looks on those little faces when you visit." Tuesday beams.

We make our way into the foyer of the facility, and I nervously approach Jasmine, feeling like I'm starring in some epidemiology thriller.

"My lands. Is that you, Poppy?"

I giggle. "I'm shocked you could tell it's me."

"I'd know those beautiful blue eyes anywhere."

"Hi, Jasmine." Broadie pops over beside me.

"Is that?" Her mouth falls ajar. "Is that you in there, Dr. Weston?"

"You're good." He chuckles. "We know you guys are on quarantine. But Poppy, my girls, and I wanted to do something to cheer up the folks here.

We've taken every precaution. I called ahead and got everything cleared with Ms. Moses, the facility manager."

"Oh, that's right. She said someone might be dropping by to bring some gifts to the residents, but I wasn't expecting all of this."

"Have they started serving lunch yet?" Broadie asks.

Looking at her watch, she says, "That should begin shortly."

"Would you mind asking the dietary manager if there's any chance I could speak with them before they start? We'd like to coordinate our deliveries with theirs."

I turn to look at him, shocked by how much thought he's put into this. And in only a few short hours. Is there nothing he can't do?

"I'll call them right now."

An hour later, we're huffing and puffing inside our protective garb. We've run all over this place, looking like some psychedelic children's cartoon, or perhaps this is what it's like if someone gets high, I suppose. I'll stick to Broadie Weston as my drug of choice. We've managed to ensure each resident received a small gift of cheer alongside their lunch. The joy I witnessed today was every bit as infectious as the flu we were trying so hard to protect everyone from.

"Just two left." Broadie winks.

My grin is instantaneous.

"You coming, girls? We've got two sassy ladies for you to meet."

As we enter Mom's room carrying balloons, daisies, and little gift bags, I have to prevent my tears of joy from spilling. It's only been a week since I've seen her, but knowing she's been in harm's way must have weighed more heavily on me than I realized.

Coming closer, I place them next to her lunch tray and bend down, hoping she'll be able to see my face clearly through the mask and shield.

"Poppy? Is that you?" she shouts.

"Yes."

"You look like a big banana!"

The girls behind me start to crack up.

"I do?"

Broadie walks over to Agnes carrying a bright turquoise gift bag with 'I'd be blue too if I had the flu' inscribed in black ink.

"And if it isn't, Dr. Weston!" Agnes announces.

"Oh my gosh, Agnes. How on earth did you recognize him in all of that?" I ask, baffled.

"I'd know that man anywhere. A body like that can't be hidden under a yellow gown."

Lauren and Lilly are beside themselves in the doorway.

"Mom, these are Broadie's daughters, Lauren and Lilly."

"You two need to promise to come back when I can see your pretty faces!" she yells.

"Yes, ma'am."

"This was so nice of you to do, Poppy," my mother adds, her voice lower as she inspects the items in her little gift bag.

"This was all Broadie, Mom. We delivered things to every single resident at Hanover Haven."

"You did?" Now her eyes match mine, filling with unshed tears.

"I don't know what happened over the last few months, Missy. But you better lock this fella down," Agnes bellows. "I already checked. He wasn't on Bumble Bee." She winks at Broadie.

I laugh, crossing my arms over my chest. "Were you checking for me or for you?"

Agnes simply shrugs.

"Okay, we probably need to head out before the girls lose any more weight from all the sweating we're doing under these gowns." Technically, we should've been taking them off and on between each patient to protect the spread of germs from one room to another, but we never touched anyone, and we're covered more than the dietary staff.

Broadie gives my mother a broad smile. "She's right. Plus, we've broken enough rules for one day. Better get out while the getting is good."

"Thank you, son. You've made our week." My mother seems happier and more alert than I've seen her in ages. But I admit, this man has that effect on me too.

I can't stop smiling as we disrobe our gowns and gear into a trash bag

Porter is holding out for us. Who could've imagined the last twenty-four hours could've gone this way?

"When's the next one, Dad?" Lauren blurts.

"Awe, I'm so glad to see you so exuberant about this. Leaning down so he's at eye level with Lauren, he continues. "This is what I was trying to tell you. You're capable of so much more. It doesn't have to be a full-time job, but I hope you two will consider participating in some type of charity work where you can share your gifts with others. You'd make your old dad proud."

They come in for a hug, and my heart swells. Looking at the three people beside me, I have no doubt this is where I belong.

This is the family I've been longing for.

CHAPTER FORTY-ONE
POPPY

"Can I see you later?"

I spin on my heel to find the most handsome surgeon on the planet standing behind me.

"Who? Me?" I beam. It's been almost a week since our crazy caper at Hanover Haven. Returning to real life has been disappointing. He still sends sweet texts to start my day, but now I get phone calls as well. "Have you got room in that busy schedule for me?" I tease.

"You've got it all wrong, pretty lady. I'm working my busy schedule around you." He bends down to put a chaste peck on my cheek. "Is eight o'clock okay?"

"Can we make it eight-thirty? I don't get off work until seven and want to look nice for my date."

"You could wear an isolation suit and turn me on." He waggles his brows at me, causing an unattractive snort to fly from my lips. "You're so hot."

I laugh. "Okay, I'll be ready by eight-thirty. You picking me up in that fancy car of yours?"

"Yes, ma'am." He winks before walking off, his hands tucked in his pants pockets. His hot ass is covered by his starched white lab coat, but I can picture it. *You can't hide a body like that.* Agnes was right.

Lifting my hand to feel the heat radiating from my blush-stained cheeks, I look up to see multiple nurses and staff members staring at me with their mouths slack. Yep. He just outed us to everyone.

"Poppy Danforth. You better fill me in right this second." Katarina squeals.

"About what?" I laugh.

"You know about what."

She loops her arm through mine and drags me with her as we head to the ER.

"I think we're going the wrong way. My department is that way." I point.

"Cut the crap, Poppy. You were just letting the hottest surgeon in the universe kiss you in front of the whole hospital. You can spare me a few minutes to get caught up!"

I fill Katarina in on everything that's happened in the last week and laugh as, with each new story, her face becomes more and more shocked. Retelling all of it even makes my head spin. "Okay, I've really got to get back to work. And I'm sure there's some patient with a situation only you can handle waiting in there." I point to the ER doors.

"Yeah. I'm sure there's a raging case of herpes waiting in a room for my arrival." She groans.

Poor Kat.

"Oh, come back down here before you leave for the day. I almost forgot that I have something here for you."

"What?"

"Not sure, really. Gavin wanted you to have it."

That's odd. "Okay, I'll be sure to pop back down before you go. Bye." I quickly make my way back to the department. Hopefully, Frank won't wonder where I've been.

～

"Hey, I'm here," I announce as I come around the corner to the nurses' workstation, where I see Kat typing into a computer.

"Hi. Perfect timing. Eve came in early for me today. I'd almost forgotten you were coming back." Kat reaches over to her backpack on the chair beside hers, digs inside, and retrieves a white envelope. "Gah, I'm dying to know what's in there, but I've got to get home. The sitter has plans this afternoon, and I don't want to be late." She stands, coming over to give me a one-armed hug. "Good ones are hard to find."

"I bet," I say, examining the nondescript envelope. "I'm sorry I didn't come sooner. I figured I'd stop as my shift was ending so I could head out soon after."

Turning the nondescript envelope in my hands, my mind comes up blank. What could this be? I'd met with Gavin for dinner the Monday after the Hanover Haven bananagrams took place. I hadn't seen him in a while and was excited to share all of my news. I'd also jumped the gun, explaining my plans to set up a trust for him. It was probably too soon, but he needed to know how important he was. That I knew Dan would've wanted it that way.

"I can't believe you are going to pass me off like this!" The disgruntled, angry voice of a male around the corner has my attention. Looking up from the envelope, I notice it's more than just mine. Most of the staff is looking down the hall.

It's not uncommon to hear frustrated voices in the ER. The tension is high here. Yet, as I walk over to where several employees have gathered to gawk as I prepare to return to my quiet department, I see Brantly Martin standing in front of Broadie. Brantly has his hands on his hips, his face red as a tomato.

"What do you mean you're not available? My wife's in need of emergency surgery, and you're going to stand here and tell me no?"

"I'm not telling you she can't have surgery, Brantly. It will just have to be with one of my partners. She'll be in perfectly good hands with any of them. But Jarod's on today. I'd trust him to operate on my daughters if they needed it. There's no need to get upset because I'm not available."

"You said it was a laparoscopic procedure. That shouldn't take you much time," he continues to argue.

I watch as Broadie's calm, professional exterior begins to crack. He doesn't seem to care that he has an audience at the moment.

He leans down, making sure he's at eye level with the surly, unapologetic Mr. Martin. "I have plans this evening. Important plans, which I have no intention of breaking. You know me well enough that if I didn't, I'd already be scrubbing in. Jarod will take good care of her, Brantly." Then he straightens and walks past Mr. Martin down the hallway as the onlookers all revel in Broadie's handling of the angry administrator.

Could I be his plans?

Two hours later, I'm pacing in my kitchen. Why am I so nervous? Curious as to whether Broadie had made some outlandish plans for us this evening that he couldn't get out of in order to perform Mr. Martin's wife's gallbladder surgery, I decided to try to reward his commitment to me by at least dressing the part. Wearing the shoes he bought me, my blue halter dress I wore in Jamaica, and the priceless charm bracelet he designed for me, I clutch onto the edge of my kitchen island and wait.

Knock, knock.

My eyes drop to the kitchen clock. 8:30. Right on time.

I make my way to the door, and as I open it, I'm greeted by my handsome date. He's wearing dark jeans and a white button-down shirt.

"Poppy." His voice cracks. "You look incredible." His eyes trail from my head to my toes before turning to himself. "Hell. I should've at least brought a suit jacket."

I usher him inside. "Why? You look nice."

All of a sudden, he looks embarrassed. "You look like you're dressed for a night on the town."

Tilting my head in confusion, I'm feeling a bit lost. Had I been wrong about what he'd told Brantly earlier?

"What's the matter?" He sounds alarmed.

"I have to admit something. I was in the ER earlier to get something from Kat. And I heard you and Brantly Martin arguing."

He shakes his head. "That guy's a tool."

I giggle. "I felt a little guilty. That you'd made some sort of big plans with me that you couldn't cancel."

Broadie comes closer, pulling me into him. "I haven't booked anything." He pushes a lock of hair behind my ear, placing a soft kiss beneath it. "You are my plans."

A gasp slips out.

"That was all that was important to me." Kiss. "Just as it should be."

I fling myself onto him, kissing him wildly. As I pull back, I realize his face is covered in red lipstick. Yet, that perfect smile of his shows right through. Reaching for his shirt, I start to unbutton it.

"What're you doing? You're all dressed up."

"Oh, have I got plans for you, Dr. Weston."

Showered, dressed, and completely sated, Broadie and I snuggle in the back of his town car as we ride to pick up take out from Carena's Jamaican Grille.

"I can't believe they're staying open late for us," I say, my face buried in his neck.

"Money talks."

I giggle. "Well, however you managed, I'm glad. I couldn't have planned this evening better."

He smiles down at me warmly. "I can't wait to take you back to Jamaica. So I can do all the things I couldn't the first time."

I arch a brow at him and grin.

"Your head is always in the gutter, dirty bird. I meant spend time with you without pretending. But the other stuff sounds good too." He chuckles.

"I'd like that."

"Hey, what's that?"

"What?"

Broadie points to my purse, where the envelope from Gavin is poking out.

"Oh. I'd almost forgotten about that." I can't believe I forgot to open it after all of the commotion with Brantly and 'our plans' distracting me. Grasping the envelope, I lift the corner of the seal and open it. There's a single piece of white paper folded inside.

"Who's it from?"

"Kat said Gavin asked her to give it to me."

Unfolding the paper, I see a small yellow Post-it attached that reads, "I thought you should know."

Scanning the paper, my eyes land on the line at the bottom.

Daniel A. Danforth is EXCLUDED as the biological father.

EPILOGUE
POPPY

SIX MONTHS LATER

"Pop, you ready?"

"Coming!" Reaching for my carry-on bag, I head for the steps.

"Porter could've gotten that, babe."

I grin down at my handsome man. "I know. But it's still kinda weird to me. I've been handling my own things for thirty-nine years." I laugh.

The last few months have been a whirlwind. It didn't take long to discover the few moments Broadie and I had together were sacred. Trying to coordinate our schedules to find time for one another started to seem senseless when instead, we could come home to each other at the end of every day if we moved in together.

So, I packed my things and moved in with him just before Christmas. It was the best gift this girl could've asked for. We often talk about where we go from here as we're lying in bed. But he hasn't formally asked, and I'm in no rush. Broadie has come so far with finding a work-life balance, I don't want to push him.

"It should be a quick flight, Dr. Weston. The weather's beautiful. You couldn't have picked a better day to fly," Porter says.

"Oh, Broadie. This seems like even more of a dream than the last time."

He winces, and I know he's recalling all of the sneaky stuff he pulled to mastermind my winning that trip, as well as the lies he kept telling once I arrived.

"It all got me to you," I coo, kissing his cheek.

"Thank god you're the forgiving type."

In no time at all, we arrive at the airport, and Porter pulls up to Broadie's jet. This man knows how to travel in style. I still can't believe this is my life now. Heck, I remember just being excited to fly first class.

"What're you giggling about?" Broadie asks.

"I was thinking about when I got randomly bumped to first class on that flight to Jamaica."

Instead of seeming shocked or amused by this, Broadie appears troubled. "What is it?"

"Poppy, I—"

"You didn't? Tell me that wasn't you."

Broadie looks up toward the heavens and rocks back on his heels.

"Oh, good grief. And the limo that came to get me out of that transportation van?"

"For fuck's sake, Poppy. I couldn't watch you bumping down the highway in that thing any longer."

"Broadie Weston, I almost had a heart attack that day."

"See. You're welcome."

"No! I thought I was being kidnapped."

"Shit. You never told me that."

"Welcome aboard, Dr. Weston," a flirty little number greets as we enter the jet.

"Hello, Samantha. This is Poppy."

"It's so nice to meet you. Can I get you anything while we're preparing to take off?" She extends her arm toward the open seating, and I follow Broadie's lead, taking the spot beside him.

"No, thank you," I say. I'm excited to get this trip underway. Broadie has joked about wanting to go back to Jamaica and enjoy our time there without the false pretenses for months. Now that spring fever is in the air, it seemed like the best possible time to travel. As much as I enjoyed the previous trip, the summer temperatures in Jamaica were brutal. I'm looking forward to spending time there when the heat isn't quite as oppressive.

Broadie leans in. "I hope you packed that sexy little blue dress."

I grin. "You don't like this one?" I was surprised when Broadie asked me to wear something white on our trip. He's always complimentary of anything I wear but hasn't seemed to have strong opinions about fashion. He advised he wanted to make a stop on the way to the resort, and there might be a chance to capture our visit with photography this time. It was sweet. I've regretted not getting more pictures the first time, even if they were of the cheesy tourist variety.

Broadie removes his suit jacket. It's a stone-colored Brioni linen that screams of money. Normally, I'd find pretension a turn-off. However, he wears it well. The clothes look natural on him. He's never flaunted his wealth. I'm not sure his patients have any idea how rich he is.

Settling in for our trip, Broadie rests his hand on my thigh as we take off. "Bring some good books, babe?"

"Yes." I clap. "I have five that I've been waiting for the right moment to read."

"Five?"

"I read fast."

"You better. Because unless we are acting out some of the spicy scenes in your books, you better make room for me."

I giggle. "Oh, how the tables have turned."

"I'll get the car and will be back shortly, Dr. Weston," Porter advises before heading for the building.

I shield my eyes as I look up at the gorgeous sky. There are a few clouds dancing about the top of the Blue Mountains in the distance. Broadie slides his arm around my waist.

"Stick with me, Pops. I don't want you falling into the wrong man's arms."

I snicker at the memory of that day.

"Here we go," Broadie advises as Porter pulls up beside us. He ushers me inside as Porter places our bags in the trunk. He seems to take longer than necessary speaking to Porter at the back of the vehicle before opening the opposite door and joining me.

"Everything okay?"

"Yes. Just wanted to verify he and Stu had everything covered."

"Oh, Stu. He's so stealthy. I tend to forget he's around most of the time."

Broadie smiles. "Yes. That's because he's good at what he does." He lifts my hand to his mouth.

"So where are we going that we needed to be all dressed up."

He adjusts himself in his seat. "I wanted to stop by Dunn's River Falls. I never got to see it on the last trip. It's on the way."

I look down at my outfit. "Wouldn't that be a place to wear bathing suits under your clothes? I thought people formed a human chain and climbed the rocks at the falls."

"They do. We can always come back if that's what you want to do. But I hired a photographer. I wanted to start our trip off right. We don't have any pictures of us together."

I laugh. "Um, *you* might not. But I bet if you asked Lauren, she has about one hundred of them on her phone." She and Lilly spent Christmas Eve with us before heading to their mother's home. "I think she spent the entire morning photographing everything."

Broadie laughs. "She takes pics for social media. I hate that she puts so much of her private life out there. But she knows full well she isn't allowed to post any of me without clearing it with me first."

"Such a party pooper."

We travel along, taking in the sights. The Sangster Airport is a bit closer than the Normal Manley airport in Kingston where I flew in the last time. Hopefully, we'll arrive to the fun part of the trip that much sooner. Not that flying in a private jet isn't fun. But the hassle of traveling to and from, checking bags, and clearing customs and security take time away from the good stuff.

About an hour later, I look up from my book to see Porter turning into the Dunn's River Falls entrance. Initially, it has the feel of a typical amusement park, but as you meander the grounds, there's a blend of both modern facilities and rustic charm. Looking at my watch, I notice it's almost midday. Yet, there's virtually no one here. I know it's an off time of year, with school in session, yet the place is practically empty.

"Are they open today?"

"Just for us," Broadie says as we walk hand in hand casually down the path.

"Are they only open on the weekends during the off-season?"

"No."

Sensing he's being intentionally vague, I stop in my tracks, nearly falling over when he continues walking with my hand in his. I arch my brow in question when he turns to make eye contact with me.

"Okay. I bought the place for the day."

"What?"

"I don't like crowds."

Blinking at him, I wait for more information. This man has lost it.

"It's harder than you think dealing with security and whatnot."

"You didn't have any problem when we went to Mystic Mountain to ride the bobsleds."

"That was different."

I ball my fists and place them on my hips. "Why?"

Broadie comes closer. "I was obsessed with the need to get to know you. And for you to get to know me. I thought we established this already. There wasn't much I wouldn't have done."

"Is it too late to rethink this relationship?"

"Yes!" He huffs, pulling me along beside him.

We meander about the place, taking in the sights. There is a tranquility garden for picnicking by the river, a splash pad for cooling off from the heat, a zip line to allow seeing the falls from a bird's eye view, and a beautiful beach.

As we make the trip back toward the front of the park, it dawns on me that there weren't any photographers around as I'd suspected, given his earlier statements. I begin to ask him where we could get some photos of the two of us together when my eyes land on the most peculiar sight. This park actually has a designated area for weddings. Covering my face with my hands, I point to the sign that reads, Tie De Knot. It's honestly the last thing I would've expected to find here. But apparently, I'm the only one shocked to see it as I turn to find Broadie down on one knee.

"Oh my god."

"Poppy, everything about our first trip to Jamaica could've gone so wrong. I lost my heart to you on this magical island. I knew if you left me, once you discovered all that I'd done, you might as well have put it in a jar on your shelf like a forgotten souvenir. Because it would never belong to anyone else."

"Broadie," I gush.

"I couldn't wait to get back here, to make sure all of our memories of Jamaica were happy ones." He stands up, holding the most incredible platinum cushion cut diamond I've ever seen out for me. "Please, Poppy? Make me the happiest man alive and say you'll be mine?"

There's no hesitation. "Yes. Yes."

He quickly scoops me up in his arms, spinning me around. As he slows us down, my eyes land on a photographer standing just to the right of the signage. Beside him is a minister.

"Broadie?"

"We don't have to. We can wait and have a big wedding or plan a big party if that's what you want. But I had the feeling since we'd been there and done that already, it might be nice to make this about us."

My inclination is to go for it. But I only have one real hesitation. "Broadie, my mother would be so disappointed if we got married without her."

"I thought you might say that."

Out of the blue, Stu walks over. "Someone wanted to say hi." He chuckles.

As Stu hands his iPad off to Broadie, my mother and Agnes come into view.

"Mom, Agnes. Hi! How on earth did you two figure out how to video-call with Stu?"

"We had some help," Agnes says, waggling her brows at the gentleman standing beside them.

"Hey, Max. I owe you one, man."

"I think you owe me more than one." He chuckles.

Is he referring to Agnes?

"Max is who helped me with the email you received about winning the trip to Jamaica."

"Ah. It's all getting clearer now."

"Sorry, Poppy."

"All's forgiven. Thank you for helping set this up for my mother."

"What are you two doing there, Poppy?" Mom says with a knowing smirk on her wrinkled face.

"Something tells me you already know."

"Well, Broadie said since your father wasn't around anymore, I'd do."

"You'd do for what?" I laugh.

"He asked my permission to marry you."

I spin toward him, amazed at how he's managed to pull this all together. "Are you okay if we Tie De Knot here without you?" I ask.

"Poppy, her hearing is so bad, she wouldn't hear your vows any better if you were in the same room." Agnes laughs.

"Just tell that guy to say he pronounces you husband and wife loud enough for everyone to hear it!" Mom declares.

We move over to the minister, who quickly reads through his prepared ceremony. There's nothing special or unique. But it's perfect all the same. Broadie spared no expense with our wedding bands. His is platinum, and mine is an infinity band decorated with the most beautiful diamonds. Heck, I really will need Stu around now.

"I now pronounce you husband and wife!" The minister yells. "Did she get that?"

We look at the screen to find Mom and Agnes smiling from ear to ear.

"Kiss her already," Agnes yells.

And he does. While Broadie gives me a toe-curling kiss that feels like a prelude to more, claps and catcalls can be heard from the iPad, Porter, and Stu. Someone walks over with two champagne glasses, and we toast the moment as the photographer takes more pictures of our impromptu wedding.

As Porter pulls up to the resort I remember so well, my heartbeat starts to pick up. Who knew this place would have such an impact on me? The car stops, and a staff member from the resort opens the door, allowing me to exit. Broadie comes around the back of the vehicle to meet me just as two rows of staff members dressed in various uniforms all clap.

"Congratulations."

"Welcome back, sir."

"We're so happy for you, Dr. Weston."

Wait?

"Broadie Weston? Is there something you need to tell me? No more secrets, remember?"

He immediately drops his head.

"What is going on?"

"I might've bought this place."

"What?"

"It has sentimental value." He smirks.

"Broadie, people buy vacation homes. Not vacation resorts."

"It's an investment."

My mouth falls open. "Are you for real, right now?"

My new husband escorts me past the cheerful staff members and down the landing toward the pool and restaurants below. Again, I take notice of how unpopulated the place appears. "Is anyone staying here but us?"

"Yes."

It's then I notice the area decorated with round tables covered in white linen, vases of colorful tropical flowers, and festive music playing.

"Surprise!"

"Oh!" I clutch my chest. As I gain my wits about me, I notice several of our friends are here—Nick and Kat, Broadie's girls, plus a few gentlemen I don't recognize. "I can't believe you did this. What if I'd said no?"

"We would've just enjoyed the resort."

"You're unbelievable."

Broadie's brows pinch together. "In a good way?"

My eyes land on Gavin standing beside Lauren, and I smile. "In the best way."

"Oh, Poppy. I'm so happy right now." Lauren beams up at the two of us. She's radiant in her sleek, form fitting, satin white sundress. Her sister is dressed similarly except her dress is A-line and flowy.

Wrapping my arms around the two of them, I give them the biggest hug. My family. I can't even put words to how I'm feeling right now. All of a sudden, I feel guilty that they weren't there to witness their father getting married. "Oh girls, I'm so sorry you weren't there."

"It's okay. We were hoping you'd say yes. When we got the message from Dad that it was a go, everyone here cheered."

Shocked, I spin to look at Broadie. "I can't believe everyone here knew but me."

"No, Pop. They only knew we were celebrating how much our lives had changed. I'm sure it may have crossed some peoples' minds, but I neither confirmed or denied what was happening. Just told the girls they could announce the news after you said yes."

Stepping closer to my husband, I cup his gorgeous face, and kiss his big, beautiful lips. "What did I ever do to deserve you?"

He tosses his head back and chuckles. "Something tells me you probably asked the same question months ago after I planned the first trip here."

I smack his chest, beyond relieved we made it through. I cannot imagine my life without him.

"Oh, it's my turn!" Kat squeals. She pulls me in for a one arm hug, pressing her forehead to mine. The joy that exudes from her is tangible. And it's no surprise. She's seen me through so many ups and downs over the last year. Katarina's beautiful dark hair is down, tossing in the wind as she holds Grace on her hip. I barely noticed the coordinating white lace dresses they're both wearing because of her huge toothy grin.

It's then I realize all of the women here are wearing white dresses and the men white shirts and sand-colored slacks or shorts. Turning to Broadie, I ask, "Did you tell everyone what to wear?"

His smile is as bright as the Jamaican sun, that flirty dimple winking at me. "I told them we wanted to take pictures and asked if everyone would match." He shakes his head. "It was Lauren's idea."

As I turn to look at Lauren, I'm interrupted.

"Congratulations, Poppy. I'm really happy for you." Gavin steps forward, giving me a hug.

My heart has ached for this young man. Gavin and I had spoken so briefly about setting up a trust for him for college with Dan's money that I was surprised when he acted on it so quickly. I'd told him if he was interested, he only needed to call Broadie's attorney, and they'd take care of all of the details, including the paternity test. He'd later shared that he'd considered taking a test before our discussion, but didn't know how to begin. There were too many questions he needed definitive answers to so he could move on with his life. He'd driven to the lawyer's office that very day and went straight to the lab.

When we spoke about it later, I recall him sharing how he was anxious to try and make something of himself. To live a life he could be proud of. One that might make Dan proud too.

Faced with the impossible news that Dan, in fact, was not his father, he fell into a downward spiral. Luckily, Nick was there to help put the pieces back together. He seems to have lost that spark he had before the results returned. But I have no doubt this incredible young man will find his way. And we'll all be the richer for having been a part of his journey.

While Gavin has become special to me, it's not my place to pry. I'm sure he's had uncomfortable conversations with his mother about this. Yet, unless he's interested in volunteering what he's found, I'll support him in any way I can. I pondered still offering to provide seed money for college, but Nick assured me he had it taken care of.

Watching these two beautiful young people, I have to acknowledge there's a weird alliance forming between Gavin and Lauren. They're an odd pair, honestly. She's so fashion forward and confident, while he's dressed like Kurt Cobain. It doesn't seem romantic. Heck, he's closer to Lilly's age. Yet, I get the feeling Broadie isn't happy they're spending so much time together.

Jarod walks over with his wife and kids. "Congratulations, you two. I'm so thrilled for you."

"For us or you?" Broadie laughs.

"Both. Who could turn down an all-expenses paid trip to Jamaica?"

Broadie arches a brow, giving me a questioning look. I have to admit, taking that trip was the best decision I've ever made.

"Broadie, introduce us to your beautiful bride," an incredibly attractive dark-haired male with an Italian accent says.

"Poppy, I want you to meet my friends." Broadie smiles broadly as he goes down the list. "This is Gianni, Devon, Becket, and Derek. And Max should be here soon. You met him briefly earlier."

I give him a bewildered expression.

"With Mom and Agnes."

"Oh, yeah." I giggle. "Hi, Dr. Hart."

"Derek," he corrects.

"And you work at St. Luke's too, right?" I ask Becket.

"Yes. I should've introduced myself years ago. Given Broadie here a run for his money."

Broadie's arm tightens around me, and I quickly realize these are his boys from the club. And not a woman in sight. "What? No dates," I ask.

"Uh, numbnuts didn't tell us he closed the resort to outside guests." Becket glares.

"That's what you get for planning to score at my wedding."

"That's okay. We'll visit a few others in the area. For research." Devon winks.

We make small talk for a few moments before sitting down to enjoy an incredible meal of jerk chicken, roasted root vegetables, rice, and fruit. The drinks are flowing, and the atmosphere is just how I remembered. Casual, relaxed, and perfect.

~

"I thought we'd never get away." We're in the town car, heading away from the resort.

"Where are we going, Broadie? I thought you'd bought out the resort for the week. Why did we have to go somewhere else?"

I wanted to spend our honeymoon at an adult-only resort.

Shifting in my seat, I look at him as if he's lost his mind. "If the only guests are those at the party tonight, then there's only like four kids. I hardly think they'll be a problem."

He chuckles. "No. They won't be. I'm just messing with you. I just wanted to spend a night or two at this resort. What better time than our honeymoon?"

After a short drive, Porter pulls into a small gated area and drops us off at the front entrance. We receive a more subdued greeting this time, but it's similar enough that I can't help but ask, "Do you own this one too?"

"No."

I giggle, shaking my head.

"We do."

My walking halts. "Of course we do."

My husband turns to the gentleman escorting us down the path to the water below. "I've got it from here, Ellison. Everything is all set up for us?"

"Yes, sir. I'm here if you need anything."

As our destination comes into view, my hand flies to my mouth. "Broadie…"

He leads me to a small bungalow built over the water. It's one of several just like it. I've seen similar structures in commercials for tropical destinations. Once we arrive, he pulls me in, hungrily kissing the skin behind my ear. Our bags are placed neatly on luggage stands by the closet. There are beautiful flowers on the dining table, a tray of fresh fruit, and champagne in a bucket of ice.

"May I take off your dress, Mrs. Weston?"

Holy crap. That's me. I'm Mrs. Weston.

"What's the matter?"

"For a minute there, I wasn't sure who you were talking to. The day has been... well, a lot." Reflecting on the last twelve hours has my head spinning. I'd be completely exhausted if being in this magical place with my new husband wasn't keeping my adrenalin going.

"Are you disappointed we didn't get married the typical way?"

"No. This was perfect. Everything is perfect."

As my strapless white sundress falls to the floor, I watch as my new husband takes in my body. I'm wearing tiny nude-colored panties and no bra, as the dress came with one sewn in.

"Yes. Yes, it is." He drags his tongue over his lower lip, and I can feel it in my belly. The air crackles between us as he reaches down to rub his hardening dick through his pants.

"Can I help you with that, Dr. Weston?" I tease, reaching out to lower his zipper.

"Ah. Such a good little wife. What do you plan to do to help?"

Dropping to my knees, I slowly tug his pants down his legs. His engorged cock bounces out and hangs heavy between us. My mouth waters. I'm tempted to grab him and start sucking him off, but reflexively, drop my fingertips to the swollen, throbbing flesh beneath my panties and attempt to rub the ache away.

"Oh, no no. No one is making that needy pussy feel good but your husband," he barks.

He gives his thick shaft a stroke.

"But you can do *that*?" I sneer playfully.

"I'm just getting it ready for you, my dear."

I inch forward, opening my mouth in anticipation.

He coats my lips with precum before pushing inside. His thrusts start slow but become more possessive. The familiar dominance emerges, as his thick cock hits the back of my throat, bringing tears to my eyes.

"That's enough." He withdraws, bending to lift me up by my arms. "On the bed, Pop. Let me see that sexy little ass." I shimmy out of my panties and climb on the edge of the mattress, digging my fingertips into the covers. I never know what I'm in for when he's behind me.

"Oh," I squeal as he repeatedly flicks his tongue over my warm, wet center.

"Fuck, you taste good."

He continues to devour me, reaching around my body to flick my clit with the pads of his fingers.

"Broadie, I need you," I shout.

I feel him back away momentarily. That's odd, he normally only does this if he's reaching for a condom. But we haven't used those since we moved in together. He returns, this time spreading my ass cheeks wide, licking me vigorously from my clit to my ass just before pushing the tip of his finger into my backside.

I let out a moan. He's never taken me here. His size is terribly intimidating. And while we don't often play there, when we do, I admit it only magnifies everything I'm feeling.

"Shhh. It's okay." His finger pushes a little deeper, before withdrawing. Suddenly the familiar sensation of lubrication drips down the crack of my ass just before his finger returns. In and out, in and out. Honeymoon or not, I'm not ready for that.

"Broadie, I'm not—"

"No, baby. Nothing like that. I'm not going to hurt you." A buzzing sensation grazes along my core before settling over my clit.

"Oh god. Broadie," I groan.

"Just give it a minute. I only want to make you feel good, Pop." I've never been one who dabbles with toys. Especially not when the person I'm with is so naturally talented. When someone like this knows how to make your body come alive, why would you need help?

This sensation is next level. I'm so wet. His left hand curls around my waist, his fingers teasing my body in all of the right places, and I worry I might faint from overstimulation. He dips the tip of the small vibrator into my ass and I shiver at the feeling.

He gently strokes his hand down my spine. "Try to relax. It's not big, Pop. Just a mini bullet vibrator. Does it hurt?"

"God, no. But I want you. Please." I sway my hips back and forth. "Please, Broadie. I'm not going to last long like this."

He places his large hand at the center of my back, pushing me down into the bed. The familiar sensation of the wide tip of his cock pressing into me has my back arching. He's so thick, it usually causes a bit of a burn when he stretches me. Yet, today, it's a relief to feel him slide inside. I'm so turned on. The fullness I feel with the vibrator simultaneously buzzing inside me is indescribable. Just when I think this man has taken me higher than I could ever go, he finds new ways to soar.

"Broadie," I whine.

"Oh, fuck, Pop. My wife's so fucking tight." He starts bucking wildly into me. The feeling sending me so close to the edge. "I'm going to come so hard. I can't wait to pull out and see it dripping down your thighs. To know you're mine."

"Oh god," I scream.

"Yes. Fuck yes." He continues to pound into me until he pulls out the vibrator and stills, emptying into me.

Unable to stay upright, I collapse beneath him. The sounds of his heavy exhales combined with the lapping of the water outside the bungalow lulling me to sleep. Safe and sound in the arms of this deliciously dirty doctor.

My dirty doctor.

BONUS EPILOGUE
POPPY

ONE YEAR LATER

BZZZ, BZZZ.

"Hello?"

"Hey, Poppy. I'm so glad you answered. Is there any chance you're available to meet any time soon?"

Kat sounds as if she's winded, her words coming out as exhales across the line.

"Yes, of course. Are you okay? You sound as if you're running."

"No, just juggling… well, a lot. That's why I wanted to see if we could meet. I've got my hands full. Literally." I can hear the sound of her car beeping in the background. "What are you doing right now." I can picture her wincing as she asks, and I laugh. It's so Kat.

"Heading to your place."

"Oh, yay! See you soon."

Pulling up to Kat and Nick's home on the lake brings a sense of calm I feel every time I see their little slice of heaven. I step out of my car and am immediately met with a cool breeze that carries the scent of the water below along with it. The leaves all sway from their branches as if waving hello.

The front door swings wide, and I'm met with a smiling Katarina, holding her daughter, Grace. As I reach the base of her steps, I notice they aren't alone.

"Well, hi there," I greet, surprised to find a third person here.

The little cherub backs away, her arms wrapped tightly about Kat's leg as she buries her face bashfully.

"This is Sara," Kat introduces. "She's a little shy. We got a call from the caseworker we've been partnered with since taking classes to foster, and she's our first blessing. I knew this day would come. And I'm excited, but I think I was expecting a newborn. So juggling both of them is going to take some getting used to." She giggles nervously. I adore this woman, yet she wears her emotions on her shirt sleeve. She looks beyond overwhelmed.

As I reach the top of the steps, I bend down to where Sara is hiding her face behind Kat's leg. "Hi, Sara. I'm Poppy. It's nice to meet you." The little girl stays hidden. "I love your name. My mother's name is Sara."

The little girl with long brown hair peeks out long enough that I can see her brown eyes before darting back behind Kat. She must be about three.

"Come on in, Poppy. I'll try to set them on the floor to play, and we can have some tea."

Following Katarina inside, I find her usually spotless den littered with toys and books. "When did you get the call?" I ask.

"I literally picked her up an hour before I called you."

After she places Grace on the floor beside a toy that looks like a xylophone, Sara follows and plops down beside her. That's when I see it. This beautiful little girl has a cleft lip. I almost didn't notice, mesmerized by her big brown eyes that captivated me with a mischievous glint, despite her bashfulness.

"I haven't changed my mind or anything. I guess I just hadn't prepared myself for the transition. Having two needy girls so close in age." Kat looks on the verge of tears.

Reaching for her, I pull her in for a big hug. "Babe, you've got this.

You're a natural. Look how well you've done with Grace. That child was born premature, fighting for her life. And now she's taking on the world." I laugh. We both look over at the sweet girls on the floor, cautiously interacting with one another. "And Sara must've taken to you right away, the way she was clinging to you when I got here."

Kat grabs her teapot, placing it under the faucet to fill with water. "I think she would've done that with anyone. That's how I met her. Clinging to the caseworker that way."

"Do you know anything about her?"

A frown mars her pretty face. "Not a lot. Unlike a lot of the kids in the foster system, she's available for adoption. Her parents terminated parental rights almost immediately."

Looking over at Sara, this makes my heart ache. "Do you think it was because they couldn't handle another child? Or because..." Turning my back to the girls, I point to my face.

"Not sure. But you can't help but wonder." Kat stands a little taller as she watches something behind me. "Gracie, you need to share. Let Sara have a turn." She turns back to me with a wearied expression.

"She's two, Kat. Haven't you seen that toddler T-shirt? What's mine is mine, and what's yours is mine." I giggle.

"I guess you're right."

It doesn't take long before the teapot starts to squeal loudly, and little Sara comes running. She collides with my leg, squeezing it tightly.

Bending down, I scoop her up and say, "Shh. It's okay, Sara. It's just the teapot." Kat holds it up so she can see. "It makes that noise when the water gets hot, so we know it's ready."

Kat fills two mugs with steaming water and carries them over to the coffee table. As I drop Sara down to her feet, I reach out and playfully tug at a light brown ringlet of hair, and she smiles. Even with the deformity, her sweet expression warms something in me that I didn't realize was missing.

Broadie and I knew the odds were stacked against us when it came to having biological children. I had accepted the fact this might be a dream I had to let go of long before he came along. Yet, I admit I was hopeful once we were married that a miracle might take place. He manages to accomplish the impossible. So why not this?

But I didn't want to allow myself to become fixated on getting pregnant. I'd seen the effect it had on so many women. The depression. Especially in a line of work where you're surrounded by so many women. Many of whom have no difficulty conceiving. I didn't want to feel envious of my peers.

We'd discussed the possibility of IVF, surrogacy, or adoption, but wanted to give ourselves the chance to conceive naturally first. Plus, our lives had been full just accommodating to married life and spending quality time with Broadie's girls.

"Can I tell you something? Without you thinking I'm nuts."

"Kat, I need to tell you something too."

She looks concerned. "Oh, you go first."

"I already think you're nuts."

She cackles, causing both girls to turn and start laughing too.

"Nick wasn't sure about how this was going to go. He was worried I was going to get too attached to these children. That I'd want to adopt them all." She takes a sip of her tea. "I'd never admit it to him. But there's a part of me that thought he might be right."

"I could see that. You're a born nurturer, Kat."

"Thank you. I feel a little guilty." She seems embarrassed.

"Why?"

"Because I don't have that feeling with Sara," she whispers.

I turn, finding the sweet little girl reaching for different toys scattered near the blanket they're playing on, handing each to Grace. "Well, maybe that's a good thing. So you'll be able to help more kids without getting too hurt at having to let her go."

"No."

My head snaps back to Kat. Is it because of her cleft lip? I'd never think that would matter to Kat.

"It's because, from the minute I picked her up, I thought of you and Broadie. I don't know why, but she never felt available."

I swallow hard at her statement. I've only just met this little girl, there's no way I can allow myself to consider something like this. "Kat, I—"

My words are cut short when Sara brings me a baby doll.

"Oh, thank you, sweet girl."

Sara beams up at me before putting a toy bottle to the doll's lips.

Before I know it, tears are welling in my eyes. As I turn to Kat, she's handing me a tissue. "Do you think Broadie could come by for dinner sometime soon?" She shrugs, a hopeful look in her eyes.

"Yeah," I answer timidly. "I think we can make that happen."

Broadie

It's been a few weeks since I met little Sara, and from the moment I saw her. I knew. I think somehow, Kat, Poppy, and I each knew. She needed us almost as much as we needed her.

We'd immediately reached out to my lawyer as well as Sara's caseworker to see what steps we needed to accomplish in order to make this adoption happen.

This little girl is shy but smart and sassy once you spend any real time with her. She's staying with Kat and Nick until we can achieve everything necessary to make the adoption legal. Luckily, my attorney has pulled some strings to get our home visits and paperwork filed expeditiously.

Now, on to the next step in this puzzle.

Knock, knock.

"Hey, Broadie. What's up?" Jarod looks up from the papers he's holding, startled to find me holding Sara. No one in the office is aware that Poppy and I have started the adoption process. I'd never considered it before, but adoption is insanely stressful. It feels similar to that first trimester in pregnancy, where you aren't sure you want to share the news in case something bad occurs.

"Who's this?" Jarod stands from his chair, wearing a bright smile as he comes closer.

As expected, Sara buries her face in my neck.

"This is Sara. I probably should've made a formal appointment to see you, so you could evaluate her. I'm hoping you'll consider performing her cleft lip and palate repair."

Jarod's eyes widen in confusion. "Me? I assumed when you were bringing her by, she was a client of yours. You take on so many pro bono cases."

"No. I'm really hoping, as a favor to me, you'll take on this one."

Jarod looks confused.

It's odd really. I'm constantly inundated with pictures of people every-where I go. Cases where I'm certain I could change their lives by performing surgery for them. Yet, you can't take on every case. And as much as I want the perfect outcome for Sara, I know it would be better if it was handled by another surgeon. The conversation I'd had about Jarod with Brantly Martin, of all people, kept coming to mind.

I'd trust him to operate on my daughters. I'd had no way of knowing back then how true this statement might be.

"Jarod, we're in the process of adopting Sara. Soon to be Sara Renee Weston," I add. Sara hadn't been given a middle name in the hospital when she was born. So, Poppy and I decided to add Renee. It's from the Latin name, Renate, which means born again.

"I don't think I'd feel comfortable in this situation with anyone but you."

"Congratulations, man. That's fantastic."

I beam at him before looking down at the overwhelmed little girl in my arms. "Would you consider performing surgery on your future goddaughter?"

He must be caught off guard by the question, as his hand flies to his chest as he blinks in response. "I'd be honored, Broadie."

Immense pride fills my chest. "Thank you. When the time comes, I'll make a formal appointment, but I wanted to meet with you first."

Placing a kiss to her head, I'm amazed at how protective I feel of her already. She's perfect, just the way she is. Yet the world can be a shallow, harsh place. I never want anything to cause this little girl pain.

I've been blessed beyond measure in this life. I grew up with a family who cared for me, a father and grandfather who provided immeasurably for me, and I managed to meet the love of my life despite myself. And now I'm about to be blessed with not just two beautiful daughters, but three.

"Bye, Dr. Weston," Beatrice says from the reception area. "Oh, who's this."

"This is Sara. We were here visiting Jarod."

"Nice to meet you, Sara. I'm Beatrice." Sara puts her face down on my shoulder, and Beatrice reaches up to rub her back. "She's got your eyes, Broadie." It's as if my intuitive receptionist knows.

"Would you look at that? I guess she does."

Returning to my car, Sara clutches her arms tightly around my neck, as I prepare to head back to Nick and Kat's place. The thought of leaving her hurts more each time we say goodbye.

I buckle Sara into the car seat just as my cell phone buzzes in my back pocket. Pulling it out, I see my lovely wife's face on the screen. "Hi, beautiful. We're headed back to Kat and Nick's now."

"Oh good. Do you mind stopping to pick up a loaf of good bread from the grocery store on your way back? Kat is making us dinner."

The instant relief that washes over me, knowing we don't have to leave the moment I return with Sara is startling. How have I gone from an absentee dad to one who wants to spend every moment with all four of my girls?

"Sure, babe. We'll be there soon."

As I carry Sara into the grocery store, it hits me how bad I've been at parenting. I look for a cart and struggle to figure out whether I need to buckle her into the front or just let her sit there with her legs dangling. "Are you going to be good and sit still in here, so you don't fall out?" I tease.

She nods up and down, her smile pulling at the cleft. Bending down, I kiss her on her head and go in search of a good crusty loaf of bread.

"Would the little one like a cookie?" the girl behind the bakery counter asks.

Well, how the hell could I say no now? Sara's arms are outstretched, fingers wiggling for the treat.

"Thank you." Her voice is soft and low. It's so rare she speaks that it almost catches me off guard.

"Oh, such a sweet girl." The woman wearing the hair net beams. "Isn't it exciting?"

"What?" I ask, dumbfounded. Had I missed something?

"Watching them grow up. Finding out who they're going to be. It's like the best gift ever." The woman's enthusiasm is infectious. "Enjoy every moment. They go by so quickly."

She's right. I'm suddenly overwhelmed with gratitude for so many things. Not only that I have the opportunity to be surrounded by these amazing girls, Poppy, Lauren, Lilly, and Sara. But that I was fortunate enough to get my act together and grow up before they did, so I could enjoy every moment from here on out.

The End.

WANT TO READ A BONUS EPILOGUE FOR THIS STORY?

Thank you for reading.
Click the link and enjoy!
https://dl.bookfunnel.com/lrsi1b9ixd

INTERESTED IN KNOWING MORE ABOUT GAVIN?

Follow my newsletter to stay up to date on how his story unfolds in future books.
https://bit.ly/3yST3pT

Keep reading for an excerpt of Mr. Second Best, starring George "Huggie" Hughes.
https://geni.us/2xItty

You can read more about Tuesday and Cygnature Blooms in Sunflowers and Surrender:
https://books2read.com/u/bwrAG9

And for readers new to the St. Luke's world, check out a snippet from Deprivation,
Book One in The Deprivation Trilogy.
This is Kat and Nick's story.

WHERE THE INTERCONNECTED SPIN-OFFS ALL BEGAN

It's been my dream to share the many characters taking up residence in my mind. I hope you enjoy their adventures as much as I've enjoyed putting them to paper. Without you, I could not continue to live this dream. To obtain more information on my current books, upcoming work, and special offers, please subscribe to my newsletter: https://bit.ly/3yST3pT

Visit me on Facebook at AuthorLMFox and my readers' group, Layla's Fox Den, as well as on Instagram @authorlmfox, X / Twitter @authorlmfox and TikTok @authorlmfox

MEET THE MEN OF
THE BILLIONAIRE BOYS CLUB

Dr. Weston
A cinnamon roll divorced general surgeon, now married to his job. He's sweet, successful, and has a way with bedside manner, in and out of the hospital.

Mr. Wilde
A tech billionaire, specializing in cyber-crime. It's going to take meeting his match to pull this dirty talker away from his obsession with the dark web.

Dr. Love
This Ob/Gyn still practices medicine, even though he made billions by creating a sex aid for older women so they can enjoy their prime. Is there one woman who could satisfy this player?

Mr. Sly
A combination of old and new money, this hard-working hotelier is the biggest playboy of the bunch. Does a woman exist who can tame him?

Dr. Hart

This cardiologist has a heart of gold. While he's worked hard to acquire his wealth, he moved into billionaire status after inheriting his deceased wife's money. Can he find love a second time around?

Mr. Black

Gianni Black is an enigma. Not even his friends in the boys' club know his true identity. This sexy Italian billionaire bad boy owns at least one sex club, but what or who makes him tick?

Mr. Banks

This millionaire stepbrother of Devon Sly is a smooth-talking Casanova. But is there one girl who can turn the tables on him and beat him at his own game?

PLAYLIST

When I Was Your Man - Bruno Mars
Broken Pieces - Apocalyptica featuring Lacey
Jaded, Miley Cyrus
Thank God - Kane Brown & Katelyn Brown
Wicked Game, Chris Isaak
Vogue - Madonna
I Don't Wanna Be in Love - Dark Waves
Give Me Everything - Pitbull featuring Ne-Yo, Afrojack &
Nayer
Something to Someone - Dermot Kennedy
How to Save a Life - The Fray
Nightmare - Halsey
Take Me to Church - Hozier
Jealous - Labrinth
What Was I Made For? - Billie Eilish
In the End - LINKIN PARK
Broken - lovelytheband
THE LONELIEST - Maneskin
I Like Me Better - Lauv
We'll Figure It Out - Smithfield
Ghost - Justin Bieber
Breakaway - Kelly Clarkson
Thank God I Do - Lauren Daigle
Vampire - Olivia Rodrigo

ACKNOWLEDGMENTS

I cannot thank TL Swan enough for starting me on this journey and remaining a huge mentor and friend. I'll always be grateful to her for teaching me to go after my dreams.

And listen up! If I can do this, so can you! If there's a wish locked deep down in your soul, make it happen.

Thank you to my team! Without the amazing work of my editors and formatters, Kelly, Cheree, Kate, and Logan I'd be lost. Each and every one jumps through hoops to help me bring these books to life. I'm honored to have such special people in my life. I'm so thankful to Wander Aguiar for his photographic genius and Hang Le for her creative vision. And the incredible work by Kate Decided to Design on my alternate covers. Working with all of you is honestly a dream come true. To Jo and the team at GMB, thank you for everything you do to get my work out there. To Linda and her incredible team at Foreword, I thank heaven for your guidance. To Jackie, Sara, Ashley, and Geissa, your posts mean everything to me! And to Brittni and my amazing PA, Kate, thank you for keeping me afloat. I'm hoping together we can accomplish great things!

Thank you so much to my alpha, beta, and ARC readers! Denise, Susan, Siri, Rita, Kelly, Kate, Erika, and Emma you've been a continued source of encouragement and support.

I want to send a special note of thanks to all of the Fox Cubs in Layla's Fox Den, my Facebook Author group, as well as the followers on my Facebook, Instagram, Twitter, and TikTok pages. Your posts continue to motivate me, and I truly appreciate all of you.

Ultimately, I'd have never completed this book without the continued support of my husband and kids. Thank for giving me the alone time to create. I love you all so very much.

ENJOY A SNEAK PEEK FROM

DEPRIVATION, BOOK ONE IN THE
DEPRIVATION TRILOGY

CHAPTER FORTY-TWO
KAT

PRESENT DAY

Rolling away from the harsh sunlight, I squint at the clock. It's 6:29 a.m. Bolting upright, I realize my day is once again starting with a bang. I rarely sleep well. When I do manage to get some shuteye, it's usually short-lived as I frequently awaken from nightmares. Occasionally, I'm able to get back to sleep. However, this time, I've slept through my alarm. I need to brush my teeth, take a four-minute shower, braid my hair, and make it to work within the next thirty minutes.

Running into the bathroom, I jump as my toasty feet hit the harsh, cold tiles. My awakening is nearly complete as I turn on the water and my tepid skin meets the frigid spray. *Holy crap!* I dart through the shower, running shampoo and body wash onto me like it's a cheap car wash, then quickly jump out to dry off and don my scrubs for work. *Ugh, no time for coffee. Please let this shift go better than the last.*

As I drive the fifteen-minute commute to work, I reflect on my chaotic morning. Rubbing my eyes of any remaining debris Mr. Sandman left behind, I try to recall anything specific about my most recent nightmare. *Nope, not a thing.* After a while, they all run together. I can't remember the last time I've gotten more than three to four hours of sleep.

It isn't like I have PTSD. No one's ever attacked or abused me physically. How have I developed constant nightmares and insomnia from years of bad boyfriends? I'm sure something's wrong with me. I know I should find a therapist, but how would I explain my reason for being there? "Hi. I'm Katarina Kelly and I'm having nightmares from the ghosts of my past relationships?" Granted, I could win an award for worst dating life ever, but enough to cause years of this? There's a reason I've avoided dating over the last three years. Quickly, I do the mental math and realize it's probably closer to four. Oh well, three or four, it doesn't matter, Gabe was the last and biggest dickwad in a string of many and I'm not going there again. Lonely or not, I'm better off this way.

As I pull into the physicians' parking lot with mere moments to spare before the start of my shift, I spot one remaining open space. Knowing I need to grab my bag and run once this car is in park, I quickly turn toward my destination. I make a harsh left into the parking spot, throw my gear shift into park, and open the door like I'm a contestant on *The Amazing Race*. Grabbing my work bag, I pull it swiftly from the back seat, close my door, and look up to see a car idling behind mine. As if everything else in the world has ceased to exist, I watch as the driver's window rolls down and the operator of the vehicle leans out.

My mouth goes dry, and I stop breathing momentarily as I take him in. *Jeez, this guy is like something out of a Hollywood movie.* He has gorgeous, tousled dark blond hair worthy of a photo shoot, movie star aviators sitting atop his straight nose, and the sexiest stubble covering his firm, square jaw. I watch as a sneer becomes evident despite the sunglasses.

"Nice. You almost took me out trying to steal that spot out from under me, Mario Andretti," he says, the angry timbre of his voice breaking through my stupor.

What? There wasn't another car waiting for this spot. I instantly feel my cheeks turn pink in embarrassment. Realizing I don't have time for this, I decide to avoid a car lot confrontation, return his menacing glare, and abruptly sprint for the ER doors.

"Hey, Kat, you ready to sew up Mrs. Barker?" I hear Jessica call. Jessica Rush is one of my favorite ER nurses, and I'm relieved to be working alongside her today. It's been nonstop in this busy emergency room for almost six hours now, and although I'm worn out, I still have six more to go. Working with people you adore can make all the difference in a stressful environment.

"Sure. You got an extra set of hands? Mildred can throw a mean left hook." I've taken care of this elderly patient before. "Dementia is no joke," I reply, sitting at my usual spot in my favorite hallway. Working as a physician assistant in a demanding ER keeps me hopping. Trying to gather my thoughts to type appropriate notes is much easier in this narrow breezeway next to the supply room. Sitting in the main work area is like trying to work at the bar at TGI Fridays. With the endless interruptions, who can get anything done? For the most part, this little alcove of three computers in this busy forty-five bed ER is my sanctuary.

"Is this seat taken?" a deep voice floats in my direction, interrupting my thoughts. I look up to see a strikingly handsome, dark-haired physician with piercing blue eyes beaming at me. He has bright white teeth which match his lab coat, a stethoscope is peeking out of the left pocket. He points to the chair and computer monitor closest to me, knowing full well there's an identical spot one seat over that's empty. *Heck, come on over. I don't mind a little eye candy sitting next to me for a while.*

It dawns on me that my mouth might be hanging open. He continues to smile down at me while I sit wordlessly, staring at him. "Um, it's all yours," I manage to reply. I notice he isn't wearing a ring on his left ring finger. Why I've looked is anyone's guess; as I haven't had so much as a blind date in three years. Oh, yeah, almost four. But if I was going to start socializing with men, well, he would be quite the—

"Kat, you ready? Mrs. Barker has been driving us crazy. The nursing home says she has sundowners. You know what that means. The later it gets, the more confused and agitated she'll become. If you don't sew up that cut on her forehead soon, she's going to let you have it with both hooks," Jessica says, halting my musing.

"Yeah, I'm coming." I stand, preparing for battle. "Get Wyatt to help hold her still. He can sweet talk the pants off of any confused elderly patient," I laugh. I take off my pristine, starched lab coat and hang it over the back of my chair for fear sewing a laceration on this spirited, unusually strong, Alzheimer's patient would have my white coat resembling a butcher's apron.

I glance over to see my appealing companion is again smiling in my direction. There's one deep, sexy dimple present in his right cheek.

"Go get 'em, Kat," he says playfully.

Feeling a flush creep from my chest toward my face, I quickly exit and head for my awaiting patient.

Thirty minutes later, exhausted from the workout Mildred gave the three of us, I return to my seat to chart my impressive accomplishment. After wiping my brow, I drain nearly half a bottle of water. Let's face it, that's probably the only nourishment I'm getting this shift. To think it required the assistance of two able-bodied professionals, one of whom is our best senior sweet-talker, in order to place five simple stitches in an eighty-two-year-old lady who weighs about ninety-five pounds. I shake my head as I review the computer to see which patients are waiting to be seen. I only have about two hours left in my shift, so I try to choose wisely. Ah, there are three quick turnaround patients waiting. I might actually leave on time today.

As I'm assigning my name to the awaiting patients, I sense an ominous presence to my left. Feeling my skin prickle and my heartrate begin to hasten, this aura is unlike the feel of Dr. Divine who graced this hallway earlier. Slowly peering to my left, I observe no dreamy white smile, no flirty dimple, no warmth or pleasant banter. The brooding, chiseled face of a dark blond god is all I see as he grabs the back of the chair furthest from me and slowly sits down. Again, my mouth is agape. Quickly clamping it shut I notice he's dressed similarly to the carefree doctor who sat in the chair adjacent a few short hours ago, but the rest of this encounter is the polar opposite. There's no witty engagement, just the briefest of intense eye contact before he jolts his view from me, as if he's witnessed an unpleasant stain.

I'm unable to look away, despite his off-putting demeanor. He's a tall, incredibly attractive man with honey blond stubble covering his jawline. Unconsciously, I rub my fingertips over my chin, longing to stroke the golden strands. Feeling parts of me awaken I've kept dormant way too long, I sit transfixed as he attacks the keyboard in front of him like it's committed a personal affront.

I practically jump in my seat as Jessica shouts from around the corner, "Kat, you ready to go downtown? I have Ms. Simmons in room four, ready to roll."

"Sure, Jess. Let's end my day with one more pelvic exam." I think this might be my sixth one today, which is sadly still not a record for me. "I'm starting to feel like I work at an OB/GYN's office," I mutter.

"Well, we don't want to deliver any babies in here. I'll meet you there in a sec. I just have to grab some peppermint oil." Jessica snorts with a lopsided grimace, her strawberry blonde locks in her hand as she refastens her hair in a messy bun above her head.

"Oh, my god, Jess, is it that bad?" I whisper, knowing we tolerate a lot of unpleasant smells in the ER, but we save the peppermint oil for some of the worst.

"Nah, it's for the guy in the room next to her. You really don't want to go in there." I hear her voice trail off as she walks away.

Glad to know I dodged that bullet. I remove my lab coat again in the hope one of us will make it out alive today. Walking past the glowering male perfection banging on his keyboard near the doorway, I ponder what it is about him that seems so familiar. Turning the corner toward my patient's exam room, I hear him utter, "Nice" under his breath. *Wait, where have... Holy heck, he's the angry guy from the car. But what does nice mean? Nice what? Nice face? Nice ass?* I'm sure he's being sarcastic. He is hot; I'll give him that, but *nice* is the last word I'd use to describe this interloper.

Fifty minutes later, I return to my computer after evaluating my last three patients. I finish the bottle of water I've accepted to be a clear substitute for dinner and momentarily place my head down on the desktop in front of me. Hoping to clear my thoughts so I can generate discharge instructions for my last three patients, I feel someone place their hand on my left shoulder. Cautiously I peer up to see one of my least favorite ER attendings, Dr. Silver.

I believe Dr. Silver completed a fellowship at the University of How to Pick Patients I Can See in Less Than Ten Minutes and Have the PA Spend Nearly Ten Times as Long Completing Their Care. If it was just completing a procedure for him so he could focus on more complex patients, it'd be different. But this arrogant son of a gun has made an art of picking up a patient requiring a complicated procedure, knowing he has no intention of completing said procedure. He'll claim he saw the individual and leave work on time while I stay an hour late taking care of his patient. I'm already so tired I can barely keep my eyes open and my shift is scheduled to be over in forty minutes.

"Hey, Kat. Could you put a sugar tong splint on the young lady in room eleven? She has a distal radius and ulna fracture. Thanks," he states, walking away without waiting for my reply.

I try to pick my work battles carefully, so in spite of sheer exhaustion, I silently agree to place the splint on a young lady who appears to have severe developmental delays. *So much for leaving on time. Again.* Ultimately, it's about giving patients the best care possible and I realize Dr. Silver is often *not* the best care. As I see him walk past me near the main physicians' work space, probably to grab his things and head home early, I mutter, "ass wipe" under my breath, just as I almost collide with a tall, broad chest. As if drawn to him like a magnet, I lean in as I inhale the pheromones which now surround me. *God, he smells good.* Ignoring the sizzle that has again crept into my loins, I hesitantly gaze up into the eyes of Dr. Broody.

"Nice," he remarks, sneering down at me with an air of superiority, shaking his head in disgust.

Wincing, I walk around him. I feel my blood pressure rise, knowing he's either heard my degrading comment or simply finds my presence distasteful. Either way, I try to shake it off. What do I care if he heard? He may be hot as hell and smell like sin on a cracker, but I don't need some condescending asshole making me feel stupid. If I wanted that, I'd call one of my ex-boyfriends.

Returning to my work station, fifty minutes past the end of my scheduled shift, I slump in my seat to complete my procedure note on the splint I've just applied. The sweet girl required sedation in order to immobilize her broken arm because her developmental delay didn't allow her to grasp what we were doing. I try to remind myself of a medical professional's call to serve so as not to want to drive to Dr. Silver's home and wring his neck while his trophy wife serves him dinner. I manage to complete the rest of my documentation in record time, now that interruptions are at a minimum and the smoldering but pompous Dr. Broody is no longer distracting me. *God, what was that cologne he was wearing? I'm sure that's what got my motor running, not him.*

Fatigue has taken over, and I find it's too much effort to pay attention to my growling stomach. I grab my bag and head for the door. I just need a hot bath, a glass of wine, my EarPods, and hopefully a few restful hours of sleep.

Heading down the hallway leading to the physicians' parking area, I see Jessica Main and Meghan Rush. I've worked with them since I started at St. Luke's, and quite honestly, every shift is better when they're here. These two nurses are crazy girls and get me through the toughest of nights with laughter instead of tears. "Finally grabbing some grub?" I ask, peering at their yummy plates of grilled cheese and fries. *Oh, there's that growl again. I knew you didn't go far.*

"Yeah, I could eat a horse," Jessica utters with a mouth full of French fry. This makes me chuckle because she literally eats all of the time and never gains a pound. She's a thin, fit, five foot seven, freckle-faced, blonde that one would describe as the quintessential girl next door. You can't help but instantly love her. Every time I see her in the department, she's snacking on goldfish crackers, M&Ms, or Skittles. "I saw you were pretty cozy with Dr. Lee earlier. You better watch that one, Kat. He's a real lady killer," she warns.

"Which one was Dr. Lee?" It dawns on me her description could apply to either of my earlier unnamed companions, particularly if said women were into arrogant dickwads. "I was surprised when they joined me in my little sanctuary. I don't get a lot of strangers in there. They usually prefer the open area with the docs."

"Which one? How many hot men were you entertaining in your lair today, Kat?" Meghan laughs. Meghan, is a sharp-witted brunette with curly hair and an endearing smile. Her humor is infectious and keeps me in stitches.

"Two, actually," I bat my eyes, teasingly. "But of course, I'm so skilled in the art of men I made a complete fool of myself with both of them." I reach over and steal a fry off of Meghan's plate. I'm quite honestly afraid to touch Jessica's, for fear she might bite off my finger. "The first one was nice enough. Heck, I think I might've drooled a little before I could get words out of my mouth when he started talking," I laugh in embarrassment.

"Oh, god," Jessica giggles. "Well, Dr. Lee is super dreamy. He has a smile that could melt lead. And that dimple, uh," she moans. "But rumors travel fast in this place, and he's definitely a playboy. He's hot and he knows it. He's a love `em and leave `em kind of guy, and as much as I'd like to get all up on that, I don't know that I want to be standing in the grill line looking at the nurse on either side of me wondering who had him last."

"Yeah, not my scene, either," I say, scrunching my face up. I'm done with playboys. "He is smooth, though. It was nice to know all my parts are still functioning as they kicked into overdrive when he spoke. I think I started sweating a little before I even laid eyes on him. That voice, it's like ear porn."

Jess and Meghan laugh with Meghan almost choking on her fries.

"How have I not heard of this guy?" I ask.

"You don't hang in the rumor circle, Kat. That's Dr. Sebastian Lee. He's a reconstructive hand specialist who primarily works out of Mary Immaculate. He'll occasionally come to our ER when it's something hand or wrist related or if the on-call orthopod is a hip guy... or if his bank account is low that week, ha. Like that ever happens." Jessica takes a bite of her grilled cheese, trailing a string of warm gooey goodness from her sandwich to her mouth.

Before the bite is completely gone, she smirks. "He's probably made his mark on plenty of nurses at both hospitals." She stops to ponder for a minute. "I think in a moment of weakness, like if I saw him in a bar and could blame my actions on one too many cosmos, I'd do him." Jessica continues to bite into her toasty cheesy sandwich as she looks at my shocked expression. "What? He's hot. When can you ever say you were able to sleep with a guy like that? It's just not possible that he could look like that, hook up with that many women, and be bad in bed."

"Well, what if he ruined all future sex for you? Hmmm?" Meghan inquires sarcastically. She turns back to me and covers her plate of remaining fries with her hand. "So who was your other suitor, Madam?"

"Heck if I know, but quite honestly, I'm not really interested in another interaction with that one. He was ridiculously hot, but that attitude. So rude! And he kept muttering things under his breath. He was very judgy. Dr. Broody can take his sexy hazel eyes and glowering stare somewhere else."

Meghan and Jessica chuckle until Jess looks down at her watch. "We need to get back or we won't have time to finish eating. I'm not leaving my food in the nurses' lounge or someone will steal it for sure." They say goodbye and wave as they head back to the ER to end their shift. Continuing toward the parking lot, I inwardly laugh at their antics while my stomach growls and visions of melty cheese and greasy fries dance in my head.

"Man, you look rough, Kat," a familiar voice blurts as I walk farther down the hall. I instantly feel a smile overtake my face as my dear friend and ER physician, Jake Harris, approaches. Jake, his wife Melanie, and their two kids are more like family than colleagues or friends. We'd met many years ago when we all volunteered as EMTs at the same rescue squad. "Are you getting any sleep at all, or did the day just kick your ass?"

I refocus on my friend and shrug my shoulders. "Today, I think it was a combination of both. You know how it is. I've been this way for years." I stifle a yawn. I've tried everything. Melatonin doesn't work. Benadryl will sometimes help, but then if I have a nightmare, I just wake up so hungover I can't remember where I am for about an hour afterward. "I think I might take Melanie's suggestion and finally see a therapist. I don't have high hopes it'll help, and I don't want to spend my free time sharing all of my troubles with some random person." I look at my watch, noticing it's even later than I thought. "I didn't know you were working today. How'd I miss that?"

"Oh, I'm off today. I had a few hundred charts to finish and needed to work on the schedule and couldn't focus at home. The kids both have friends over. I put on scrubs in case I get pulled in to help someone while I'm here." He looks directly at me and begins to speak more seriously. "Kat, you know I'm happy to write you a prescription for zolpidem. I've worked night shifts for so many years, it's the only way I get any sleep at all. Just try a few and see if they make a difference. But that being said, I think Melanie's right. It wouldn't hurt for you to see someone. I just have insomnia, no constant nightmares. Maybe if someone could help you sort that shit out, you could put it behind you and move on. Hell, maybe you could even meet someone and get laid. God knows you need it."

"Hey! I expect that kind of talk from Jess and Meghan, but not you," I shout, punching his shoulder playfully with my fist. "Besides, if I keep meeting men like the two I met today, you can count me out."

"More of your patients hitting on you?" he snickers.

"No. Apparently, I'm not up on the gossip, but Jess and Meghan educated me on the first, Dr. Lee," I state as a matter of fact. "I don't know who the other one was, but whoever he is, no thanks."

"Ah, the illusive Dr. Sebastian Lee. All the women want him, and all the men hate him," he says without hesitation. "Well, except me. He's kind of a smug bastard, but he is good at what he does and he's come to my aid when no one else would more times than I'd like to admit. He's professional and willing to help when he's on the phone. Yet, if the whole world doesn't revolve around him once he arrives, look out." He scratches his head and smiles. "So long as he doesn't put Melanie under his spell, he's okay by me. But he can be a condescending motherfucker, so he tends to rub a lot of his colleagues the wrong way. And he leaves a trail of women in his wake, so as much as I'd like to see the dust knocked off of your girl parts, I'd recommend you start with someone else."

I stare at him in disgust. I don't like him worrying about my girl parts. They'll rise to the occasion when someone who isn't a complete douche nozzle shows up. "On that note, I'm heading home to a hot soak in the tub and then bed. Don't forget, you and Melanie promised to take me out to the new club that's opening soon. I need to get my groove on," I say, dancing in place.

"Kat, you're twenty-nine, not twenty-one. Can't you get your groove on at The Sports Page down the street?" he groans. "The food's better, it isn't as loud, and you don't have to wait an hour to get a beer."

"Well, we can go there until the club opens. You know going out dancing is the closest thing to sex I get," I joke. "We need to get the guys together for beers soon. It's been way too long. Maybe we could meet up Friday. I'm actually off." Thank God for my guys. I know I'll never meet anyone hanging out with a bunch of firefighters, police officers, and medics who all think of me as a little sister, but I'm okay with that.

"Sure, I could do Friday," Jake says with a little more excitement in his voice than I expect. "You're actually doing me a favor. I think I saw Melanie write something on a piece of paper about book club at our house this Friday. Hell if I want to be there for that noise."

~

On the drive home, I think about how lucky I am to have the Harris family in my life. Don't get me wrong, I love my mom and dad. I was raised in a traditional two-parent household, in a suburb in central Virginia, with parents who remain married after thirty years. I have a younger sister, Rachel. We didn't have a fancy house or car growing up, no brand name clothes or electronics. Yet I never really felt like we wanted for anything. I was never hungry. I wasn't truly neglected. My mother stayed at home with us until we were in high school and then returned to working a clerical job to help with expenses. She was always there for us, but there wasn't the closeness I yearned for. Maybe I'd been watching too much of *The Brady Bunch* and *Leave It to Beaver* when I was young. Unattainable family standards were great entertainment.

I always felt I lived in Rachel's shadow. Two years my junior, she was beautiful and charismatic, and regardless of my grades and hard work around the house, I was a small star eclipsed by her dramatic rays of sunlight. Any boys of interest, or friends for that matter, quickly fell under her spell, and I was pushed into the background. Poor, plain Katarina Kelly. I love Rachel, but I can only handle being her shadow for so long before detaching from her and her throng of admirers.

I eventually distanced myself from everyone but my grandmother. She was my rock. My immediate family was never warm and fuzzy, but my grandmother wouldn't hesitate to hug me every chance she got. She tried to care for Rachel and I equally. Every birthday, she'd bring gifts for both of us, so the other didn't feel left out. But I knew when she looked into my eyes there was a special soft spot in her heart just for me. Now that I'm older, I miss that more than I can admit. If she were still around, I wouldn't need to consider seeing a counselor about my constant bad dreams and lack of sleep. She would be all the therapy I needed.

Nick

Heading home after another long day, I rub the back of my neck as I drive my Audi toward my neighborhood. After work, I left the office and stopped by the ER to introduce myself to the physicians that were working. This took longer than I planned, as they were all busy taking care of patients, but hopefully leaving my business cards and asking to be invited to their next quarterly meeting would bring more referrals. I'm not lacking in business, but I'm new to St. Luke's and want to dive into work there and shrug off the feeling of being an outsider. I wear that cloak enough in my personal life, I don't need to be that way at work, as well.

At almost thirty-six, I'm divorced and still living in the home we shared as a married couple. The neighborhood is nice enough, but the house was Sophia's choosing, along with everything in it. When we split, she initially demanded she take all the furnishings, until she met with her high-powered divorce attorney who must've enlightened her on the windfall she was coming into. Now, it's new everything for her. New townhouse, new furniture, new man.

As I park my shiny black Audi R8 in the garage, I grab my keys and work bag and enter the house. Walking into the kitchen, I look into the near empty refrigerator and stare like something edible is going to materialize. *Unless I want a mustard sandwich, I guess it's take-out again.* Thankfully, I have beer. I pop the cap off of a lager and lean back against the kitchen island, looking around the house. There are no fond memories of our life together here causing me melancholy. The place doesn't fill me with dread. Quite honestly, it's utterly and completely flat. It's just a place to park my car and my body until I head back to work. This home feels like the type of place you'd start a family. While I realize I'd wanted that when I proposed to Sophia four years ago, it no longer looks like a future I'm interested in. I'd suffered enough betrayal at the end of my marriage that I don't foresee ever risking a relationship again.

I hadn't planned to marry after my mother died. I saw what losing her did to my father, but Sophia had seemed different. I cared for her and thought she'd make a good partner and a good mother. I can't say it was the type of love I witnessed between my mom and dad, but I planned to avoid that sort. The kind which could only cripple you if the other person was no longer around. The more I contemplate the last few years, I realize I was more disappointed about the possibility of never having kids than the loss of my marriage... Well, that and the utter humiliation of the way it ended. I abhor liars. Particularly a liar and cheat who made vows to the contrary. Making a clean start and moving to a new hospital just felt like the right thing to do. Sophia didn't work in medicine, but gossip about my divorce had spread through the hospital and I needed a break from all of the drama.

Coming to St. Luke's seemed like the right move, but why did I feel so irritated? I'd dropped off my business cards and was eventually able to meet the physicians on duty in the ER. They appeared receptive to referring patients my way. Dr. Silver seemed a little suspect. He reminds me of talking to a politician, but there's one in every crowd, so that isn't terribly surprising. The nurses seemed nice enough, when they weren't gawking at me.

I accepted long ago that God granted me with features physically appealing to women. Even as a teen, my mother would laugh when young girls and older women alike would stare and giggle. It was ridiculous. It's just skin deep. I had nothing to do with it. Granted, I don't mind it allows me to easily obtain a willing participant for a night of pleasure when I desire it. I just have to be upfront that one night of hot sex is all I'm interested in, nothing more. I do not entertain those dalliances often, and when I do, I try to avoid dating women where I work. I don't need that reputation, and quite honestly, it limits the chance of bumping into them again. But that girl, that brassy, brown haired, beautiful girl... *Why can't I stop thinking about her?*

I stop my wayward thoughts and type my Thai food order into the delivery window on my phone. As soon as the payment is sent through, thoughts of her return. They aren't necessarily alluring, more like annoying. She's definitely not my type. Sure, she's educated and capable or she wouldn't be employed at such a busy ER. But she isn't the most professional PA I've encountered by a long shot. First, she rolled into that parking space like a race car driver. Then, I find her sitting at that messy work station with various scribbled notes, headphones, pens, and reference material all scattered about her computer area in a heap. Yet seeing her slumped in her chair, chewing on the end of her pen, I felt an instant magnetism pulling me toward her I couldn't put my finger on. I have no business considering anything with that one. Looking her way caused a conflict of emotion, intrigue versus irritation. Taking orthopedic consults in the ER, I'll see her frequently. With no plans to date in the future, I don't need that in my life, no matter how mesmerizing her big brown eyes are.

I finish my Thai food and clean up my kitchen. The food is always good, but I still feel unsatisfied. I'm sure all of these changes just take time and are affecting my eating. It's been a year and a half since Sophia moved out. The divorce was ugly and took months to finalize, but I've been a free man for three months. *Maybe I should consider moving. Getting a place that's more my taste and fitting of a lifelong bachelor. That'd probably improve my mood.* I head up the stairs to the master bathroom to take a hot shower. I want to make it to bed early so I can get in a run before work tomorrow. Plus, I have soccer this weekend, so that'll take my mind off of things. It's a recreational league, but a good group of guys who love the sport as much as I do, so it's a great way to spend a beautiful Saturday. *I should also visit Dad this weekend.*

I love Dad, but he's no longer the man he was when Mom was alive, and the visits always leave me depressed. I miss her and our life together as a family more every time I drive away. *I'll see him early Saturday for breakfast before my game so I can shake off the past and focus on soccer.*

I enter the large marble bathroom and turn on the shower. It's meticulously kept, but it's just me now, so it doesn't take much effort. I drop my discarded clothing into the hamper then enter the hot, steamy shower. *Yes, this is what this day needs. Finally. Maybe the Thai food and beer were the foreplay I needed for this epic moment.* I adjust the setting on my shower head to allow for increased water pressure and feel the scalding water pound into my head, neck, and shoulders.

The more relaxed I get, the more thoughts of the crass creature with the long brown braid flash in my brain. Soaping up my body, my mind begins to drift. Like a movie in my mind, I watch as her soft pink lips nibble on the end of the pen in her mouth and picture it is my cock. I reach out to stroke her hair, removing the tie that keeps her dark locks braided, and I run my fingers through her coffee-colored strands as she sucks me in deeper. I can feel her soft hand reach up to cup my balls, and as I look down at her I'm captivated by her big brown eyes staring up at me while she services my thick length like a pro. She starts moving her head up and down greedily over my shaft, and I feel my hands gripping her long, gorgeous, wet tresses in my fists. The sensation is building quickly, and I don't want it to end. But I'm abruptly brought back to reality when I hear my phone ringing on the bathroom counter. *Dammit.* I quickly jump from the shower, grabbing a towel to see if I've missed a call from the ER.

"Nick?" I hear Sophia inquire on the other end of the line. Well, I won't need to return for a cold shower now. Just hearing the sound of that self-righteous bitch on the line has caused my dick to soften. "Are you there?" *If I said no, would she hang up?*

"What do you want, Soph?" I spit out.

"Well, there's that sweet disposition I don't miss for a second."

"Is there a point to this phone call, Sophia?"

"Yes, I just wanted you to be aware I plan on coming by the house this weekend to pick up a few things and didn't want to walk in on you with a guest." Not likely, but I guess I can at least appreciate the warning.

"What could you possibly need from the house after all of this time that you haven't already packed up?"

"I've joined a cooking class and wanted to grab some of the cookbooks I left behind. I'm certain you won't be needing them, as you barely know how to use the microwave."

"Well, I could say the same for you. I can't remember the last time you ever cooked. What's the occasion, trying to impress your new man?"

"Maybe. Does that bother you, Nick? That someone else might like me to cook for them?"

"Uh, no. I just wish you'd waited until we were separated to decide you wanted to impress someone else with your culinary skills," I jibe. "I'm going to visit Dad early on Saturday morning. Please come then to retrieve your cookbooks, and take any other items you may suddenly decide are essential enough to require interrupting my evening."

"Oh, so touchy. What on earth did I interrupt, anything important? The game, a riveting read of the *Journal of Orthopedic Medicine?*"

"No, just the best blow job I've ever had!" I bark, hanging up the phone without another word. Sadly, what I'd told her was true, in spite of the fact I didn't come...and that there was no one else in the room, just visions of *her*.

Amazon universal order link https://geni.us/qVoIg6

ENJOY THIS EXCERPT FROM
MR. SECOND BEST

https://geni.us/2xItty

"What's all this?" Seth asks as the front door closes behind him.

"Are we making the pie?" Ruby bounces up and down with a hopeful look on her face.

"We're going to try. Seth, I'm begging you. Man to man. Will you please help us out with this thing?"

He laughs. "Well, after I left you alone to play Pretty, Pretty Princess with her, I think this is the least I can do."

The kids wash up, and I give Seth the chore of peeling the apples and chopping. I tell Ruby we're in charge of the pie crust. Lord, help us. She's apparently baked with Melanie enough times she knows how to spread out the flour and lay out the dough for the top of the pie.

"Oh, wait!" Ruby yells.

Seth and I stop dead in our tracks as she runs to grab a stool, drags it into the pantry, and starts to climb up.

"Woah, woah, woah. I thought we talked about this."

"Sorry. Can you get that green box up there?" Ruby points to what looks like some type of Tupperware container on the top shelf of the pantry. Hell, she would've broken her neck trying to reach that thing.

Pulling it down, she grabs it and returns to the kitchen table to retrieve the items.

"Found it!" Ruby runs over and holds up a cookie cutter shaped like an apple.

"I thought we were making pie, not cookies, Rubs."

"It's for the top. I saw it on a cooking show once."

Bending down, I smile at her. "That's all you. You are way past my kitchen skills on this one."

"No! You have to help." She pouts. Hell. This little imp has me almost as wrapped around her finger as her mother.

"Okay." I huff.

"Come here," she says, pulling my arm with her to the kitchen island. "Move all this stuff over there, and we can spread out the dough."

"Bossy much?" I tease her.

Ruby gives me that look. The one she no doubt inherited from Melanie. She carefully places the first layer of pie crust in the bottom of the pan and tries to mold it without tearing the pastry. I'm pretty impressed. She seems to have a grip on this. She spreads a liberal amount of flour onto the countertop and unrolls the second layer of pie dough. "Now you start making a few apples," she directs, pointing at the cookie cutter.

Okay, this can't be that hard. "Seth, you doing okay over there?" It's gotten quiet, and I was starting to get concerned until I realized he's eating as he peels. I place the metal-shaped instrument in the center of the dough, and a replica of an apple easily comes out. Moving lower, I repeat the process several more times.

"Huggie."

"Yeah?" I'm expecting her to tell me what a great job I'm doing like her mother might do until…

"If you keep spreading them out like that, we'll be here all day."

What the hell?

Ruby shoves me to the side and gathers up the remaining dough, squeezing it into a ball before spreading more flour. "You need to cut them close together to get the most apples out of it, so we don't have to keep rolling it out." She pulls out the roller and pushes back and forth over the ball of dough until she has it spread back out. Reaching for the cookie cutter, she artfully arranges the shapes so she uses up almost the entire thing.

"Show off," I tease.

"I think we can get a few more."

"How many do you think we need? The pie isn't that big."

No, but we could put butter on them and sprinkle them with cinnamon and sugar," she says like a pro.

"That's what mom does," Seth adds, mouth still full of apples.

As Ruby dumps more flour onto the marble surface, it flies everywhere. "Oops."

Looking down, I notice that I'm covered in it. So is the floor.

"Okay, but this is the last of it. The kitchen looks like it's the middle of winter."

The kids laugh.

"Laugh all you want. You're helping clean this up."

Ruby places the apples on top of the pie after Seth pours in the pie filling. I melt a little butter for the remainder of the dough that Ruby's turning into cookies. Once it's ready, I swing back around to retrieve the sheet pan with Ruby's remaining apples and hear the door fly open. In a flash, Ruby shrieks and runs toward the door while the room goes topsy-turvy.

Thud!

Instantly, I slam into the floor in a cloud of smoke. No, a cloud of flour. The pain from the impact of hitting solid travertine causes a sharp stabbing sensation. Fuck, I'm too young to break a hip.

"Huggie!" I hear Melanie shout before all three of them are crouched around me in the small space between the kitchen island and the stove. "Where do you hurt?"

"I think I broke my ass!"

"Hugs!" Mel rolls her eyes and pinches my side as the kids cover their mouths and guffaw.

"You asked," I tell her incredulously.

"Let me see."

"My ass?" I blurt. "Ow!" Melanie pinches me again, making the kids howl with laughter.

"Do you think you broke anything?" she whispers.

"My pride." I chuckle. "Ow. Why does laughing hurt my—"

Mel quickly covers my mouth with her hand. Her beautiful dark hair cascades down, enveloping either side of my face like a tent. Looking up at her, I just want to pull her down on top of me, kids or no kids.

"Is the pie okay?" Ruby suddenly interjects.

"Rubs. I'm sorry. It was your little apple cookies. I think there was too much flour on the floor."

"Yeah. It's not 'cause you're old or anything."

What? "Old? I'll show you old." I attempt to get up off the floor and tickle her but don't make it far before realizing I might be older than I'd like to admit. It's taking an effort to get up.

Melanie and Seth come to my side, and I'm able to get myself upright between them and the use of the kitchen island.

"Thanks," I say. Looking about the kitchen, it looks like a flour tornado hit it. "Oh, Mel. I'm sorry—"

"Stop! Are you kidding? You managed to get this pie done. Cleaning up is the least of my worries."

My gaze drops to my clothes, which are completely covered in flour, sugar, and who knows what else. "I'm going to get a shower."

"Do you need help?" Melanie asks.

My eyes widen, and it's all I can do to ask if she's offering before she realizes where my mind has gone.

"Getting to the bathroom?"

"No. I'll be okay. Might just take me a day or two."

"Okay." She laughs. "I'm going to start dinner." She steps away for a moment, going to her purse to retrieve something. Walking briskly back to the kitchen, she fills a glass with water and hands me the tablets in her palm. "Ibuprofen. Please yell if you need something." She gives me a light tap on the ass as she walks away.

"Hey!"

Well, that took me forever. I was able to drag my sorry ass, no pun intended, up the stairs and strip everything off. It just took me a while to prevent having her bathroom also covered in flour. I think showering has taken me an hour.

Stepping over the bathtub into the steamy room, I try to see if there's a big bruise on my backside, but I can't see it from this angle. Not to mention the mirror is fogged up.

Scanning the bathroom, it hits me. I didn't bring a change of clothes. I attempt to dry off as best I can before wrapping a towel around my waist. Gazing down, I note my tattoos are on full display. So, I drape a second one around my neck until I reach my room.

I open the door, hoping to make a dash for my room when I crash into Melanie. I breathe in relief that it wasn't the kids until I realize my towel is lying on the floor. And not the one that's hanging from behind my neck.

Bending quickly, I attempt to retrieve it when a sharp, searing pain stabs through my right ass cheek. "Fuck!"

"Are you okay?"

Pushing through the pain, I quickly cover myself. I notice Melanie staring at my ass out of the corner of my eye, and I stand to my full height. Well, I guess it beats what she could've been looking at. I can't discern her expression. But she doesn't look shocked or embarrassed.

Then, what?

https://geni.us/2xItty

ADDITIONAL TITLES BY LM FOX

Amazon Author Page: https://amzn.to/3xT25BJ

The Deprivation Trilogy, Book One: Deprivation
The Deprivation Trilogy, Book Two: Fractured
The Deprivation Trilogy, Book Three: Stronger
Deprived No More, The Epilogue

Interconnected Stand-Alones:
The Bitter Rival
Sweet Surrender, The Epilogue to The Bitter Rival
Moonshot
Mr. Second Best
Naughty & Nice, A Man of the Month Club, 2022 Sycamore Mountain
Series Novella
Sunflowers and Surrender, a Wild Blooms Novella
Hot Chicken, A Man of the Month Club, 2023 Christmas in July Spin-off
Novella
Nuts For Jeremy, A 2023 Holidates Series Novella

Upcoming Titles

Luca

My Best Shot

Hard Hat Hottie

Sam

Chasing Mr. December, A Man of the Month Club, 2024 Series Novella

ABOUT THE AUTHOR

Born and raised in Virginia, LM Fox currently lives in a suburb of Richmond with her husband, three kids, and a chocolate lab.

Her pastimes are traveling to new and favorite places, trying new foods, a swoony book with either a good cup of tea or coffee, margaritas on special occasions, and watching her kids participate in a variety of sports.

She has spent the majority of her adult life working in emergency medicine, and her books are written in this setting. Her main characters are typically in the medical field, EMS, fire, and/or law enforcement. She enjoys writing angsty, contemporary romance about headstrong, independent heroines you can't help but love and the hot alpha men who fall hard for them.

www.authorlmfox.com